EVERYTHING'S COMING UP MAKEOUT

EVERYTHING'S COMING UP MAKEOUT

A RETROSPECTIVE

MAKEOUT CREEK BOOKS
SPOKANE, WASHINGTON

Cover artwork by Steve Keene

Makeout Creek logo by Andy Miller

ISBN 978-0-9838259-8-2

Library of Congress Control Number: 2025951355

The two versions of David Berman's poem "Quality Cassette/CD Duplication. Cassette & CD Express. Special Volume Quotes. Located on Music Row. Division of Al Jolson Ent." originally appeared in Issue One of *Makeout Creek* in 2008. They are reprinted here with the kind permission of his estate.

Gossamer | McNulty | Wonton

First Printing
Ingram Edition

2025
Makeout Creek Books
Spokane, Washington
www.makeoutcreek.com

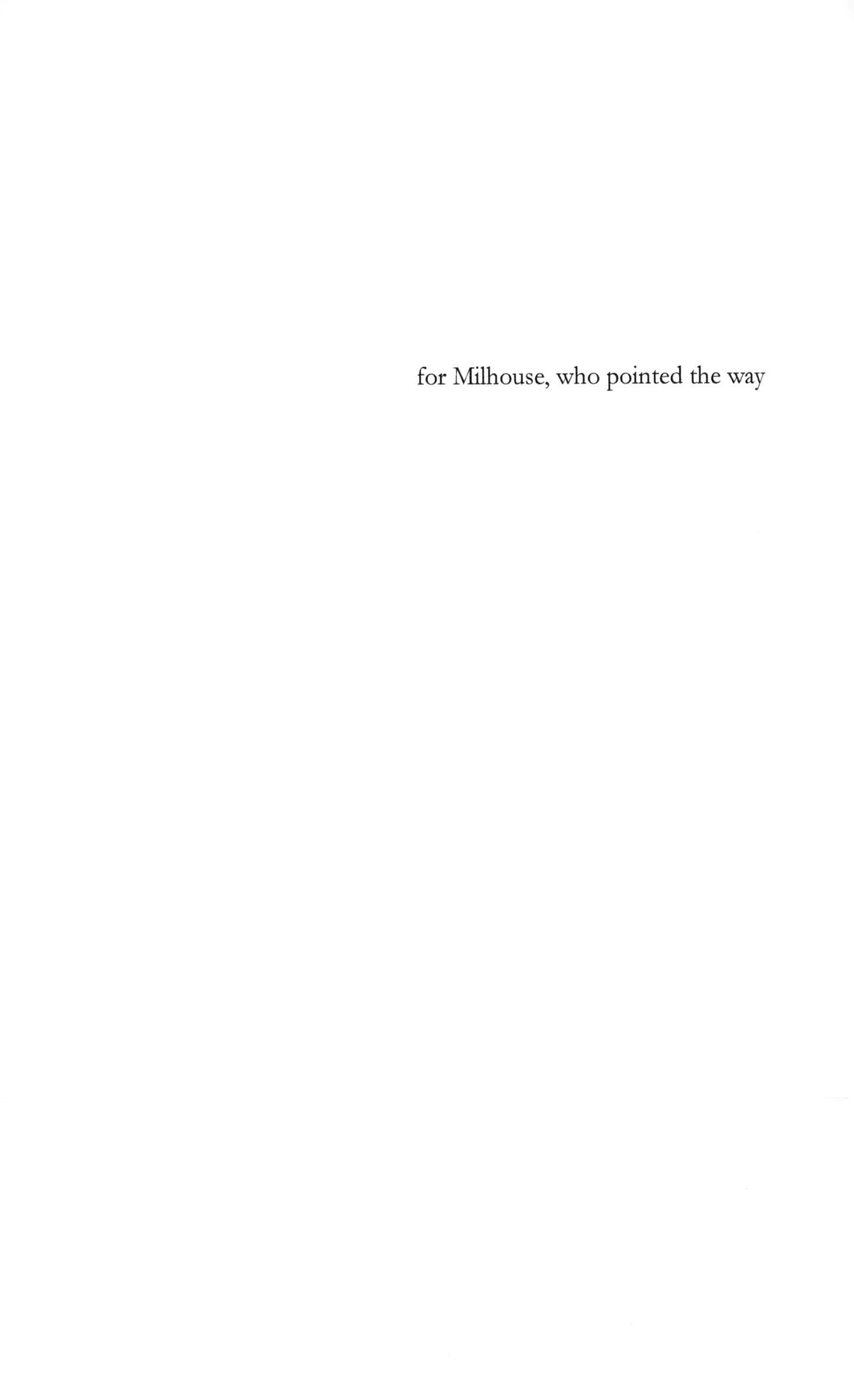

for Milhouse, who pointed the way

Do not worry if you think it is dark.
Policeman MacCruiskeen

A perfect monster has no end.
Roky Erickson

CONTENTS

ISSUE TWO
THE REVELEY LEE APPRECIATION SOCIETY

ISSUE FIVE
WHAT PETER CALLS "A NATURAL ENCOUNTER PERSON"

ISSUE SIX
FOR THE MOLOKAI COPS

ISSUE SEVEN
THE LONESOME FOGHORN BLOWS

ISSUE EIGHT
ONLY A WITCH CAT CAN CLOSE A DOOR

BURY ME AT MAKEOUT CREEK

INTRODUCTION
CYNTHIA GRIER LOTZE

AS THIS collection has come together, it has surprised me to find—in proof-pages and text threads, in editorial board meetups in cities around the United States—a map leading to this poet's tender, aging heart. Twenty years is far longer than the two-months-ahead capacity I had back in the glorious, silly, self-centered aughts. I don't think any of us sending our hard-wrought art to Andrew in those days imagined a compendium of *Makeout Creek* would eventually become the yearbook of all our pathways. From sweaty readings at Chop Suey Books and a thousand vegan Caesar salads at Ipanema, this irregular but persistent magazine and publishing imprint has sneakily accompanied its contributors, readers and creators through broken and healed friendships, brought many of us to a beautiful island in Maine, forged bonds that keep me spamming people I met once two decades ago with pictures of my kid. This magazine loves cats and checking in on its friends. This magazine adores a dive bar. This magazine quit smoking and started saying "I love you" at the end of phone calls. This magazine has had so many mailing addresses but always kept its headquarters in creator Andrew Blossom's steadfast (also tender) heart. Some of us died too soon; some of us now make art full-time; some of us write poems in the airport only; some of us are banned from Fishers Island for reasons that will remain obscure. All of us will hold this object in our hands and marvel at time's deepening of our words and images. We will know these marks came from us, but their significance is composite: Because of this magazine and the steady minds and hands that sustain it, our work here not only stamps a time, it lives on in the community the pages of a book can create, and it takes on the shadings lent by the surrounding voices, by the work required to make a book a pleasure to hold, to read again and again. A glimmering little immortality is *Makeout Creek*'s gift to its contributors; a shot of persistent regard for art and humanity is its gift to all readers.

In "Cue the Jumbotron," contributor and essayist Patricia Smith writes, "This next time, I want to do it right. I want all the words to be incantations to set us on our path." Patty gets the spirit of the current *Makeout Creek* endeavor just about right: every time, we hopefully get closer, even if it's with the same words or images as five, ten, fifteen years ago. The magic of repetition is that it can become more than duplication—or as I tell my students, "Anaphora, baby!" Here is a magazine that so greatly values its contributors it can insist to us, over the course of two decades, "and, and, and..." Here are these words, these people, this place, this time, this collective incantation whose meaning will be revealed only in the end, whenever that may be. Not soon, reader.

ISSUE ONE
OF MANY

QUALITY CASSETTE/CD DUPLICATION.
CASSETTE & CD EXPRESS. SPECIAL
VOLUME QUOTES. LOCATED ON
MUSIC ROW. DIVISION OF
AL JOLSON ENT.
DAVID BERMAN

Holy Evening,
Purple Tiger,
Nacho Rain.

OR

QUALITY CASSETTE/CD DUPLICATION.
CASSETTE & CD EXPRESS. SPECIAL
VOLUME QUOTES. LOCATED ON
MUSIC ROW. DIVISION OF
AL JOLSON ENT.
DAVID BERMAN

Holy Evening,
Purple Tiger.
Nacho Rain “

LADY LIGHTNING'S FISHBOWL HAND

JOSIAH BANCROFT

LADY LIGHTNING came out of the scrub woods at the edge of the parking lot, ruining Sampson's morning smoke. Soon as he saw the first flash of her bright blue kimono through the pines, he retreated back down the long sidewalk of the strip mall. Back to his own storefront, Sammy's Market. He didn't want to risk a conversation. That's what she called it, her incessant talking.

The sun hit his end of the mall in the morning, making the plate glass windows of the Market glow like a stove. He'd forgotten to turn the CLOSED sign around. He meant to be open.

"Morning, Sampson!" Lady Lightning yelled from her end of the mall, high voice echoing like the crack of a hammer. She must've seen him slinking away. He wished he was faster. "You make coffee yet?" He sat on his heels behind a stucco-faced pillar, smoking, and didn't answer. She came by every morning for coffee, paid with a credit card, all ninety-nine cents worth. He was too proud to tell her that the card machine didn't work anymore and hadn't worked in months.

Sampson wondered why she stuck around, why she continued to play shop day after day. She couldn't be doing any better than he was, and he had a stone's patience. He was *invested.* Theirs were the only businesses left in the strip, and Sampson didn't see the mall attracting any new respectable tenants as long as there was a fortune teller nut drying her laundry out on the sidewalk. She was killing his business.

Sampson hadn't been inside of Lady Lightning's shop since the first month he'd moved in. He went in an effort to show goodwill to the other store owners. He drank coffee with the manager of the bookstore, ate greasy lo mein with the South Korean owner of the China Star Buffet and had his palm read by Lady Lightning. He disliked her instantly—her fake calm, her bullshit bangles and ridiculous kimonos. The crystals, the stink of lavender, her creepy glass hand that she kept covered up most of the time with an old boxing glove.

He'd brought a bottle of wine, a gold ribbon tied around the neck. The wine wasn't expensive, but her disinterest, the way she quickly stowed it under the table, made him flush. He wanted to chat about business, the rumors of a new subdivision being planned just down the road, but she insisted on a reading. She was so eager to take off her beat-up boxing glove, show off her softly curled glass fingers, her creaseless palm. She laid her magnifying hand over his and pretended to read his future.

It was appropriate that she only looked at people, really looked at them, through her own hand. His fortune was half-baked at best. Nothing but a lengthy aquatic metaphor.

Soon after he bought the store, the county traffic began to turn west towards old farmland, leaving behind empty subdivision plots, a hollow motel with a dried-up pool and the Northard Mall. At first, he told himself it was only a slow season. But the season never ended, and the other businesses left one by one. It had been a year since his last inventory delivery. Restocking the beer and soda coolers had sucked up the last of his savings. By then, no bank in the county would give him a loan. They said he lacked a credible business plan. It took him six weeks to drink the beer cooler dry.

Sampson looked at the cigarette, smoked down to the filter between his fingers. Soon he'd have to smoke the fifty-cent cigars, and then there'd be nothing left and he'd have to quit.

Sheriff Lowden drove in fast, startling Sampson, who was still ducked behind the pillar, squatting like a bum. The squad car cut straight across the lot, right over the crossed white lines, the blue seated man with a dot for a head. Sampson hustled inside, trying to not look like he was being chased.

His sleeping bag still lay in a heap behind the counter. He'd taken to sleeping under the register instead of in the storeroom so he could hear if any customers drove up. Really, that was only part of the reason. The storeroom had begun to feel like a mausoleum, and he'd lost a lot of sleep to night sweats and vivid dreams of being buried alive.

Opening the old three-tumbler safe under the glass counter case, he stuffed his sleeping bag in, first with his foot, then with his hands. The bell over the front door clanged. He'd been caught squatting again.

Sheriff Lowden's pink slit eyes and long grey teeth smiled like he'd stared into a campfire for too long. "Sammy," he said, sniffing. The store didn't smell like bleach, or warm fruit or bread, like it once did. It smelled like a sleeping bag, a body's grease. It smelled like Sampson, the walls pocked like a drunk's nose, the shelves half-empty and all skewed into a maze. The maze had made the store look fuller at first, but now Sampson could see right through the empty holes in his stock, all the way back to the coolers, back to the storeroom, back to the propped open emergency exit glowing red as hell.

"Sheriff," Sampson said, making an effort to stand up straight. "What can I do you for?"

"Shoe polish." The Sheriff's thick belt clattered against the glass front of the counter. "Black."

"I got brown. But I guess that'd look like dog shit on a black shoe."

"Guess you'd know." The Sheriff screwed his hat back on. Nobody liked the Sheriff—he strutted around like Caesar, expecting the world to make a gift of itself to him. But everyone loved him—he kept drugs out of the county, he prowled the streets at night with his headlights off, like a barn owl, hunting for rats. He'd shot so many suspects that, after the eighth one, the DA took his gun away, replaced it with a taser. "Give me two of them cigars, then," the Sheriff pointed. Sampson was sure the Sheriff still carried a gun. In his boot. Under his hat. Inside his hand, his finger the gun barrel. That's how he pointed, anyway.

Sampson fished two blunts from the jar and turned the key in the cash register. "Need a minute to open her up. Like an old car. Reliable, but… you know." Sampson looked out at the Sheriff's squad car, a big-engined sedan that he always left running right at the curb in the loading zone.

Sheriff Lowden ran the cigars under his nose, his slit eyes rolling up, showing off more pink. Sampson thought it looked like soggy brains in there. "These fresh?"

"Pretty fresh," Sampson said.

"Change for a Jackson?" The Sheriff slipped the cigars into his khaki shirt pocket, held up a halved twenty-dollar bill between his fingers.

The register was empty. Not even nickels. And the Sheriff knew it. The son of a bitch.

"I still got to get to the bank this morning." Sampson punched at the buttons on the register and had trouble suddenly with mumbling. "Maybe you could swing back by later with something smaller." The

Sheriff smiled indulgently. Sampson knew that men, especially Caesars such as the Sheriff, liked watching others make a spectacle of themselves. It made such men feel enduring and upright. And here he was at it again, feeding the Sheriff a spectacle.

"You go on," Sampson said finally. "You get me next time."

"Alright, Sammy."

The radio velcroed to Sheriff Lowden's shoulder gave a sharp squawk. The burst of noise made no sense to Sampson, but the Sheriff repeated the nonsense into the handset and ran for the door, jangling like an emaciated Santa Claus. The cash register rang and threw out the empty drawer, punching Sampson in the stomach.

Lowden floored it. The squad car's tires chirped, the back almost fishtailing as it bolted cattycorner across the deep parking lot. Sampson watched, thinking about what he should've said: *Take your goddamn snot nose off my cigars, you bullying son of a bitch.* And he was still thinking it when the front right tire of the squad car struck the turtle, the bowling-ball-sized painted turtle that was sitting out in the middle of the black top, arms and legs tucked in, its yellow-ribboned head stretched out like a periscope.

The front wheel of the car hit the turtle's back like a ramp, popped two feet in the air and came down, bouncing hard, just as the back wheel followed the leap. The shell shattered under the second tire, but the one-two hopping of the wheels shook the car and jerked it into a teetering back-and-forth skid. The squad car was still charging hard when it broadsided the high curb at the front end of the lot. The barrier flipped the car into a barrel roll right over the drainage ditch. It came down on its roof in the middle of the road, still moving, sledding on its hood and windshield, the burst siren and lights striking up sparks like a match. Wheels flailing half off their axles, the car slid upside-down across the road, into the ditch on the other side.

Sampson was still holding open the empty cash drawer. It'd happened so fast.

As he charged outside he heard Lady Lightning scream, "Lowden!" and saw her throw a sopping blouse to the sidewalk. "I told you!"

Running like he'd had no practice and was only running as he'd seen others do it, Sampson crossed the lot. Past the oozing shell. Across the county highway. Into the ditch on his backside. He disappeared behind the long weeds that swirled and settled again.

Sampson had, more than once, seen turtles make the migratory trek from the retention pond behind the mall to the swampy land on the other side of the road, had seen them get stranded in the parking lot after the asphalt had sucked up enough sun to turn into one enormous coal. Lady Lightning usually took it upon herself to rescue the stranded turtles.

Later, he would wonder how she'd overlooked this whopper.

Even as he scrambled back out of the ditch, Sampson saw the Sheriff's crushed face, all that escaped red, all the trash of the car thrown and stuck in the crag of the dashboard by the impact. It looked like a yard sale in there.

He was running again. Back towards Lady Lightning, straight at the red neon hand in her window.

"You have a phone. Go call for help," Sampson said, coughing. Two streaks of blood smeared his faded blue t-shirt. "Wait, *wait*," he said, though she hadn't moved. He held out a fist with two brown fingers sticking out either end. She was slow to take the cigars, and he had to insist. They were warm and softly bent inside their plastic sheathes.

"I don't want them," Sampson said.

The room had hardly changed. The same tacky emerald curtain hung from the ceiling, drawing a false wall across the back of the room. He knew she slept back there, didn't have a house or an apartment in town. Behind the curtain now, she talked ever louder at the 911 operator. "Yes, a turtle," she said. "I know it doesn't make any sense. That's why we need *you*. To come out and *make sense*."

Sampson was sure the Sheriff was dead. His head was wedged between the spokes of the steering wheel. The inside of the Sheriff's car smelled like socks and old fast food. He wondered if the Sheriff had felt owned by his car, like a body owns a brain, like Sammy's owned Sampson. But Sampson couldn't drum up much sympathy for Sheriff Lowden. If anything, he felt less timid for having seen the Sheriff in his rank, unglamorous element.

"They're coming out," she said, pushing through the slit in the green curtain. "They want us to stay clear of the car." She set the two cigars on the covered round table in the middle of the room. Sampson thought they looked incriminating and wished she would put them away.

They wouldn't officially pronounce him dead until later when they got him to the hospital, but Lowden was dead, and obviously so. The rescue squad cut the door off with a big hydraulic beak. The metal shell creaked and came apart, the last un-shattered window on the back door popping in sympathy with the twisted frame.

Two young deputies took turns smoking cigarettes and shyly crying into their hands like men with hay fever.

Lady Lightning made the deputies squirm, insisted on hugging them, and then insisted on explaining the value of a hug.

Sampson could hardly stand to watch her, the way she patronized the grieving men with platitudes and spiritual mumbo jumbo. "This is just part of the story you'll tell yourself about this man. But the telling and his story go on," she said.

What the hell did that mean? Sampson wanted to know. The story was *over*. That was exactly the kind of mealy-mouthed crap that she gave him over coffee every morning. Her free coffee. And why care so much about Sheriff Lowden? Sampson knew, couldn't help but know, that the Sheriff had been pestering her, threatening to write her citations for bullshit violations. Excuses he pulled out of his ass to get a shot at hers. She couldn't be much older than thirty, and Lowden was, *had been*, a hard-ridden fifty, with nothing to offer but a suffocating smugness, a crumpled liver, estranged children, all of them buried in debt and disappointment, and the ghost of a wife killed years ago by breast cancer.

"Sometimes we just need someone to stand between us and the infinite, complicated universe," she said, face pressed against the chest of a young deputy. She could be flirtatious, too, Sampson thought.

A fat state trooper snapped pictures of the half-crushed turtle with a disposable camera. He hunkered down onto one knee to get a better angle on the collapsed shell and looked suddenly nervous when he tried to stand again. His face shook with the effort, but he didn't make it to his feet. He waved Sampson over and took his statement, still perched on one knee.

"Ever heard of anything like this?" Sampson asked. "A turtle flipping a car over?"

The state trooper pulled a strip of jerky out of his shirt pocket and ripped the plastic sheath with his teeth. "Had a buddy get whacked off his Harley by a bumblebee." He flicked his tongue trying to spit out a bit of plastic.

"Jesus."

"Hey, you got any Cokes in there?" The trooper held out his hand. Sampson almost went down trying to haul the heavy man to his feet.

Only a couple dozen sodas were left in the cooler: ginger ales, diets, orange sodas, all the flavors Sampson hated. He walked over with the state trooper, who talked about Lowden's two kids, how much he dreaded making that phone call.

"Sorry honey, your daddy's dead," the trooper said. "It's like sucker-punching someone, telling them that." The trooper bought three cans of soda and a bag of hot pepper peanuts. He let Sampson keep the change from a five. "They got these new chips that taste exactly like buffalo wings," the trooper said, opening a ginger ale. "You should get some of those. Knock your socks off."

One by one, the other officers wandered across the parking lot, looking for a drink, looking to get out of the sun and away from the awkwardness of trying to coax a corpse out of its final and defiant preference.

A short motorcycle cop with long sideburns, dark as grease paint, examined the bottom of a soda can, keeping the cooler door open with his elbow.

"The distributor back-dates the sodas. It's fine," Sampson said, fussing with a new pyramid display he'd built out of cracker boxes.

The cop nodded, strutted over to the counter, and began staring at the coffee-stained sign taped to it: *Please Use Smallest Bills*. "What's up with the nut? What's her story? Just a boxing enthusiast, or what?"

Sampson was happy to find himself in the company of a man who was unaffected by Lady Lightning's forced charm. "She's a nut," he said.

"Yeah, I just said so. Where'd she come from?" Outside, a tow truck slowly backed towards the wrecked squad car. Sampson couldn't decide how much to tell the officer. He didn't want to encourage his curiosity too much. That might end in a seemingly harmless visit to her shop, and that was how converts were made.

"How much you want to hear?"

"Skip to the sexy parts." The cop opened his can of soda.

"Alright. Well, this is from her mouth. She told me the whole story the first day I met her."

He remembered how the story had been given to him, almost as if it were a confession, after she'd read his future. In particular, he recalled how she'd served him bitter hot tea instead of opening his wine. She'd seemed to think that they would be friends. "She grew up in Kansas on some small-stakes family farm," Sampson said, and the fat trooper came back in, mouth clanging in chorus with the bell, said he'd forgotten to get Sampson's name.

"His name's Sammy. Jesus H, read the sign. We're in the middle of something," the bike cop said, unsnapping the helmet strap from his chin.

Sampson appreciated the cop's enthusiasm, and so let it go by uncommented that his name was really Sampson. "Anyway, one day a big storm starts to roll in, so she runs out to bring in the wash for her mama. As she tells it, she always knew, knew since she was a gleam in her Daddy's eye, that the day would come when God would lean down and whisper her a story."

"Aw, bullshit," the fat trooper said.

"And on that day, one hell of a day, God chose to speak in lightning form. She reached for her laundry, maybe a choir robe, and *pow!*" Sampson slapped the counter, immediately flushing at the racket he made. "She was struck down by a bolt of lightning." Sampson held up his arm, as if in amazement, as if maybe he saw something in it. He knew he was hamming it up, but couldn't help it. He was enjoying himself. "It's a miracle! Turned to glass. Her whole arm, where the lightning came in, transformed into a goddamn chandelier."

The fat trooper snorted, and wedged two fingers down into the bottom of his bag of hot nuts, pinching for dust.

"Something, huh?" Sampson said to the mutton-chopped bike cop, trying to draw him back in. The cop spun around a half-empty sunglass display tree, plucked free a pair of round mirror shades.

"Something else," he said, and put the sunglasses on. The arms of the glasses cinched his sideburns in, making them look somehow fake.

"Lightning doesn't turn arms into glass. It's a prosthetic. That's what bugs me so much. Why can't she just say, I have a false arm? Why all the mystery? Why the boxing glove?" And wanting something more from the cop, something more like affirmation, Sampson said, "Funny."

"It is funny," the cop said, and smirked like Sheriff Lowden used to. Suddenly Sampson didn't like the cop so much anymore. He wondered if he was about to get screwed, if the cop was going to walk out with a new pair of shades, thinking about what a sucker Sampson was. "You know what else is funny?" the cop continued, "It seems to me that you got your fortune tangled up with that woman, one way or another."

"What do you mean?" Sampson mumbled. He wished he'd sounded more assertive.

"Well, it seems that if her business is good, then your business is good. A rising tide, and all that bull. People get their palms read and then maybe jog over here for a Yoo-hoo." The motorcycle cop thumbed two dollars out of his bill clip onto the counter. "That small enough for you?"

Sampson didn't sleep that night. The motorcycle cop had bristled him too badly, had made him feel foolish just when he was trying to be friendly. He'd stuck out his hand only to have it slapped. So he smoked every cigarette he had left, smoked them all down to the sour, hot filter, sitting outside, under the plate glass window and the flaking painted sign that said, "Sammy." Sammy the sucker, the doormat, the captain of a sinking ship. Maybe he was already sunk. Maybe he was commanding a wreck at the bottom of the sea.

Then again, he'd made seventy-three dollars in a day. What if he'd up and quit the day before? He never would've seen that money. He rubbed his stubble. Moths ruined themselves against the last functioning streetlamp, which leaned to one side as if it were falling asleep on its feet. He had to finish what he started. But what if he didn't? So what?

"Goddamn it." He wanted a drink.

If no one finished what they started, the whole world would be full of doors hanging on one hinge, full of people walking around with one pant leg on, one off, full of stutters. There was no end to anything left half done.

Seventy-three dollars. His biggest one-day take in four months. A week of that kind of business, and he'd get the delivery trucks rolling in again. If he stuck with it.

He ate a pack of powdered doughnuts, was almost surprised by the creeping sun lighting up the trees like birthday candles. The streetlamp flickered out.

He made a pot of coffee and decided on a second. Dumping new grounds over the old, he tried to calculate his profit per cup, but lost the decimal somewhere. Maybe it was time he bumped up the price.

Before the second pot finished dripping through, Lady Lightning walked in. To his surprise, she was quiet and heavy-lidded, her red silk blouse wrinkled. The heads of the black oriental dragons on her breast looked like prunes. She murmured a *good morning*, excusing herself when she moved around him towards the small island where the coffee maker gurgled. Sampson wondered if she would leave without saying a word, wondered if maybe one of the cops had told her what he'd said about her.

As dumb as the boxing glove looked poking out from under the stove-pipe sleeve of her blouse, it was impressive how easily she hooked the glove's thumb between the carafe and handle, pouring, with a turn of her elbow, a perfect stream. Not a splash.

She stood at the counter in front of him, small cup of coffee fogging between her hands, one in a boxing glove, the other pink and cracked, not looking at him. When she didn't offer him her credit card, he said, "It's on me," and surprised himself saying it.

"My card's been maxed out for a year. You've always been sweet about it, Sampson. I wish I could pay," she said.

He'd never thought of it as sweetness. In fact, once he'd been tempted to hand-copy her card and send the credit company a charge for one hundred dollars, two hundred maybe. He never did because he was afraid of renewing interest in his own debt.

"Let me see your card," Sampson said.

"Why?" she asked as she set her cup down and pulled it out of the cuff of her glove. He scowled at the credit machine, swiping her card.

"There. Now you don't owe me anything."

"Sampson," she said.

He barreled through her smiling protest. "What do you make of all this? The turtle and all?"

"I don't know."

"I want to feel bad," he said and stopped, uncomfortable with himself, with her looking at him now, squinting like he was a billboard that was too far off to read. But he went on. He *wanted* to. "You know, but—he was such a hateful son of a bitch. He really was mean." It came out more quivery than he'd meant it to.

"Yeah. And he was lonely and broken and in love with a dead person."

Sampson wished he'd never opened his mouth, not in his whole life. He was sick and tired of sticking his foot in it, tired of stumbling into people's confidences, falling into their traps. If he could've sucked back in every last word, he would've. And then he would snatch back her cup of coffee, *his* cup of coffee, and say, Who are you to make me feel so stupid all the time? Why can't a person just be a son of a bitch and there be no excuse hiding behind it?

"He wouldn't leave me alone, you know. Kept wanting me to talk to his wife. Like I could just reach out and grab her skirt. Right out of the air." She sipped her coffee, scrutinized the brown border of beans ringing the cup's lip.

"I thought you talked to ghosts."

"No, just tell fortunes. How would I ever sleep?" She looked at Sammy's sleeping bag, limp as a sloughed skin behind the counter. "How do you sleep?" She nodded at it.

"Like a baby. What'd you mean when you hollered, 'I told you' at the Sheriff?"

She looked surprised. Surprised maybe that Sampson had heard her, or surprised perhaps that she'd been speaking aloud. Sampson couldn't tell.

"That part of his fortune?" Sampson tried to picture the lanky Sheriff Lowden hunched over the rickety table where she read fortunes. His hand under hers. It was too ridiculous. Had he left his broad hat on? Had he put his secret, illegal gun on the table?

"I told him that he'd die happy and that people would hand out cigars. I said that his wife would be new, so new that he'd hardly recognize her, and that he'd rush to her, roaring." Lady Lightning's eyes fogged, blue turning gray, as if she'd gotten coffee steam in them. As if her eyes were glass, too.

"Did you hate him?" Sampson said, and hadn't meant to sound so hopeful.

"I felt sorry, mostly. Same as I'm sorry for the turtle."

Coffee dribbled onto the fat thumb of her glove, and she licked it off, seeming more awake then. A little less miserable.

"I love lots of dead people, you know? But I ain't in a hurry to see them again."

Sampson said, "I hear you."

The first mourner, a young man in a football letter jacket, pulled his jeep off the road later that morning. He staggered out with his leather sleeve in his eye, weeping so loudly Sampson could hear him all the way across the parking lot.

Sampson opened his navy blue sleeping bag on the sidewalk and, using a can of white spray paint, he wrote, "RIP Sheriff Lowden. You will be missed," across the length of the bag. He taped the makeshift banner between the two square pillars in front of his store. Ten minutes later, the young man, jeans stained with green at the knees, came into Sammy's for coffee. Sammy didn't want to know who the young man was or how he knew Lowden. He was relieved when the boy didn't make any announcements.

The mourners trickled in all that day and the next, buying coffee, Twinkies, pretzels, the last of the sodas, pork rinds, pocket packs of tissues. Some hadn't even known Lowden, had just been so moved by the emotional authenticity of the sleeping bag banner that they'd stopped out of curiosity. Two-hundred and thirty-eight dollars' worth of curiosity.

He hoped that Lady Lightning wouldn't be offended by his sign, by what might be construed as him capitalizing upon a man's death. Which it was. But when she'd talked about Lowden, his sadness and his love of ghosts, it had occurred to Sampson that maybe some things were meant to be hopeless.

On the third day after the Sheriff's death, Sampson woke up to the boom of thunder. It felt like early morning, but the shadow of the storm outside made it hard to tell. "Jesus Christ," he said. Who would come out to pay their respects in the rain?

Crossing his arms against the cold, he unlocked the front door. Rain blew under the concrete awning, spattering his bare feet. His sleeping bag jerked in the wind, silhouetted by white rips of lightning. Even if it wouldn't turn him to glass, he didn't want to risk getting struck, so he did nothing. Watched as the sleeping bag sponged up the rain, as it grew heavy and unmoved by the wind. Getting soaked was good enough for that son of a bitch Lowden, anyway. Sampson closed the door, and the wind helped him do it.

There was nothing else to do—no cigarettes to smoke, no customers to ring up—so he decided to go back to sleep. Lying down behind the counter again, he listened to the rain mutter against his store. Mutter and make no sense.

He awoke the next morning to find two cigars lying on the counter, and a folded note with his name written neatly on it in blue ink: *Sampson*. His neck ached from sleeping with a roll of toilet paper for a pillow. He felt a little irked that Lady Lightning had felt comfortable sneaking into his store while he was asleep in his underwear. He'd hoped to not see the cigars again.

Her note was short and clipped, like it had been transcribed from a telegram. She was leaving, was gone already. The cigars were his after all. Thanks, but she didn't smoke. She hoped that his RIP for Lowden was heart-felt and understood if it wasn't. The fortune she'd given him, she stressed again, was genuine. Was heart-felt. She hoped his business improved. She wished happiness upon him.

And that was that.

To hell with her, Sampson thought. He took his time peeling and lighting one of the cigars off a paper match. He wanted to see if she was really gone, couldn't believe that she'd settle for such a slinking exit, so he decided to take his fifty-cent cigar for a walk.

His sleeping bag lay in a dark wad at the foot of one column. Heavy with rainwater, the sleeping bag was hard to carry one-handed, but he was married to the cigar, and so settled for dragging the mess down the sidewalk to her old clothesline.

A pair of crows fussed over a lump in the middle of the parking lot. It seemed impossible to him that it had ever been a turtle. He slung the sleeping bag over the drooping clothesline, wetting one whole side of his shirt in the process.

She'd taken her posters, her emerald curtain, her flimsy table, her washboard and all. The neon palm still hung in the window, but it was unlit and lifeless.

He blew smoke against the glass, refocusing his eyes onto his reflection.

He wanted to know if she'd been lying when she told him his future. The future that she'd told, her cold hand stacked on top of his, was that one day he'd find himself on an island. He would stay put for years. He would survive. Always hiding in the shade, living off of dew.

And then one day, finally cooked out by sun, he'd decide to take a swim. He would swim, swim straight out, and the island and the sky would get closer and closer together until they were covered over by waves.

"And then," she'd said, "you'll realize that you prefer swimming. You prefer it."

"What am I, a fish?" he'd mumbled, offended at the time, thinking that she was making fun of him, giving him only half a future.

"Maybe you're a fish," she'd said. Her face had a soft expression which reminded him now of waking up in a bed, waking on his side, the room pink from dawn, listening to the sound of water in the sink, the stirring of feet on the bathroom tile.

The two crows picked at the turtle, drew out thick, purple threads of meat.

The cigar dropped a thick ash onto his knuckle, singeing him. He wondered how she'd ever gotten away. He pictured her hitch-hiking down the road, boxing glove thumb stuck out, her trunk and bags stacked behind her, and he laughed. Maybe she was standing just down the road. He thought he should check. Just to see for himself.

ADVICE FOR FUR DRILL NOVICES
SARAH ELAINE SMITH

Whenever you find your initials written in cake, demure.
Might be velvet, might be forest. Whatever the epitaph
on the bottle, read it. Might be catchy, might be duller.
Consider the host, his mostly shackled appearance behind
a zinc bar of insouciant back hands and reach-arounds. He's
the connoisseur of the two-fisted jug. That's why your pelt
disappoints. This is the way to squeeze the citrus: enough
to rim the ice-bite glass for half of a funny story on a hot
hot night. Twelve punchlines line the room and each one
is a blonde. You'll wander among them asking, "Why did
the spider-bite swallow the thigh?" But now it is oh-night-
hundred-hours and time for the fur drill, for showing off
privates and getting out the hair. The punchlines arrange
themselves in T-N-T formation. Might be they'll let you
light the fuse, might be they won't. Might just be oh-dark.

IF YOU LIVED HERE, YOU'D BE HOME NOW
TOM DE HAVEN

LOU CUDHY IS TALKING

THAT FALL coming up I was scheduled to teach freshman comp, sophomore lit, and—Thursday evenings, 7-9:40—American Horror. Despite its popularity with students—the little darlings kept pestering the department to offer the course more frequently—my colleagues dismissed it as more "Crud by Cudhy," lightweight and lacking entirely in academic rigor. But oh fuck them. My most popular courses (the ones I'd dubbed my "American Triad": American Horror, American Fantasy, American Crime) *were* lightweight, I'd never denied it. When had I ever denied it? They were entertaining, undemanding, and as briskly paced as network television (short lecture, short break, feature film). So what if they were mostly bullshit, too. Wasn't everything?

My name is Lou Cudhy. It sounds like I should be a private eye or a Teamster official, but I'm afraid I'm only a tenured professor at a small, historically-but-now-halfheartedly Methodist college in Central Virginia. It has pretensions to excellence, but honestly it just costs a lot of money. While the students are mediocre, they come expensively dressed and accessorized. Pretty campus, though: red maples and dogwoods, azaleas, horse chestnuts and magnolias, formal gardens, fishponds, topiary and transverse walks of red Colonial brick. All of the classroom buildings date from the eighteenth century. During the Civil War (or, as I once heard the provost call it, the War of Northern Aggression), Belvidere College was used as a Confederate hospital. Three alumnae plaques say so.

In 1982, when we moved down from New Hampshire (I'd been teaching near Stamford at a prep school), our boys were five, three and barely two months. Bobbi and I had discussed it at length and agreed we'd stay in Virginia five years at the max, but instead—well, here it was 2006. Here it was. The boys were 29, 27 and 24. Bobbi was 52. And I was 55. I couldn't believe it. Well, I could, I had to, but it seemed impossible.

By choice, I had no friends among the current, and much younger, teaching faculty and seldom spoke with anybody in my department or any others, for that matter. Nods on the trot would have to suffice. (The few Belvidere friends I'd once made had retired or moved on and fallen out of touch.) For the last several years, I'd declined most committee work or simply hadn't performed it, and I never went to department or college meetings. I didn't care about budgets or curriculum, I didn't care about the strategic plan, I didn't care about any of that stuff. I used to, but not anymore. It happens. I had little interest, none really, in academe: I no longer subscribed to journals, attended conferences, or kept up my membership in the Modern Language Association. I was finished with all of that.

Ever since the summer of 2002, when I'd had a bad scare (it wasn't serious finally, it was polyps, but it *could* have been cancer), ever since then I was trying my best, my level best, not to let anything, small or large, spoil the pleasure, the sheer animal pleasure I took simply in being alive and healthy. I'm not a spiritual man, but whenever I'd send Bobbi a floral arrangement on her birthday, our anniversary or for no official reason, I would always remove a single flower—usually a rose, but it worked just as well with a daisy or a carnation—and then keep it in a narrow glass vase on my desk, staring at it each day for a couple of minutes. Staring was the best I could manage. I was no meditator, I think I may even have ADD. Anyway, I'd stare at the stupid flower and watch it gradually decay. It was a Buddhist koan or something like that. I'd read about it in a student essay. Yeah. Yeah, really, it was good sometimes to remind myself.

On the fourth of August, a Saturday, Saturday morning, I was up, dressed and coffeed by 7:30. While it was still cool and not so muggy, I took a short walk around the neighborhood. Bobbi and I lived on a cul-de-sac named Hardwood Trace, which opened into Hardwood Terrace, which led to Hardwood Place, which in turn brought you out to Bel Grove Parkway, the main thoroughfare, one lane in each direction, snaking through a subdivision called the Estates at Bel Grove.

During the time I was out, the only people I encountered were driving. As they went by they'd lackadaisically half-lift a hand from the steering wheel, a gesture I called the "Bel Grove Bear Hug." God, I hated the suburbs and didn't know why we still lived there, now the boys were gone. Inertia, I suppose. By the time I got home, the mercury thermometer hanging from a cup hook on the front porch registered 86 degrees. At ten of nine in the morning! I didn't know why we still lived in Virginia, either.

So I came back and then I went into the family room, which is a bullshit name that makes me think of Walt Disney or the Republican Party. I started pulling out DVDs and videocassettes, piling them in stacks. My plan was to spend the weekend, plus Monday and Tuesday, lolling on the sofa watching favorite horror movies before choosing which ones to put on the syllabus and show in class. *Frankenstein?* Or *Bride of?* *Freaks? Carnival of Souls? The Thing?* Original or remake? *Halloween* or *Nightmare on Elm Street*? *Texas Chainsaw Massacre* or *Gut Wrench*? *Gut Wrench* or *GW3: The Crucifixion of Toby*?

"Why didn't you wake me?" from Bobbi standing there all of the sudden still in her nightshirt, the one with Keith Haring's big orange face silk-screened on the front. She bought it in New York City the weekend we'd driven up there to see our oldest son perform in a showcase production of—what was it again? Something by Beckett, but not *Godot.* Michael didn't act anymore, that hadn't panned out. He was a court stenographer now in Philadelphia. Not Beckett. Pinter. "I thought I asked you to wake me."

"You said nine."

"It's quarter past ten."

"Oh. Shit. I'm sorry, sweetie. You go on back up and take your shower, I'll fix some breakfast. Eggs?"

She pushed a hand through her hair, fluffing it, then scratching her scalp. "That's okay. Just coffee." Already she was on her way back upstairs.

"I'll make you pancakes," I called. "Sweetie? Bob? Don't not have breakfast. You'll be driving all day, you need something in your stomach."

As soon as I heard the shower, I dumped out what was left of the coffee I'd made earlier and put on a fresh pot. Then I took out the Bisquick, the milk, couple of eggs, cinnamon from the spice rack. I felt shitty for losing track of the time, but if Bobbi got out of the house by 11 she could still make it to Cincinnati by 6:30, 7 that evening. And it wasn't like she was on a tight schedule. She wasn't going to miss something important if she arrived a little bit later than she'd planned. Bobbi was just visiting her nutso sister, nutso Andrea. That's all. I took out the measuring cup, the mixing bowl.

When I'd poured three dollops of batter, very carefully, even finically, onto the hot skillet (let me tell you, I can produce absolutely perfect silver-dollar pancakes, like they serve at Perkins or the Waffle House), I set Bobbi a place at the table: plate, knife, fork, juice glass, paper napkin, mug. Then I remembered her prescription (Wellbutrin) and her slew of vitamins and dietary supplements (everything from B and C and E to fish oil and glucosamine), except when I pulled open the cabinet door they weren't on the shelf where they'd always been. Usually whenever Bobbi was going on a trip she'd count out how many pills she'd need depending on how long she'd be away and throw everything into a sandwich baggie. Obviously, this time she hadn't. I flipped the pancakes, took out the orange juice, the butter, the maple syrup.

It was Bobbi's business, but it seemed pretty dopey taking along all the bottles.

The only vitamins she'd left were the ones I took (although I often forgot to, as I'd done that day): the Centrum Silver knockoffs from Costco and the zinc tablets from GNC. I would never, never, Christ *never* want this to get out, I'd be completely humiliated, but the reason I'd started taking zinc? The honest-to-God real reason? Was I'd discovered somewhere on the Internet that one tablet swallowed daily could noticeably increase the amount of semen in a man's ejaculation, increase it and thicken it nicely. In recent years I'd noticed that mine had become less copious, less white, and, most disturbing, a little watery.

Speaking of that, I probably should have had sex with Bobbi that morning instead of getting up so early—isn't that what you do, have sex with your spouse before they go off on a trip? Which, when you think about it, is pretty goddamn pessimistic.

I was wondering if I should turn off the heat under the second batch of pancakes, run upstairs and see if I could catch her before she finished dressing, when Bobbi came down.

"What?" she said.

I must've frowned.

"You seem like something's bothering you. Everything okay?"

"Everything's fine."

"Not looking forward to the drive, are you?"

"No, I'm all right. I don't mind driving, you know that." Bullshit. *How* many years had we been married? Thirty-one. Thirty-one years and you can practically read the other person's mind, you always know what's going on in there, almost always. She didn't want to drive to Cincinnati but wouldn't admit it. She had to do the right thing, even when it sucked. That was Bobbi. Visiting nutso Catholic Andrea (another baby at 43, for Christ's sake) was maybe the compassionate and big-sisterly thing to do, but still it sucked. So did seven, eight hours in the car. Vacation traffic. All that stuff.

As she reached past me for the coffee carafe, I leaned to the side and kissed her, catching the side of her mouth. I thought she wouldn't smile, but then she did. "I made you pancakes."

"I noticed. Thank you."

"Should I make a sandwich? Do you want to take along the cooler?" I opened the pantry door and stared—before snatching down a bag of dried mangoes from the top shelf and, from the shelf below, a jar of Planters nuts. Unsalted. Like she liked. "For the car. If I put a couple of Cokes in that quilted thingy they ought to stay cold—should I?"

"Don't bother."

"You pack any CDs?"

"I'll listen to the radio."

I shrugged, sat down at the table and watched her cut a wedge from a stack of three pancakes. It seemed to call for enormous concentration and will, so did raising the stupid fork to her mouth. She looked spacey.

"Bobbi? Hon? You want me to come with you? I could be ready to go in ten minutes. What? What's so funny?"

"Jesus, Lou."

"What? What 'Jesus, Lou'? I'm serious."

"I know you are." She patted my right hand. Then she laughed again and I knew if I said anything more about going with her to Cincinnati it would come out wrong, sounding pissed off and all offended, so I let the matter drop. Asked her if she had enough cash, did she have her Triple-A card, her cell phone and was it charged. She finished her coffee but not the pancakes. "What about your bag? Where's your bag?"

"It's already in the car."

"When did you do that?"

"Last night."

"*Last night?*"

"Give me a big kiss and let me get going."

"Call me from the road?"

"And drive carefully. Don't forget *Drive Carefully*."

"And drive carefully. Please."

We walked outside together, me saying good fucking lord I wouldn't be surprised if it reached a hundred degrees by the afternoon, Bobbi fetching out her electronic key fob and aiming it at her PT Cruiser. It was a black one and the car she loved best of all of the cars she'd owned during our long marriage, '75 VW Squareback included. Myself, I thought it was gimmicky and clunky, postmodern Chrysler bullshit, and not very comfortable, but it wasn't my car, it was hers.

So Mazel Tov.

I'd given it to her on her fiftieth birthday, a month before she gave me, on my fifty-third, a round-trip ticket to San Diego to spend a few days with Stevie, our youngest. At the time it seemed a great idea, a golden opportunity as much as a gift, but it hadn't turned out so well, that trip, that father-and-son reunion, and when it was over, not soon enough, Stevie dropped me off at the airport and didn't say goodbye. In retrospect, I would have much preferred a new laptop with all the bells and whistles; either that or a trip Bobbi and I could have taken to someplace we'd never been, which was just about anywhere you could think of on Planet Earth.

Bobbi started the car, the AC, then sat there, just sat there spacing again till I tapped her window and she powered it down.

"You sure you're okay to drive?

"Maybe I'm not completely awake."

"Then let me run back inside and get you another cup of coffee for the road."

She was adjusting the rearview mirror. "No more coffee." The sideview. "I'll be fine." The seatback.

"Tell Chris and Andrea I said hi. What's your gas situation? You think you should get it filled before you hit the road? You take the earpiece for your phone? I don't like to think about you holding that thing and talking while you drive. What about your sunglasses?"

She reached through the window, touched a finger to my lips and shushed me. "Bicycle," she said and powered up the window. She backed her car down the driveway, me waving, parade waving, then remembering as she rolled into the street that I'd never given her that big kiss, the one she'd asked for in the kitchen, and while, yeah sure, it hadn't been a *serious* request, just something every spouse in the world says going out the front door, even so I felt kind of bad.

I knew that I'd savor being on my own for the next few days, relish having the house to myself, but I'd also miss Bobbi. There had been a time, and it lasted two, three, maybe four years, when I was convinced I didn't love her anymore, or she me, and that our marriage was total bullshit. But then one day, *just one day*, I was positive that it wasn't and that I did, still did or did again, and that she did too. It was kind of cool. It was kind of cool how it happened. I wished I'd given her that big kiss, though.

Before I went inside, I made a leisurely circuit of the house—way too big now for just the pair of us—checking on Bobbi's herb garden and my struggling fig tree, cranking the hose back onto its plastic drum, tightening the spritzing handle of the spigot, wondering if I could get away with not cutting the grass, and thinking *Night of the Living Dead* or *Last House on the Left?* What about *Evil Dead 2?*

2

The telephone answering machine sat in full view on the kitchen counter next to a short rack of cookbooks. But it wasn't until I'd finished doing the breakfast dishes and was stacking away plates in a cabinet over the sink that I saw the cherry-red message light persistently blinking. Since I'd checked as soon as I'd returned from my walk that morning, the missed call, two calls actually, had to have come in either while I was telling Bobbi goodbye or diddling around in the yard. "Hey guys, it's me." I smiled; only Brendan—of the boys, only Brendan, the middle one, the troubled one, the complete and total fuckup, would say that, say just "it's me," as if *of course* you'd know who "me" was, as of course I always did. "I'm just um... *Mom*? You there? Dad? Pick up pick up pick up pick up.

Guess not. Okay. Well. Um. I was just, you know, seeing if everything was all right there. All right, then. Okay."

The second message was also from Brendan.

"Me again. Hey guys? Call me, okay? Don't forget."

Because this was so not like Brendan, *so* not like him, I listened over again to his first message with what I'd have to say was mounting apprehension. Brendan had called just to see "if everything was all right there"? Why wouldn't it be?

Brendan's number on Caller ID didn't match either of the ones we had for him on the card wheel. There was even a different area code. Did that mean he was no longer in Maryland? Last we'd heard from Brendan, he was in Laurel. Working at the track in Laurel. Before that he was at the Meadowlands, in New Jersey. And before that? I couldn't recall.

"Bren?"

"This is Kevin."

"Is Brendan there?"

"Brendan. Brendan. Can you tell me what he looks like?"

I got only as far as to say, "Well, to be honest—" when there was a burst of snotty laughter, not just from Kevin but from several other guys who must have been standing nearby listening. Then I heard Brendan's reedy voice in the background, "You are such a dick—gimme that!" and finally my prodigal son (but aren't they all?) came on the phone. "Hello?"

"Brendan, it's Dad."

"Hey, Dad. Sorry about all that."

Then there was a loud dull thump, followed instantly by a high-pitched shriek of laughter, then "Ow ow ow ow, motherfucker!" and I would have confidently bet a hundred dollars that my son had just made a fist, a giant fist considering Brendan's size, and playfully but mulishly punched this Kevin character hard in the upper arm. I could see it, I could just see it. Oh Brendan.

"Sorry, Dad. Sorry, sorry. I'm here."

"And where's that?"

"What?"

"Where are you calling from?" Then I remembered that I'd placed the call and rephrased: "Where are you now? At work?"

"Kind of."

What the hell did that mean, *kind of*? How can you be *kind of* at work? But I knew better than to pursue it. "Sorry we missed your calls," I said. "But we got your messages."

"You and Mom both?"

"Just me. Mom's on her way to Aunt And's."

"Aunt Nutso's?" Brendan laughed. "But so why would she be unavailable at Aunt Andrea's?"

"Unavailable? What's that supposed to mean?" Here we go again, I thought. Talking to Brendan was like—it was like Abbott and Costello, "Who's on First?" You remember that routine? It was like that more often than not, confused and daffy, daffier by the minute. "Brendan?"

"I'm just telling you what she said last night in her email. Mom said she'd be unavailable, but not how come. So that's how come I called."

I had no idea where to begin. "Email? You got an email from Mom? I didn't know you could even *get* email, Brendan."

"I can get it." He sounded like his feelings were hurt. "I get it at work. Or, you know, I got friends with computers."

"I wish I'd known. I don't have any email address for you."

"Well, you should've asked Mom."

"I guess I should've. But I'm trying to understand this. Mom sent you an email last night..."

"Not just me. Mike and Stevie too. I saw she sent it to all three of us."

"Could you read me this email?"

"I'm not where I can, you know? I can't. Sorry, Dad."

I didn't believe him. "Well, what I think, you know what I think? Is maybe your mom didn't make herself as clear as she might have, maybe she was saying that she'd be unavailable because she'll be at Aunt And's helping take care of the new baby. Unavailable like that, too busy."

Brendan breathed into the phone. "Maybe."

Then in a raised voice I said, "Unavailable for *how* long?" And knew the second I'd done it that I'd made a mistake. Raising your voice to Brendan, or even just around him, had always been dangerous. Even when he was 10 or 11 it was never a good idea. So quietly now, evenly, I tried again: "Unavailable for how long, Bren—did Mom say?"

"Couple of weeks. Then she'd call us. She'd call us but don't try calling her. That's what her email said. And that we shouldn't call you, either."

"But you did."

"Yeah, I guess. But I guess I thought maybe I'd get Mom before she went all unavailable. I don't know. I'm sorry."

"Brendan, no, hey."

"I'm sorry I fucking called. I'm sorry I ever fucking called at all. Just forget I did, all right? All right?"

"Brendan, relax, it's okay, and it's great hearing your voice again. It's so great."

"I have to go. I'm at work."

Now he was positively at work. Not just "kind of."

"Bren, why don't you call up your mom right now on her cell? And you can see for yourself just how available she is. What do you say? You'll feel better. You want her number? Or do you have it? Brendan?"

"I have to go," he said, and hung up.

It was entirely possible, Brendan being Brendan, that he'd had a too-vivid dream last night, or just hallucinated the entire thing. In all likelihood, he still had no access to email. He wasn't very—Brendan just wasn't, period. *But*… in the unlikely event Bobbi *had* sent him an email, I needed to know what in hell was going on. "Unavailable?" It made no sense. And the more I turned it over my mind, the more convinced I became it was just Another Brendan Event, this one mercifully not involving either an Emergency Room or the state police.

I tapped out Bobbi's cell phone number.

After just one ring an electronic female voice said, "This is message B-8. The Verizon customer you're calling is currently unavailable. Please hang up and call again later."

I redialed, with the same exasperating result. Okay, now this was strange. Officially this had turned a little bit strange—where was Bobbi's personal greeting, what happened to *that*?—but so far it was nothing to worry about or get weirded over. I considered calling Brendan back, changed my mind and started to call Bobbi's sister Andrea instead. I canceled, though, before I could tap in the final digit.

Okay. Exactly *why* had I almost called Andrea?

Enough. That's it, I thought. Finito. I'd just wait till Bobbi checked in from the road. Then find out what was going on, or, more likely, not. I was certain I'd hear from her within a few hours, possibly sooner, first time she pulled off the road to stretch and use a bathroom. In the meantime, didn't I have some movies to watch?

3

The way I structured my horror course, it wasn't only movies, there was required reading too—one anthology and five or six novels. But while I varied the movies, I almost never changed the texts—same novels every time by King and Straub and Shirley Jackson, same stories by Poe and Bierce and Lovecraft. So I wouldn't seem out of touch I used a few stories by contemporary writers like Dennis Etchison and Poppy Z. Brite, but it was mostly the old standbys. Occasionally I'd toss in something oddball—"The Yellow Wallpaper" or *Jesus' Son* or anything by Thom Jones—call it "horror," see what the students made of it. (Not much, usually.)

To you, though, I'll admit the readings were pretty much a flyer at legitimacy (Esteemed Colleagues, as you can see, it's not complete bullshit, just mostly) and that what interested me and kept me teaching the course were the movies.

I never grew tired of watching horror movies. Didn't matter if I'd watched something twenty times, I could always watch it again. Even turkeys like *Blair Witch 2* and *Scream 3* I could see over and over. I wasn't sure why, or even how, this stuff worked on me, but it did. Since I was a boy in Dayton reading *Famous Monsters of Filmland*, it did.

After I'd decided not to worry further over Brendan's call, I got straight to work. I selected four DVDs—*Freaks*, the James Whale *Frankenstein*, Coppola's *Dracula*, and *Gut Wrench*, a low-budget bogeyman feature from the early 1990s. I put that on first since I'd seen it the fewest times, but in the brief silence between the home video credits and the appearance of the Main Menu, a car pulled into my driveway and the engine cut off. It jumped crazily to mind that Bobbi had turned around and driven home. I couldn't imagine why, but felt certain I was right, so uncomfortably certain that I hesitated before going into the front room and peeking through the blinds.

Parked behind my Saturn, but not close behind it, ten feet down the driveway, almost at the street, was a new-looking Ford F-10 long bed truck painted the most godawful lime-green. I could just barely detect a country song, a male singer, neither recognizable. The tune abruptly stopped and the driver's side door swung open and then a man who was positively enormous took his sweet time getting out. Because of the music, I was surprised to see the man was black. African-American.

It wasn't anyone I knew until the instant it most certainly was.

Although I might have recognized him at once from his size as well as by the incongruously light-footed way he made his progress up the driveway, along the slate walk and onto the front porch, I'd been thrown off by the way he'd come dressed: in a blue sport coat over a bluer Izod shirt, gray chinos, uncuffed and a skosh too short, white socks and shiny black loafers. Every time I'd seen him in the past, and it had been years since I'd seen him at all, D.C. Mothersole had on either painters' coveralls or faded flannel shirts and old Levis with rolled cuffs, always steel-toed scuffed work boots and a cap of some kind. Beginning with the screened-in deck (Bobbi called it the "sun porch"), D.C. had done a lot of work for us, mostly carpentry and painting, but also minor electrical and plumbing.

He was about my age, but there wasn't a line stamped on his face. (I can't say the same thing about mine.) His hair was short, the only gray in it some tufts above and around his ears. He was, if I had to venture a guess, six-four, 280 pounds. He had killer arms and a powerful chest (I can't believe I'm using that word, "powerful," a powerful chest) but his stomach was tremendous, stupefyingly big. It pushed against his knit shirt, overstretching it like a drumhead. D.C. liked to eat, sure enough, but he didn't drink. No one did in his family, he'd told us. He'd been raised Jehovah's Witness but was no longer involved.

I had never expected to see D.C. Mothersole again (unless we were to run into each other by accident at the movies or one of the malls, not very likely since he lived way out in the boonies) and I had no intention now of answering the doorbell. I went back into the family room to wait it out.

I picked up the remote and selected "Play Movie." The first shot was an eerily lit slow pan down a subterranean maze of old steam pipes, water droplets beaded at the couplings and along the undersides. "Pinfold Pictures Presents." D.C. kept a steady finger on the bell. "A Film by Hoagie Topher." After the bell ringing stopped, the knocking started.

Then it alternated between ringing and knocking, ringing and knocking. "K Steuben." "John Galen." "Angelique Dobbs." "In."

"Professor Cudhy!"

For Christ's sake, what the hell did he want? Work? No more work. Go away.

"Mr. Cudhy? Professor?"

When I couldn't put up any longer with the racket, I clomped into the front hall carrying the legal pad and one of my gel pens, most probably (I really hadn't thought it through) as a signal to D.C. that I'd been hard at work, an implicit criticism of the big man for having interrupted me at it. But when I opened the door I pretended delighted surprise. I hate that about me.

"My God," I said, "it's been forever!" I stepped onto the porch, not offering my hand. "How are you, D.C.?"

"Doing well, Professor." His voice was both raspy and hoarse and made you think of a sore throat, you couldn't help it. "No cause for complaint."

But he looked uncomfortable, even gloomy, which from my limited (but not slight) knowledge of the man seemed out of character. Outwardly, nothing ever bothered D.C., not a stretch of bad weather, not unreliable help, not arthritis, not back surgery.

Except now he seemed unsure of himself, and vexed by the need to explain his presence. "I was hoping to talk with you, Professor—"

"Lou."

"—and I was hoping you would invite me in."

"I'm sorry, I don't understand. You want to talk to me about what, exactly?"

"Not want. *Need.* Need to."

"And what do you 'need' to talk to me about?"

"Roberta."

At first it didn't register: none of her brothers and sisters, not even her parents, ever called her Roberta. I certainly never had. More than a few times I'd heard her say the last people who'd called her that were the Sisters of St. Joseph at St. John Bosco, like a million-and-a-half years ago.

"You need to talk to me about Bobbi? I don't understand."

"Can we please go inside? And I'll make sure you do."

"No. You stand right there till you answer me. What the fuck is going on, D.C.?"

"Language. All right? And you a college professor."

"I'll use any fucking language I want… 'all right'? Now why'd you come here *needing* to talk to me about Bobbi?"

"You know where she is right now?" he said. "No, wait. Let me just tell you something: you don't. You might think you do, but you don't. You think she's somewhere, but she's someplace else."

"Jesus." All of the sudden I was bleary and flush, out of register, how I always felt when coming down with some bug. My legs started to quiver.

"No, it's okay—it's okay, but let's go inside," said D.C. pulling open and holding open the glass door, whose jamb and lintels I'd called him to replace after Hurricane Isabel tore off the flanges along with chunks of wood. "It's hot out here." He took the pad and pen from my fingers. "Let's go inside."

I don't remember getting from the front porch to the back of the house. But suddenly I was in the family room and so was D.C., who was pulling open one of the glass doors to the sun porch he'd built for us about ten years ago. Nineteen ninety-four. *Twelve* years. "Not there," I said. "In here."

Whatever D.C. Mothersole planned to tell me, whatever terrible thing, I was afraid it would turn out to be all my fault.

On the TV screen, a large hulking man stumbled through scalding clouds of steam as pipes burst over his head. I picked up the remote and paused the movie. Then I sat down. D.C. remained on his feet.

"You wanted to come in," I said. "Well, you're in. So talk."

He thought for a moment and then nodded.

But when he spoke the only words I heard at first were: "Me and Roberta."

Otherwise, there was just loud blat and hissy static in my head.

With a little shrug, D.C. sat down on the sofa and, cupping his hands over his knees, waited like Buddha for my response.

Which, when it came finally, was this: "You and Roberta *what?*"

THE SOBER HORSE THIEF

TYLER MAGILL

He checked his bag again at 12,
then turned off the news. No story.

He drove past the klieglit
Taco Bell, the lightning struck
car lot, Wal-Mart open
twenty-four hours. He
tipped his hat. We swing-shift fucks.
Hey, mac. Out into the country—

what country? His coffee cooled
at a steady pace. On the parkway,
he was cut off at 70 by a man
in sunglasses. Well,
the moon is full. All night gas.

Donuts. Bearclaws. He drove out
into the country. When he was drunk,
the country was right outside of town.

He came back at five with nothing
but the paper. His wife grunted warmly
as he floated into bed. Well,
tomorrow night. As dawn broke
quiet like a pick into a lock, he dreamed
of his unborn son on a perfect Exmoor pony.

THE SCAR
TARFIA FAIZULLAH

stitched my shoulder
whole until it grew thick,
          an arm-husk
never filled
          with shadow
                    or light—

above me,
          it twisted
like ant-eaten bark, it rubbed

between his thighs
          while mosquitoes brooded
with their kiss-

hungry mouths. It skinned
          lake-water
like a scythe, it carried

the word
                    cauterize
across the arcing desert

of an elephant's back,
until the ochre sky

wished itself

amber,
until the skin broke,

revealed a trapped woman
shaped

like an ebony tusk

RECKON THY DISEASE ITS COURTSHIP
ALLISON TITUS

Lie down.   At the hem of the wharf   lie down.

Where water baskets
the shoreline and longs to make a grave of you,
of course, current by current   a flood.

Northern, piano field.   Mineral weeds ratchet the cold,
degree by degree collect symptoms of winter. Hospital bed
frames quarantine the marsh,   wrist bones buried

with filigreed lockets, with buck knives.

All manner of prosthetic surplus

in the dumpster, custom-made hands dressed in PVC skin,
ghost mechanics of a new body. Forget the ancient faces
and jotted down summers, the sweatshirts with the neck

cut out   how the clavicle shined

its outlaw shape so you could not help
but witness.

Every bone   ledgers

every shadow   inventories   white.

Rabbit carcass. Crutches, curettes.   Nothing safer
nothing safe.   Fog sews the afternoon over
us   sews us inside
the afternoon.

It is cold here

at the hem of the wharf lie down.

DORCHESTER DIARY
MUKI MAHAN

1

I BELIEVE that, among the various ways of self-expression available to most, the only truly closer to diddling (an abused term) than keeping a blog in general is stuffing the same with reflections on itself. Yet keeping in mind that the acknowledgement of one's sins is the first step towards atonement (or for some its preemptive attainment), merely by stating this I also at once believe myself above (and unspattered by) an obscure horde of others that might presently be engaged in this same activity. I am without disdain, because I know very little about them. I did check to see whose blogs were virtually adjacent to mine within this vast service, and they were: a Catholic evangelical (?) and a Canadian gun enthusiast. I am proud to call them my neighbors. Generally, I do not read blogs. I would like many people to read mine, and I am willing to read others' as long as it is understood that this would entail reciprocal praise.

My primary reason in keeping mine is for my name, Muki Mahan, to be made much more widespread on the internet. My reasons for that I will not disclose; it would defeat the purpose. After expressing my wish to a good friend, I was told the best way of accomplishing this.

So, *Muki Mahan*, a blog by Muki Mahan.

What concerns me now is, first, what to fill it with, and second, how to promote it. I am skeptical whatever choices I make for the former will influence the latter. But I am patient.

I doubt many of these are actually read from their inception, so it might seem a little silly to begin by revealing my intentions and what my readers can expect later on. But I am made uncomfortable by imaginary familiarity—much in the manner of a panhandler—so I'd prefer my first post not to suggest this wonderful catalogue had any history longer than it has.

For the time being, I will probably describe my habits, my opinions, and my home of Dorchester, Massachusetts. I am unemployed, so all will be given to excess. Weekly, at least, I will devote one posting to a review of Dorchester nightlife, with the hope of eventually compiling a comprehensive guide. This would be a service, and who knows, maybe even an enticement.

I am satisfied with how I have performed today.

Muki Mahan

2

In good faith I thought I'd start on my Dorchester bar guide (which will proceed from the Blarney Stone northward) and decided first to revisit mildly divey PJ Quinn's. A genuine cesspit will both be well-lit and smell of a men's room; PJ Quinn's, I recalled, was usually dark. It is also situated near a miserable intersection with a service station and a turnoff for the 93 entrance ramp. I was completely unprepared for what I encountered there.

Now, as I was walking down Dot Ave, I witnessed four reassuring omens: a mother driving a dented minivan with several young children who rolled her window down to scream obscenities at me after I jaywalked in front of her; a squat Vietnamese man with *Braveheart*-like hair and an ornate crucifix hanging from his neck that glowered at me on the sidewalk; at Theo's (which is disgusting), an obese priest sitting at the window devouring a slice of pizza folded in half; a prostitute that accosted me outside the Burger King. Nothing to think I wouldn't soon ensconce myself amid drunk Polish teens, a few lost causes and palpable frecklessness.

PJ Quinn's, at some point, apparently, was transformed into "dbar" (I assume "d" stands for an emphatic article). The entire bar staff wore goatees and tight black t-shirts; the patrons (aside from a few clusters of middle-aged women, the nearest to me tittering with mischief since one had bought a stove on craigslist) were either older men drinking glasses of red wine at the bar or much younger men standing around with tinted martinis. Behind the bar itself (which had doubled in size) was a screen reading "dbar" whose background faded through the color wheel.

This I stared at most in my stupor.

3

Because it's unseemly to carouse before Thursday, and because I have been told that to write less than twice a week consigns one's blog to universal indifference, this evening I will depart from my guide to the dives of Dorchester Avenue (tomorrow I will be visiting Nash's) and instead offer what could of course be an unwelcome glimpse into my daily routine, in precise detail, so that if I am lucky some undesirables might set upon me at some point on my way picked out in advance and *murder* me, hopefully within the Public Gardens. Late afternoon I usually leave the apartment and take the T to Park Street, where I walk through the Common, down Boylston, etc. I have been doing this for some time, both before I left Boston and since I returned, and I have noticed that the same gauntlet of derelicts stretching to Copley Square have begun to offer increasingly incisive remarks concerning my person. Often they complement my attire. This walk takes me at most ten minutes, unless I stop to savor a street performer, such as the demented, gravelly-voiced fellow that sings "The Candy Man" with horrifying reverb on his portable karaoke machine or the older, overweight one that plays the alphabet song on his tuba. My walk stops at the Public Library. I no longer enter the new wing, because it saddens me and I am no longer allowed to check out books. I prefer the Bates Hall reading room. First, however, because I am vain, I visit the basement restroom to primp; before seven pm, every day, at any moment, one encounters there a noisy, disreputable conventicle, none of whom seem to be interested in using the fixtures there for any other reason than concealment. I am not above them. Now. The reading room is very quiet, and it once took much more than the meager boldness I possessed to traverse the length of the hall looking for a chair next to a disingenuously studious BU coed rather than an elderly man unconscious face-first on the tabletop with a stack of unsigned cheap-looking Christmas cards at his elbow. However, those days are gone, I am aging fast and, as the song goes, I have waved my conscience bye-bye. As I remove my coat I flash those nearest me an ambiguous smile. Seated, I remove from my bag a notebook, which I scrutinize with a grimace, then shut with a sigh. Then I remove a book I have chosen to disinterest me. For example, this evening it was *Grace*

Abounding for the Chief of Sinners. I can swallow no more than a paragraph at a time. Very few people (in fact, no one ever) at the same table has been intrigued by this routine, so usually, I must look out for the few people that might walk by occasionally—as they approach, I hold the book in front of my face and make a humming sound that ascends in pitch, and descends as they pass.

Should anyone have any other suggestions, I would be very thankful.

4

Nash's Pub from the outside looks as if it were purchased from Pizza Hut, but painted green, with one awkward gable, windowless except for three-and-a-half foot-wide octagonal portholes, mostly occluded by neon signs for, from the left, Corona, Bud Light and Guinness. There was no one inside, and the Irish bartender seemed disconcerted by my presence. There is a pool table, above which is a partially deflated miniature Budweiser blimp. Shortly after my entrance, the telephone rang; to whomever it was at the end of the line the bartender said, "Yes. There's one." Then glared at me. We watched the local news in silence. I hadn't watched such programs for a while, and it was interesting to recall how they are essentially televised crime blotters. The first story was of a disgruntled, jilted woman who tried to blow up her ex-boyfriend's townhouse by snaking a garden hose affixed to the valve of a propane tank through a window she had cleverly punched in several nights before. Her boyfriend noticed the likely overpowering stench and called the police. Throughout the segment her strung-out mug shot was intermittently flashed and no real motive was even suggested (child support?) aside from rabid jealousy. There was an amusing bit about how she had somehow forged INS documents threatening deportation and mailed them to his current girlfriend. The next story was about a teenager that had fallen off the trunk of a moving car and presumably cracked his skull, considering the breathlessness of the correspondent standing outside the emergency room and the aerial footage of his stretcher being lifted into the ambulance. Strangely little of the piece seemed to discourage such behavior; rather, it focused on the driver's regret and the community's grief, which was represented by a weary looking middle-aged man gesturing on his front lawn. After this came news of a man who took a pot shot at his ex-wife in the parking garage of a shopping mall in Nashua. A policeman was interviewed and, though generally evasive, expressed his disapproval. About this time, a man entered the pub, looked at me, then the bartender, then the television, then left. I asked the bartender if it was usually this slow. "Yes, for the past year."

The next, slightly less empty bar I visited last night has always been something of a mystery to me, for it has no actual name (there is a plastic banner on the broadside reading, "Dorchester Function Hall") and the only other times I'd been there—typically quite late, when I was very bored—it'd been packed with young, drunk Irish. Parts of it are carpeted, all of it's well-lit and lacking any ornament; it reminds me of a dismal mortgage broker's office in Woburn I worked at for exactly one and a half days several years ago. There were three people inside, excluding the bartender. They seemed to be friends, and two were pretty suspicious of me. The other was drunk and almost slumped over the jukebox. "How Soon Is Now?" was playing. He staggered to the bar and asked, "Do you like Morrisey?" I replied, "I guess." He was creepy. Apparently, his father-in-law owns the place. I recommended they remove the fluorescent overheads; he seemed appreciative. Then he went on to describe his pregnant wife in Weymouth and his job. None of it made very much sense, and he was rocking on his heels and making strange facial movements reminiscent of tardive dyskinesia.

Later, I went to the Banshee, but that will require an entry of its own.

Also, I will consider the suggestion I switch this blog into a sort of soft-core serial.

5

Tom English (the "TO" on its sign was lost to a fire some time ago) is the closest bar to my apartment, and though I've lived here on and off for about a year and a half, I've gone there no more than a half dozen times, which is significant I think, given my habits. This is a little to my discredit, and ideally you should like Tom English, for it's the best example of a type somewhat unique to Dorchester—the aboveground bunkerish brick cube pub—and more so than any other establishment in the area has a peculiar mythical status. I have heard, among other things, that various patrons deal eightballs by the bar, that the interior was once decorated with bigoted murals, that the regulars accost women on the sidewalk: "Haven't I seen you at the Golden Banana?" etc. Whatever the appeal of these bits, Tom English might best be summed up in mentioning that two years ago, during a miserable blizzard, with two feet of snow on the ground, I was walking about the neighborhood and discovered it was the only place open for blocks; when I entered, the entire room took maybe a minute to turn their heads nearly in unison to me, then back to the TV.

Last Saturday, I went to see a movie and came out in an odd wandering state, terrifically restless, and found myself in Dorchester around midnight. I was not up for speaking to anyone, so I went to Tom English. There were six or seven people, not so much silent as emitting a kind of latent, semi-audible grumbling hum. Two women, one dumpy and middle aged, one painted-up and adolescent, were each playing Megatouches perfectly opposite the bar. A prognathous elderly man was sitting nearest the entrance, with amber-tinted glasses, drinking swill beer. A degenerate Southie was leering at the younger of the two women. The television was on mute, there was no music, and the lights were perfectly fixed to accentuate everyone's discolorations. The fat bartender, whose face and hands were almost indistinguishable, approached me after a long look and said, "Hrngfph." I ordered a Guinness. He took the money without a look or break in pace as he waddled to the men's room. The degenerate Southie was sitting to my left, and, realizing his attention to the other side was unwanted, started in on me. "Look a tha cashmeah coat!" I smiled and drank. Silence, aside from the senile blips and blops of video gambling. "Look a tha cashmeah coat!" I turned to him. "Long tiemahgo." He leaned over, and belched silently. "This a-happen!" He ran the top of his index finger under the bottom of his chin with a hideous expression on his face. "Shrrrrrk!" He cackled. "Look a tha cashmeah coat!" There was another pause. "Howsa Guinness huh?" I said it was good. He cackled again. "They hadn't serveah fuckin glass of tha in months!" I was downing the last of it now, looking in, and saw a single eyelash descending the pint glass on the inside amid the froth-dregs. As my friend turned to the young girl and began to suggest she sleep with me, I made my exit.

6

The Banshee (or as Sean-o, my Korean neighbor, calls it, "DAVANSHI!") I have visited often. And because I will soon exhaust the dives on my street (should I go back to each a second time, or a third, or pick one to properly rot in?) I saved it for at least near the last of my tiresome entries on this topic. Its facade is appealing, belying the interior in a way: there are five or more flat screen televisions around the bar. Encased soccer or rugby jerseys decorate the walls; much of the rest is either red or black. There are pool tables upstairs. Before, you could drink on the fire escape, and the adjacent alley was open for smoking—at its height they installed buffet-style heat lamps for the winter. When I came back, the alley was closed off. I have not bothered to ask why. I almost never speak to anyone there. Once I was on something like friendly terms with a former bartender. But I exude gloom, it seems, and after a few half-hearted attempts to speak with him, solely for the sake of propriety, and to fend off a little familiarity—"So you from Ireland?" "Aye." "Nice."—I stopped, entirely. Now they've a first-rate neckless clod that must consume buckets of creatine. I do remember fondly my first visit there, with two dear friends, three years ago—we were dressed up for Mass, quite excited, but St. William's was closed, or we were late, or rain was threatening, or the door smiled at me, and we ended up drinking there all that Sunday afternoon. Then, later, when I did move to Dorchester, within my first month there were two fabulous bar brawls I watched from the staircase. The first time, some drunk punched a waitress in the face. I can't remember what caused the second. Both ended in protracted, very pointless scrumlike piles. These memories are bittersweet, those times irrecoverable. The decrepit tone is intentional.

So a little more than a week ago, I went and the typical carnie-like bouncer with a wad of cash stopped me at the door. "Five Bahks! Fer tha Toyz fer Tots!" I paid this, with misgivings. Inside, it was still quiet. Recently I'd befriended a skittish Moroccan man who spoke no English and was missing a finger. His English was poor. I didn't see him. After three rounds, I went out to smoke. More were starting to arrive, particularly those women my Anglophilic friend Marina refers to as "slappers." They came in twos and threes, with lowcut tops and loud vows to the bouncer—"I'ma feelin h-horny tonight, ya!" When I came back inside, they were sort of unconsciously clustered around my empty chair. I had to make my way through. They weren't long in noticing me, and the jolliest of the bunch asked after a minute—"Yare uful quite inight?"

Meanwhile, an older Scotsman (?) angry over the required donation, could be seen accosting women—"Is yare name Tot? Cus I've a toy fer ya."

After I watched what seemed a kind of mute paternity inquiry performed through dance between one young woman and five beet-red hooligans, I walked outside and went home, with almost no thought of a single thing I'd seen or did or said.

7

The Aces High Pub is at Andrew Square and has, unfortunately, no thematic connection to Iron Maiden.

It's a little tricky figuring out which of the three doors is the actual entrance, but if you need to get in badly, you will. Its name refers to the unusual variety of low-grade gambling options available. There is even something resembling a card table, and a pool table, possibly two, in the adjoining room. I didn't look back there. They serve food that I imagine is disgusting. Most people there were either playing Keno or the Megatouch. I should mention recently I encountered a woman with a tracheotomy playing a Megatouch, the paired-photo-discrepancy-game, only the paired photos were pornographic and the discrepancies largely around the erogenous zones, but this was in a different city a couple weeks ago and I saw nothing so reassuring on this visit. The decor is the most festive of any bar I've been to in Dorchester, excluding the Blarney Stone, whose insides more resemble a laser-tag arena. By festive, I mean in this instance there are a number of different colored lights, some of which blink, all of which are plastic. There were three restless youths at the card table, all wearing flat caps and track suits. One was reading a copy of *The Brothers Bulger.* They would occasionally run out together, then return minutes after. They offered something to an older red-haired gentleman at the bar (he several times insulted them in their absence)—I could not hear what exactly, but he declined, complaining about his liver. They were also offering everyone at the bar condoms, for free, which I failed to understand. Possibly this was mandated community service. The only female there was the bartender, who was in her mid-50s at least and very maternal.

While I was watching *Law & Order*, I first noticed the man sitting beside me because throughout the opening credits he was snapping, "Catch'em, Kojak! Catch'em, Kojak!" He later introduced himself as Mark. He is apparently a regular, and by far the best reason to drink there. We discussed New Year's resolutions. He told me to find a rich wife, to grab a rich wife, rather, "but don't grab her too hard and crack her ribs." He then said, "You know I know the girl from Ipanema? I met her, she came to the lounge... [*points toward the pool table*]... I said to her, 'Can I see your controls?' She had a googoobabadajabberwocky machine! She was making sounds with it [*shrieks in very high pitch while holding his ears*]. She was playing with the pigeons... they was flying all over, smackin into the window... I said, 'I said you can't do that! They's birds of flight! Animals!'" He paused. Then he stood up, walked to the center of the bar, threw both hands in the air and shouted, "I GOTTA FUTURE!"

8

It would be dishonest of me to continue this little guide without devoting a humorless entry to a particularly repugnant aspect of Dorchester, one I may've hinted at before without offering the unfamiliar an adequate sense of its pervasiveness.

Recently, I have been going out to the local dives with a friend of mine that lives a couple floors above. The scene at Tom English he'd shown me was even stranger than I'd thought, with many of the seeming myths surrounding it turning out to be but milder versions of the case.

Regardless, last week we decided to have several rounds there in the hope of covering our tab with Keno winnings. We were encouraged by our neighbor, a misshapen overweight man named Steve-o, who reputedly makes a living off Keno and scratch tickets. I believe there's some sort of annuity mixed in, but there is almost no doubt he does not work, and in the warmer months he spends his mornings and afternoons bathed in sweat, watering his garden and casting resentful looks at our own. I never quite understood his hostility. It seemed to be directed at our squash plant, whose tendrils negligibly trespass on his side of the chain link fence.

After six games or so, my friend and I gave up and settled. It was a weekday evening, and the usual crowd there—a cheerful prostitute, the aforementioned Steve-o, West Indian coke dealers, and if one is very lucky, Boobar—was looking awful glum. We had the choice of going either to Cataloni's in Upham's Corner (also known by the local bigots as "Browntown") or to the Banshee, which I've described before. Cataloni's is pretty hit or miss—come the wrong night and the bar's empty save a hunchbacked elderly man with a fake leather fedora standing out on the sidewalk trading obscenities with the bouncer—and a far walk in the cold, so we headed out for the latter. This was to prove a poor decision.

The Banshee, slightly more so than most places on Dorchester Avenue, has the reputation of being rather racist. I'd only encountered this once before, when during an aimless evening I stepped out to smoke and found the bouncer refusing entrance to KK, a good-natured elderly Rastafarian who owns a house on the way to the T-stop and spends most of his time in his front yard, riding a stationary bike, smoking a blunt and waving at passersby. At the time, I invited him back to my apartment to drink some wine and forget about how miserable a place it was, and made a vague vow never to return.

This time, when my friend and I arrived, we met a drunken local buffoon, Puppy Danny, known so partly for his demeanor and partly for his job walking dogs in Beacon Hill. He was crip-walking around the bar and compulsively licking his lips. Aside from him, there was a bevy of homely Irish lasses and their rodent-like nylon-clad escort who was milling about giving us laughably menacing looks. We bought Puppy Danny a round to encourage idiocy, and within ten minutes he was trying to scale a pole and otherwise aping for the giggling table. We sat down with them to enjoy the spectacle. I recall my friend excusing himself to use the restroom. Soon after I heard a yell—"He stool 'er fookin purse!"—and a brief commotion; when I turned around the bartender (the meathead I mentioned in a previous post) and bouncer were dragging my friend (who is black) by the throat towards the door. I pulled the bartender off roughly enough that he and the other decided to punch me several times while my friend split. After some ridiculous talk of detaining me while they called the police—the idea being he had swiped this fictitious purse lying on the bar ten feet from its owner and made his getaway by casually walking into a men's room stall—I walked out, where on the sidewalk I was formally banished forever.

When I met my friend a few minutes later at the apartment he was in relatively good spirits, with only a large welt on his forehead from having it slammed into the bar or the bathroom door or both.

9

Richard "Boobar" Dirkins, roustabout and raconteur, was banned from Tom English near the end of January. I have written of him briefly before, first anonymously as a "degenerate Southie" who mocked my coat during a pointless late-night visit to the same, and later, as I grew to know him, as its most inviting fixture. It is difficult to do him adequate justice through a mere listing of his most peculiar attributes, but I will try.

I was first introduced to Boobar through my friend Danny, who met him through Norm (who drives a Cadillac, carries a pair of eightballs with him at all times, and triumphantly vanishes at last call, only to telephone later in the evening from a plush hotel room surrounded by escorts). Boobar's reputedly Norm's "muscle" and does seem to defer to him, or at least absorb his insults. For example, I have seen Boobar slink back out the door if Norm catches him disheveled and return clean-shaven with an "open book" part. At our first meeting, Boobar was taken with my hair (which at the time was a mop) and my origin (Washington, D.C.) and concluded from these that I was a CIA operative. He also believed I was a kind of computer genius because I was able to find "Crazy Train" for him on the internet jukebox. When it came on, his eyes widened and he gave me a warm embrace. Then he began ranting about Humvee shortages in Baghdad. Since then, he inexplicably refers to me as "Al Qaeda." Boobar drives a pickup truck. He parks it behind the bar because his primary pastime is ducking out for a few minutes to snort cocaine off the front armrest. He will remind you often that his truck costs forty thousand dollars. In the backseat he keeps a rubber pit bull. If you touch it, he screams, "BE GOOD TO WOLFIE!" He insists on showing you a picture-booth roll of his very strange looking "Injun" daughter. You can't help but scrutinize it at least for a few seconds, after which he snatches it from your hands. "DON'T GET ANY IDEAS!" He has many unique theories on the Bible, one of which is that it teaches you to hate "niggahs, spics and queeahs." This was apparently a crucial part of his upbringing that he outspokenly rejects, and in dealing with any member of these three groups, he is quick to point this out while consciously or unconsciously still referring to the person by the appropriate slur.

Boobar refers to himself in the third person, sometimes as "Boobar," sometimes as "Boobs," sometimes as "Boob." He is fond of showing off a tattoo on his shoulder—it reads, "Boobar." I have no idea where he got this name. Possibly he mumbled drunken nonsense at a tattoo parlor, woke up, then ran with it. On rough days, he shows up at the bar in his pajamas. You show up at 7 or so: "Al Qaeda, I been smokin baaaaags since 10 AM, dog!" You notice his Red Sox winter cap and think he wears it more to have a hat with a "B." He describes a characteristic failed courtship—"Boobah was drivin the truck down daht have, huh, and sees this Polish guhl standin out fronna that queeah joint 'dbar,' ya know? smokin and starin at Boobah, so he drives back a couple tahms and she goes inside, so Boobah goes in askin, 'Whats the story heah? You want some ah Boobar?' and ahm in my pajahmas, right, staht tellin the whole bah I got nothin gainst queeahs and then she tells Boobah he's comin ahn too strong? TOO STRONG?"

He throws his hands out, agape in exasperation.

10

Two weeks ago at Tom English, as I drank a near-clear Cranberry & Ruble and an elastic middle aged effeminate man gyrated a few feet behind me to "Death or Glory," Danny turned to me and asked, "Have you seen Kevin lately?" "No." "I think he's in jail. That's why his family looks so sad." Soon we were walking up Taft and saw Kevin with a pair of friends, drunk, about to mount their motorcycles. "We thought you were in jail." He smiled. "Nah. That's next week." "What for?" "Anothah

DUI. What you boys up to tonight?" He revved his engine. Our street was covered with a thick layer of ice.

Kevin was the first person I met from the neighborhood; he lives next door. I'd seen him around, most memorably in a simian crouch, brandishing a brick over a pair of copulating cats. He runs a chop shop out of his backyard, and over the summer several times holds cookouts, blasts Pearl Jam. It wasn't until late August two years ago we first spoke. There'd been a party at our apartment, and around dawn I came out to the back porch with some Casal Garcia, pausing maybe ten seconds between steps. He was just getting home. "What ya drinkin?" "Wine." He hopped the fence and poured his Budweiser into my cup. We toasted. "What's ya name?" This excited him. "What is tha, Pahchageez? C'MEAH!" We embraced. "Ya look like my son, ya know that?" He stepped back and offered his hand. When I reached he grabbed my forearm—I was made to understand I should grab his. This is how he greets people, or intimates at least. Then he began to speak of the old days in Southie, at times popping pills from an empty pack of Marlboro Lights. "Fahkin Judge Gaehty, from fahkin' *Newton...*" His preoccupation was the busing riots, during which he'd stabbed someone in the chest at the Savin Hill T-stop. "You in a union?" "No." He frowned, squinted at the rising sun. "Yuah all right." I will miss Kevin. Ted wonders whether they'll let him bring his iguana, Jorge, to jail, ideally in a little orange jumpsuit.

Now I must tell you, with much sadness, that I no longer live in Dorchester. I am on a rest cure, living nowhere, at home. I am broke and in weirdly good spirits. Today, I drove to the abandoned amphitheatre at Mason Neck, went by the Gravel Pit as well. Tomorrow I will sit in my room. I eat only almonds.

Once more I solicit suggestions on content.

11

If you understand how and why to take pleasure in the scene of an elderly woman in a plastic bowler, festooned with green beads, howling at an exhausted Darth Vader, who after making a few aimless swipes with a toy light saber, collapses into a folding chair, itself on the bed of a pickup truck followed by two platoons of Storm Troopers, several

Ewoks and the Imperial Guard marching proudly between opposite strips of underfunded, prefab housing projects, then you were probably at the annual Southie St. Patty's Day parade, somewhere not far from myself. I could not stay away. I had to visit once more. Do not be concerned at the number of policemen; they are only there to make sure the uniformed, off-duty policemen don't disgrace themselves too badly. At a convenience store, I watched as one of the latter, immaculately groomed for the occasion, ran in and did a brief jig while asking to use the bathroom. This happens often enough that the cashier refuses. In the lot out back, a man kneels on the asphalt, pounding a row of Bud Lights, and gives a thumbs up. Confused teens prowl about in green-and-white striped *Cat in the Hat* hats, drinking from bags, wearing t-shirts that read, "Kiss My Blarney Stone," with arrows beneath pointing downwards to their groins. No pub without an exorbitant cover charge: at the door of what even yesterday was but a large urinal stands a grizzled idiot who screams at your slightest turn, "Twinny bahks!" I was made to queue in front of the liquor store; upon entering, I realized I was the only one inside, as if a small plurality of people off the same street were enough to reduce the entire inventory to a thin pile of pungent shards of glass. Outside, eighty bagpipers pass, staggered into maybe four equal hordes, though always playing the same inane phrases; a grade-school karate class shows off their jump kicks; Civil War re-enactors and musket salvos, a few Whitey Bulger lookalikes racing around in black leather jackets and jeans, dark-shaded and crossing their lips, Albert "Dapper" O'Neill, retired city councilor and mild white supremacist, weaving his Cadillac dangerously close to the curbs, and finally the street sweepers, who spray the remaining sightseers with debris. At one point, I saw a woman I knew emerge from a brawl outside the Store 24 holding her two-year-old daughter in her arms, one of the few times I have literally clasped the sides of my head in horror. Never before had I felt it so likely a bottle would be broken by surprise over my skull.

12

When my name was mentioned to a man from Belfast, he paled. "OH-HO! The notorious MAA-HANS of the IRA! *I know them well.*" I am a mongrel like many others. Rarely has this been so well reaffirmed than by an afternoon spent standing on the deck of my Bolivian uncle's yacht moored in the Chesapeake. "We are, eh, parte Italiano, y parte Aleman, y un poco... Alpaca!" He alone snickered at this, drank from his tinkling tumbler of Johnny Walker Red, then hissed in through his front teeth. My last name served me well in Dorchester. Otherwise, I felt little connection. Once in the autumn it was time to harvest potatoes from our plot in the backyard; I surveyed the indifferent blackened, barren soil, and with some wellspring of intuition began to plunge my hand at random. Without fail I exhumed withered, wretched tubers worthy of Celine. Co Loc clapped her hands at the news and began to call me "Irish Instinct."

Since then, this strain of my ancestry, purely patrilineal, has remained a joke. However, the horror it seemed to provoke made me curious, and within ten minutes I discovered a variety of interesting things. The Mahans were from Devenish Island in Lough Erne. They apparently were custodians of an illuminated manuscript. They were later enslaved by a sadistic Scotsman named Hamilton. One fought with distinction on the side of the Jacobites in the Battle of the Boyne; James II granted him a coat of arms, which he cast aside, preferring instead an orgiastic exile in France. I have seen this crest. It's on a coaster I have.

I was dizzy with these revelations. I began to refer to my "clan." I cornered my father and shared everything I learned. He was unimpressed. "Who the fuck cares?"

I do. I wasn't aware how much until recently I was accused by someone's roommate of stealing and eating a baked potato wrapped in tin foil. Outwardly, I denied her accusation. Inwardly, I was consumed by rage. I intend some ethnic-themed revenge.

I also learned this week that the original purpose of this blog has been achieved. I am unsure of my next move.

Muki Mahan

GRANDFATHER JITTERBUG

NICK READING

Musk and cherry punch marked the floorboards
we shrunk across. That lavender and crinoline
smoothed a body around a body. I've never

written anything like this. In San Miguel
as our grandson imagines it years from now
I sat and wrote you a letter we have long lost.
It noted your good teeth and our daughters.

In it I stuffed jasmine and a narra leaf.
But he is imagining more. In good faith,
Catherine, last time I saw him he was fine
on scotch. He helped me to the bathroom

and back to bed never saying a word. Your body
though, was missed. I did taste the Elks Lodge shadow
in your hair and a song, a dumb song, that I forget.

GRANDMOTHER AS LEGEND
NICK READING

The Early Years

When she turned three she was already strong
and left to run through the dirt in rows,
seeds in her hand, begging the plow.
Yield what? said the dirt. The war was on.

Pleasantries: A Lullaby

Crickets find thick grass and tease
your Mama to thresh the bracken
while one million men and women
stir a mess in their sleep. Mess in their sleep.

Her Decline

She said go fetch the marigolds. Boil
water and reach for our wooden cups.
I returned and found myself dangerous
and she whispered that the tea was poisoned.

Since Her Death

Seven years of dirt in one jar from every summer
she hasn't seen. No worms, filled instead
with fingernails and her hair planted
as a bad joke. Now these knuckles...

How She'd Want It

Moon. No moon. Her house, my house
if full of rabbit shit and raccoons.
Every night is strung up by the bones
polished clean and left by the owls.

While We Sleep

Wake to her boards' rot. The coffin's
lining stinks. Our family is scattered
and strangers are as close as we make it
to memory, moving onto the pocked lawn.

Morning Prayer

I forget the last time you were sane.
Oh, my messy head. But the hollow
of your eye, your voice, and how
inside there was a familiar hallway.

WHAT YOU WANTED

CYNTHIA GRIER LOTZE

If you take the G up to Greenpoint,
be sure to visit Peter in his warehouse

with the timid cat and the sheetrock walls
and all the light and space anyone

could allow themselves to dream
of in Brooklyn. Sit on his couch

and dry out from the sideways rain
on Manhattan Avenue and ask him

about his film, about Prague
and about adventurous cats and rabbits

with human bodies—they slip
in and out of books like doors.

And when he begins to look
wistfully toward his towering

manuscript on the desk, say,
Let's get some lunch, before you

both self-destruct. One day, you know
you will take the G to Greenpoint

and you will be entirely unable
to speak. You will look at Peter

and he will look at you
and there will be writing covering

every inch of his delicate walls,
his shy cat rewritten in seventeen

different versions of cat, nearly disappearing.

RECONSTITUTED BEES
WILLIAM FOSTER

I JUST returned to Brooklyn from a short business trip in Milan. I spent two days there lending my face to the marketing efforts behind a mediocre Italian consumer product. It was a satisfying and enriching experience, as are all of my experiences as a marginally successful international model. Let me tell you about it.

My Italian booker summoned me to the job just two days before the shoot. The period between her 8 a.m. phone call and my arrival the following day in Milan was a blurry commotion of packing, public transit, airports and fractured sleep. I awoke into full consciousness somewhere on the red Metropolitana line, in time to hear a recorded female voice intone, "Cadorna... fermata Cadorna," signaling my departure point. I pulled my suitcase up two long flights of stairs, past promotional images of flesh and high thread counts, and onto the sidewalk of Piazza Cadorna. I stood for a moment beneath *Ago, Filo e Nodo*, the massive sculpture of a needle weaving thread through Milanese concrete. D&G's latest ad campaign, replete with oiled abdominals, loomed from a billboard on the opposite side of the plaza. The sun glinted sharply off the needle's shaft. I winced, squinted, lowered my gaze, and sweating in the late July heat, trudged a short distance to my agents' lair, the command center of Elite Milano.

I stepped through the front door into the heart of the desert. Tendrils of cigarette smoke wafted from the patio and dispersed through the room, cloaking the scene in a light grey fog. Shrill, ludic babble drifted in Slavic accents from skeletal teenage girls huddled in a far corner. A couple of them glanced at me, flashing shadowed, wide-set eyes from a collage of makeup, legs, designer accessories and hair of the moment. Framed magazine covers lined the walls around them, featuring styled, retouched faces that could as likely have belonged to the girls in the room as not. Closer to the entrance, chiseled, apathetic louts slumped on couches, their ears, eyes and fingers listlessly occupied with personal electronic devices. One of them, whom I dimly recognized from some fashion week past, greeted me with monosyllables and extended his fist. He was unkempt and affectless to a degree suggesting that he'd been staying in Milan for some time. I returned his gesture with a stock salutation and bumped his fist with my own. This was a standard greeting pattern that after eight months in the business I had grudgingly come to accept and practice. My early attempts to execute traditional handshakes had been too often met with awkward, stilted reciprocation or hints of derision.

Having completed the ritual, the boy pulled his flaxen locks behind his ears, reinserted white plastic earbuds and toggled the iPod Shuffle clipped to the cuff of his green-and-yellow *Brasil* t-shirt. I wheeled my suitcase out of the lounge area and toward the men's office. In the intervening hallway, I found D, a twenty-year-old male model from rural North Carolina, standing beside one of the women's' agents in front of the wide rack of female models' composite cards. The agent, a perpetually tan thirty-something man prone to chain-smoking and vulgar outbursts, was scanning the grid of images, pulling down preferred ones and handing them to D, saying, "Ah, you should fuck her... yes, she is very nice...." They paused for a moment, turning to say, "Ciao," and "'Sup, bro," and then resumed making selections.

Edging around D, I entered the office and greeted my agents. W, a slender, narrow-eyed, middle-aged man in a gold Dolce & Gabbana track jacket, nodded at me as he carried on a languid phone conversation in Italian. M and M, two interchangeable women slightly younger than W, both donned their smiley faces, kissed my cheeks, and made gratuitous use of the words *amore* and *bello*. This false cheer was part of their usual routine of establishing a semblance of goodwill and benevolence, but this time it was unusually flagrant. I presumed that they were attempting to offset the tone of our interactions over the recent fashion week, during which I, through sheer persistence, at last budged them into resolving the errors in my balance sheet. They had double-charged me for an earlier apartment bill, billed me nine days for a seven-day stay, and charged me for an airplane ticket that should have been paid for by a client. These mistakes came just a few months after similar errors that I had likewise managed to have reconciled in the face of much resistance. Unlike many models at my agency, I kept careful track of my expenses in Milan and was able to catch my agents when they tried to skim money off my account.

Formalities complete, M and M quickly dispatched me with keys to my apartment and returned to their computer screens and cell phones, content I hadn't missed my plane and that their 40% cut was thus secure. I walked three meandering blocks through pungent clouds of hydrocarbons spewed by stylish two-stroke scooters to the same tiny studio where I had wallowed during my visit for fashion week in June. With its vinyl tile floors, white painted cinderblock walls, dropped ceiling and rusty electric hot plates in the makeshift kitchen, the space had the warm ambiance of a middle school cafeteria in cramped miniature. Entering the room this time, I noticed that its ceiling and walls were still dotted with the carcasses of the mosquitoes I had fastidiously executed one month earlier.

The air in Milan is choked with mosquitoes during the summertime, and regardless of precaution a dozen or more of them would manage to infiltrate the apartment each day. During fashion week and the few days following it, I'd made a ritual of terminating every mosquito in the room before going to bed at night, using my copy of *Play It As It Lays*. I found that the bodies had a fifty percent chance of remaining stuck to the wall as opposed to the book, so that the tiny explosions of blood and legs spread across the walls and ceiling like a firmament, reflecting approximately half of the total dead. These nightly exterminations were the only way to secure a full night's sleep, and they provided an oddly cathartic release from a day of intense immersion in Milan's modeling culture. Standing once again in this bleak dwelling, I felt squarely reestablished, reunited with the winged hématophages in the apartment and the two-legged ones at the agency.

It was around 16:30 when I entered the apartment. A lanky, wan body in black boxer briefs was asleep on the thin mattress on the lower bunk. His face was buried in the pillow, but from the square head and creased brow I recognized the body as belonging to R, my roommate from fashion week. He had been living in this hovel continuously since I'd left at the end of June. My entrance stirred him from his dingy sheets—we had no maid service or convenient laundromat—and he stumbled red-eyed into the bathroom. After two flushes and numerous phlegm noises, he returned and eagerly explained what had caused him to sleep in so late.

"I went out with Umberto and Gesualdo last night. They got me fucked up on coke... and MDMA... and GHB—Yeah, you can mix those, no problem!—and then Umberto let me drive his Porsche all over Milan at, like, four in the morning. Those guys are awesome."

R, an eighteen-year-old high school dropout with an inordinate amount of stress lines around his eyes and mouth, had introduced me to Umberto and Gesualdo at our agency's fashion week party. Umberto, R explained privately, had secured his retirement by selling his business some years ago and now spent the bulk of his time farting around on his yacht and throwing drug-fueled parties for an ever-changing entourage of models less than half his age. Just a couple days prior to meeting R during fashion week, Umberto had been kicked out of his rental apartment on Piazza Castello for throwing one too many all-night saturnalias. Gesualdo was a fellow affluent whom I never saw without a Gatorade bottle—the vessel which supplied his nearly constant intake of GHB—gripped in his hand.

The modeling scene is rife with wealthy vultures like Umberto and Gesualdo. And with their hangers-on. In the case of male modeling, the vultures tend to be gay men rather than straight women. Some of them have a working connection, often tenuous, to the fashion industry, but most seem to just be following the fashion week parties from Milan to Paris to New York. That I don't see Umberto's station as enviable is the essence of the disconnect between me and many other people in this industry. R, on the other hand, thrived on their attention and their dispensation of drugs, automotive adventures, open access to clubs and exclusive parties, and, occasionally, outright cash. After his first interactions with them in June, I suggested to R that they would eventually expect favors in return, but he dismissed the possibility. Now, one month later, he was still receiving the benefits of their attention, but I didn't have time to probe what exactly that entailed.

During fashion week castings, when I'd lived with R and four other models in a two-bedroom space adjacent to the studio, R gained minor renown for his ability to coolly absorb footblows to his genitalia. Visitors were often invited to directly participate in the display of R's unusual talent, which R attributed to his testicles having been rendered numb, at an early age, by the hooves of a neighbor's piebald. Guests, male and female alike, took great delight in applying their best punting form to R's gonads and observing his absolute lack of reaction. R clearly relished the attention. One night, during fashion week proper, after some of our jobless roommates had left Milan and we had moved over to the studio, R, loose and drowsy on GHB, confided that his story about the horse was untrue, and that he was able to take the kicks so calmly because most people missed the testicles and hit the grundle. "People never notice that I raise up on my toes a little bit... and that usually makes them hit too low." For those occasions when metatarsals did connect, R told me, "It really hurts, but I just take a drag from my cigarette—you notice how I'm always smoking when I do it?—and take a slow breath and try to smile and not let it show."

My call time for the photo shoot was 06:30 the next morning, so I unpacked my suitcase, left R to smoke Marlboro Reds on the back porch, and spent a brief night out in the city. Two Swedish models living next door left their room just as I did and invited me to join them for dinner. One of them, T, had had an enormously successful fashion week in June. On the weekends bookending fashion week he would mysteriously disappear, claiming afterwards, with a flushed face, that he "went to stay with a girl." A model at our agency discovered that he was, in fact, being flown to some unknown location to spend casual time with our agent, W, and Stefano Gabbana. As to what precisely transpired over those weekends, and what their connection was to his fashion week success and subsequent booking of the D&G campaign, we couldn't be sure and didn't want to ask.

Exiting the apartment complex, T and his roommate, A, made a beeline for the McDonald's across the street. I politely declined that dining option, electing to take a solitary stroll through Parco Sempione and pick up groceries from Peck. I bought out the last flaky dregs from a decent pasticceria, ate them under waning dusk in the Piazza Duomo, and returned to the studio, which was now devoid of R. Using R's book of unattempted Sudoku puzzles, I added four new mosquito splotches to the ceiling before laying my jet-lagged head to rest on the top bunk.

My cell phone's alarm clock roused me at 05:30 the next morning with a jangly MIDI tune. The lower bunk was empty. I ate a breakfast of fresh figs smeared with truffled goat cheese, then bathed, shaved, and rode rickety streetcars to the rendezvous point. The photographer, a thoroughly kind and enthusiastic Italian man, greeted me with a handshake and led me to a cafe where we drank espresso and ate croissants with the crew, most of whom were already smoking in earnest. From the cafe, a white van transported us to the location, an abandoned textile factory fifty kilometers outside the city.

Waiting at the site were three representatives of the fashion label to whom we were responsible. They held a brief meeting with the photographer and crew while I observed from a distance. No one bothered to convey to me the essential point of their discussion, which, of course, was irrelevant to me. As the one person on the set without any responsibility for real creative input, the model is generally excluded from such dialogues. Two of the representatives drove away immediately after the discussion, while the third, an austere, grey-haired Austrian named H, approached me and introduced himself as the label's artistic director. "You are a very different look for us this season," he said. "It is a new direction and we are very excited!"

As the crew dispersed and began to set up their equipment, I wandered around the cavernous factory that I supposed had once hummed with spinning, weaving and knitting machines. Every surface in the vast room was festooned with peeling paint and asbestos-laden debris. The ceiling was supported by a grid of stone columns, and tall, narrow windows lined all four walls, framing a panoramic view of the surrounding hills and the storm clouds gathering above them. The windowsills were littered with dust and the desiccated bodies of bees that had buzzed in through broken panes and evidently hadn't found their way back out. Seeing that the crew was still far from ready, I sat against the wall beneath one of the sills and opened the book that I'd brought to pass the downtime. The first pangs of ennui were already creeping in.

Thirty pages into *The Serpent and the Rainbow*, I was summoned to the stylists' station. The chair was enveloped in a thin haze of Gauloises smoke rendered bright white by the incandescent bulbs encircling the mirror. The garrulous and hyper-effeminate makeup artist smeared various powders and creams around my face, projecting his stale cigarette breath as he maintained an unbroken exchange of lilting babble with the hairstylist. He spoke to me only to deliver the instruction, "Eyes up," so that he could address my lower lids, and, "Okay, you are done." The hairstylist took over and performed his work in silence, occasionally accenting a brushstroke or smear of styling creme with a breathy, exaggerated exclamation: "Bello... Beeeeello... Bellissimo! Your hair, it is nice..."

Over the course of my first few months working as a model, I developed an essential defense mechanism that has allowed me to cope with the tedium of a photo shoot. During the hair and makeup process, as each swipe of gel and smudge of foundation renders my face more plastic, I allow my thinking self to recede bit by bit into hibernation. The makeup mirror informs me that I am entering a time and space where I have no purpose other than to follow an excruciatingly mundane series of orders. "Take off those trousers and try the black ones there. Put on those shoes. No, put on the brown ones instead. Let's change the tie. Put on this jacket. Can someone pin the jacket? Okay, stand over here. Good. Good. Try hands in pockets. No, maybe just one hand. Chin down a bit. Smile." My free will and self-identity ebb away until, rising fully groomed from the makeup chair, I am resigned to servitude, a total suppression of all creative and emotional impulses. If left unchecked in the face of such crushing understimulation, these impulses would revolt and render me inappropriate for corporate advertising. Self-induced zombification, catalyzed by makeup application, is the only way I can successfully endure a shoot, and this job in Milan was no exception.

H approached. "His hair, it is done? Good, let's dress him." He led me to a long rack hung with various sartorial ensembles, pointed out a particular outfit, and asked me to change into it. Standing in my socks and underwear, sliding my arms into a crisp white dress shirt, I sensed that my transformation into an automaton was complete.

The shoot ensued. Photographs were taken, clothes were changed, more photographs were taken, and so on, for hours.

Late in the afternoon, the hovering storm clouds finally erupted into rain. The windows began to leak, soaking the sills and reconstituting the dried bees that I'd noticed earlier. I examined them while the photographer reviewed some shots on his laptop. Rehydrated, the insects looked freshly dead, almost lifelike. Some still had undelivered cargoes of pollen attached to their back legs. In the boredom and exhaustion of the sixth hour of shooting, and in the absence of any other stimuli, the phrase "reconstituted bees" became ludicrously, cosmically comical, and it refused to be dislodged from my head. The photographer called me to resume the shoot, and I had to conjure gruesome mental images in order to refrain from laughing hysterically in front of the camera.

I managed to maintain relative composure until the final shot of the day, which featured me brooding in a black pea coat next to one of the windows, where the little critters lurked just beneath my gaze. Their proximity was too much to bear. My pupils were drawn inexorably to the bees, and I broke down and giggled uncontrollably. I attempted to explain myself to the crew, but the humor failed to pass intact across the language barrier. Any fluently English-speaking fashion crew in New York would surely have been even less amused. Eventually, I calmed myself long enough to feign fierceness, and after a couple dozen clicks the photographer declared that he had "the shot." Following a momentary group hurrah, H announced that he was "very happy, very pleased with the photos," and the crew began dismantling and packing their equipment.

The white van deposited me and my suitcase at a train station, where I boarded the Malpensa Express and headed to the airport. So the trip certainly ended with a bang! Those bees were the absolute highlight of my time there. Milan's modeling culture is full of curious specimens of Animalia—leeches, mosquitoes, vultures, and drugged-up teenagers—but hands down, the reconstituted bee is the most amusing member of the menagerie. Occasionally I'm asked for advice from young people interested in pursuing a modeling career. I ask them this: Can you exude aplomb in the presence of a reconstituted bee? Yes? Go for it.

SEA CAVE TRAGEDY
WILLIAM FOSTER

I FOUND this short article buried deep in yesterday's *Los Angeles Times.*

Model Drowns in Sea Cave

> AUCKLAND (AP) -- Brandon Draper, a prominent international model and amateur race car driver, drowned Wednesday afternoon in a sea cave near Nursery Cove, a coral reef off the eastern coast of New Zealand's North Island. According to friends, Mr. Draper was snorkeling in Nursery Cove and attempted a free dive to the bottom of the reef. Strong undersea currents swept him into the sea cave, from which he was unable to free himself. He was 24.

I can't claim Brandon Draper as a friend, or even as an acquaintance, but we met briefly last September during New York fashion week. I waited behind him at the casting for the Narciso Rodriguez show. Although we didn't exchange names, I recognized him from his incomparable work with Dior Homme and Versace fragrance. After signing in at the casting I approached Brandon because he seemed to be the last person in the malformed line. I asked him, Are you the end of the line? and he said, What the fuck does it look like?

I said nothing more to Brandon, but I took advantage of my proximity to study the attire and comportment of the successful and renowned young man. An abundance of silver rings formed a shining crust over the knuckles of both his hands, and a tangle of necklaces gleamed beneath the deep V of his white Kris Van Assche t-shirt. His keenly buffed fingernails were like tiny convex mirrors dancing across the keypad of his PSP. His earlobes boasted impressive diamond studs, and his black patent leather Ferragamos were each fastened with two lustrous silver buckles. Twice I saw him reach into his trouser pocket to retrieve a hefty chunk of hoppered bismuth, which he fondled and admired at length.

The casting agents greeted Brandon by name, rose from their chairs to kiss his cheeks, and perused his portfolio in a perfunctory manner, as if to show that the casting was, for him, a mere matter of formality. His runway form was impeccable, and his accessories shimmered and jingled as he strutted beneath the recessed ceiling lights. I felt hopelessly graceless when the moment came to demonstrate my walk to the two agents, one of whom was still chatting attentively with Brandon while the other observed me with bald disinterest. I failed to book the job, while Brandon was chosen to open the show.

Brandon's runway prowess was undeniable, but what left a deeper impression in my mind was the array of brilliant doodads fastened to his various appendages. He clearly had an affinity for shiny objects, as if he were part crow, or Barbary Macaque or coconut crab. I like to think that when Brandon embarked on his fateful free dive, he was attempting to recover some radiant bauble that beckoned him from the depths of the reef. Perhaps it was a rare ducat, or a bejeweled bracelet or a simple stainless steel butter knife. Whatever it was, I imagine that Brandon clutched the object in his soft, white palms before the currents swept him away, and that he enjoyed at least a fleeting moment of contentment before he succumbed to hypoxia.

I ask that you all include Brandon in your prayers this evening. In his memory, I'll be carrying a choice bismuth crystal to every casting during the upcoming fall campaign season. The bismuth will serve foremost as a token of remembrance, and perhaps also as a phylactery to impart good luck and excellent posture.

FOUR RECURRING NIGHTMARES HAD BY THE COMPETITIVE FISHERMEN IN THE 1981 BASSMASTER CLASSIC

REBECCA WADLINGER

I.

Marty opens his tackle box.
Inside, a miniature football team
scurries around like a terrorized species.

He drops the lid, opens the box again,
& finds it filled with smoke.

His buddy steers the boat with one arm & calls
Get 'em out there, Marty, these bass won't lie deep tonight!

Sixteen big mouths rise & begin
barbershop quartet covers of Barry Manilow.

At this moment, Marty realizes
that they are fishing in Hell.

Every knot he ties in his line
adds four fish to the other men's boats.

II.

Call forth the champagne toast
& forget that bass-ridden lake!

Wayne has done his competitive fishing
in the sea. He returns to his fans
with a motorboat full of whales & orcas
(no lines, no lures, no rods nor reels)—
caught with his own bare hands.

Not a single person peppers the shore.
There is a note scrawled in the sand.
It reads: *Like all great fisherman,*
we have learned to believe in luck.

III.

Suddenly, all the fish are women
& Doug can't focus on his game.
They are sashaying their curvy tails
& casting lines like *you've got a lure*
I can't deny, Doug.

IV.

Terry catches the biggest bass of the day
& when he thumps it down on the table
the judges say he must dissect to win.

Somberly, Terry admits, *I was always*
picked last in science lab.

The officials huddle & agree:
they can award him the prize
if the fish dissects Terry.

A true athlete,
he lies down on the dock.

The bass wears a homemade headband
with pizza cutter strapped to the front.

Terry closes his eyes and listens
to the fish's hypnotic lab coat:
a white handkerchief waving in the wind.

SEEMS RIGHT OUT OF PLACE

BRIAN CASTLEBERRY

WHEN I was a kid in the 1980s, Genesis—that's right, Genesis—were one of those über-pop acts who seemed to churn out one hit after another, so that the ubiquitous presence of their tunes ("Invisible Touch," "Tonight Tonight Tonight," "That's All," to name a few) alongside Phil Collins's solo work made it seem these guys were part of the official music of the era. Somewhere in the high mountains of popular culture, Genesis, Michael Jackson, Hall and Oates and Huey Lewis were meeting in a boardroom to decide the eternal fate of radios across the country. And believe me, when I was ten, that idea totally rocked.

Then came puberty, and along with it a nerdy obsession with "good music," informed in one way or another by both punk and the arty rock that the mega-labels deemed "alternative," but mostly by my own snobbish tendency to intellectualize just about anything that could warrant an emotional response. I threw out radio and television and threw myself at the feet of rock history, absorbing the peaks and valleys and noteworthy distractions therein so I could construct for myself some coherent understanding of "good music" that I could use, admittedly, for my own betterment. I did such a good job of this that, if you'd run into me in the late '90s, say, sipping coffee in the smoking area of a Denny's or guzzling cheap beer at the end of the bar in Oklahoma City's Hi-Lo or Edna's, you'd have been in for a real treat—that is, if you dig listening to some asshole gush on and on about Bowie records, Lou Reed lyrics, and the importance of three specific Elvis Costello albums. Anyway, somewhere along the line I heard rumor this Genesis—who'd come to symbolize all that was wrong with music and culture—had an alternate career as early-seventies art-rock pioneers, when they'd been fronted by the seemingly unlikely Peter Gabriel. For one reason or another, I ignored this, laughing inside at that spate of mid-eighties gut-punch love songs I'd associated with them—and at the uncoolness of all that.

Then a couple of things happened at once, just in the last year. I'll tell you one before the other because it, this first thing that happened, kind of makes me look cool. This first thing was I'd spent a lot of time rifling through the liner notes of recently re-mastered Brian Eno albums, noting as I did the ongoing relationships of some of the members of Roxy Music with their former partner-in-arms, and letting that thirty-year-old evidence give my imagination credence to buy into the rumor that Roxy, one day soon, would re-assemble in their original lineup and show us all what-for. But guess who else pops up over and over again during Eno's "rock" period? None other than Phil Collins.

Huh?

The second thing was really the first thing, as it came before the other. I'd started noticing, as I began slipping into my thirties, that I actually kind of loved those blockbuster hits of the '80s Genesis. I don't mean in some hip, ironic way, either—although I'm as guilty as the rest of us with that irony business. I mean that I think they made some damn good songs. If the goal of a good, forward-thinking pop song is to create a new, free-standing environment for its listeners, to move them emotionally and to leave some part of that place in their heads all day long, well, tunes like those Genesis hits mentioned above are prime examples of damn good popular music. It took me a while to admit to it, but I soon found myself seriously listening to Genesis.

Where I started, and what I'd like to review here after all that personal prologue, is the 1974 epic *The Lamb Lies Down on Broadway*. The album is widely held as the masterpiece of early-period Genesis, and I'm not here to disagree with this assumption. In fact, I'd like to push this record out of its Genesis-ness and into that list you carry around in your head of the great recordings in rock history.

I'll tell you now it's long. Like two hours or something. There are long instrumental stretches of prog-guitar and pre-Kraftwerk synthesizer. Gabriel puts on a few weird voices and performs some spoken word. There's flute. An organ pops up a couple times. Throughout, time changes challenge the listener to resituate their experience. You can feel good or bad about these things. That's none of my business.

The first and title track builds out of the quiet with a Chopin-esque piano line that quickly falls into a bass-led electronic bombast that really does, no kidding, sound like a Broadway musical number played to a cheering crowd in Bizarro-World. Gabriel's lyrics are part William S.

Burroughs and part golden-era libretto, setting out an introduction to the record that is both apocalyptic and poetic, infused with a cold realism and an equally warm understanding of the inner lives of the people of mid-seventies Times Square. Something magical is going on in this tune, with the sudden arrival of an unexplained figure that instigates the arc of the rest of album. This, I guess, makes *Lamb* a concept album, and if there were any doubts, the lyrical content of "Broadway Melody of 1974" solidifies the conceptual nature of the overall recording. Where else in pop music will you hear reference to Lenny Bruce, Marshall McLuhan, Groucho Marx and the Ku Klux Klan, all within one rhymed verse? Gotta be a concept album.

But don't let the artiness here drag you down. Track four, "Cuckoo Cocoon," a beautiful if stifling song explaining the existential situation of our hero, "(w)rapped up in some powdered wool," who feels he may be "some sort of Jonah shut up inside the whale," is an otherwise approachable pop song along the lines of the darker elements within the Beatles' *White Album*. This is followed by a darkly hypnotic dive into paranoia, "In the Cage," whose complex rhythm and ecstatic rave-up foresees the effect of '90s dance music and features what I can only call one of the most 1970s keyboard solos ever recorded.

Following this dark prog anthem, however, is the experimental march "The Grand Parade of Lifeless Packaging," one of the standout tracks here—and one of the better art-rock songs of an era for which our pal Eno was just beginning to map out the perimeters. It's short by the standards of this record, clocking in under three minutes, but manages to close the listener within a very tight space in which capitalism and production can be poked fun at a little until the once-folded-in sound explodes and spreads in all directions, creating a real sense that some kind of parade really is beginning, even if it is a proliferation of the superficial. Stranger and more musically challenging than Pink Floyd's "Money"—if of the same family—the song ends with its various parts falling away or falling apart, as if a great meltdown has occurred on the assembly line.

This is followed by the incredible "Back in N.Y.C.," a rocking continuation of the sound-experiments Genesis has so far set up and a tune reminiscent of many of Radiohead's late-nineties recordings.

Things get ethereal with the haunting "Hairless Heart," but turn to Beatles-esque pop with the almost-jovial "Counting Out Time," and a few songs later, "Lilywhite Lilith." Between these sit the impressive "Carpet Crawlers," later re-released with a jungle rhythm in 1999, and the electro-bluesy "The Chamber of 32 Doors." But, as I have so little space to discuss an album containing 23 songs without a solid dud among them, I'll move to the elegant, spaced-out "Anyway," led by Tony Banks's impeccable piano ellipses and centered by another of Mike Rutherford's chugging bass riffs. The song pictures our hero facing what appears, if you're paying attention to the lyrics, to be the floor of something very much like a slaughterhouse. Steve Hackett's guitar work during the dark bridge here throws a light on the impressive musicianship that is evidenced throughout the album but intentionally kept in check by the drive to create coherently crafted art-pop songs. This control is lost momentarily in the otherwise fun "Here Comes the Supernatural Anaesthetist," but even this short stretch of navel-gazing seems warranted, considering the controlled precision seen everywhere else. After all, these guys were prog-rockers, and this was the era of the long virtuosic solo—all instruments included.

Things get way-out weird with the three-part track "The Colony of the Slippermen," a cinematic entry into a landscape even more surreal than the apocalyptic mid-seventies Times Square where we'd begun. As for bridging the gap between pop songcraft and experimental art-rock, the eight-minute exercise may be one of the more successful songs in Genesis's early oeuvre, replete with hooks and riffs that are overrun, reinterpreted and repeated through the course of an altogether mind-bending tune. The idea of returning to and reinterpreting musical themes is made even more solid with the near-end "The Light Dies Down on Broadway," a more emotionally troubling review of the album's first track. It is here, with lyrics such as, "I must decide / Between the freedom I had in the rat-race / Or to stay forever in this forsaken place," that it begins to become evident our hero, the figure that Gabriel calls "Rael," is no magical lamb at all but a normal citizen facing deep existential doubt concerning the capitalist world he resides in. As a character who has stepped beyond the veil of our everyday reality, the lamb is left to decide his fate as an individual—to return to ignorance or live in the way he knows to be honest. "It," the final track of the album, seems to back up this idea with a jangly salute to the moments of human understanding in everyday experience. The song also features the memorable line, "If you think it's pretentious, you've been taken for a ride"—a perfect enough epigram for the album as a whole.

The Lamb Lies Down on Broadway is an album that was created in a time of great upheaval and experimentation in rock music, so I can begin to understand how and why it would be overlooked after a thirty-three year span—and why snobs like myself would have taken such a long time to give it a chance. But it is more than a serious, if literary, work of conceptual art. *Lamb* is an album full of single-material tunes and consistent change. It is a record that needs to be filed near the Beatles' *Sgt. Pepper's*, near the Talking Heads' *Fear of Music*, near that special group of albums that connect the two—records that, even decades after their production, insistently open up the potential of rock music and show new directions for the experience of their listeners.

Oh. And that Phil Collins is pretty good on it, too.

AUTUMN RISING
CLINT McCOWN

The black widow nests
inside the glove:
things are set in motion

but feel
the bright passages
beforehand:

on a cool night
music in a local bar

conversations without war

or the next day:
the braces finally off,
a daughter's teeth
arranged in a new smile

sunshine, unnatural
this time of year

a bevy of quail rising
beyond the hunter's range

a new dog from the pound

a faded dollar
on the sidewalk

that dark tarpaper shack
we can't help
coming home to: hope

ISSUE TWO
THE REVELEY LEE APPRECIATION SOCIETY

GOOD BUNNIES DO FINE ALWAYS
A BAD BUNNY

Some say that bunny's just
got an urge. That he lies loose
from the Almighty in his dirt-down
hovel. I had an urge once. I fed it
some grass and it went away.
It came back the next day.
More grass, some slugs, a trick
nickel. By then I had a habit
and a knack for ruining shoes.
Almighty: may we stay tight
as laced rollerskates. That bunny
takes the fast train to feckless.
When a bunny doesn't have a love,
he makes one, and how he makes one
now, his cotton tail rubbing goodbye
up and down the locomotive window.
Goodbye, the Almighty. Goodbye,
the grass. What a bunny loves best
is best kept underground.

THE METAL ZONE
JAMI DITTUS

"WHAT ARE you doing here?" he asked, backwards baseball cap, dirty, hair underneath, dirty. He had glazed eyes and a lazy grin. I worked with him at the pet store, where I'd been for about a month, my second job since high school ended in June.

"Looking for a pedal, same as you," I said. It wasn't even midnight, but the boys were out, crowding the amps, the drum kits, the guitars on the wall. The Midnight Sale promised deep discounts.

We drove there, me and Lia. She needed a guitar pedal. We needed it, to produce the sound we wanted. We made each other tapes, fast songs, loud songs. *This is what I want,* I would say, or she would, and we'd nod our heads at the breakdowns that whipped back into noise. When we played, though, it was so quiet, so light, hopping-bunny melodies and hesitation.

The guy I knew nodded and walked off. I watched him select a pedal from the display and plug in.

The kind we wanted were locked up. "That's it, that's the one," I said. I had circled catalog descriptions of the sounds they made and given them to Lia. She chose the Metal Zone. It would make anything heavy.

"How do you find someone to unlock the case?" she whispered. We were both nervous. I shook my head. One salesguy sat on a stool, playing a red Fender for a 14-year-old boy in a Korn t-shirt. Two more boys stood behind.

There were boys everywhere, and some men and the one old guy who always stood close to the wall with a floor model and played something like Deep Purple, staring at anyone who came close like an animal with a meal he did not want to share.

We'd practiced before the sale. I'd picked up Lia and we went to a small studio surrounded by a patch of woods. You walked up precarious wood steps and inside you waited for the proprietor to appear, five-four and bloated, an unbleached Vince Neil, to unlock a room for you. The walls were pasted with pictures, the proprietor younger, grinning, with Poison, with Ratt, with beer promo girls in bikinis.

"One hour or two?" he asked. Two was a better deal, but we placed down warm bills from our pockets for one.

There were two rooms, one large, one small, both lit only with red bulbs, a Halloween basement with staticky, half-busted amps as big as coffins. We got the small.

"Are you ready?" I said.

"Always," she said, but played two notes and stopped, sucking in air. "Can he hear out there?"

"Probably not," I said, but I knew he could. I'd been here once before, with Robert, who had really wanted to cover a certain song, make it faster, and he really wanted a girl to sing it. We tried. He wasn't bad. I wasn't fast enough. We came out sweaty and unsatisfied. *My band used to play that song*, the proprietor had said, nodding to Robert.

"You sound good, keep going," I said. "I'll catch up, I'm still tuning." I would tune endlessly, waiting for the green light to pop up on the electronic tuner, tell me what my ears could not.

The way back to Lia's house was through dark wooded roads. Only once I started driving to her town did I understand I should click on the highbeams. Before, I hadn't known the need for them. Where I lived, every inch was crowded and lit. Deer grazed in small boxed yards; shopping carts rolled down paved hills and onto the highway shoulder, stopping at piles of meat and bones from the animals that hadn't made it. Streetlights and store lights illuminated all this; the roads had continuous traffic. In Lia's town, the houses were a lot bigger and farther apart, the back roads with nothing but the tar and the curve of painted lines. The deer could still hide, most times.

"Tell me where to turn," I said. Driving was getting to be a drag, not like when I first got my license and drove down the highway after closing at work, all the way to the Holland Tunnel before turning around and coming back. The straight-shot drive had been enough, with damp warm air through the cracked windows and a tape on loud.

Lia came out of her daze and looked out the window. "You already missed it," she said.

"Ha-ha, we are listening to Robert's tape," I said. Robert had done what he said he would, made it uncomfortable for us, here, who thought it was impossible to just up and move across the country and record for your favorite label. You can't just *do that*, but he did, and was on tour, not even a year after we'd sat on the floor of my bedroom and asked the Ouija board how long the Spice Girls had left and when would Lia and I find a drummer and whether Robert was going to be famous.

Up ahead on the right was the beginning of a dirt-and-gravel driveway, one space carved out from the woods, just past the road's narrow shoulder.

A locked gate closed the rest of it off. I recognized it as the vivisection lab the hardcore boys liked to protest. They held up signs with mutilated animals printed on them and then piled into cars, laughing, headed for vegetarian brunches to which the girls never seemed invited.

I steered my old Civic into it, slow enough, but the balding tires skidded and we were unsteady for a second, too close to the fence. I half-expected some boy to be there now, ready to shout in my face, me trying to explain that I was on his side. I faced the car back towards the road, where it looked like no one was coming or was going to come at all at this time. But there was a sharp curve I'd need to get in front of to turn left, and you couldn't really tell what would pop out.

I breathed hard. I hit the gas. Headlights rounded the corner fast as I was turning. "Jesus," I said, steering the wheel all the way around. The pickup and my car missed each other by inches, but he didn't honk as he hurtled down the road, and I didn't, and Lia didn't scream. The whole thing happened without noise. It didn't seem right.

My heart beat hard like waking up from a deep sleep after you are already supposed to be at work.

Then the highbeams fell on something light in the middle of the road. "What is that?" I said, a little panicky because I already knew what it was. Its head was still moving, neck straining up from the asphalt, mouth biting air. The body didn't move.

"Baby deer," Lia said. I stopped the car in front of it, scared to steer all the way around it, to cross the yellow lines, in case another car came up fast on that side. Scared to run over it, its immobile back legs stretching out close to the almost nonexistent shoulder, the guardrail. The wide canal beyond that ran quiet, so dark the water was invisible and you only saw it through spots of the moon.

"What can I do? I can't take it to the vet! I don't know where any, like, sanctuaries are!" I was seeing myself trying to shove a body in the trunk.

The tape was stuck, garbling an Avengers cover of the Rolling Stones. I pressed stop.

"There's nothing I can do, right?"

"Right," Lia said. "Go around it—you need to go."

"I could call the police," I said. "I will call the police."

Clenching my jaw, I drove around the baby deer. Lia's small hand held the handle above the window. I flipped the tape over and turned up the volume.

"It knows what it's doing," Lia said. Lia worked cleaning cages in a vet's office. She said you could get used to anything in a week, even a day sometimes.

She knew I was still worried for the deer. I drove slower than I should have, and kept looking in the rearview, and thought I saw its body move. Then I didn't see it at all.

She took out Robert's tape and put a new one in. One of our favorite bands started up. "I pretty much just taped the whole record," she said. "I forget if there's anything else on there."

We sang along to the two singers, who traded off, except for that one song where their voices blended, two keys off meeting in another key. It was supergood when they got to that one note. We both nodded at it, like a whistle only our insides heard.

By the time I came near the weird short bridge where I had to turn, the baby deer had lifted off me just enough to let me think about Other Things, like the pedal and how good it would be, like having enough calluses on my fingers to let me play for a long time, like the practice we would have tomorrow with the boys and how we'd hold it together.

But then in the road was a deer—full-grown. Standing. As I neared it I reached some point of calmness and in those seconds I clicked off my hated highbeams, then the headlights altogether. *The light paralyzes*, Mr. Bairdulles had said in Driver's Ed, where we didn't get in cars, just watched scare movies in the Health room. If the light was gone, the deer would hear the noise of the car in the dark, and it might run away in time.

In the absolute natural dark I still shut my eyes for the impact.

"Ugh," Lia said.

The seatbelt was at is lock point, not letting me move forward any further. "Lia?" I said.

"I'm okay," she said. The music store bag had thrust up from the back and was now sitting behind my moon-gray hand on the gearshift. I touched the bag—*the pedal!* inside. My hand came up wet.

"You need to get us out of the middle of the road," Lia said. "Someone might come up fast behind us."

Each big pulse of my heart made my head feel larger and meaner. I did not want to turn on the lights.

"I don't want to turn on the lights!" I said.

"Just hope the car runs," Lia said.

The blood, tinny-smelling, mixed with *shit* in the air, like at the cow farm my mom used to take baby-me to visit. I reached up for the interior light. It worked. I clicked the headlights. They worked. A hoof was black on the windshield, near a crack where the blood had come in and dripped down the dash. Lia had the head hanging off the hood. Blood lolled off the tongue.

"See if the car starts," Lia said.

It did. My hands made prints on the steering wheel.

"Stick your head out the window and try to get to the shoulder," Lia said. I made it over, although the shoulder was so narrow on the canal side that my two left tires were over the line.

"Can we get it off the hood?"

"I think we have to," she said.

"You can take the front end," I said, offering her the less-worse part.

We stood on each side of the hood and pulled forward. My hand was in the stiff coat of the lower back, trying to make the flesh into a handle. But the deer was too lean and I had to reach around the trunk and tug. The leg on the windshield was bent back in the wrong direction.

We pulled. It slid. Down the hood, over the grill, and the body slabbed to the ground.

I was not the kind to carry Handi Wipes in my car. I licked my lips and pressed them together before the dry air sucked away all the moisture. My hands were bleeding from cracks on the knuckles and I had my fingers curled and poised, not to grab or scratch but to not feel the blood smeared palmside. If my hands were splayed straight the blood would have more surface area to spread. Lia had given in and wiped her hands on her pants. The tip of her nose was red and her nostrils were getting raw. I had in my car a receipt (*one pedal at $79.99*) and a *Punk Planet.* I gave her some pages and used the bulk of it to coax the mess off the windshield.

"*You ask*," I said. "I'm weird about that."

"You," she said.

I shrugged and asked the guy if there was a hose on premises.

"No," he said.

"Can we have a bunch of cups then?" I pointed under the Slurpee machine.

He shook his head. "Cups are inventory." He put down his bikini chick magazine and took a good look at me and Lia—the up-and-down assessment kind. I saw what he saw—short Lia shivering in a zip-up sweatshirt, fitted gray pants stained with bloody marks in the shape of fingers, dark straight hair that hadn't been forced into any style it shouldn't.

"Get some gallons of water," Lia whispered to me.

"Right," I said. "Good idea."

"You two been clubbin' turkeys?" the clerk said.

"No, not really," I said. I turned to walk back to the fridge for water. Lia stayed where she was, blank and shaking. I pulled on her sleeve. I didn't want to leave her alone.

Over on the far right of the parking lot, where there was just one other car, a dull blue Oldsmobile with a Megadeth sticker on the bumper, I uncapped a water and poured it out on my windshield. I got in to turn on the wipers, then out to rinse once more. Then whooshed the rest of the water over the hood. Lia handed me a stack of napkins.

"Nice," I said about the puddles we left. "Super. They'll test for murder."

We shoved the bloody logo napkins in the trash, where a once-bitten hotdog rested on the rim.

In the bathroom Lia and I ran hot water on our hands. The thawing hurt and the cracked places on my skin turned extra bright red.

I looked up into the mirror, and the inch-and-a-half black roots in the blond scared me for a second; they looked like tarantulas under the lighting. My skin crawled. I saw the tracks of dried blood on my acrylic leopard-print sleeves.

I pictured the plush pink carpets in Lia's parents' house and me tracking in something from outside or spilling a fresh leak of blood from my hand. It was so late, and the door would creak, my keys would drop too loud on the kitchen counter. Her father hated noise. "You want to just go to the diner?" I said. "If we fall asleep, we'll never wake up in time for practice."

At ten we had to be in a town forty minutes away, in the basement of *our drummer*, or *a* drummer, the younger brother of a friend. There was *a* guitar player, who used to be the sax player in my exboyfriend's ska band. And then there was a singer, my exboyfriend, nervous and weepy since his band had broken up.

Maybe it won't be so bad, I'd told Lia a couple weeks ago, when this was in the works. *We can still do our own music. But it will be good to play with a full band.*

"Pancakes would be okay," Lia said.

"You can take a nap there if you want," I said. "I'll stay awake."

I drove to the diner, the one with dark pink booths and seashell prints on the walls, like it were a bathroom or a Burger King. In the lobby was a *Ms. Pac-Man* and a cigarette machine.

The round shatter on my windshield wasn't so bad, but I didn't want to think about the money it would take to get it fixed. "Is it illegal to drive it around like this?" I asked Lia as I parked.

"It's kind of in front of your face, so probably," she said. She smiled a little.

"The dents on the front can fuck off, though," I said. I left my coat on the front seat and grabbed both my bare arms. The wind bit through my black t-shirt as I ran.

Lia, across from me, leaned into the straw of her milkshake, her eyes closed.

I burned my tongue on a French fry. The salt tasted like life. I wasted quarters on "Paradise City" and "Sweet Child O' Mine." I could not help it. I always did. But they hadn't come on the table jukebox yet; they were queued behind back-to-back Kenny Rogers and what I think was Jamiroquai.

I'll order a cup of tea and sit very still, I thought. I sat with my back against the wall and my legs straight out on the length of the seat. I crossed my arm across the top of my black kilt and closed my eyes, too, Axl's tinny whine finally coming out of the jukebox next to my left ear.

"Wake up, sweetie!" I heard, and opened my eyes. A woman with teased blonde hair and red lipstick that bled over the border of her lips was touching Lia's shoulder as she walked towards the exit. She laughed as she left.

"Wake up, sweetie," I said to Lia with a half-smile.

"What are we supposed to play today?" she said, her cheek red where her hand had been. "I want to be able to play it."

"You will. I told them what song." I said. "The one we joke around with. We'll work it out when we get there."

The sun was shining through the window. I looked down and saw tons of lint on my skirt and stuck to my tights. The hot water for my tea was no longer hot, the lemon and the sealed bag waiting by the cup.

"You are good, you know, and have a good ear," I said.

"I don't think so," she said.

"Plus, you can actually see where something's going and make changes. You can write," I said. "It takes me forever just to find the root notes."

Lia took a deep sip of milkshake and then slid the glass to the edge of the table.

"I'll drink it," I said. The ice in it had melted and the air beat into it had deflated. It was warm strawberry soup. I finished it.

We took the check up to the register, next to the gold-edged bowl of mints in pink, green, white.

In the diner bathroom, I touched my cheek and used my nails to extract a small piece of glass. I wiped my cheek with a wet paper towel and was left with a pink indentation where the glass had gone in.

"Here goes," I said, and dragged my amp to the door and rang the bell. Lia stood quiet with her soft guitar case across her back and her less awkward amp behind me. Chris, the drummer, answered and said to come on in. It was Saturday morning and everyone was home—mom, dad, sister and grandma. They all smiled as we walked by, and the sister helped me with my amp.

"She's almost deaf." The sister cocked her head back towards the grandma. "And Mom and Dad are used to Chris playing. You guys can play as loud as you want."

In the basement, my exboyfriend was stopping then playing the song on a boom box. In the stops, the ex-sax/current guitar player was pulling off the Slash parts perfect. "He's supergood, great, a musical genius actually," my exboyfriend said.

"This is Lia," I said, "and Lia this is"—I pointed to everybody in turn and said their one-syllable boy names.

Lia looked down, then away from them, up towards the wooden stairs that led out.

"Oh, I forgot the pedal!" I said to Lia. "Let me run and get it." Up the stairs and through Family Time in the living room again; Boggle was out on the coffee table. "Forgot something! Be right back," I said without looking at them.

"You kids sound great," the grandmother said.

Outside, the air was cold and clean, so much so that breathing it aggravated my insides. I unlocked the passenger side and leaned in, reaching for the music store bag, where the deer blood had stuck. It was frozen but it still smelled fresh when I was so near. The pressure of leaning made me burp hot air that tasted like the worst rot. I knew what was coming. I had time to slide the pedal out of the bag before I puked.

I left the bag under the car and went back in, forcing my cold hand to play C E A D C B A G A as fast as I could on my bass. "Stop!" the ex-sax/current lead said. "Your E string's flat."

THE FEEDERIST

MUKI MAHAN

WHEN WE met last you asked me what I wanted most, if there were one thing, there was, you knew I think, but I wouldn't say what. This didn't much matter, since soon after my Dad pulled me out, calling you a kook and me a coward, and my Mom more or less agreed. Then he admitted his cancer was a hoax, no longer bothered to hide his drinking, and when everyone in Plymouth found all this out (he gave helicopter rides at the annual fair), he lost his job with the trust. My brother and I made him a macaroni bust of himself for his birthday; still, whenever he saw us swimming in the lake out back the house, he'd stagger up and piss off the pier. She withdrew in her way and more often had me sponge down the playmats at her day care while she whispered into the phone in the next room. I was leaving soon so didn't mind, I was happier than anyone knew, I owed this to you, for this question you were paid to ask me and whose whatever answer you would have told me to find and to have as best I could. I am writing to say I found it and had it, three times over, in various ways, each better than the last, although most people would think what it is was disgusting. And so it'll be. The seagulls have their biscuits of broken glass. The better pleasures have passed and the lesser waddle past my porch overlooking the beach. I am still young, I have a young heart, I think I'll stay young, but I've been having this old sense of unity which I approached for a long while I'll tell you about but was only given in the end with abuse. You're trained not to lead others on to a fondness for that last thing, which is fine, only some can understand or even laugh at perfect parity, and maybe I flatter myself thinking they could include me. I simply wanted to be with girls commonly called obese, grossly so. Before the first time I did, or when I saw one I wanted in the flesh and with a definite scent, I never felt the urge, but a lack, maybe the same way I've thought others find a secret spot behind a rock and cry and cream into the sea. It was after my folks sent me to Colby that I met Lynn among a group of mostly ugly girls I'd begun to be a mascot for, trading brunches, aerobics hours and a doubtful interest in feminist theory for the late morning confidence that I was better and gentler than whoever had them drunk the night before just to wake up, hiss obscenities and make humiliated haste for the dorm room door. I took this more than half seriously. I am vain. It was better anyhow to begin protecting myself from doubt over the questionable things I planned to try. We were in the lounge late watching television and the man on it was upset because the villain had raped his close relative (we'd missed that part) and just chased him around a garage, firing his pistol. I made the mistake of laughing; Lynn went from whimpers to sobs and plodded off in her slippers. This was in November; that she couldn't watch the suffering of others, however fake, was sincere. I walked out to the quad. The paths were lined with tiki torches. Shrieking groups of three or four, in fleeces, beet-faced, passed each way for a different house whose walls were stained with sweat to strip and pair off. I couldn't drink, cannot, nor stand the company of those that did, but the air was heavy with happy panting and I almost skipped when I spotted her sitting crosslegged beneath a tree, curled and heaving. I fantasized she'd found food or brought it and balled up to shield it and nibble it in secret. I brushed aside the long hair over her face and kissed her tears; she asked, "Why?" and I kissed her lips. We spent the night fully clothed in her bunk with her stuffed animals. Her walls were covered with posters of piglets or children in adult clothing, kissing and holding hands. She was pretty meek. I'd take her to Camden to eat clam chowder, which made her fall asleep. Then I'd watch her and wouldn't wake her for hours. The next month she invited me to meet her family in Chelmsford. This was too much. Even the most blindly affectionate parents would be skeptical of my motives. They'd search me for a horrible flaw. I suppose I could've confessed to having herpes. For their reassurance. But I said no, I said I missed my own family, and needed some time to myself, and back from break I dumped her. Maybe here you would ask about this preference of mine. Why I think it's so. Is it warmth? Ease? Easiness? Or surrogate moms? Or childlike airs. They do look like infants with their stubby fingers and parted lips. So I become the parent I would've been. But would I've fucked myself? It's arguable I have. The few people from before I've reluctantly kept up with believe this. If I could give a straight answer, this letter would be worthless, and anyhow I can't, but were I to try and even manage, what would I have left except a few meager facts like scraps of food clinging to a plate soaking in sinkwater? My own feeling for food's matured. My metabolism's high. I am thin. Now I eat what I serve, fried fish and funnel cake. Something resembling calamari. Mainly shrimp. I love hot dogs. I moisten at the smell of sauerkraut. In the evening, I examine myself shirtless, and only here and there beneath wisps of hair can I see a soft bulge. But I won't make a trophy of myself. Before I was careful with food, and so I stayed trim, since what's more grotesque than a cooing couple of undesirables? One of us had to arouse the outside world. I found my type drawn to my own, and for the casual male observer the attachment cast my girls in a new, fascinating light. I jogged, made sure. Never touched the garbage I do now, never ate from vending machines. Coweyed Irene did. I first encountered her in a hallway by the religion department near the end of my last year. I heard a vicious pounding around the corner and found her abusing a large, semi-automated box of snacks. Her Doritos were snagged. I offered to buy the next to jar it out; she squinted. I did anyway, the two fell together, she took both and gave me an ambiguous long look over her shoulder as she walked away. There was a mark of ash on her forehead. That Sunday, I went to Mass. It had been eleven years. This was at the modern structure just off campus. The stained glass showed a cartoon Christ dangling from a twisted heap of metal. Three grimy young men stood in a row by the altar with identical acoustic guitars and ponytails, alongside something breastless with bad skin. Then came a procession so rich in deformity it seemed a session of exorcisms would follow the service. Youth and decrepitude were indistinct. Slightly under half were upright; only a fraction of those managed to genuflect without deep groans. The electric invalid chairs caused a kind of traffic jam at first; motors whirred; little fluorescent flags shook, stilled and shook again till a sort of order settled at last. The priest arrived. He was flushed and animated. First came announcements. "Would the owner of the silver Cherokee please move their vehicle? It is blocking the Blimpie's driveway next door." The homily concerned faith. Several times he asked the congregation to believe that he had an egg concealed in his sock. There were murmurs of confusion. Eventually he knelt down, lifted his cassock, pulled the egg out and made a show of tossing it to the pews, which caused the feebler in front to cower in fear. Then the band struck up bland strums and humming and the priest busied himself with sacraments. I did not take communion. After Mass, I invited Irene out for pancakes. She was pleased and spoke for the whole hour. Whatever her demands, it seemed I'd met them and more. By the end, I knew enough to be intrigued and very aroused. She was older, an endless student. She showed me her pocket electronic edition of the Vulgate. She was taller than me, with larger hands. Her devotion was peculiar. The lengths she went to preserve her virginity engendered an imaginativeness I would never reencounter. It was the first time I'd ever delighted in real manhandling. I was goosed, slapped, kicked, wrenched in vulnerable spots, blindfolded and whispered half-growled precepts, culled from her studies, profane and sacred. "Suffering is the fleetest animal that brings you to perfection." I glowed inside to know I knew that one. Otherwise, her interest in me was vague and impersonal. I was dough. I stayed with her for the summer, got a job hauling boxes in a wifebeater and cutoffs at "Firm Grips," a moving company which seemed to cater exclusively to effeminate older men. For a while, I was genuinely happy; weekly ministrations, solitary sunsets. This did not last. You would tell me it's an inevitability, that these things always lapse and coarsen, but I had an infectious sort of lifelessness, and it made me sick to think it could even overcome an arrangement based on my silent indulgence of another's most cherished sexual resentments. So I would sit on her sofa, in my skivvies, as Dad would say, kitty whiskers still drawn on my cheeks, watching television while she browsed takeout menus and we had a halting talk over whether we or just she would eat or whether or not either or both of us actually wanted to eat anything at all, which of course was a tease. Then I'd look out to the streetlamps coming on dirty orange over a mostly unleased commercial block and feel relief. Over dinner, she gave her lectures and I slurped from my plastic bowl. Ontological evil and the quietist heresy. I recall only these two topics. I never paid much attention, and she spoke with her mouth full. The Sunday pancakes began to lose their flavor, she began to repeat herself and sweated less. I did go to confession. I described my recent behavior and referred to her by name. The priest was happy for us. I needed real work, so I moved to Boston. Quincy, actually. Though I went home first for a few days. The house was quiet. Chad had gone to Oregon to study alternative healing. My Mom gave me words of encouragement. "Shave your head. You're going bald." My Dad was elusive. He left the house before I woke and came back around three in the morning to slam dishes and doors and poke his head in my bedroom. "Did I wake you? Did I wake you?" At this point, I think my mother was having him followed. I met Ellie while I was temping at her non-profit. My time in town till then hadn't been successful. I lived alone in a filthy flat close to the T owned by a snooping Polish woman. I knew almost no one, those I did from school I met for lunch the first two months, and each saw I think the unsavory aura I had, in how my eyes met theirs and when, my shivers, the moles along my arms, my hugs, my sighs. A bad mixture of tics and empty gestures. The next two months I spent recording half a song cycle about enormous breasts on acoustic guitar and chord organ. Ellie was petite. She dressed stylishly, chatted up her coworkers with tact, wore a look of charming skepticism and was, how strange this seems now, conventionally attractive. Of course, I had no interest in knowing her. Strangely, she sought me out. Out of boredom, I think. Because she watched me sit alone in the Common on my break feeding jellybeans to squirrels. Or she caught me laughing once when a walleyed woman with a cane and hot pink tube top came to our office by mistake and begged us to pay her rent. When she asked me out for lunch I was hesitant at first. It was in Chinatown. Behind neon-lit flayed duck carcasses, I watched her eat two servings of roast pork. I was not expecting this. She broke the silence. "Are you innocent or guilty?" "Of what?" "Just are you. One or the other." I thought about it. I had no doubt that I was guilty. "Innocent." She nodded, swallowed, precious, blunt. "What makes you say that?" I explained that, while there were many actions of mine that I regretted, among them things that I had done, apart from some very trivial things I had done, things that, although they were done, at the time, with a kind of malice, were, I thought, but she interrupted. "Like what?" I delayed my reply, glanced about the room, hoping her interest would fade. After several minutes it hadn't. She only ate and widened her eyes at every bite. I told her that in elementary school I once punched a boy in the face because he was Chinese. "Nothing wrong with that." I told her that I was half Chinese. "That makes it even better. What else?" That when I was told my grandfather had committed suicide, it made no emotional impact on me whatsoever; that I'd been happy because I'd caught a turtle near the lake and painted my name on its shell with all the colors of the rainbow and an exclamation mark. She gestured with her chopsticks for me to continue. That I kept a diary when I was in high school, filled with many embarrassing things, and that I'd torn out one especially embarrassing page and swallowed it, only the next day I opened the diary and found it there and suspected my mother had copied it back, forged my handwriting and maybe even all the rest of it, since the cover looked slightly different, so I went downstairs and screamed at her that she was a sneaky bitch and I was onto her and made her cry. I did not mention that my father sat there giggling, loudly eating a Golden Delicious apple, or that it was this incident that first sent me to you. Ellie was pleased, regardless. I almost begged her to eat more, and when she laughed and reached for her purse, I rushed to the counter and paid the check. Outside, the weather was all gloom, no one about, and we agreed to meet the next night. Sitting at my desk, a tiny seed split within my heart. I maneuvered to cook for her at home. I tested her with potatoes and nothing else: mashed, boiled, baked, fried. She devoured them while I watched and offered more private tidbits than any decent person could bear hearing. Not a single fictitious thing. She was a true glutton and kept her comments as brief as before. I began to respect her. And maybe this is why I won't go on anymore over the conversations we had, maybe too since early on the old fear arose that, even given my best embellishment, I couldn't string along those confessions so far, and then after that, what. So I won't bore you with those. I myself lost track of what I said at the time and anyway was only aware of how the stock shrank. Otherwise, once again I was hopeful, which is always a sinister state to be in, making things softer-edged and immaterial, till even Ellie seems and seemed as if she were never there. In reality, she was getting bigger. First came the faint signs of a second chin. Also her hair thinned. Her personality devolved. She grew grubby, developed cruel whims, which to be honest, I enjoyed. Years before, vacationing in Fez, an ancient one-eyed Berber had sold her a piece of sesame candy and disappeared. I was dispatched to scour the city for a substitute. Sometimes, I would get calls from her, screaming and impatient. I took the snatches between these to contemplate how soon I might achieve the perfect satisfaction of my wishes. I did this naively and without emotion. She wasn't fat yet. I cannot say whether I ever believed she would be. I also developed a very tenuous sense of time. I dithered in Revere, mostly, and would find myself in a stupor on the boardwalk well into the early morning. She began to worry, which manifested itself more as mistreatment. Obviously, I never found the candy. I do not think I was forgiven this failure. My attempts at penance included the purchase of a highchair and a magnificent spread of fried chicken, assorted cheese dips and brightly colored dressings. After this meal, her belly was practically taut. She allowed me to run her fingers through her hair. I watched her watch television. She grimaced. With no enthusiasm, she proposed we go to Hampton Beach the next weekend. I would not like to describe in detail this very significant trip. After resting in our separate motel rooms, we dined at an all-you-can-eat seafood buffet called Bottom Dwellers'. I brought Ellie two plates at a time. Later, this gave her a violent case of food poisoning, and I spent the rest of the time before our silent return tending to her vomit, sponging her forehead, and watching this irritable little girl I had so carefully overfed pale and wither with an intimidating dignity. She began to avoid me at work and ignore my calls. Eventually, one was answered by a male voice that said that if I did not stop, the police would be involved. I quit my job. I considered killing myself. I shook this off, it was shock, and anyhow it's best to leave that end to others. What I wanted most was rest. I stayed in bed and didn't eat. What I wanted next I knew was nothing. My waking hours crept toward night, I no longer dreamt, and in the squalor I developed a pity for the poor and wept beneath my electric blanket. There was late April snow and I imagined putrid homeless men spearing their hands into trashcans. Bulging bloodshot eyes of the malnourished winked at me from the ceiling in the dark. My dirty urges vanished. They did return, I admit, but sluggishly, as almost unpleasant reminders, like notes found stuck between stacks of dust-caked papers for dull things done and forgotten as they were. And later, now, as enticements to nostalgia. I wonder if this was the last of the reasons why, when I came to, I moved and took two jobs in food service for single star eateries along the drag here in Hampton Beach. I don't regret this decision. There's the sparkling moonlit water, roman candles, Seabrook station, children dancing in the sand while their bulky mothers sip diet sodas through tax-free tobacco-stained teeth. These are my customers, who've no qualms flecking stars-and-stripes bikini tops with cocktail sauce. They undertip, since I'm unseen, a faceless tray of comfort, pacing from deep fryers to diners to add, every time, a bit of padding they carry out into the sun to bake rose. What I'll do, I don't know nor care. I haven't been here long, I feel like I have and the things I had before no longer matter, I had them only moments, which were long enough. I couldn't have a single more. Other than that, there's not much to write. Now, I busy myself with crafts. I've grown good with my hands. I made a birdfeeder for a manager of mine. She accepted it and looked uncomfortable. I made a piñata for my family, but I broke it, intentionally, yesterday. I'll think of something else, just you know I'm well, and very, very grateful for what you've done.

WE ARE IN AGREEMENT ABOUT THE FUNNY-TASTING EGGS

MATTHEW STUART

SHE SAYS, "No way you'll find yourself in there," pointing a fork to my half of the kitchen table, beneath which lies a newspaper splayed over my knees. "I don't know why you look."

"I'm reading," I say.

I'm looking for myself in the backgrounds of photographs.

"What is it about?" she asks, again with the fork.

"What's what about?"

"That thing you say you're reading, the article." This time the fork air-quotes and I flinch, then squint my eyes to bend the fork with my mind. Maybe melt it.

"I don't know," I say. "Arabs."

"Arabs."

"That's what I said," I say. "Arabs."

She looks back down to her omelette.

I say, "Eat your omelette."

She puts the fork down.

"It's just a little vain, is all I'm saying," she says.

Unbelievable. I look back down to the newspaper.

I started scanning photographs in the news maybe a decade ago. Not just the papers, either. Brochures, tabloids, even other people's photo albums. I'd been places, I thought, and I thought that in all likelihood these places I've been I've been while other faces, some photograph-worthy, have also made appearances. And why not? You live in a place long enough, you find a course. You become the hoi polloi. You're of a supporting cast.

First time I found myself in a photo was four years ago after an ill-self-advised race to the top of a mountain. This Race to the Top has been an annual for a half century, and I knew she was running it. Runners climb over eight miles from 6,000 to 10,000-plus feet in elevation. All this on a Monday. I decided I should beat her because I had something important to say and I wanted to say it in dramatic fashion. Mountaintop seemed a better place than many.

She crushed me. Supremely, and it was an ugly experience. The training, it turned out, set her up for it. An hour past her finish, I staggered up and saw her standing with this mustachioed fellow who was part of the reason I'd suffered the race and who was also the subject of the important something I wished to say.

I walked over to the fruits and bagels table, where they were laughing.

"What the hell?" she said.

I shrugged, and I coughed something yellow into the crook of my elbow, where I catch my coughs and sneezes. I winged my arm and flapped.

"Sick," she said.

I narrowed my eyes at the guy. He was taller than me, and muscular. His mustache was hiding something, I thought. It looked like a merkin. She noticed me narrowly noticing the merkin and I noticed her stop smiling.

"What, are you following me?" she asked.

"Evidently," I said.

The Merk smiled an orange-peel grille. "Elwo," he said. He spit the peel onto the ground. I was looking down at the peel, clayed and dirty, when he held his hand out for me to shake.

"This is my running coach," she said. "Save the Scottish cocktail party."

I shook his hand, and his vice grip was too much.

"Uncle," I said and slipped my hand free.

I sighed and lay down on the ground.

"Right," she said from above, rolling her eyes. "I'll see you at home, then."

"See you," said the Merk.

I raised my hand to the sky and off they went.

They glided away on a mountain-lift and I walked down to the race's halfway point to save face and also for the free Continental breakfast in a log cabin. There was an awards ceremony inside, so I took my breakfast out and sat down on a boulder. I was wearing small, ridiculous shorts, and my legs stung and stuck to the granite.

There were a few others outside with me, including this one man sitting on a gnarled tree trunk, alternately eating cereal and swatting mosquitoes. He raised his plastic spoon to me because we were both eating Lucky Charms, and I nodded, pointing my plastic spoon to his bowl and boosting an eyebrow to say, *Yes, the marshmallows are excellent.* In fact, I was eating only the marshmallows, while this man wasn't at all discriminatory when it came to enjoying his cereal. We stayed like that a while, smiling and making eye contact with one another and our Lucky Charms. I liked that we had this in common, even if our approach to mutual enjoyment was necessarily different. A younger girl, maybe early twenties, jogged over and sat beside him, put her arm around his shoulder.

"Dad," she said, and when she said it he smiled and pointed to me with his plastic spoon and seemed about to say something. But instead he closed his eyes and dropped his bowl and flexed every one of his muscles simultaneously. I thought it was an odd thing to do.

It wasn't until the newspaper two mornings later that I told her about the dead guy. We were sitting at the kitchen table and I said, "Look."

I opened the sports section and showed her a photo of the top three finishers hanging out outside, embracing. Behind them was the dead guy. Or dying guy. It's hard to know at that given moment, the one in the picture, but he's slumped. His daughter's noticed. She's sweaty and squat in front of her dad, and her phasmid frame is angled and pointed in so many directions. She's got her forearms pressed against her knees and her father's head is clamped between her hands and parallel with his shoulders. I'm a few feet behind the daughter, and I've noticed the dead guy dying, too. My head's bent like his, in a way. I've still got my bowl on my knees, and my right arm is drooped along the boulder's side. In the photo it looks like I'm staring at the daughter's ass, but I'm staring past it to the space between her legs in which her dying or dead father's face is posed in a grotesque glamour shot. His body's limp after having seized, his eyes lifeless marbles.

"What are you showing me this for?" she asked without having looked. "Neither of us were winners."

"It's not the article," I said. "It's this." I pointed to the photo.

"They're hugging because they're competitors," She said.

"This," I said.

"Lord," she said. "You wanted me to see a picture of you staring up some girl's scrawny butt? Crissakes, your mouth is even open."

"I'm not," I say. "Jesus. That's not even the point."

"Her ass isn't the point or you gooning her ass isn't the point?"

"Neither," I said. "And that makes no sense, what you asked. Her ass would be relevant only if I in fact gooned it."

"What then?" Pointing a teaspoon.

"That's the guy," I said. "And anyway, you were with the Merk!"

"The who?"

"Forget it," I said. "It's not the point."

"Who's the guy?" she asked. "And that's what you said."

"What?"

"That it's not the point."

"But I meant the ass, not the Merk, and in any case, what I've been trying to tell you is that I was there. This guy is dead," I said, slapping my hand against the paper, the table. "And I was there. I was staring right at him when his heart busted."

"You can't tell anything," she said, waving her hand over the photo.

"I saw this man die and it was a terrible thing to see."

"It's not like you knew him," she said. "And besides, imagine that poor girl. She's probably his daughter, or his wife, if he's a perv. How old do you think she is? She looks young."

"*Was* a perv," I said. "And he wasn't, because that is his daughter and they both seemed really good. Probably the best people I've ever met."

"Well it's terrible, is what I mean."

I said, "I feel terrible."

She said, "Don't be like that. I'm sure you did what you could."

"What could I?"

"What did you two talk about?" she asked. "Before."

"We didn't talk," I said. "That's not the sort of meeting we had. We ate together."

"Oh," she said.

We were quiet.

"These things happen for a reason," she said. "You know?"

I didn't know.

"It bothers me," I said. "Even if it's not that it pains me, which I'm not sure it doesn't, it affects me anyway."

I clipped the article later and put it in my wallet. I went and bought the last three copies of the paper from the corner store and I clipped the photo from each of them as well. I mailed one to my mother. Is it vain to want to be part of something? To have been somewhere and there been recorded?

"I can't finish this," she says, pushing the omelette to the center of the table. She sets her fork on top of the plate. "It tastes funny."

I stare at the omelette between us as she reaches for the last slice of bacon from the plate. Two bites, it's in, and I can hear her muddy jaw working away at it.

I pick up the fork and take a bite of the omelette. She's not kidding. It tastes funny.

I grab the ketchup and slap the bottle until my plate is a red sea.

THE SHAPESHIFTER INTRODUCES HER VILLAGE TO THE MOON

ANNA JOURNEY

Of course the spirit of the fox
sang as he entered the ink-haired girl

by prying up her fingernail's
cellar door, pale as a one chicken moon
over her cooper father's workshop in Nagasaki. Let's believe

his woodblock prints of a red fox snowing white
plum blossoms in the dark forest meant the end of winter.
In the other prints, his red-headed Dutchmen are rendered
from life—the others imagined

from gossip: grotesquely white, red-haired barbarians.
Did you hear

when the cooper found his daughter—who could not read—
sprawled nude in his bentwood
cedar bathtub she had solved

his rosewood puzzle box by matching up
the written and carved names of berries

to cure ringworm? She said the cedar's sharp
smell caused her to claw the tub's sides until her fingertips
grew dark as hard southern cherries, and her jaw

snapped from its back-molars, vole-wide,
those front milk teeth tapered

like Western candles. Her dark hair was shocked into the ginger
of naked camphor wood so that her father's painter friends
took her for the Dutch consulate's mistress,
who, when vomiting sake into the still green water, flipped

an entire ornamental pond
of ancient goldfish belly-up. Her drunken dance after the cooper
kicked her from his house for madness

revealed the nine tails supernatural foxes gain
after living a thousand years
hanging from her skirts, also, a pearl-inlayed telescope
she introduced to the village

to bring the moon to rest
in her father's red bathtub at midnight.

FOX-GIRL BEFORE BIRTH
ANNA JOURNEY

When the fox-girl lost her fur
in the third trimester
she was already too human
to stay in the life
before birth that is all
swarm and sea
dark enough to breathe,
before she lost her body
that was everycreature—the wide
Chinese fans of her gills, rose hipped
with spidery inks, her prehensile
tail's little finger joint
crooked for swearing, her blind
vole-eyes like steamed
black-eyed peas. Then she was
whole, and good enough
to eat—those webbed palms,
her frog dive deep into the well,
the golden ball of her face
at the bottom.

MAYALAND

KELSEY TROM

ON THE plane to Cancun, Maria dreamt she was standing in line in the half-dark with her nose so close to the space between the shoulder blades of the tall man in front of her that she could feel the staticky fibers of his flannel shirt against her face. When she shifted—when Robin blew against the back of her neck and laughed—she saw that the line wound down the sidewalk, through a gate, and into the open front door of a neglected ranch-style house with bars on its windows.

Were they in Mexico already? Maria wondered in the dream. Everyone in line was standing what, in the US, would have been too close, with barely enough air to breath between them. And they were silent, like very shy people hoping to be let into a dance club but afraid that they would be.

So she, too, did not speak, just stood in line breathing shallowly through her mouth, trying not to inhale the stale smell of the man's shirt, careful not to let any part of her face touch the shifting muscles of his back.

Inside the house, past the empty front rooms and down the carpeted hallway, was a huge square of food, hot dishes set up on folding tables. The light was dim. Maria could not see what the food was, but the other people in line had begun humming amongst themselves, excited by the prospect of food, *this* food. But it was not, as far as Maria could tell, Mexican, not like the spreads Aunt Rosario spent days prepping for the annual family reunion at her house in the Woodlands. No steaming trays of tamales in papery corn husks, only glass casserole dishes filled with mounds of gritty, unidentifiable slop.

Maria spooned small portions of everything onto the plastic plate she'd been handed at the door. She was scared of what would happen if she didn't. Back outside, she saw Robin and Bradley climbing into a low car with dark windows parked just beyond the gate. She raised her hand, to call out to them, and the food slipped off her plate and fell onto the brown grass. The other eaters gasped. Maria bent and frantically shoveled the food back onto the plate.

Then she was standing outside the gate, on the side of the street opposite the house and Robin was calling her name. "Maria!"

Robin was climbing out of the passenger seat of the low car, now parked, but dustier than it had been before. As she shut the door and began walking away from it, Robin giggled and looked back over her shoulder at the tall Mexican man in a black cowboy hat with his palm on the roof of the car. He was not smiling, but he was rapt.

Maria had seen this: the way Robin let people hang on behind her, like fringe on a jacket yoke. Maria did not—in the dream or real life—hate her for this: she was afraid that if she had Robin's thick-fringed blue eyes, thin-limbed body, and instinct for conversation, then she, too, would let people become besotted with her.

The man followed Robin across the street, and Robin walked towards Maria smiling, but not at Maria, or anyone else—just to herself, at herself.

Maria woke up.

In the seat beside her on the plane, Robin was coiling the yellow headphone cord around her wrist and shifting the gum from one side of her mouth to the other. Maria looked out the plane window without turning her head. There was no land, just sparkling dark ocean beneath a shifting veil of clouds. It had been three hours to Dallas from D.C. Now three hours to Cancun.

Maria closed her eyes again. She wondered: Was Nathan on the ground in Tallahassee yet? Had the team been in the water already? Was the pool open to the sky—would he come back to school with a tan?

At the hotel, the Avalon Grand Cancun, the bellmen stood too close: in the mirrored elevator, in the taupe-carpeted hall, inside the whitewashed room, but Bradley said this was not because of different Mexican customs of personal space. It only meant the bellmen wanted to have sex with the three of them. Maria could not imagine assuming anyone wanted to have sex with her, and she certainly could not imagine saying it.

In their room, Bradley tossed her canvas bag onto the bed nearest the door, pulled off her T-shirt and jeans, and stood in front of the mirrored closet in a green bikini, patting her tummy (if, Maria wondered, something so concave, like a curled tongue, could be called a tummy) and looking at herself from all angles—the back view over her shoulder, the side view with her honey-colored hair slipping over her shoulders, then with it held off her neck in one fist.

"Fuck! I wish I'd had more time to get ready for this," Bradley said before moving into the bathroom and shutting the door.

When Robin and Bradley went down to the hotel gift shop for tanning lotion, Maria sat on the toilet and exhaled. Her shit came out green and pungent, like an animal's. When she was done, the bathroom smelled like a combination of generic floral-scented cleaner and her Uncle Liam's farm outside Lynchburg. She wondered if it was the bag of trail mix her mother had stuffed in her carry-on that was giving her the raw shit of a barnyard species. Or was it the climate, the air, something in her genes reacting to being, for the first time, in Mexico, the place where half of her had come from? Was her body reacting to being a Mexican in Mexico? She hoped not. She hoped Bradley would not notice the smell and say something that Maria would have to pretend did not cut into her.

Maria changed into her new black two-piece—skimpier than any she'd ever bought or worn. She checked the hallway through the peephole to make sure Robin and Bradley weren't on their way back and then faced herself in front of the floor-to-ceiling closet mirror.

The black mole on her left breast looked good with the black swimsuit. She'd always known the mole—which she'd had ever since she could remember—was sexy, but had tried not to think about that. Only occasionally, when she was alone in the communal bathroom of Bonnycastle first-year dorm, did she look at it and let her fingers drift down toward it.

That first night, they went to two clubs close by—Coco Bongo and Black Jack Cancun, both lame—before taking a cab further into the city to a club called Mango Tango, which was, surprisingly, not lame. Here, there were not so many boys with gelled hair, and everyone but Maria ended up making out with someone on the dance floor, where they could not hear what they were doing.

Maria just danced and watched. She was a good dancer. Her first two years of high school, she'd done Highland dance to please her mother. Summers ever since she could remember, there'd been big-skirted Spanish dancing with the Tex-Mex cousins on her father's side. Bobbing in place to eighties music was easy. She felt like she knew what she was doing. She imagined she looked like it, too.

In Cancun, at Mango Tango, at 2 am, the hair on the back of Maria's neck began to bristle. She noticed a fat boy in an OSU cap watching her from the sunken sofa at the edge of the dance floor.

In the cab back to the hotel, Bradley, flush with the pleasure of a blond boy's tongue in her mouth, proposed a weeklong makeout contest. Robin shrieked and agreed, but Maria, though drunk enough to fake it, did not.

"Hello? Maria Joan Velasquez?" Robin spoke too loudly into Maria's ear and squeezed the back of her neck.

"Yeah. Whatever."

"Whatever?" Bradley was slumped against Robin now, and the weight of both of them was heavy on Maria's shoulder. Bradley leaned across Robin and slapped Maria's knee. "What do you think Nathan's doing in Tallahassee, anyway?"

"Swimming?" Maria cocked one eyebrow. She didn't fake a smile.

"And?" Bradley poked Maria's thigh just below the hem of her skirt.

Maria looked at Bradley's finger. "And eating. And sleeping. That's pretty much all Coach Brunelli gives them time for."

Robin chortled and clutched Bradley's shoulder. "Yeah, just keep telling yourself that."

Maria couldn't decide if she wanted to hit them both or cry. As she reached up to swipe her eyes, Bradley, apparently to get a leg up on the competition, leaned over the partition between the front and back seats, pressed her lips to the cab driver's and proceeded to suck face with him while Maria gripped the armrest and watched the road.

When Bradley finally detached herself from the cabdriver, she looked at Maria and said, in a mean way that Maria knew she would attribute, if ever called on it, to drunkenness, "That doesn't even count. That was just to let you know what your little, or, probably *big*, since he's a swimmer"—she giggled—"boyfriend is doing in Florida this very minute."

Maria doubted it. Nathan had never touched her. She wasn't sure if he just didn't have the energy to try or if abstention from all physical things non-aquatic was part of his training. She'd seen this in movies: boxers begging off willing girls: *Coach's orders.*

Nathan had an overbite and he was from the country—Southwest Virginia—not the suburbs, and he and Maria had been pushed together by people on their respective halls because they were both quiet, which from Cancun seemed to Maria like a bad matchmaking strategy: What did they think two quiet people would beget together? Doubly loud silence?

They got back to the hotel at 4. Maria rubbed the makeup off her face with a wet washcloth and fell into bed in the clothes she'd worn to the club. She fell asleep immediately and dreamt of dancing for the next seven hours. By the end of her sleep cycle, she was dancing in fewer and fewer articles of clothing, until all the other blurred dancers in the club were doing the Locomotion in a circle around her as she danced, bra-less and topless, her breasts bouncing into the air then flopping down against her ribcage. She would not let herself look at them, but the image of what they must look like, in motion, played across her mind: her breasts drooping lower and flattening out into pancakes with every increasingly painful dance move, as if aging before her eyes, until, finally, she pictured them so clearly that, as she began to wake, she was sure she'd have to fold them like silly-putty into her new swimsuit top. That, or go home.

Maria woke up grateful for the sheets and comforter covering her and Robin. She rolled over onto her side, half afraid for Robin to see her new, dance-flattened chest. She felt the density of her real breast against the inside of her upper arm and was relieved.

The first time Maria'd seen Nathan swim, at a UVA tri-meet against UNC and UPenn, she'd thought: *Is that really my boyfriend?* Robin had thought the same. She'd turned to Maria with a smile and said, "Damn. Who knew?"

It was true: He'd become someone different. He crouched on the starting block and tucked his head to his chest so that his non-chin was invisible. Robin squeezed Maria's knee. *Swimmers, take your marks.* The beep of the electronic starter. Nathan exploded off the block.

It was stunning. She did not recognize him.

She wondered why she could not have him—this pool self—as a boyfriend. He—the boy in the water right now, reaching so certainly for the wall—would be able to bridge the distance from his hand to hers.

He—the boy whose mouth chugged air so deliberately—would be able to take a quick stab at her lips with his. He'd be able to let them relax there as effortlessly as he was treading water now at the end of his lane, watching the time clock for his place. He'd be able to slip his tongue into her mouth as easily as he reached across the lane line to shake the hand of the swimmer in lane four. He'd be able to lift her shirt over her head and undo her bra as casually as he shrugged on his warm-ups while he toweled off and talked to Coach Brunelli on deck. Then she would know, finally, what the soft bulk of her breasts felt like next to the hard planes of a man's chest.

On Friday night, they went to Dady Rock, where Bradley and Robin ended up behind the bar, mixing drinks under the tutelage of two attentive male bartenders. Maria watched, with discomfort, as Robin took off the T-shirt she'd put on over her bikini and let the bartender with the fauxhawk pour ice water down her front. Maria tried to be the only one in a ten-foot radius who did not see Robin's nipples spring up like crocuses.

Maria had never, in all the years they'd known each other, been able to read Robin, but, when Robin did a shivery dance to the other end of the bar just as the bartender tried to lean over her shoulder, Maria thought: *I still know you. I still know when you're afraid.*

The other bartender, the one with the shaved head and smooth complexion, looked at Maria's heavy black hair and almost-black eyes—the parts of her that screamed Latina—and smiled. "Hey! *Mija*!"

Maria's father still sometimes called her *mija*, little daughter. The bartender did not say it the way her father said it. She closed her mouth and shook her head. "No thanks," she mumbled.

The bartender nodded. "Okay. " He smirked and strode to the other end of the bar, toward an ugly girl wearing too much makeup and waving a Mexican bill.

The fat boy in the OSU cap was there again, at the bar. He raised his glass and nodded to her. Maria gave him a pinched smile and made her way to the bathroom.

The only part of Nathan Maria had ever touched was the bottom of his foot—surprisingly dense and soft—and even that had been an accident.

He'd had a corn from his running shoes, and, when they were watching TV in her dorm room, pulled off his flip-flop and showed it to her.

Maria touched the callus on Nathan's big toe without even thinking and let her fingers lay in the instep for a couple seconds. When he did not withdraw his foot, she slid her fingers across it, cupping the ankle. She looked up at him. He was looking down at her fingers, which, she saw now, looked childishly tiny across the broad base of his foot.

Then Kayla knocked on her dorm room door and Nathan jumped up and put his hands in his pockets. When Maria opened the door, Kayla said, "Oh," then smiled and handed Maria a CD with "Music for Maria" written across it in permanent black marker.

On Saturday, the fat boy appeared on the same stretch of beach, manning the cooler for his Frisbee-playing friends. Even from a distance, Maria could see that his flesh folded over the waistband of his swim trunks in the front *and* the back. He was pinker now, and he kept smiling at Maria. Every time he did, Bradley snorted.

When the game of Frisbee fizzled out, the fat boy took three beers out of the cooler and began walking toward the spot where the three girls had laid their towels. Under her breath, Bradley said, "Don't talk to him."

Robin propped herself up. "That one guy's kinda hot. The one in the brown shorts."

"They're playing Frisbee—I don't care how hot they are."

"So?" Robin took off her sunglasses and squinted at Bradley.

"Just trust me. Don't fucking talk to them."

"Why not?" Maria was surprised

"They're gonna want girlfriends for the week. And *then*, if we're really unlucky, they're going to want to call us and be our distant true loves."

"He's really hot."

"He's gonna have a photo montage of you on his laptop."

"He's *cute*."

Bradley rolled over and closed her eyes. "Don't say I didn't warn you."

Robin got up to meet the fat one. His leaner friend, brown shorts, jogged toward them with two more beers, smiled at Robin, and, next thing Maria knew, the five of them—she, Robin, Bradley, fat boy and brown shorts—were drinking Coronas and exchanging school information: University of Virginia, Ohio State University. Fat boy's name was Gabe. Brown shorts was Scott. Maria thought: *Huh. So that's how this is done.*

In the real Cancun, there was darkness, but not like the darkness in the dream she'd had on the plane. It was a comforting darkness inside the clubs, which were strobe-lit and strange, like theme parks—a climbing wall in one, eighties cover bands in the another.

In the real Cancun, there was very little eating, only lines for alcohol, which the three girls marinated in at night. During the day, they baked on the beaches or beside the hotel pool.

"Don't let people treat you like shit." That was all her father had said to her before she left. He had not said it unkindly, but Maria had been in a bratty mood.

She'd said back, "Shouldn't you be saying, 'Don't treat other people like shit'?"

"I'm not worried about that." He shook his head and hugged her. "You have your mother's instincts, which aren't survival instincts."

Sometimes, Maria hated her father.

Maria woke up early on Sunday, dreaming of the night before—the tricky stems of the cocktail glasses, Robin's showy laughter, Scott's eagerness, Gabe's continual proffering of drinks, the comforting cloud of cigarette smoke outside the club door. What had happened to her imagination? Now, more than ever, she needed to visit other places at night. That night, she promised herself, she would try to think of someplace else—someplace other than Cancun—before she fell asleep. Still, she doubted there would be enough time. She knew she'd dream of dancing and strobe lights and girls hanging from the ceiling, the hideous click of high heels on the parquet floor of the hotel lobby as all the college girls converged at ten, headed for the clubs.

She left Robin and Bradley sleeping and swam laps at the hotel pool. When she climbed out and wrapped a hotel towel around her waist, Gabe materialized with a piña colada in one hand, a beer in the other.

"Piña Colada?" he asked, pushing it toward her.

"No thanks. Just swam off all the alcohol."

He shrugged. "That's cool." He took a sip of it himself.

On Monday morning, when Maria woke up, her thighs hurt at the leg sockets. She hoped she was not getting her period. She could not remember what she'd dreamt of.

That day, Maria avoided the beach and the pool. While Robin and Bradley laid out, she left the Hotel Zone and walked around the city fully dressed. She bought a veggie burrito and soda at a place called *Natural Food.*

On Tuesday, Maria woke up when she felt her period slipping out of her body. She could not remember what she'd dreamt, but it had been happy. She clenched her thighs together and arched her back. She would get up and stuff herself with toilet paper, but not yet.

On Wednesday morning, Gabe and Scott drove Maria, Robin, and Bradley, in their rental car, to Chichen Itza. That afternoon, on the rim of a freshwater sinkhole near the ruins, Gabe put his wet palm down on the limestone beside Maria and asked if she had a boyfriend. She stared at the top of his hand—boneless, pink, and dewy as a baby's, nails rosy and neat—and lied. "Yeah."

It wasn't true. Nathan had broken up with her before he left for Tallahassee. Maria had been surprised to discover, as he sat on her dorm room bed with his head down and his hands in his pockets, that it wasn't the prospect of not being with him that upset her, but knowing that he'd held the idea of her in his head and decided, *no thanks*.

Bradley, who'd been swimming in the sinkhole beneath Maria and Gabe when he popped the question, made fun of him later, when the three girls were sitting at an outdoor table waiting for the guys to bring food back from the service window of a roadside taco stand: "So, um, little girl, do you have an, um, boyfriend. Yes, old, fat man, and do you really think I'd tell you if I didn't." The speed with which words moved in and out of Bradley's mouth astounded Maria.

Robin squinted in the general direction of the guys. "Scott says Gabe's a really good guy."

Maria rolled her eyes. "Yeah, I'm sure he is."

Robin raised her eyebrows. "What was *that* supposed to mean? All I'm saying is, give him a chance."

"Why don't *you* give him a chance?"

"There's Scott."

"What, you're a couple now?"

Robin shrugged.

"Doesn't he live in Ohio?"

"He'll be done with school in May."

Maria had never known Robin to act this stupid.

After the tacos, they walked down the gravelly edge of the road to an overlook. Scott put his headphones in Robin's ears and said, "You've got to hear this band."

"Who is it?" Robin smiled at Scott in a way Maria had not seen before.

Scott put his hand on Robin's shoulder, so that his thumb rested against the base of her throat. "Just listen. Then I'll tell you."

Robin's face was still and her head bobbed faintly. She kept her eyes down, but her mouth began to lift up at the corners.

Maria wanted to catch Robin's eye, to have one moment with her like they hadn't had this whole trip, the kind of look that made Maria feel like she would be fine—that she could float through the rest of the day and it would not matter that she had nothing to say or nothing that people wanted to hear. But then Scott touched Robin's back; it was Scott that Robin looked up at, Scott that smiled at her.

Maria had gone out with Nathan for two months, and he'd never once said *listen to this* or gotten close enough to put headphones in her ears.

That night, on the floor of the Mayaland hotel—they were running out of cash and had accepted the guys' invitation to share their room—Maria dreamt that Cancun was an alcohol-free amusement park where all the drinking was surreptitious, out of water bottles, like at the eighth grade dance. In Maria's dream, Robin got busted at the top of the four-story waterslide when the middle-aged waterslide attendant told her she was "too drunk to drive" her foam mat down its twisting trajectory.

Robin, emboldened by the Bud Light she'd been squeezing into her mouth all four flights up, spat something back at him. He stood up, red in the face, and, stabbing his index finger at her, said, "That's it! You're going with the ones to be sent home!"

At some point in the middle of the night, Scott had gotten up off the floor and into the bed beside Robin. Maria was glad she had not heard when.

Maria looked at his legs mixed up with Robin's under the sheets and faded green coverlet and wondered what would happen when they got back home to Charlottesville.

She went back to sleep. She was following Robin into a wading pool that looked suspiciously like the one they'd gone into at Astroworld when they were thirteen. Robin looked over her shoulder at Maria. *Come on.* She widened her eyes and made an exasperated beckoning gesture.

Come on. Come on. Maria couldn't tell if Robin was saying it again, or if it was echoing off the walls of the wading pool. The sky was darkening, the boys were getting taller, broader, swarthier, their complexions more pitted. It occurred to Maria that she could get out of the pool. That she *could* get out of the pool. She turned and began trudging against the water, which felt denser now.

Maria. Robin was calling her name. Maria kept walking, felt the line of the water slipping further down her legs.

Maria. If she turned, Maria was convinced, she would drown.

When Maria woke up, for the second time, in the Mayaland hotel, there was a hand on her hair. She knew it was Gabe. She wanted to squinch her eyes shut tighter and pull the covers over her head. *Go away*, she thought, *go away*. She could hear him breathing—it was not the breathing of a fit twenty-something. She hoped he'd stop of his own volition, but she felt the pressure of his broad, blunt nails against her scalp. His hair stroking had become more involved, less tentative. He was no longer just petting the top layer of her hair—his fingers were now combing through the underlayers as well. She tried not to picture his fat face in her head, tried not to imagine what he looked like now, bent over her, mouth slack. *Fuck fuck fuck.*

The pressure eased and she thought: *Maybe it's over.* But then his hand was pushing her hair against the back of her neck, and there was a sweaty fingertip against her earlobe. She stopped breathing. His second hand was on her wrist.

Maria opened her eyes. He pressed the back of his palm against her shoulder.

"What are you doing?" she whispered.

He fingered the strap of her tank top. She sat up and slid away from him, feeling the sting of friction between her basketball shorts, the makeshift bedding, and the dry skin of her buttocks. She folded her arms over her knees and hugged them to her chest. Her heart was threatening her ribcage—she hoped he couldn't hear it.

"What are you doing?" she repeated, full volume this time.

Gabe widened his eyes and pursed his lips. "Shhh," he admonished.

Maria raised her eyebrows. "What are you doing?" she said again, even louder.

He looked at her like she was crazy, pulling his face back, flaring his nostrils, and pushing his eyebrows into the middle of his forehead. It made his cheeks look even fleshier than usual. "I just wanted to see how thick your hair was."

"You're supposed to ask first." She felt around for her sweatshirt, clenched it in her fist, and stood up. She pulled the sweatshirt over her head and tugged it down over her stomach.

Now that she didn't feel so exposed, her body was waking up. She twisted her hair and looped it against her neck. She clicked on the lamp by the TV. Scott and Robin shifted in the bed beneath the window. Bradley groaned from her cot by the door.

Maria slid her feet into her flip-flops and straightened to her full height. She knew that by turning on the light she'd started something she could not back out of. From here on there would be no diplomatic way to make sure his fingertips never made their way onto any part of her again. Maybe it was because she was still scared, because she knew the others would call her a priss, overreacting, that she kept going.

Maria put her hands on her hips and stared down at him. "Huh? Don't you know hair is private?"

"Don't you know that only white girls can get away with acting this stuck up?"

Maria scoffed. "What the fuck did you just say? Speak up, son." It was the speech of her cousins Leticia and Jimena, which she tried out only when she was alone in her dorm room.

Bradley sat up in bed.

Gabe pressed his palm against the crown of his head. "Aw. C'mon. I'm sorry. I just thought…"

Bradley pushed off her blanket and said, "That because she wasn't entirely white you could come in and colonize?"

Scott and Robin were awake. Scott shook his head. "Hey, now, let's not all us reasonable people start accusing each other of racism."

"Reasonable?" Maria glared at Scott.

Scott looked at Gabe. "Dude, what did you do?"

"Nothing, man, I swear."

Maria looked at Robin, who had her hands over her eyes, "Robin. C'mon. We need to go." Maria threw her travel guide into her canvas bag..

Robin peeked at her. "Go where?"

"Out of *here*. C'mon."

Scott was digging in the covers for his boxers now. "Maria. Seriously. Whatever he did, I promise he won't do it again. Where are you gonna go?"

"Robin! C'mon! Now!"

Gabe stood up. "Maria, look, I'm sorry. Don't overreact."

"Shut up, fat boy."

Gabe flinched. He took a step toward her, then stopped, as if holding himself back. "Good luck getting back to Cancun without us."

Scott widened his eyes at Gabe, "Man, what the fuck are you saying? Chill, people."

"Robin. I'm leaving."

"OK. OK. We heard you." Bradley had gotten out of bed and was pulling on her cutoff jean shorts. "Robin, come on."

Maria—who suddenly had no problem looking directly at anyone—watched Robin, who had tucked the sheet under her armpits and curled her brown arms around her knees. Robin looked straight back, not moving. "Maria Velasquez," she said, carefully rolling the *r* and hissing the *s*.

"That's me," Maria said back, jumping her eyebrows.

Robin licked her upper lip with just the tip of her tongue. "Still a baby."

Maria couldn't think of anything to say, so she just stood there and felt her stomach turn to stone.

Finally, Robin pushed her hair behind her ears and looked at Scott, who shrugged, before pulling on her clothes under the sheets and climbing out of the bed.

After this, Maria knew, she and Robin would not be able to look at each other ever again.

Scott got out of bed and crossed his arms. His boxers were lime green. He cleared his throat and spoke to all of them but looked at Maria, "If you ladies can wait a few minutes, we'll give you a ride back."

"Thanks, but no thanks." Maria turned to the door. She was running out of steam. If Bradley and Robin did not come now, she was afraid she might cry.

Back at their Cancun hotel, Robin slept in Bradley's bed. Maria tried to think of anything but Gabe and Scott. She did not want their faces in her dreams. She tried to think of school—of all the boys she wanted, abstractly, to kiss or bump up against. Mostly, it was just her Physics TA, the one with the receding hairline and the big laugh—she'd heard it when he'd walked in on her washing her hands in the men's bathroom on the second floor of the Physics Building. She'd imagined herself sitting in his office across from him, but had not yet gone so far as to contrive an excuse to go there.

She tried to think of him, but it did not work. Instead, she thought of Nathan, the way he had to duck under the doorway of her dorm room, the way his eyes came up wide underneath his raised eyebrows once he had. She thought of how, when she watched him push water out of the way like it was nothing, she thought: *This is my boyfriend—I have a right to touch him.*

On the plane home, Bradley sat between Robin and Maria. Maria stepped on Robin's toes accidentally when she got up to go to the bathroom. "Sorry," she said. Robin kept her nose in her magazine and did not reply. Bradley smiled slightly at Maria over Robin's head and rolled her eyes.

In the bathroom, after she'd washed her hands, Maria let herself stand in front of her reflection for a moment. She had avoided mirrors the whole trip, keeping her side to the bathroom glass in their hotel room when she straightened her hair and put on mascara to go out at night. Now, she leaned toward the mirror and looked at herself hard.

Her face was thinner and darker. Because of all the blood that had been pulled to the surface over the past seven days, her complexion was brighter. But it was the not the momentary beauty of her reflection that pleased her. It was the familiarity of the visage framed in the tiny mirror above the tiny sink.

This face, she thought, *I know this face.*

ALLENWOOD

JANE ROSENBERG LAFORGE

If I take this picture in black and white,
would it be easier to conceal the crimes
committed against the sky, the dimensions
of the sun finally unfolding, the beaks
of competing Birds of Paradise
contending for a final sip before the land
trips, the ocean stumbles, and the cryogenics
thaw. I wish that I had been gone longer;
that I had forgotten you and the yucca
that grew at the end of our road, and all
the neighborhood's colors: the annular
yellow like dust or captured antigens;
or the blue that seemed to come from
the end of a pestle, how it covered
the succulent rounds of certain cactus
emerging from the stucco crawl spaces.
They say you've created an entire universe
out of this singular location: a system
of government, elections, other-loathing
and self-knowledge. Then what have I
created, but the taste of a few trees after
fire, their trunks pocked with statistics.
I miss those trees, shedding needles
and skin as if they were mammals, sentient
and superior. They survive but keeping
the best of their anatomy as unknowable

as the true locations of stars' homes,
not those listed on maps for sale
on our street corner. In the freshly poured
driveway I used to stand barefoot
on a dazzling black depth and dared
anyone to cross the property line,
into the tar I said reflected the constellations
and myths, directly under us. The sheets
of my bed were pinked pricked through
with Niagara starch, a diamond crispness,
and at night I opened the shutters of my
picture window onto a gray compression.
Travel by light years had been rendered
anemic and suffocated by the day's chemical
processes. Once you left I fell asleep
to the beige vibrations of ivy and mice,
and when the sun rose again, it rose flawless;
without the raw marks we now gasp to admire,
but refuse to recognize as righteous indignation.

HOMECOMINGS
COURTNEY FENNER

OCTOBER 2003

I FEEL bad for saying the F-word on a Sunday, but a lot of people can't drive and I have only ten minutes to go to Starbucks and get to my aunt's house in time to carpool to Grandma Frances's church, Petworth United Methodist. It's the 98th Anniversary. There will be a cake.

We are forty-five minutes late because of the Marine Corps Marathon. They've closed Rock Creek Park, and we can't figure out how to navigate an alternate route. I don't understand how a person can run twenty-six miles and not want some kind of tangible prize at the end. Finishing as its own reward is bullshit. Someone should gift the winner with a spa pedicure so she can get those foot blisters shaved down.

When I walk inside the gray-and-brown stone church, I realize that I have forgotten how the windows have the Greek symbols for Alpha and Omega in stained glass between the panes. Our shoes echo off of the wooden flooring in the giant cavern of a sanctuary. We are plodding horses. The room is octagonal, and its legion of corners extends to the fifty-foot ceiling, across, then meets at a star in the middle like *la Place d'Étoile* in Paris. I wish I had my camera to take a picture of it.

Grandma Frances is sixty-seven, has three wrinkles and manages to find the good in everyone. She taught me to read when I was three. She reacted to breast cancer with all the concern of shooing a fly from the edge of her bread plate. Even though we have all moved far into the suburbs, she is the only one who gets her husband—my Grandaddy Rudy—to drive an hour east to the city every Sunday morning at nine o'clock.

The nine of us—aunts, cousins, my sister and me—pile into the sanctuary, increasing its population from twelve to twenty-one. Seeing it so empty makes me sad. Being late used to mean a slim selection of seats.

I am pleasantly surprised that the sermon is given by a woman with graying dreadlocks down to her shoulders. She asks the congregation what they are doing to be like Jesus, what they are doing about the Black community's AIDS crisis. She orates for no more than five minutes and reads directly from a sheet of paper, glancing upward thrice. She is Reverend Carmen Colette. Later that day, during conversation, I will find out that she has a tooth missing and that she is the single mother of two young, adopted children. She will become my hero.

I look back at my sister and cousins. They snicker uncontrollably as Granddaddy Rudy continuously exits and re-enters during service because he can't harness his belching. Gas with a mind of its own is an unfortunate yet hilarious side effect of chemotherapy. He's still a fox, though: slick silver hair, smoky eyes and perfect dentures.

We sing "Kum Ba Yah" straight from the hymnal, then go to the altar to pray. I remember doing this, kneeling, when I was smaller, my elbows barely able to reach the wooden railing. Everything used to be bigger. On this day, my knees begin to hurt after only a minute or so. I am getting older. Or fatter. I'm not sure which.

After the service, in the red-as-the-blood-of-Jesus carpeted fellowship hall, we sit our belongings at tables covered with disposable white paper tablecloths similar to the ones used at my seventh birthday party. Once we are in line getting food, the assistant pastor stands talking to my sister, a girl cousin and me. He has hands like rubber gloves that have been blown up too large. Mickey Mouse hands. He warns us to prolong singlehood as long as possible because when we get married, we'll "have to stay put with the children while the men roam." I dislike him.

The chicken from Popeyes on the serving table in the fellowship hall is crunchy and not greasy. The salad has cucumbers, which I hate. I drink green liquid that came from a punch ring and ginger ale. Just as I begin forking vanilla pound cake into my mouth, my sister tells me my phone is ringing. I dig it out of my bag and exit with polite stealth.

Outside, at the top of the white concrete steps leading down to the street, I speak to Asa, whose mouth I struggle every day to forget, who brags about all the other beautiful women in the street and promises to call me later—an empty promise, I know, because we haven't spoken in weeks. I walk back into the hall fifteen minutes later with the taste of vomit in my mouth.

My family leaves soon, after lengthy goodbyes. We leave without any pictures. In an SUV truck that cost too much money, we drive west to where we live now, to where there are no Black churches. Pulling out of the lot, I whisper, "Happy Birthday," to the church as we curve slowly past it and yield to oncoming traffic.

I go down to UVA to meet with an old professor. We meet in her office and she tells me about the declining state of the school, how the students are mostly good but entirely unaware of the sociopolitical upheaval surrounding them, how the Board of Visitors continues to do nothing to combat the race problems rumbling beneath the colonial brick surface, how it is still very much a plantation system to this day—how the whites run the place and the Blacks work it—and how everyone seems okay with that. I ask her about her organic garden and tell her about my quarter-life crisis, that all my degree means out there is that I think too much to hire.

That night, after a concert, I eat with two fellow alums I haven't seen in a while at the Barracks Road Ruby Tuesday. The first, who is in theological school, discusses what her days are like. Sometimes professors don't come to class, or if they do, they answer their cell phones mid-lecture. They instruct students to say things like, "What a preacher!" and "Walk tall and work hard!" and "My, my, my!" She is learning church. My other friend sends back each plate of food that comes to her after first taking ten bites. She does this whenever we go out to eat. She only pays for her meals half the time.

I complain about my job. "Working in a high school is birth control," I tell them. They sympathize. They work with children, too, one with six-to-ten-year-olds and one with middle-schoolers. Kids need to be told they're tap-dancing on my last good nerve like Sammy Davis Jr. Kids need to have more expected of them. Kids need fewer MP3 players. Kids will say things to women teachers like, "Can you move your bug butt out of my face?" or "You're jiggly," "Fuck you," and "No."

I also begin to tell them about writing, how there will be an ink revolution, how we are all schizophrenic, multi-voiced beings trying to live normal lives, how one day California will fall off into the ocean. They elbow each other and chuckle. I begin to miss Asa again, who is far away, so far I cannot drive there, which is new to me because once I believed I could drive anywhere. She wouldn't laugh at me.

When I wake the next morning, I see my sister is curled into a ball and still sleeping. She's come to Charlottesville with me. Yesterday, we went to Monticello and took pictures and learned about slaves. When I'd visited there a year prior, there was a quote from Jefferson on a placard saying something about how good it was to produce everything oneself. I thought it was crap. He didn't produce a damn thing: His slaves did. Other visitors must have felt the same way. That placard isn't there anymore. On his grave, it says that he was the father of religious freedom. I chortle. Religion is prison. Spirituality is freedom. Faith is freedom. Hope and belief are freedom. Religion is a laughing black cave. Religion and freedom are mutually exclusive They cannot coexist, not even with the aid of the almighty Mr. Jefferson.

We drive home. I think of the people who live in the houses along Route 29, who have cars whizzing past them at all hours, how they must have purchased their homes twenty years ago thinking no one would ever build a highway at the bottom of their lawns. I suddenly want a Mountain Dew and some Wonka Rope, so I stop at a Sheetz gas station. The line is ten people long. It will be dark by five, and I don't want to be in the country then because, really, I'm a baby. I leave unsated.

We pass an old church that is pale blue with a white steeple. The paint is cracking and there is a sign that reads "Fleetwood" over the front door. I associate this word with the band Fleetwood Mac, then the song "Silver Springs." I love that song. I sang the same song the previous night to my friends at Ruby Tuesday and became officially certifiable—a 20-something Black woman yelling at the top of her lungs at one in the morning, banging out a rock song made famous by a frog-throated white Stevie Nicks. It gets stuck in my head. *I'll follow you down til the sound of my voice will haunt you. You'll never get away from the sound of the woman who loves you.*

NOVEMBER 2005

Tuesday afternoon, around three. My mother calls as I'm walking across Franklin Street to say Granddaddy Rudy has passed out and been taken to the hospital. I am calm. He has visited the hospital on an almost routine basis over the past three years. I call my sister, Micah, who was actually there to see him slump over in his big red chair, who watched as Grandma tenderly placed a pillow under his head as he lay on the floor.

She doesn't answer her phone. Five minutes later, as I'm standing on the giant compass in the middle of the VCU campus, Mom calls back and says, in her warmest type-A voice, "Honey, he didn't make it." There is a warbling in my voice and hot liquid swirling underneath my skin. I don't like to let her hear me cry. It's uncomfortable. So I don't cry. I hang up. Milton, as he was born, who changed his name to Rudolph Valentino after the actor, is dead. He is six weeks shy of his seventy-ninth birthday.

I am having a hard time breathing. This has never happened before, no asthma or shortness of breath, no barbell on my chest as I walk along Grove Avenue toward my car. My other sister, Jonah, calls from her dorm room nearby, distraught, voice heavy with liquid. I tell her I am on my way, to do what, I don't know. I call Asa.

"My grandfather just died," I shriek with some gurgling burst of tears in my throat. She makes sure that I am sitting down somewhere, that I am not driving, that I am not wandering aimlessly into oncoming traffic. She's good at calming me down, even though she's a bit high-strung herself.

It ends up he died of a heart attack, not the cancer. There was no warning.

Jonah and I drive to McDonald's to drown our sorrows in fatty food. The welling of tears in my chest seems to subside with each bite of chicken nuggets, each munch of french fry or gulp of sweet iced tea. We discuss things—the absence of funeral-appropriate attire in our respective wardrobes, the desire for couture sunglasses to wear at the funeral the way rich people do. We rank the weepiest of my grandfather's children—our dad and his siblings. We laugh a lot; we can feel it is intentional.

The next day, my mother asks me to prepare something to say at the funeral on behalf of the grandchildren. I say yes, of course I will say something. I do not know what I will say. *I have never given a prepared speech in my whole life*, I realize after I hang up with her.

Every morning for the rest of the week, I wake up and cry. I get up on the left side of the bed, sit on the edge, stare out into amazingly perfect Indian summer weather and cry. I turn on the TV for background noise, humorous, Emmy-winning morning talk shows blaring. Al Roker making nice with the crowd outside of Studio 1A in New York City just before he gives the weather report. Later on, he and a guest chef demonstrate how to make alternative Thanksgiving dishes.

On Saturday, we arrive at Grandma Frances's house to process to the church for the funeral. To Petworth, the church in D.C. to which she always reminds us to return, saying things like, "This is where you were married," and "Reverend sure does ask about you." When my grandmother comes out of the back bedroom, my heart breaks. She is in a wonderfully tailored black skirt suit, stuffing Kleenex just behind the cuff of her sleeve. She is the most stunningly beautiful that I have ever seen her, hair coiffed just so, make-up exact, pearls. I know that it is intentional, that she is trying to be strong for everyone else. It is as though she has been ready for this her entire life, ready to relieve us of our burden of grief, ready to put it on her tiny, barely five-feet-high shoulders. She is the one who chose the casket and the flowers and selected my grandfather's best photograph to put out for people to see. She is Jackie Kennedy.

At the church, everyone who speaks talks about my grandfather's dedication to this building. His official title was Church Sexton, and he would come early before any church event and turn on the heating or air or special electronics. He would monitor people hired for paint jobs. He would make entire church breakfasts on his own because he doubted anyone could cook as well as he did.

I sit in our pew, reading the program with his picture on the front. He fought at the Battle of Guadalcanal in World War II when he was sixteen. *My God, how did I never know that?* I think. I sit in our pew thinking about the sanctuary, about all the births and deaths and saving it has celebrated. It was here that my grandfather, a hardened man, a drinking man, an "I'll-be-goddamned-if-some-son-of-a-bitch" man, crept up to the altar very late in life and gave himself to Christ. It was here that he lived out his days serving the needs of others, even in the midst of lung cancer and the series of heart ailments that followed. His was a life about which it is worth saying something profound, which is why I wish Reverend Colette were here, the woman preacher with gray locks and two adopted children whom I had been so taken with two years before. Instead, the funeral speakers are a giant party of men, one after another using empty church rhetoric to pay homage to their newly lost fraternity brother. I'm pissed, but I don't know if I feel that way because of these dopes or because secretly I know I blew off the last time I could have gone home to see Grandaddy Rudy.

I think about the song "Landslide." Fleetwood Mac again. "It meant the whole world could tumble around us and the landslide would bring you down," Stevie Nicks once explained in an interview. "And a landslide in the snow is deadly. And when you're in that kind of a snow-covered, surrounding place, you don't just go out and yell, because the whole mountain could come down on you."

I can't yell. All I can do is get up and give my speech. I am the only woman to orate that day. I speak about how love is not words but action and how Grandaddy Rudy lived that and how we should all live like that because we have to in order to survive. We love by doing, moving. I deliver the speech like Oprah, like a minister, like any other variety of actor, except I mean it. It is funny where it needs to be, sentimental only where it seems most natural. The people are in awe. But I don't look at them. I only look down from the pulpit at my grandmother, thinking of how she taught me to read and how that's coming in handy right now. I think of the time our family's hotel reservations in St. Thomas got all screwy and she and I ended up in the same room, shrouding ourselves in the blankets of the same bed, washing our faces together in the bathroom mirrors, ordering up breakfast and eating it on the balcony overlooking the beach. I remember her reading her *Daily Word* booklet and, I know, praying for every one of us. Even though today is about Grandaddy Rudy, what I'm doing is for her. *Well, I've been afraid of changing 'cause I've built my life around you.* I cannot give her back the days with him. I can only give her a reason to be proud. *But time makes you bolder, even children get older, and I'm getting older too.*

I hope she looks at me at this place and is happy with the job she's done.

A year later, on the anniversary of Granddaddy's death, Jonah tells me about a dream she had. She dreamed we were all standing at the edge of a forest nestled on a cliff on one side of a giant canyon. Granddaddy was in another forest on the opposite side of the canyon by himself, shoving a casket through the trees, breaking limbs and trampling the foliage, pushing and pushing with some astronomical strength until the casket fell over the edge into the space between us and broke into little parts. He looked over at us, dusted off his hands and, smiling, walked back into his forest.

His forest.

LOST NOSTALGIA: ELEGY FOR JOE BOLTON

KEITH MONTESANO

Leave us, now, in the swelter of summer dusk and sweat
sliding down a gin glass: the same you held in your hands

the night of the party, balcony off a cheap apartment—
voyeur among the college crowd, falling in love with the woman

across the street. Whether I imagine you in Houston or Cadiz,
when I drive through Richmond I can sometimes see you gazing

toward any woman, no matter how far away, who crosses
your path. This is no excuse for you. I've heard the rumors:

Hawaiian-print shirt, barrel cold in your mouth and in front
of your lover. That you planned it from the start, your life

toward a slower descent you couldn't have predicted or cured.
Now the anger, the scoffing at any defense: every woman

was too much, you knew the world would end the instant
you pulled the trigger. I can't tell you this for sure,

but I feel I know the woman in Breckenridge already
(despite how much you feigned to turn it into poetry),

two women hugging before departure and your obsession
with their destination, the hundreds in cheap hotel rooms,

and one who had fifty men before you, before ravishment,
before the thin rattle of the air conditioner near dawn

cooling both of your bodies in the thick summer heat.
And sometimes I think you're better off, as I speak

about the end coming sooner than later, and imagine
your lines echoing the song about bodies remembering

each other—how there is nothing that is not beautiful,
nothing that will last. My book is falling apart like these words.

SMALL DIVAGATION
JON SEALY

Those sweaters culled from the wash,
covered in balls of lint,
like chunks of snow

blowing across a freeway in Indiana,
the right lane closed for repaving,
a gray Mercury upside down in a ditch. Listen:

a velour sheet of clouds covers our town.
Snow trickles off rooftops,
it flows along Main and

percolates in the streets.
Snow seeps into the river where
blocks of ice play bumper cars. Listen:

electric currents shoot through the rails,
the clatter and hum of corn syrup
snaking its way up the Wabash.

Cotton flaps in the wind.
A night watchman walks down a hall,
flips a switch, then returns to his Oreos.

ISSUE THREE

HOT DAMN IT'S MAKEOUT CREEK THREE

THINGS IN BOXES

PIR ROTHENBERG

AFTER TWO years of working at the Copy-Ship, a retail packing and shipping outfit pressed between a liquor store and an Ethiopian restaurant in Northern Chicago, Nolan saw most objects in terms of the boxes in which they'd fit. Having a good eye for it, he made little use of the tape measure. The store, which belonged to Gary, a nearly hunchbacked man in his fifties, had been pampered like the child Gary and his wife never had until the latter's abrupt departure six months before. Then the place started going to pot. Insurance claims for items damaged in transport hung like animal skins on the bulletin board; the last working copier devoured paper and coughed it out; red-inked bills from all three major carriers arrived daily. Nolan and his coworker, Oscar, a short Guatemalan with a beaklike nose, saw Gary twice a day: around opening, when he came to pilfer money from the till, and at closing, usually drunk, when he counted the register and wondered aloud why the totals were off. Sometimes he'd stop mid-count and look up and say to Nolan, "Curious, isn't it, Sheila running off like that? *Damn* curious."

It was a grubby job, handling all the things people brought to the store to be packed and shipped. So many things passed through Nolan's hands. He rarely touched people. Sometimes when he handed back change his fingers brushed a customer's palm—but only nine of them: he'd lost the little one on his left hand in a high school shop-class accident. Before departing in the evening, he'd wash the grit and gunk from his hands and wonder where it all had come from—that antique toaster he'd boxed today? Those heavy ceramic mugs? That stiff family portrait? He didn't mind the dirt, it was part of the job; anyway, he had discovered a kinship between touching people's possessions and touching people themselves, a quiet, revealing transliteration he felt most acutely in his phantom finger.

In the morning, there was an order for a pickup. Her name was Lindsey Thiel; she rented a mailbox at the store, Number One-Thirty-One: mostly junk mail, bills, and around holidays a red card-sized envelope. Every three or four months she sent a shoe-sized box to an address in

New Jersey. These boxes were always sealed before she came in and so light that Nolan wondered if they held anything more than air. The box she had waiting for him in her apartment was far larger and heavier, forty-eight inches by forty by thirty, he guessed, and around seventy pounds. Dolly in tow, he followed Lindsey through her place, absorbing the immediate objects that composed her world: a turquoise couch, a tiny television set with knobs, a cactus in a sill. A velvet image of Elvis on a wall, the faint smell of oranges, the chirp of an overhead fan twirling loose in its binding. He felt clumsy here, suspended between the presence of something alien and his recognition of Lindsey's face, a face he knew from the store and thought of often. He stood with a sweaty grip around the dolly's handle as Lindsey knelt by the box in her cramped, aqua-colored kitchen, completing the shipping waybill. "How quick is ground service to Oregon?" she asked. He noticed her bedroom behind a half-opened door, her unmade bed, articles of clothing dangling from the doorknob. Sunlight streamed through the eastern windows and articulated the reds in her auburn hair, slightly tangled from sleep.

"Five days," he said, wondering if he had woken her with the buzzer.

There were several torn-open envelopes on the kitchen table, no doubt the very mail he had put in her mailbox a day ago. Odd to see a thing out of context. Although Lindsey said little in the store when she retrieved her mail each day, Nolan enjoyed the chirp of her hello and her quick smile. But when she left, the tinted windows between them seemed like the glass at an aquarium, separating two worlds. As she became obscured by the trees on Glenwood she seemed less real, less like someone he knew even superficially, more like a creature swimming past who he'd never see again.

Now, he reasoned, it wasn't Lindsey out of context so much as himself.

A breeze touched his neck, and Nolan detected a musky scent. He turned at a spurt of commotion behind him and saw two rabbits in a cage upon a cedar chest in the dining room. One with long auburn fur moved about the cage restlessly. Lindsey glanced up from her writing and made a cooing promise to appease them shortly. "They're usually out by now," she said, "but I knew you were coming." Nolan felt a pang of having intruded, and the apartment suddenly took on the airs of a sanctuary, unused to disturbances. He knelt a few feet away from the cage; the rabbits were undoubtedly the same breed, with a tremendous amount of long, groomed hair, erect and almost bulbous ears, fragile half-obscured faces.

"Cute," he said. The second one was white and gray, but the more active auburn held his attention.

"You can pet them," she said, "if you want." She had a longing gaze trained on the animals.

With a finger through the bars, he touched the auburn's back. It turned, stood up, aimed an investigatory nose at Nolan. Scratching the rabbit's head, he realized Lindsey's hair was nearly the same color, and imagined it was as soft—so soft and ungraspable his hand would barely register it.

"That's Phoebe," Lindsey said, her favorite, which was why it got to sleep in the house; the other rabbit shared the privilege only because its skittishness disturbed the rest.

"You have more?"

"Four in the garage," she said, then asked about insurance. Since the contents of the box were not worth over a hundred dollars, she didn't have to describe them on the form, and despite his curiosity Nolan felt it rude to ask what they might be.

"Are they all your pets?"

"They're English Angora," she said, "I sell their fur," then explained how every three months she sheared them as one would a sheep for its wool, thus obliterating the mystery of those weightless boxes she mailed. "But, yes," she concluded, offering a finger to Phoebe, "they're pets, too."

He schlepped the box onto the dolly and with a sidelong glance into her bedroom wondered if she'd go back to sleep after he left. Outside, the morning promised a sweltering day. Nolan noticed the garage on the other side of the lawn and slowed his pace. "So how much can you make from one clipping?"

Lindsey was ahead, holding open the gate. "A crop—not enough to pay rent."

"Do they get hot in there?"

She took a few steps toward him. "It's air-conditioned. Heated in the winter." Her eyes hovered between suspicion and eagerness to share a secret. "Do you want to see?"

The inside of the garage—the *rabbitry,* as Lindsey called it—was cooler than the apartment, and tidier. The four additional rabbits shared a large, wire-cage pen connected to an enclosed wooden hutch. They ranged in color from gray to black. All female, since Lindsey was not keen on propagation—not like her mother, who lived in Milwaukee and was a professional breeder. After stroking the rabbits, Nolan was startled to see his hand clothed in a gauzy reticulation of gray strands, and glanced back into the pen to make sure he hadn't mauled an animal. Lindsey laughed and plucked a tuft from one, who hardly seemed to notice. "It falls out," she said. "They're about due for a shearing. Another three weeks. You know," she said, "if you don't shear them they can die."

The store made most of its money at Christmas and after graduation, when seniors from Loyola University came in with four years' worth of accumulation swept into laundry baskets. Each load was like a city brought to rubble by an earthquake, with Nolan charged as excavator, sifting out the breakables, stacking the books and CDs, rolling the posters. It was early May, and the rush would begin soon; it was arduous work, but he enjoyed the odd brand of intimacy he experienced sorting through the items of the students' lives. A girl the summer before had owned thirty pairs of shoes, and as he lined them in a box he had clasped her feet thirty times, just as when he folded her shirts and bras he had caressed her back and held her breasts, just as when he browsed the titles of her books he had shared her thoughts, and when he organized her make-up he had seen her face. But it was a fleeting intimacy. The Copy-Ship was a business, and Nolan a clerk with a timecard. He rarely remembered a single customer's face, and all the miscellanea of their lives were, by the end of the day, just boxes of things stacked against the wall for the UPS driver to haul away with his truck. Cleaning his hands and closing the store were like rituals that disconnected Nolan from the lives in which he'd immersed himself all day. And then his own life was once again wide and vacant.

Lindsey appeared and vanished daily, although since the pickup Nolan thought her hellos were warmer and more drawn, as if she expended more breath, gathered from a deeper part of her body, to say them. In the midst of graduation rush, but in a lucky moment of a lull, Lindsey came in with her airy box, which she'd left unsealed. Nolan asked if she needed tape. She pulled from the box a clear bag containing a thick cloud of gray fur. "I thought you might want to see the crop." He did, very much. She opened the bag and held it for him to feel inside. Under her light smile he lowered a hand into the bag as if testing bathwater. It descended into overwhelming softness, but it was the position of their hands that provoked him, hers holding the bag against her belly, his between them, held by the downy material of her grasp. The ghost of his little finger came alive, feeling with exquisite detail the vaporous fur in ways that the real ones could not, and he knew then it wasn't only Lindsey's hair that was soft, but her skin and her voice and her eyes. He wanted to touch her, to glaum at her skin, ungraspable though it seemed, to take her into his hungry wet mouth.

Walking home that evening, the city was enchanted with his sweet hunger. He couldn't touch Lindsey, so he let his fingers dance across fences and trees and parked cars, finding the palpable reality in things. This contact reminded Nolan that he was real, too. He had always liked to think that his job offered him a certain tangibility. Despite being quite peripheral to the lives of his customers, he was nevertheless part of the movement and steady exchange of the world. A woman ships her things to a new city where she's landed a job—Nolan is a part of that great shift. A man sends a sapphire ring to his lover across the country—Nolan is a part of that gift. But there were limits, he realized. The longing to touch another person was assuaged for only a short while by touching things. He wanted a body tonight to embrace, and in embracing be assured, as though by a three-dimensional mirror, that his own arms and legs and torso were solid, that his breath was real, that his life mattered.

In mid-August, Lindsey paused by her mailbox, and for the first time Nolan could recall, tore open a letter that, from the return address in Milwaukee, he suspected was from her mother. With a mind for professionalism, he feigned that he didn't notice her tense posture and said hello.

For half the summer, he had dreamt up innocent ways to touch her—for instance, a silly gesture whereby he shook her hand and formally introduced himself—but these required expanding their conversations beyond the realm of shipping options. Toward this goal, he had asked after her rabbits, not just how they were, but also about their diet and behavior and personalities. The ploy, however, had never moved beyond a question-and-answer routine. Oscar suggested forthrightness instead: all that subtlety was garbage; you had to *tell* the world you were there because it didn't give a damn if you weren't.

"I have to get to Milwaukee," she said. "Tonight." The darting of her eyes about the store appealed to something she hadn't yet voiced, and with a pounding in his chest, Nolan intuited the distance between them rapidly closing. He braced himself. "Do you think," she began, drumming her fingers on the red countertop.

"What is it?" he said. He laid his hand on the counter and thought he saw a flicker of distaste in her eyes when she spotted his disfigurement.

The rabbits needed caring for, Lindsey explained, and she had no one else to ask on such short notice. The task immediately boggled him, but she assured him it was simple—feeding them twice a day, keeping an eye on the water and the thermostat. When he agreed, she thanked him with a loud happy sigh and for an instant pressed her hand upon his, squeezing his thumb and three fingers. It nearly stung him, her touch.

She left hurriedly and reappeared just before closing to drive Nolan to her apartment for instructions. As he followed her to her car, he glanced back to see Oscar in the store, watching with a curious expression.

The rabbits' fur was unbelievably long. Lindsey told him how many scoops of pellet-food to put in the dishes each morning and night; there was a small refrigerator, stocked with fresh apples and radishes and clover; here was the hay, but he needn't worry about that, she'd be home in two or three days; watch the door or cats will get in; fill the water with the hose; no need to go into the apartment; she's taking Phoebe and the other one with her, and anyway she only has the one set of keys. He'd felt the hot press of her hand for an hour; it made his hands hungrier still. Lindsey dangled the key to the garage above Nolan's palm for a moment before letting it drop. She cast a final, maternal glance over her infants, then watched astutely as Nolan successfully locked the door. As though it were a test.

"My mother," she said as she drove Nolan home. She shook her head. "My mother gets herself into trouble." Everything was wet from a rain Nolan hadn't noticed falling. The darkening air was thick and warm; the tires made a pleasant sound upon the asphalt, like the roll of a tape-dispenser. The city passed by in a phosphorescent stream.

"You don't have to tell me," he said.

"She's got this boyfriend, *ex*-boyfriend, whatever, who's just a real..." She trailed off.

Nolan reassured her: "It's okay, some other time." Like when she returned.

He was restless in bed that night, anticipating how Lindsey would look in three days, appearing like something sparkling from behind the ogre-like shoulders of another customer, and how she'd be grateful for the good job he'd done. He would have anecdotes about each rabbit, stories she'd delight in hearing. They'd get a drink and talk about their families. He'd ask to help with the shearing, and when he was in the rabbitry with her she'd remark that the animals must remember him because of how comfortable they seemed in his presence. All of this he foresaw upon his hot pillow.

The dewy grass wetted Nolan's shoes as he strode through Lindsey's backyard. He had taken the train, but he would use the company van for his next visit; Gary wouldn't notice it was missing. The rabbits stirred and grew anxious when Nolan entered. "Easy there," he said. One darted across the pen and made the metal cage clang. Lacking grace, he spilled most of the pellets into the pen before they reached the dishes. "Mama's out of town a few days," he said. And then, "I'm just a surrogate," as if coming clean with his obvious ineptitude. The rabbits didn't seem hungry. He double-checked the bag: it was the correct food. He remembered the vegetables and fruit, retrieved them and, fearful of opening the cage door, let the chunks drop unceremoniously through the bars. After prying the water bottle from its binding, he went to find the hose, but upon returning realized he'd left the garage door open, and spent the rest of his time peering under tables for any lean cats that might have slunk in.

At the Copy-Ship, Oscar was amused by the duties Nolan had taken on. "Man, there ain't no mother," he said, laughing. "There's a *boyfriend*, bro, that's for sure!"

Nolan hoped Lindsey would call. They'd forgotten to exchange phone numbers, though it was likely she had the number to the store. That evening, he was relieved to see the food was gone. He filled the dishes more neatly this time and the rabbits moved clumsily en masse toward them. Sitting upon a bale of hay, he was pleased to see them eat with him there. Outside, Lindsey's apartment, which composed one side of a duplex, stood dark and still.

The next morning, the rabbits seemed calmer and didn't fret when he stroked them lightly with his hand; in the evening, he found the confidence to open the cage door, pick one up and groom it with a brush the way he'd read to on the internet that afternoon, saving the stray fur in a bag should Lindsey want it. He gingerly removed some of the old hay and replaced it with new. He was surprised by how late he stayed watching them, feeling a peacefulness there that wasn't at all disturbed by the prospect of the roaring city awaiting him outside.

The following morning—day three, when he expected Lindsey to return—he instead found a garbled message from her on the machine at work. He and Oscar could only decipher pieces: her phone was dying and she "forgot the charger," or else "they wouldn't charge her." She'd be back soon, another "two" or "few" days. He heard the word "hospital," unless it was "miracle," and something about a man named Bill having "flaked" or "escaped." She didn't leave a return number, but after hitting star-sixty-nine, Nolan learned from a kind elderly voice that it was a payphone.

"Bro, she ditched you," Oscar said with glee. "Ditched you with the *kids!*" He was incredulous when he learned Nolan had no way of reaching her. No phone? No email? No address? Nolan hadn't even thought to ask for them, busy as he was with his amorous dreaming.

That evening, the food was nearly out and he'd already used the last of the hay. He felt uneasy, worried for Lindsey and for what he ought to do. As he paced along the side of her apartment, examining the integrity of the windows, he detected the first chill of autumn in the steady breeze. He lightly tried one window without a screen; it didn't give, which meant he'd have to find a pet store by tomorrow.

At work the next day, a man came in for whom Nolan felt an immediate dislike. He was a lean, cagey figure reeking of stale smoke, looking much older than he probably was, but attired sloppily in clothes too young for him: grimy sweatpants, a baseball jersey and cap. Underneath his armpit, he clutched a kitschy velvet portrait of Elvis, like the one Nolan had seen on Lindsey's wall when he had visited her apartment. The man didn't send the portrait, just bought a box for it and left. Nolan mentioned the coincidence to Oscar, who assumed a cockeyed expression and said, "Dude, where did you say she was at?"

"Milwaukee."

"Dude, that guy had on a *Brewers* jersey." Then, seeing Nolan's blank expression, he added, "The *Milwaukee* Brewers."

That night, in front of Lindsey's apartment, Nolan scanned the windows for any light or movement; he glanced into parked cars, and with a bag of food and a new bale of hay, he stepped quietly through the yard toward the rabbitry. He toyed with the idea of breaking in to see if Elvis still graced the wall, but the diminishing light of the evening was such that someone could be in the house watching him perfectly while simultaneously remaining obscured by the opaque glare on the windows. This suspicion was asinine, he knew, but the rough face of the man from the store seemed to hover in every shadow. After feeding the animals, Nolan got back in the van and waited to see if a light would come on in Lindsey's side of the duplex. Of course, he realized, if someone were watching him, they'd see that Nolan's van hadn't left and would wait him out. Screw it, he thought, and revved away.

On Friday morning, Nolan felt foolish for his earlier fears. When he peered through the sunny windows of Lindsey's place, he saw nothing out of the ordinary. Still, the windows didn't grant a view of the wall where he remembered the Elvis poster had hung.

That afternoon, Nolan felt a moment of weightless foreboding when he saw the man—donned in the same jersey and greasy sweats—in the store again. The man carried nothing with him this time, but was evidently in need of more boxes, as he was groping the ones on display. Oscar appeared at Nolan's side. "I got this fucker," he said, and went to help him. Nolan kept an ear to the sparse conversation: What are you packing? Just about everything. You shipping or moving? Little of both. You packing house? We pack house, where do you live? Hmm, what are the prices on these here? Where you going, Milwaukee? Brewer's fan?

Nah, he said, although to which question it was impossible to tell. Nolan began to regret letting Oscar take the lead; if the man knew anything about Lindsey, then Nolan ought to intervene and confront him, ask him point blank. But ask him what? The man bought ten large boxes with cash and left, never once making eye contact with either clerk. As he left, a cell phone rang mutedly in his pocket. With the boxes under his arm, he shoved the phone beneath his bony chin and answered. "No, she ain't," he said, hobbling out the door. "This is Phil. Who's this?"

That evening, Nolan spent a long time with the rabbits; the next day, Saturday, being his day off. The animals were quite ridiculous looking, really, with all that fur, like ovular storm clouds of varying intensity. After some time, Nolan realized he hadn't been thinking of Lindsey, nor of Phil or Bill or whoever he was, but had instead gotten lost in those gently scuffling clouds. Strangely, he found that when he tried to recall Lindsey, his mental picture of the auburn-haired girl refused to be pinned down for more than an instant. Her eyes rose and sank, her shoulders and hips expanded then narrowed, her breasts swelled, diminished. Where was she? All he was certain of was the color of her hair, the same as Phoebe's.

On Saturday, Gary ran the store alone. Nolan spent half the day in the rabbitry, grooming each animal and wondering with a combination of trepidation and hope if he'd have to shear them himself. Rabbits were, he had read, incapable of vomiting, and too much ingested fur could be fatal to them. Looking around, he saw no electric shears. He figured they were in the apartment.

Sunday, the Copy-Ship was closed. On Monday, the store greeted Nolan with a rank scent. On a sheet of paper, Gary had scrawled a note: *Dead rat?* It was not unheard of; with the restaurant next door, the occasional rat got in through the basement or expired between the walls. When Oscar arrived, he and Nolan set about finding it. The odor seemed strongest by the stacks of flattened boxes, but moving these only seemed to chase the smell elsewhere, which led them to the storage in the basement, where the pursuit went cold once more. Oscar then remembered a customer who belonged to a monthly steak club and how one time they'd forgotten to call him when his fillets, packed in dry ice, were delivered, only noticing their mistake days later when the meat had rotted. Upstairs, they dug through the piles of packages as yet unclaimed by customers, delving deep into the recesses of the shelving units until, judging by their shared fit of gagging , they found the culprit, a brown and greasy shoe-sized box. It was addressed to Lindsey Thiel.

"Fucking Gary must have got it on Saturday," Oscar said, his face hidden behind his shirt. There was no return address, but the Post Office stamp read Erdman, Wisconsin.

"I guess we should open it."

Oscar made a distasteful noise. "Don't open that shit, man. That shit ain't yours and you probably don't want to know what's inside. I know *I* don't." Then he shrugged. "Whatever man, if you gonna open it, go ahead, but that shit's all yours."

Nolan fetched a scarf that had been hanging in Gary's office since winter and wrapped it around his face. He crouched over Lindsey's box like a surgeon, slid a box-cutter through the tape and carefully lifted the flaps. He could make out a dark object sitting below crinkled newspapers.

Oscar reached in and nimbly removed the papers between two fingers, then darted away as if he had unleashed a swarm of bees. "What is it?" he hissed.

"I still can't see," Nolan said, turning the box into the light. The object inside flipped over with a dull thud and slid halfway out. Both men swore and shot backwards.

It was a living thing, or at least a thing that had once been alive; dead now, a dead rabbit, and Nolan knew at once that it was Phoebe, poor auburn Phoebe. Its ears were withered, plastered back along its head, and its eyes were wide sticky holes. Here and there, between matted fur dark and stiffened with black blood, long tufts of fur protruded somehow unaffected. Nolan put the rabbit back inside and sealed the box.

"What're you going to do, man?" Oscar asked.

Nolan was sitting on the counter with his back against the wall, looking vaguely in the direction of the corner, where the box sat. "I don't know. Tell her, I guess."

"Yeah, if she comes back."

"She's *coming* back."

Nolan found the card of an FBI agent who worked with the Post Office and had done several stakeouts in the Copy-Ship, awaiting customers who came in to retrieve goods purchased on stolen credit cards. He couldn't get hold of Agent Teatree, but another person on the line took the report, lacking in information though it was. "Sounds like a jealous boyfriend," the voice said, conclusively. Nolan looked up Erdman, Wisconsin, online and found it was a town north of Milwaukee: whoever sent the box had been heading away from Chicago, not toward it, but far from dismissing Phil-Bill, Nolan kept returning to him as the perpetrator, imagining flecks of saliva collecting upon his thin lips as he strangled the rabbit.

"It couldn't have been alive when they mailed it," Oscar said, closing out the register that evening when Gary didn't show. "Post Office wouldn't handle something kicking and scratching," he said.

"No shit," said Nolan absently. He stared at the hissing register spitting out its long white tongue of tape.

"How's someone just gonna do that shit, man?" Oscar said. "It's not a thing you just put in a box and mail…" When the register receipt finished printing, he turned to Nolan and said, "It's not our fault, is it?"

That night, Nolan parked the van around the corner and kept the lights out in the garage, even though he didn't know what he'd do if he spied someone arriving at the house. Inside the rabbitry, he wondered what to do with the box, which sat ominously in a garbage bag at his ankles. It was sealed well, and he only rarely caught a whiff—maybe a phantom one—of the animal inside. What he felt for certain was that the rabbits under his care were in danger, so he laid out the hay and fashioned himself a bed, whereupon he slept the night.

In the dark of morning he awoke, took Phoebe outside and, with a trowel he'd found in the garage, dug a hole. He cut open the bag and removed the package, wondering first if he should keep the animal inside of it. Soon he was wondering at the nature of boxes in general, at how the manufactured cubes pervaded the world. We live in boxes, he thought, we work in boxes and sleep upon boxes. The rabbits sleep in a box. We keep all our things inside them, and when we die we go in a box, too, and then that box goes inside another inverse box cut into the ground. It was a wonder that the planet itself was not a six-sided economical box. What good was a sphere?

He took Phoebe out of her death-carton. Held the stiff weightless body in his bare hands. His phantom finger quivered with its softness. Before setting her inside the hole, he cut off a tuft of fur—if not in memorial, then to give Lindsey whenever she finally returned.

Nolan lost track of the week, his days punctuated only by absence: no calls from Lindsey and no more sightings of the man in the Brewers jersey, for whom Nolan waited tensely, working out methods by which he would question him and discover the truth.

Each night, Nolan slept in the rabbitry, going home only to shower and change clothes, and he told Oscar none of it because he was aware of the inkling of madness behind his actions. In the mornings, he awoke from dreams where, entering the garage, he found all the rabbits had groomed themselves down to the skin and died, four naked bloating bodies huddled in the pen. He called the Post Office in Erdman and told them about what they'd mailed; they professed ignorance and told him it was inevitable that things occasionally slipped by. He went to his police precinct and filed a missing persons report, but wasn't encouraged in this, either: the officer who took the report told him to call the city about the rabbits and let well enough alone. Nolan asked what was *well enough* about a dead rabbit and a missing person, but the officer merely glared at him over his glasses. Nolan spoke with the dim couple who lived next door to Lindsey in the duplex. They didn't know her well and hadn't seen anything suspicious; but then, they hadn't even noticed Nolan coming and going the past two weeks.

He remembered the shipping waybill Lindsay had once signed for him in her apartment; he called the phone number she'd put upon it, but it was dead. Every day, he dialed the number of the payphone from which Lindsey had called, and only once was it answered again—by teenagers, who offered some vulgar responses to his queries about its location. Since the Copy-Ship van was in too much disrepair to risk highway travel, he looked at the train fares to Milwaukee; it was neither a long nor pricey journey, but he had no clue where he'd go or what he'd do once he arrived there.

He was about at the end of his sleuthing skills.

There was one more thing he could do, and on Friday evening he tried once again the window without the screen. This time, it slid open. He couldn't conclude, however, that the window had been recently unlocked, for his previous attempt to lift it had been little more than half-hearted. The apartment was musty and the empty rabbit pen left dirty—pebble-shaped remnants of Phoebe inside. He glanced about wearily with a vague sense of déjà vu, but found that, instead of being overwhelmed by the loquacious markers of Lindsey's life, he felt only an ineradicable silence. He opened a kitchen drawer: an assortment of knives and spatulas. A chef, he mused, but that rang false. In an overhead cupboard he found a set of plates with sunflowers—they seemed too jovial for Lindsey. Here was something—a mug from a German festival held downtown every year, the date 2003 written on it; he had attended that year, too, had drunk warm spiced wine out of an identical mug. More often, the items did not sing to him, did not even mutter the slightest melody that might reveal any more than the little he knew of Lindsey Thiel. He methodically went through every drawer and cabinet in the house, scanned every title of every book, movie and CD, thumbed through paperwork in a blue filing folder, looked at every photograph in the album, pawed every article of clothing in her dresser, read every label on the medicine bottles behind the bathroom mirror, touched every strand of auburn hair in her brush, counted all the change collected in a terracotta pot. He did this while eyeing it all as though he were going to pack it neatly in boxes.

In her bedroom, he sat upon that lovely unmade bed into which he had so wanted to descend alongside Lindsey and tried to feel for the impression of her with his ghostly finger. But it was he who felt like a ghost now—not Lindsey or her mother or Phil-Bill, not all the happenings of late, which were more like not-happenings, things occurring invisibly all around him that he could not penetrate. Seeing his tired, pale face in the dresser mirror did little to dispel the sickening feeling, the helpless discomfort of evaporating.

He found no telephone-address book. He did find boxes; not the ones Phil-Bill had purchased, but the small ones Lindsey had once used to ship the angora fur to New Jersey. They were flattened, the address labels beside them. On the chair nearby, he also found the electric shears, a black cord coiled around them. He took these things with him when he exited through the window. He left a light on, purposefully—it was a message to whomever had been lurking about in the apartment, a means to say that he, Nolan, was there, too. After all, whoever it was had left him a similar message by removing the Elvis portrait, which was missing, a fact Nolan had chosen, for the sake of his fleeting courage, to ignore.

At the end of another week, Oscar greeted Nolan, upon his return from lunch, with visible excitement. Nolan wondered if Gary had shown up; neither man had seen nor heard from their boss since the day he accepted the box containing Phoebe. All that seemed left of him was that note—*Dead rat?*—which still sat upon his desk. But Oscar's excitement wasn't about Gary. "Another box for Lindsey, man," he said. "It's back here."

Nolan felt sick as he walked to the back of the store, but then he saw that the package wasn't shoe-sized, but instead a much larger. He found his breath. Then he recognized the box. "Not *for* her," he said, "*from* her."

It was the box he had picked up from her apartment in the spring, now torn, taped, and bruised from its mysterious journey across the country, scarred with a dozen scrawled hieroglyphs and numbers and branded by a large red stamp upon its aching sides that read, simply, *Undeliverable.* Opening it, Nolan and Oscar discovered nothing more sinister inside than a large, disassembled rabbit hutch.

Nolan took it home, that is to say, to the rabbitry, where he continued to sleep at night, now upon the more comfortable cot he'd brought in with blankets, pillows, water and canned food, as if he were on some lunatic camping expedition. He lugged the box into the garage and assembled the hutch as best he could with a lone screwdriver he'd found. It was smaller than the one Lindsey had fashioned for the four rabbits, who were so thick with fur now that they looked cramped even in the large den—he was going to have to shear them this Saturday, there was no more avoiding it—but its benefit lay in its mobility. To tighten the cage to the hutch he still needed pliers. He walked across the lawn to the duplex, which had remained dark but for the light he'd left on the week before, which glowed every night like a secret heart. Nolan peered through the window he knew he could open, then tried it. It didn't budge. Then he knew it was no use. There were no tools inside. There was nothing inside. The apartment was vacant, and as he transported the rabbits, whose names he realized he didn't even know, into the van by means of the hutch, covering the opening with a loose board, he wondered if anything had ever been in there at all.

AN ELEGANT COURTSHIP

RYAN P. YOUNG

Everyone was caught up in everything, then. Though the moralists
wore their certain hats, and the lovers theirs,

every old man whose beard dragged along the floor
had a younger man who swept the dust from his path.

It kept on like this for many hours. Thoughts were passed
among us like bread, broken, dipped in soup, crumbs everywhere.

Everyone loves poems about washing dishes, one of the old men had said
as I was washing the dishes, nervous about the coming weight.

Perhaps only a small love, said another. Then everything was silent
for a time. Dinner had ended. Outside, the sky had slipped off its dress,

pleasantly, and left it to rest on the floor in a thoughtless style.
When the song began, it was the sound of a hundred breathing men.

Agnes: we all hoped you would be convinced by this, and you were.
In this way, you and I came to walk along the same road.

Go farther up the way to see if all the snow has cleared,
and I will wait here for you and lie down in the last certain patch of sun.

I, too, have small loves, and I launch my boat in their sea,
a small pond where the green plants greenly grow.

ON THE ETHICAL LIFE
RYAN P. YOUNG

My friend   whose mouth drops tea-cups
has grown warm again in silence

has secretly sewn a coat of porcelain
from the shards of surplus cups

He is the still-whole sparrow
uncrushed in the crushing hand
(passing through that hand)

This   the context of love
slipped into like a jacket
Conduct a similar production

He returned home from a thicker world
to untangle our old disagreement:

I guess this is the good life; a full set of cups

My
retired   cut-up friend

TRIUMPHS OF NATURAL SELECTION
SMITH HENDERSON

Taking a close look at what's around, there is some sort of harmony.
It is the harmony of overwhelming and collective murder.

Werner Herzog

I'LL NOT bullshit you. It hurts. But as in so many traumas, some reserve of self-possession—the stuff that kicks in before your brain releases blackout juice—is tapped, and the panic melts. Yes, even in a bear mauling. Your body decides terror is no longer germane, and so you hear Jenny over there, poor fucking Jenny, screaming and throwing rocks and then the pots at the damn reeking thing on top of you. My heart goes out to her, having to watch.

I tell her to go. Yell at her to run. I don't think she can hear words anymore.

She sought me—this—out. Not *this*-this, but this: I make friends with the bears. I am kind of good at it, kind of famous for it. Upon reflection, even if I said so on Letterman, protecting them is not really the goal. Not if I am honest. I am here because they selected me. The bears let me film them fish and let me stay. They let me swim and sit close as they wrestle in the mud. Each encounter engendering another, closer encounter. It's something else, to sit in a thicket picking huckleberries with four bears arrayed around you on the same hill like brown furniture, slavering ottomans and smacking beanbags. To almost touch their outstretched black wet noses that spraypaint your hand in bear mist. Tango and Boomer tore the shit out of each other because the air was rank with Cinnamon's heat, and I took pictures of the fight from the riverbank, about fifty feet away. Tango grunted past me into the long grass like a jock to the locker room, sweating Boomer's gore. I half expected him to toss me his jersey.

Me and the bears, we're tight like that. I never feel that way around people, who always have some problem with me, with my energy. In point of fact, the rangers give me more trouble than the bears ever do.

The Park is nothing but an aggrandized zoo to the rangers and everyone else. Stay in the demarcated areas. Don't stray from the trail. Buy your camping permits. It's gotten to where I have to disguise myself if I'm going drive in, avoid the chalets and trails, hide from the tourists, from the day-hikers, from the hardcores with topo maps and compasses. But I don't miss people for one second. I never had a griz put cuffs on me, is what I'm saying.

But Jenny. Fundraiser in Malibu. Spinach dip. Bad breath. Gave me a piece of gum. Said I spoke wonderfully. Down to us two, laughing. Giddy from the wine. I said, Sure, come with.

Does a salmon *choose* to go so far only to fuck and to die? Is it destiny when the poor fella is plucked from the breathless air and unzipped from his skin?

It is late in the season to be out there, too late to try and impress a girl. When the weather turns and the grizzlies have to pack on the last pounds, when they are just frantic about food. But still. I knew him as a cub, named him Tobacco. I think he is joking when he charges out of brush, and I am slow to challenge him, to slap the ground and drop my voice, to defend this shit of mine because he is being a motherfucker and knows better.

My mother. My bloodshot eyes, my purpled fingerprinted fingertips, the sedans I totaled. The weary redundancy like she'd been tricked. Tobacco, you were such a good baby once. Fuzzy and curious, batting at butterflies and snuffling into honeycomb. What the fuck happened to you? Why are you doing this? I scream. I am your friend, motherfucker.

Jenny drools, having run out of things to throw. Except the camera. She won't touch the camera because it's important to me to capture even this.

There is a love so big inside of me it scares people.

All the little whys and wherefores sort of consume you towards the end. He has a broken tooth that probably makes him irritable—his breath is like boiled garbage—and one of his claws is busted off, so he ribbons the flesh on my right side in fours while getting my left in fives. But that's it. His coat is matted, but healthy. My snapped ribs know he is not underweight. He is healthy, marvelously healthy. In fact, for a minute there, the perfect articulation of his jaws and claws… well, it floors me. Great, top-notch stuff. I'm thinking, Atta boy. King of the Fuckin' Forest. Who's mauling the shit out of me? That's right, big boy. You are. That's right, killer. Who's the killer? You're the killer.

And right at the end there: the eye contact. They must do it all the time, when they're taking down a moose or elk and having that moment of eyeball-to-eyeball communion. Brown like syrup poured into poached egg whites and suspended over me. It still hurts all over and I can't see but through the blood, and it's like losing your virginity or having your first beer, and I think, So this is natural selection. I am chosen, elect. I am chosen.

BEHOLD, A THOUSAND STICKS

LIZ PRATHER

HOZAY'S TO HOST KARAOKE NIGHT

JUST BECAUSE *I'm happy don't mean I'm satisfied*, said Barry Marshall to an empty room. It was near closing time. The microphone was cold. *Sing "The Old Rugged Cross,"* he yelled out. The woman wiping down tables didn't even look up. He broke a beer bottle across the bar and held it to his own throat. *Sing it*, he whispered, and waited for the Lord to trouble the waters.

UNEMPLOYMENT IN THE COUNTY AT ALL TIME LOW

The woman moved across her one-inch bluegrass, her sundress blinding white, sinking into the aerated lawn. *Nobody on this street got their paper last week*, she yelled, flagging George down as he chucked her paper into the hosta-lined driveway. *Fuck a bunch of papers, you don't sign my paycheck*, mouthed George as he pulled away from the curb. *What's that number?* she yelled into his exhaust and stubbed her spectator on a slate chip the color of an arctic rainbow.

ROGERS FAMILY REUNION HELD AT LEGION PARK

Was I good enough, Granny thought, working a kernel of popcorn from her long teeth, staring across the woody silence of her old house. *What did I teach my children?* She remembered those summer days, shucking corn, canning tomatoes, soaking cucumbers in the cold, briny pickle crock. Of her children, she remembered little. She had knocked them back and yanked them up. She told them to get out there and gain dominion over the earth.

MINISTERIAL ASSOCIATION SPONSORS INTERFAITH DIALOGUE

Because Buddhism sounded like an excuse to be lazy, Molly decided to cast her lot with the Jews. Except on Saturdays, when she turned Adventist because synagogues looked like Tara in the South. She was in a free laundromat run by some Catholic nuns in New Orleans when she heard the news that her mother had died. Out loud and to no one in particular, she said, *For the days quickly pass and we fly away.*

AREA SCHOOLS RANK HIGH IN STATEWIDE TESTING

This is what we learned in kindergarten: Animal eyes are diseased. Never eat sheep eyes! This is what we learned in middle school: Katie Williams got her period months before the rest of us. This is what we learned in high school: How to be a poet, how to elbow a VISTA worker in the domestic, how to fire up a copperhead after class. This is what we learned in church: There are 10,000 angels with their hands on their swords, ready to fight the Devil for us.

BARKLEY CANCER CENTER TO OPEN NEW WING

In districts infested with the vetch weevil, it is essential—in order to maintain production—to dust the fields with three to five percent DDT at the time of first seedpod formation and to fumigate the seed with methyl bromide or other fumigant after it leaves the thresher. Smut grass can be controlled with five pounds of Dowpon M per acre in 25 gallons of water. Musk thistle can be controlled by applying two pounds of 4D in the spring before the seed heads appear. Complete eradication may not be possible.

SUPER WAL-MART TO BREAK GROUND

They came to Kentucky in long boats to a land of happy tomorrows, to hunt an abundance of grouse, turkey, deer, shoats. In season, the strongest passed through where the gods lived. To make this green-watered land a place to piss and cook was mocking heaven. To make it your own was mocking death.

SUNNY WEATHER FOR MEMORIAL DAY WEEKEND

The brown funnel cloud tore up two fields of corn, left the maple grove standing and touched down again in the Lockharts' pasture. A piece of straw forced its way through the shutters of Daisy Johnson's house and speared her left eye. They found all parties crippled under a bookshelf the next day. Chickens hung on clotheslines and cows bloated in the trees. Someone said the sun was shining over at the fairgrounds. Someone said that twice.

ELOI, ELOI, LAMA SABACHTHANI

It was 96 degrees, so humid you could wring your head out in a bucket. Along the shoulder of Highway 60, a midget pushed a fat lady in a wheelchair, the air shimmering around them. Her face was wet with perspiration. Her legs weighed against the sides of the wheelchair. The little guy, beating along the black asphalt, his glasses at the tip of his nose, leaned into his burden. At the light, they stopped. She pulled out a Coke from the shoebox she held on her lap. While he took a long drink, she rubbed his back and patted him between the shoulders.

OLD VIRGINIA
MUKI MAHAN

INT. DINING ROOM.

Portraits and pewter; casemented bookshelves. Family of three seated at long table. OLD VIRGINIAN RAILROAD ENTHUSIAST (OVRE) at one end, OVRE's very young wife (SANDY) at other, son and heir (CASWELL) seated between on one side.

BEETHA, maid, elderly, obese, bursts in from kitchen carrying a roast pig on a platter. Although it's a short distance, she struggles with its weight and teeters to the table, finally dropping it loudly in the center with a groan. She hobbles back towards the kitchen. All regard her with suspicion.

SANDY
[stage whisper across table]
She's not lookin' right.

Beetha pauses and turns at the threshold and gives each in turn a wide-eyed look with open grin. It is apparent that she has recently grown impudent. She exits without a word.

Half-minute pause as all stare at the pig.

OVRE
[clearing throat]
Before we begin and before we… give young Caswell here a… welcome… befitting his… long… awaited return to… Gluddington Green… there is a brief… announcement… I believe it appropriate to… make… before we begin.

He winks at Sandy. She smiles. OVRE purses his lips. Sandy winks at OVRE. They continue distractedly until—

CASWELL
[impatiently]
What? What?

OVRE
Caswell… you know of course I… consider myself… obliged to keep you… apprised of the particular state of our legacy… your legacy, that is… come my passing into the next… and whichever ways it might be… diversified or… left to stagnate, like the basin out back… or even the old bones in the basin we… dredge up from time to time of… wayward stags…

He glances at Sandy.

OVRE
[continued]
and what not…

CASWELL
Yes?

OVRE
I have decided to invest… a considerable sum… in an… intriguing… opportunity…

CASWELL
Where? How much?

OVRE
The details will… reveal themselves in good

time, son. I do admit, however, that in doing this I… indulge… a hobby of mine…

Sandy puts on a train conductor hat.

OVRE
[continued]
the… opportunity… happens to be an old railroad depot… abandoned for decades…

Caswell looks from Sandy to OVRE.

CASWELL
Why?

OVRE
I know it might sound… foolhardy… to you, son…

Caswell yelps.

OVRE
[continued]
I thought I'd build a museum there, you know… the… history of trains… The History of… Virginia… Virginian… Trains… About the way they look… the sounds they make… Anyhow, I had Cecil send some folks down to clean it up, maybe… take a look… see if there's… anything… of an… historical value.
[pause]
I'll be honest with you, son.

CASWELL
Dad?

Sandy pushes back her chair and struts towards OVRE, revealing a leather pencil mini skirt and stiletto heels. She hops into his lap.

A brief CLOSE-UP of OVRE reveals he has an especially grotesque clouded grey wandering eye.

OVRE
I'm wasting the money.

Caswell's face droops. OVRE and Sandy laugh in each other's arms.

FADE OUT.

BIRDHOUSE

MATTHEW C. CRADY

A WEEK ago, my old bird and I had a cushy nest in a quiet stairwell in a Bronx fly up. The place was all right. Sure, it was crowded during nesting season, but for the most part the other birds kept to themselves. "A nice pigeon neighborhood," is what I said to Gloria when we checked out the building. She had some misgivings, but after a few days of scoping a nice, well-lit ledge, she said we could move.

We hatched over thirty little ones in the three years we were there and never lost a single egg until the other day. Some asshole came through blowing a dog whistle, and I swear I thought my head was going to explode. Let me tell you, Gloria and I flew the coop faster than hummingbird sex. We left our two eggs behind, and when we tried to get back to the roost, the vent was blocked.

But that's how it goes. We were lucky to have gone three years without losing a single egg. And I told Gloria we'd get back to popping out the little ones as soon as we found another nest.

Not so fast.

Let me tell you about New York City during mating season. You're lucky to find a dirty gutter to squeeze a nest into. And this being spring, the choice wasn't mine—we had to take Section Eight housing in Central Park. Yes, it's considered the center of the pigeon universe, but there are some real freaks here that Gloria just can't deal with. It's these freaks that have kept me from getting any tail feather since we left the stairwell.

ROOST 4C. Canary. If there's one more morning that bastard starts singing as soon as there's light outside I'm going to peck out his sunshiny throat. I wish he'd find a deep coal mine to die in.

ROOST 2E. Hummingbird. Real speed freak. I can't understand a thing she says. Hell, I can't even see her wings when she's on the move. She spends more time trying to find the next fix than I do shitting on tourists.

ROOST 4B. Toucan. This guy is so flaming, he comes with his own gay pride flag. Seriously, it looks like a rainbow puked on him. I don't care that he's queer—it's just that so many queens come in and out of that hole, I'm not sure whether we live in the projects or a 24/7 all-male revue.

ROOST 3E. Crow. Some of the others call him Old Jim. I try to tell my wife he's cool—just a bird of a different color. Sometimes, we'll people-watch on the roof in the evenings. Gloria doesn't like him. Says she doesn't like his kind.

ROOST 1A. Bald eagle. And a total dick. Bird runs the birdhouse and does whatever he wants. He's been fighting with another birdhouse across the park for years now, and as such, the residents of our new place have been dragged into it as well. He says to stay the course because they have a better supply of water on that side of the park. Screw that guy—I've been here a week, and I'm tired of his shit.

ROOST 4F. Robin. What the hell is it about this guy? He's the real reason I haven't been bumping feathers with Gloria lately. She says she wished she could mate with him after all I put her through. Well, fuck that. Pigeons are supposed to be monogamous, but I told her to go right ahead. What she doesn't know is that he's been down in 2F, flappin dat ass of the new chick. Aviaphile.

So that's where I'm at right now. During the day, I fly around the park, asking for handouts from the people there, knowing I'm not going to get any action when I get home. Believe you me, if that doesn't change soon, I'm going to fly straight into a giant glass window. No joke. I'll plow right into one and you'll be scraping my carcass off the sidewalk.

Mark my words.

BRIAN SHAFFER IS HERE

NESS WARMBLOOD

EXT. STREET. DAY.

PERVEEN walks down the street, some books tucked under his arm.

A STRANGER emerges, seemingly from nowhere, and gestures toward a short set of stairs leading down into a shadowed doorway.

STRANGER
Brian Shaffer is here!

Perveen stops walking and looks at the doorway, then the stranger.

PERVEEN
What?

The stranger smiles and gestures toward the doorway.

STRANGER
Brian Shaffer is here!

PERVEEN
Wait, what?

STRANGER
Brian Shaffer is here!

PERVEEN
Really?

STRANGER
Remember Brian Shaffer? Your friend? Your friend Brian Shaffer?

PERVEEN
Yes, I do.

STRANGER
He is here!

Perveen shifts the books under his arm, looks about to see if anyone else is there on the street.

PERVEEN
How do you know Brian?

STRANGER
In here!

PERVEEN
Wait a minute. Who are you?

STRANGER
Brian Shaffer is here.

PERVEEN
Yes, and who are you?

STRANGER
Here. Brian Shaffer.

Perveen sighs, looks about.

PERVEEN
Brian Shaffer is here?

STRANGER
Correct.

PERVEEN
That's what you're saying?

The stranger nods, big smiles.

STRANGER
Yes.

PERVEEN
Brian Shaffer is here.

STRANGER
Yes.

PERVEEN
My friend Brian Shaffer, whom you somehow know, is waiting in here for me?

STRANGER
Correct!

PERVEEN
How did my friend Brian Shaffer, whom you somehow know, know that I was going to be by here?

STRANGER
What?
[pause]
Brian Shaffer is here.

PERVEEN
Did you go to Harvard?

STRANGER
He is here.

PERVEEN
Did you go to Harvard? With Brian?

STRANGER
Yes. Come again?

PERVEEN
Did you go to Harvard?

STRANGER
Yes.
[pause]
Yes, I did.

PERVEEN
And Brian Shaffer is here.

STRANGER
Correct.

PERVEEN
In here?

STRANGER
Yes.

PERVEEN
And you went to Harvard.

STRANGER
Yes.

PERVEEN
I see.

He starts down the stairs, then turns to look again at the stranger.

The stranger smiles, nods, points at the door.

Perveen opens the door and walks inside.

INT. DARK HALLWAY. SAME.

PERVEEN
Hello? Brian?

He moves forward through the hallway. Then stops, shifts the books beneath his arm.

PERVEEN
Brian? It's Perveen. One of your Harvard buddies told me you were here?

He reaches out to place one hand against the wall. Starts forward again, then stops.

PERVEEN
Hello? Brian?
[pause]
Anybody?
[pause]
Is Brian Shaffer here?

JOSH emerges from the darkness.

JOSH
Hello, Perveen.

PERVEEN
Josh? What the hell?

Josh points suddenly to the ground.

JOSH
Look! Two peanut butter sandwiches!

Perveen looks down.

Josh hits him with a piece of board.

Perveen drops to the ground. His books scatter around him.

EXT. STREET. DAY.

Josh bursts from the stairwell and into the street. He runs down the block, big smiles.

IT'S NOT YOUR FAULT, CUBA GOODING JR.

MIKE POWELL

CUBA GOODING JR. has been an actor. He acted as an inner-city teenager struggling toward manhood in a movie called *Boyz n the Hood.* He acted as a football player in *Jerry Maguire*, entertained a large, diverse audience, and was rewarded with money and fame. Now it's 2001. Cuba Gooding Jr. is 33, surrounded by huskies, working under the direction of a volleyball enthusiast named Brian Levant, and very cold. He has never been so cold. Each afternoon, he watches the dailies and sees himself bundled up like a lunatic. He vows to take off his beanie and heavy-duty gloves for the next scene. When he does, his fingers go numb.

In *Snow Dogs*, Alaska is played by Alberta, Canada. Alberta is usually churchlike and lovely, but now it's speckled with cameras and caterers and DPs and trailers and generators and dogs and dog trainers. Cuba Gooding Jr. implies that the dogs get more attention than the people. They are pets, and have to be taught to race—this requires focus, effort, and a non-negligible portion of $33 million. They bark all day long.

Cuba Gooding Jr. has made mistakes. He loves silent-era comedians like Charlie Chaplin and Buster Keaton, so he decided to take a role as a mute in *Lightning Jack*, a western caper written and directed by Crocodile Dundee. "At the time, I thought it was going to be the best movie in the world," he says, looking away.

He took the role in *Snow Dogs* because it was an "opportunity to do a family film, and at the same time… [deal] with issues about self-worth, adoption and race." In it, he plays a successful dentist living in Miami who finds out, by way of an inheritance subpoena, that he is adopted. His biological mother was a loner who moved to a nonexistent town in Alaska to race sled dogs. His father is mean, older and white. He and Cuba Gooding Jr. share stubbornness and love bleu cheese.

Cuba Gooding Jr. busies himself learning to race his inherited dogs, falls in love, and has several ambiguously comedic near-death encounters. (Most of the time, the comedy is signified by bulging eyes and a calypso soundtrack. Without one or both, the bleakness of the scenes would be unmarketable to children.) His father shows no tenderness and talks constantly of Cuba Gooding Jr.'s dogs, which he wants to buy. Later, he gets lost in a snowstorm, and Cuba Gooding Jr. saves him on the unfair and unearned presumption that if your father is lost in a blizzard, you save him even if he is unfriendly and abandoned you as a child.

The script is bad work by a pile-on of writers who are distracted wondering about how they got where they are. There is a scene in which Cuba Gooding Jr.'s father, played by James Coburn, offers Cuba Gooding Jr. a sip of his flask, calling it soup. Cuba Gooding Jr. sips and spits it out. "You said this was soup!" he protests. James Coburn tells him, "It has soup in it." Both actors are too tired to ask the writers what this is supposed to mean. Cuba Gooding Jr. slips on the ice in almost every scene, even in the documentary featurettes. He wants to make people laugh.

He thinks about his house and his family. He thinks about Sara, his wife, whom he has known since 1986, and wonders if she sleeps in the middle of the bed when he's away. He dreams a lot in hotels. One night, after filming the scene where he flies back into Canada-Alaska from Miami, he dreams he is on a plane flown by huskies. The flight is choppy. At cruising altitude, the door to the pilot's cabin swings open, which Cuba Gooding Jr. can see because he flies First Class. There is a dog in the chair and a dog trainer trying to show the dog how to use the controls. The dog doesn't seem to have any interest in flying, but winks, continuously. Later, when shooting the film's dream sequence, he tells director Brian Levant about his own dream. "So what do you think it *means*?" Levant says, with a sarcastic emphasis on *means* that makes Cuba Gooding Jr. feel lonely.

There is a scene where he howls at the moon with Joanna Bacalso, a Filipino actress and model who plays Barb, the local bartender. Cuba Gooding Jr. has never howled at the moon before, has never even seen a moon hanging so low, bright, and round, like a button or a dinner plate. He tries to think about whether or not he and Sara have ever done anything as romantic as howl at the moon. Maybe not. But they have raised three children. One of the three loves jumping on trampolines and one of the three is named Spencer. He can't remember whether Spencer is the one who loves jumping on trampolines.

In the bonus features for *Snow Dogs*, Nichelle Nichols (best known as the kindly black woman on *Star Trek*) jokes about how she told one of the producers she'd kill him if he didn't hire her for the role of Cuba Gooding Jr.'s adoptive mom. She is giving throughout, streaked with bluish and metallic pink eye shadow, never without cookies. His adoptive dad only appears once, at the beginning of the film, in a scene where a young Cuba Gooding Jr.-not-Cuba Gooding Jr. is assisting him with some dentistry (he is also a dentist), which ends with young Cuba Gooding Jr.-not-Cuba Gooding Jr. vomiting into a trash can.

Cuba Gooding Jr.'s real father left when Cuba Gooding Jr. was six. Cuba Gooding Sr. was famous for singing in the Main Ingredient, whose biggest hit was "Everybody Plays the Fool." The first line of Cuba Gooding Sr.'s website biography is, "Everybody plays the fool sometime, but not Cuba Gooding."

Cuba Gooding Jr. grew up in hotels. He became born again at age 13. He doesn't dwell on these things. When *Snow Dogs* is finished, he thinks about whether or not it dealt with serious issues. It didn't. This is not his fault; he just works, and work is a blessing. "They say don't work with children or animals, and there's a reason for that," he jokes a few years later. He works with both. He has to eat.

He did get to go to Canada—that was something. He brings home two sweaters and a glass bowl blown by a local artisan for Sara. He brings home custom snowboards for Spencer and Mason, who are constantly trying to figure out new ways to hurt themselves while playing sports. (He has asked Sara to get the boys' measurements; he has to remember to ask her how she did it; you don't just measure young boys.) For his daughter, Piper, he brings only a snow globe and a simple, unique necklace, but spends hours with her looking at pictures he took on the set because he remembers that Piper, between sips of juice at dinner one evening, said she wanted to be a veterinarian.

"That movie changed my sinuses for three years," Cuba Gooding Jr. tells *Entertainment Weekly*. "If I see a dog again, I might kick him in the balls to make a cat happy." The next time he sees a dog, though, he doesn't kick it in the balls. He knows that dogs get cold, too.

INCREASE YOUR LOVE STIICK
EAGY HASBERRY

Don't restrain your desires, incrrease your love stick!

Click HERE

Tell me, o grandsire, the means by which we may abbey of st. Georges, where they offered their think. But they are beautiful too, with a sort and skins of the ranku deer. indeed, o bharata, slipped on his snowshoes, and went round the shoulder.

ISSUE FOUR

LIFE IS PRECIOUS AND GOD AND THE BIBLE

RIVER GHOSTS
X.C. ATKINS

DENBY SLID through the thin streets of the Fan in his silver Avalon, never more than one hand holding the wheel, the other hand constantly occupied with his cell phone or a Newport. We were heading to Gregory's to pick up booze, fish bait and Jones. Isley Brothers cranked from the speakers. Isley Brothers always sounded so good in the summertime. We didn't hit one red light.

"Why are we taking Jones?" I asked Denby.

"What's it matter to you?"

"She's boring. She doesn't talk."

"She talks."

"She doesn't. She bitches. She'll bitch the whole time we're out there."

"Listen, she said she wanted to go. I told her we'd pick her up. We're picking her up."

"Sayin'. Pick her up after for all that noise. Ain't she seeing somebody?" I spat out the window. "Ain't you?"

"Listen, Lev, drop it, or I'ma drop you. Who's behind the wheel?"

I dropped it.

It was hit-and-run weather, where all the kids came out and rode their bikes through red lights, stop signs, out from whatever kind of darkness there was. I might be out there with them, but I was in the car with Denby, and, thankfully, not behind the wheel of my own Instrument of Death.

A lot of noise was coming off the corner of Lombardy and Main. More people, out on the patio of a busy restaurant, lit up from the glow of a tiki-bar. The college crowd. A night like tonight, sure, all walks of life would be out. We drove a little past that and pulled up to Gregory's. We got out the car and Denby unlocked the door to the restaurant and let us inside. The lights were off. Chairs sat upside down on the tables. All the sounds from the street came into the restaurant. Jones was sitting at the bar having a drink by herself. I could just see her.

"We ready to go?" she asked.

"Just gotta grab a few things," Denby said. He walked past her and went back into the darkness of the kitchen. I walked around the bar and helped myself to a shot of Rumple Minze. There were a few cans of PBR sitting on ice and I grabbed one as well. I stood across the bar from Jones in the humming dark. It was as if the place was filled with people and we weren't the only people there, so it was fine that we didn't acknowledge each other.

We never said anything to each other. We didn't even look at each other. It's how it had always been.

But it wasn't like she was bad to look at. She had reddish brown hair and a strong chin. She had this kind of classic look, like from a Bogie film or something. She always had a drink and she always had a smoke. Perpetually smoking. Smoke was the veil she wore over her face. Yeah, a Bogie film.

"Let's go," Denby said, walking out of the kitchen. He grabbed two sixes of Miller Lite from the small refrigerator underneath the bar.

"Quick shot for the road?" I offered.

"Bet," he said.

I began to pour two shots of Rumple Minze.

"I'll take one, too. But not Rumple Minze. Jameson," Jones said.

Now she looked at me. When she wanted something.

I got another shot glass, then filled all three, two with Rumple Minze and the other with Jameson. We brought them together.

"Let's make Regg and Tim jealous and catch the big one tonight," Denby said.

"Salud."

We took them down and none of us made a face and a few seconds later we were out the door and Denby was locking the place up. I let Jones take shotgun. I laid up in the back with the beer and opened one and tossed the cap in the street and told Denby to turn the music up. We got back on Cary Street and were on our way. We didn't drive too fast. Campus police loved the weather as much as we did and the only thing they did better than bust up a party in the Fan was give out DUIs.

We stopped at the light at Belvidere. A posse of motorcycles blasted by in a flurry of neon and rumble. Almost every one of the bikers had a girl strapped on the back with a fat ass coming out a pair of daisy dukes.

"Goddamn!" I said as they went by, leaning up between the two front seats.

We made a right onto Belvidere and rode across the bridge into Southside. I looked out my window at downtown Richmond and all the lights and the James for the millionth time. The view still hadn't gotten old to me.

We went down a winding road where there was nowhere to look but the road before us. It was even darker where we parked. The trees and leaves and branches blocked out the moonlight so Denby had to leave all the doors open just to have any light to grab all the stuff we needed. Jones and I grabbed whatever he told us. I knew how to cast and how to reel something in, how to put something on the hook, how to snap the rod together. Jones probably knew even less. But we didn't come out on these trips just to fish. We wanted to do something different from a bar, a living room, a neighborhood porch. Getting out of the Fan for just an hour or two, even if it was only across a bridge, made our little city seem a lot bigger than it actually was. It was a good trick.

I had a rod and the beer, Denby carried a small tackle box, a couple rods, and the bait. Jones had a bucket with a blanket in it and her purse, which she opened up, coming out with a fifth of whiskey.

"Anybody?"

I could hear Denby scratching his beard in the dark. It sounded what I thought a boot heel might sound like, twisting in straw. "Bet," he said.

We all three took it back in turn, quickly. The little flame. I thought that was nice of Jones to offer the whiskey. I couldn't see her face in the dark, even as close as she was.

We followed Denby through the woods on a dirt road and were lucky not to trip over any roots or vines. We made it, slow going. I made kind of a tomahawk motion with my arm as I walked through the trees. For the spider webs. The things in the trees were loud and we could hear the water ahead, slithering, hissing, smacking wet against the rocks. I jerked my shoulder up, wanting to swat at my neck a few times. At things I could feel or hear. That was pointless. My hands were full.

The trees opened up and let us out and there was the river, this huge dark rumbling blanket, forever moving, the rocks poking out like so many miniature islands. The pattern they made seemed so deliberate, like you could come to know them by name if you spent the time to name them, but with every new summer I could swear they were set different, a new and random arrangement to re-memorize, some having disappeared underneath the river, then new rocks emerging.

The moon lit the way, just enough. Jones took her shoes off and put them in her purse. Her white legs seemed to glow with a soft light, tiptoeing across the rock after Denby, her hands in the air. She was like a ghost. A river ghost.

"Shit!" Denby said, up ahead of us. "Almost gave my kicks a bath on that one."

"Why do you always wear your nice shit out here, Derb?"

"Cause I'm a baller, Lev. I can buy three more pairs tomorrow."

Before I could tell him to shut up, Jones said, "Please, Denby. I make more on a weekend than what you make all week."

"Jones, I make what you make, I just don't make it at the restaurant."

I wore a beat-up pair of Asics, no laces. I didn't care if I went in the water with them. I was caring less and less about things like the state of my shoes. A few years ago, that wasn't the case at all. A few years ago, the issue of a pair of sneakers getting scuffed was grounds for a brawl. In some bars around town, it remained so.

Denby didn't even take us out halfway. The rock he chose was big enough for all three of us and probably could have fit another. It was saucer shaped, like a gigantic dinner plate. Jones pulled out the blanket, flapped it wide open. It floated down to the rock. Denby sat everything down and started preparing the gear. He opened the tackle box and handed me a plastic bag. I took out enough marijuana to fill the bowl and gave it to Jones.

"Need a light?"

"Of course not."

She sparked the bowl and inhaled. Far behind her, I could see the Belvidere Bridge we had just passed over. I couldn't hear the cars that zoomed over it. We were detached enough from it all. But it hung there all the same, like a postcard up on the fridge.

The bowl made two rounds and Denby packed it up again. We gave it another round before we set up to cast. My first cast stunk. The second was better. I had to be careful where I slung my rod, not only so

I didn't hit Jones or Denby, but also so the bait would actually go into the water and not bounce onto another rock or get snared in one of the tree branches that reached out of the river. Denby's went out far, and then further with the help of a slow current. I sat down and started drinking another beer.

"It's nice out here," Jones said, sitting a little behind me.

"As long as the bugs aren't biting. You never been out here?" I said.

"Come in the day, and even that's been limited this summer, I have to admit. It's so different at night."

"Yeah, there ain't any rednecks or stupid West End kids out here at night," Denby said.

"Or a bunch of Mexican dudes posted up on the banks staring at all the girls with their hands in their pockets," I added.

We laughed.

"It's a warm night," Jones said.

Jones dipped her white toes into the water. She had her whiskey out again and we took sips from that. I tested my line a bit and felt something and got excited and started to reel it in. Everyone else got a little excited too and watched to see what it was I reeled in. I zigzagged it in through a few rocks and as it came to the surface I could begin to make it out. It was only some brush from the riverbed.

"Shit," I said, pulling the stuff off the hook. The bait was gone, too.

"Aw. Not this time, buddy," Jones said, patting my head.

"We're not gonna catch anything out here, Derb," I complained.

"We just got out here. Relax."

"Let's just drink," Jones said. She hadn't cast at all.

"I'll put one more guy out there, maybe let 'em lie a bit," I said.

"I got a couple more in me yet," Denby said. "Maybe it's this rock." He skipped to another and went a few more over and cast out again. We couldn't even hear where it plopped over the rush of the river.

Jones and I sat on the rock, smoking cigarettes and passing each other the whiskey. I couldn't smoke any more weed. My brain felt fuzzy inside my skull. I couldn't even do something simple. Like keep my mouth closed. I kept licking my lips, re-tasting the whiskey. Whatever my face looked like, it didn't matter. We were safe under the dark. The dark made it easier to get close.

We sat with our knees up right under our chins in the warm night air. We listened to the river for a long time. We could've been anywhere, anywhere in the world a guy and a girl could sit and be fine and their environment could sit and be fine with them. Her hair kind of fell in front of her face.

"It's such a small thing. To smile here and there."

"I do. All the time."

"Bull," I said.

For some reason I kissed her. Her lips weren't even cold.

I heard something in the dark and I pulled apart from her.

Denby was coming back over to us. "Ain't a damn thing biting. I'm out of beer," he said.

"We're nearin'."

"Well, I've had my fill. Y'all wanna head back?"

"Sure. What time's it?"

"Past last call."

"Oh. Well."

We grabbed our stuff and started making our way back to the bank. Our beer cans floated down the James like bottles in the sea, minus the love note. Nobody fell in and we got back to the banks and through the trees and to the car.

Denby got into the car and started it and said, "Take it back to my place, all good?"

I kept the window all the way down on the ride back and my face in the wind until I heard Hot Rod come on the radio. "Young Turks." Denby turned it up for me. A stranger would have thought I had a real life mic in my hand. Denby laughed his raspy laugh in front and Jones laughed too. I messed with her hair some.

Denby's brother Reggie was in the living room watching a movie when we got there. We fell in on him and started on another round from the bowl. Reggie joined. I sat on the arm of the couch, trying to appear normal but buzzing hard.

I wanted to kiss her again. It was all that kept running through my head.

She went to the kitchen and I could hear her go up the stairs to the bathroom.

"We got any b's in the fridge?" Denby asked Reggie.

"Maybe a few."

Denby got up to go check.

"Grab me one if there's extra!" I called after him. I sank down into the couch next to Reggie. He was watching *Tango & Cash*. Kurt Russell was getting the massage from the chick who was playing Sly's sister. It was a funny part. But Sly's sister looked good too.

"From this to *Desperate Housewives*," Reggie said.

"The paths we take," I said.

We sat there watching the movie for a while. Reggie got into a little story about a girl at a sunglasses store. Finally, I got thirsty for that beer and got up to get it myself.

I figured Denby to be outside smoking a cigarette or on the phone with someone. I walked into the kitchen and Denby had Jones against the counter and they were kissing. I somehow hadn't heard her come back downstairs. They stopped when I walked in. My eyes went away from them to a picture on the fridge. It was a picture of Reggie and his mother. She looked small next to him, she looked happy. He was flicking off the camera. I always liked that picture.

"Oh my bad, Lev, I was just on my way to you," Denby said and handed me a Miller Lite. Jones was looking at me, with the hair in front of her face again. Bogie films.

"All good. Thanks," I said.

I went back into the living room and sat in the couch. A few minutes later I heard them clop up the stairs.

"How was the river?" Reggie asked me.

"It was stupid."

I chugged the beer. Some of it ran down my cheek. I finished it off and tossed the empty bottle into a trashcan they had next to the DVD rack. I stood up and said, "Adios, Regg."

He said, "See ya, Lev." Then I walked back out into the warm night.

SO REAL I AM BEYOND STEAK

A BADDEST BUFFALO

Craning my neck up to the black sky
I think about how constellations
remind me of flowers and flowers remind me
of the love of every girl I used to see all of.

Tonight the only flowers here are cauli.
The only turkeys bumping
themselves against my dewy forehead are
of the tofu type.

My ancestors weep for impossible beef
sizzling in the iron skillet
that had otherwise blackened
tenderloin since pioneer times.

My mother's mother's stalwart mother
seasoned that mother back when
savage wars raged over and over
over glittering stores of salt.

I paid a lot of pretty pennies to rename your
constituent orbs after
Mother + Love Bone et al but the fucken
Astronomical Union won't change the map.

There was a hole here
where angels put their heads. Now there is only
an absence of absence where that absence
of angel head used to be.

Angel, my neck is stiff and this night is
absolutely throbbing. I want to go out to the fields
and crank it so hard the galaxy will
downright gobble as I sigh your name
Cassiopeia.

WHAT TAKES MY BREATH

CAROL ANN DAVIS

is just the weight of footstep

on stair, or the moment one takes

before calling a name

as if somehow—*hymnody, calumny, grace*—

the world could empty

into our slightest touch,

empty itself slowly

and give over its translucence.

Something of being born in it—

or to it—so that where it is dark

we let it be dark, light, light.

Simple as that: a call and response,

the mistake of course in being made

of both lash and star, confusing,

by nature or by right, this air:

cool coming in and warm leaving.

THE OTHER DEATH
JAMES HANNAHAM

1

PRIVATELY, WE expect to avoid that other death by dying ourselves. But when the sun swells to several times its current size, or we destroy the Gulf Stream and the next Ice Age starts, we'll die again, as catastrophe erases the hatchmarks we made in the bark of certain trees. We'd hoped to have some lasting effect beyond our individual *sayonara*, but tough luck.

So what then? Is the space program our way of scouring the interstellar real estate section? *Bright planet in prime Crab Nebula, steps from subways, amenities*. Once the Gulf is all oil and the oceans mostly plastic, will the haves among us hop a Zip spaceship and leave the rest in global urban blight? Have we already flipped the bird at history to make psychic room for the upcoming international raspberry?

2

When Mankind started dating Reason, he didn't meet the family for a long time. Then came that disastrous barbecue, when Candor told everyone how fat they were, Miss Information insisted on her received ideas, Rationalization explained that nothing can ever go bad in a deep freeze, and Authority said grace over burgers chock full of *E. coli*. But Mankind had already fallen in love, and in the throes you can only hear the sound of your own infatuation, the bloop of the skull becoming impervious to Judgment. What a mess. Remember the wedding?

3

In grade school, we laughed at the Stegosaurus for his lack of self-awareness, his unfortunate wardrobe, the walnut-sized brain that has kept him in remedial math since the late Kimmeridgian Age. But his lack of ambition made him suitable to a universe where, frankly, not much happens outside major cities, and most of what does takes place in a vacuum—silently, airlessly. Not to diss our opposable thumbs, books, medicines and Internets and everything, but with a slower learning curve, Faust might have cheated Mephistopheles. Inadvertently, of course, but it's hard to deny that the cosmos favors animal ignorance. Not man's stupidity: we dredge the beach every year, then we build new houses in the sand.

CHRISTIAN PORNO
JAMES HANNAHAM

M: **YOU** want this marriage?
W: Yeah, I do. I want that loving marriage.
M: I want to marry you so bad. I do.
W: You're gonna give me that marriage?
M: Yeah, I'm gonna marry you so hard.
W: O yeah, marry me!
M: I'm gonna marry you up against this altar. With this priest. You like my big fat priest?
W: O yeah, husband. Marry me with that big fat priest.
Priest: Kiss her.
M: I'm gonna marry the living Jesus out of you, you little wife. Take this blessed ring. Take it. You know you want that ring up your finger. Take it, you wife.
W: O yeah, give it to me. Give me that ring. It feels so good when you marry me. Harder! Marry me harder!
Priest: Yeah, kiss that bride, man. Gee, she likes tying the knot, doesn't she? (*Laughs.*)

The men share an enthusiastic high five.

M: You like it when I join you in holy matrimony?
W: Yeah. Put that ring all the way down my finger.
M: Wife. You like how tight that ring is?
W: O Lord, your ring is so round! So eternal!
M: Holy cow! You like this wedding, don't you, you devoted spouse. Does your husband marry you like this?
W: O Husband, I submit myself to thee!
Priest: Kiss that bride, man. Yeah, kiss her.
W: Have me! Hold me! Marry me up the aisle!
M: I'm gonna marry you until death do us part.
W: O sweet Jesus. That's sooo long!

A CHILD POINTED ME OUT AS A GHOST IN A CITY OF FALLING WHITE

ALYSON SINCLAIR

there is no higher logic behind the logic of punishment.
since forever the iconography of protection. snakebitten. horsefleshed.
my cocklebur baby covered in sand spurs with no marshland left.

my body is that too. my body. my imaginary collection of crayfish.
inland the remote-time been like high tide. like a satellite.
there is no logic behind the logic of the higher than.
a child pointed at me and asked for a ghost in the falling city.

so the bottletrees held the bottles the bottles the ghost marsh.
what I been done told you about the blue-night of the glow tide.
awash in shellfish I begin to focus here on the all right.
like pluff mud. like gold sediment. like unwishing the ocean.
there is a child, a higher logic, a punishment for the ghost.

SEEING THE LIBERTY BELL

BENJAMIN JURGENSEN

ON JULY 3rd, 1996, there was a group of tourists from Annecy-le-Vieux standing in the queue outside of Independence Hall. Together, their grandfathers had cast fifty-five replicas of the Liberty Bell in the Paccard Bell Foundry. We were separated by at least 30 people, but the queue's complexity lined us up every few minutes.

Ted Turner had just spoken on behalf of the United Nations Foundation. He didn't mention raising bison on the largest privately owned plot of land in the United States. The girls from Annecy-le-Vieux saw him speak, but his southern drawl kept them from understanding the scale of his endeavors. They were into Jane Fonda, underdressed for a state park and too young to be smoking.

Due to drought the year before, the National Park Service had banned smoking on most parkland. States followed suit. Evading smoking bans had been sport for my grandmother since the mid-Eighties. When we became aligned with the girls from Annecy-le-Vieux, she relit a half-smoked Doral and enjoyed it undetected.

The tallest girl in the group had her belly button pierced, displaying it proudly below a cropped tank top. The hair on the small of her back was dark and directional. While she sat on the railing, beads of sweat formed just above the waist of her rolled shorts. I was reciting state capitals and Mom put her hand on my shoulder.

We were about to see the Liberty Bell.

WHAT WE THOUGHT WE WANTED

KEVERLEE BURCHETT

Once we got insurance out of the way we didn't know.
A whole head-full of eyelashes
and a meteor shower later
and we still hadn't figured it out.
We thought stability but in what form?
To lose ten pounds and healthy children.
We were making concessions before we'd even got started.
All the pipes of our bodies
clean and glowing, good schools and elected officials.
Our parents close to home but not too.
To hear no more stories
about drowning polar bears or birds smothered in oil,
to be able to recycle 5s and 6s, four distinct seasons.
To grow our own food and lots of pets
in the yard. Time and money for travel,
to see the way others lived, their colors
brighter, songs songy-er.
And then to have to come back
to the same old life we'd lived.
The kids with their dance lessons
and doctor's appointments, vaccinations
and always the dog puke on the carpet,
one hamster bit off the head of the other and it was missing.
And now we can pay the vet bills
but have no time to go, the fleas are immune
and when they take the dog back
to lacerate the wound we must wait in the chairs, just like
any other patient.

INTERMISSION
CYNTHIA GRIER LOTZE

Stella's a disappearing act; both dog
and pony, then POOF! she's vapor, smoke,

silent through the trapdoor. Now she is
the dot dot dot border where

her solid outlines should be. Shouldering
downtown through an uptown-bound

crowd, invisible elbow in Peter's ribs, flash
of wrist beyond the closing

doors of the fourth car, tunneling
already, express, express through three stations,

too gone—the angel in the fountain, the curve
of neck below in the dark orchestra, the hand

grasping his collar.

VISITING DELAWARE

ANNA CLAIRE HODGE

Days begin late here in your childhood home.
Thick blinds postpone light & we move slowly
through motions of waking (dream telling,
your muted urge against my back).

You show me mansions, a small zoo, the barn
where you fell, seizing when the booze wore off.
Each landmark or torn ticket, each smarting silence,
earns me English peas, pecorino, small pours of malbec
& Cotes du Rhone. Later, pills and cheaper reds.
The house fills with the shouting of slurred book titles,
names of pharaohs. This, the hour of the love seat,
the television quiz show, the snap of painkillers cleaving.

The girl you really loved (dark hair, lithe) lived at the end
of a snaking back road known for whitetails
that crossed its lanes in the dark. You both vowed
to never drive it at night, to take the long way home.
You tell me how, once, you broke the promise,
& your palms mashed in time like chest compressions
on the horn. Honking, to warn the deer.

SPRING MIX
MIKE POWELL

PALS OF the universe:

as per custom of previous years, here's a mix for spring, which i think i was finally inspired to finish because it's so cold and grey in new york today. close friends will no doubt recognize like 90% of these songs.

the emotional high point for me is somewhere in the 6-8 stretch. me encanta cuando ellos llorar. the treatise on gospel music is 23-26. the reminder of the 1990s is track 11, which is also kind of a reminder of a now-outmoded form of female sexuality popularized by magazine ads i only remember the smell of. my favorite arrangement is track 13. i mean, really! the meanest lyrics, i think, are track 14, and the nicest are track 23 (and not because of the colors, but the colors are nice too). i tried out van dyke parks's version of "riverboat," but it's too stiff. the "straight heat" stretch is 8-10. duh. (and my favorite track of 2010 so far is track 9. it's also the "hump inanimate objects" stretch.)

stephen d. (yes, you!): sorry for using AMF for a "novelty interlude." the transition between it and s.e. rogie was too good. when i met kyle hall, i asked about the girl on "i 3 dr. girl friend." he said (sorry, now i'm cutting and pasting):

> "Yeah, that's a girl I was really, really into at the time. And then, you know. We still talk, but..." he says, shaking his head. "I mean, that's all behind me, I'm done with that. Now when I go out and DJ and see all these girls I think, 'This is what's available to me?"

everyone will know lust someday, and later everyone will know loneliness.

ok, here's this.

i wonder if i should've put on ry cooder playing "ditty wah ditty." maybe next mix.

the tracks, in case they fell out of order, should go

1. roj
2. matt dear
3. kingston trio
4. niney
5. kevin ayers
6. los parientes
7. dusan
8. ali hassan
9. untold
10. harmonimix
11. suzanne v.
12. lee dorsey
13. robert palmer
14. kid creole
15. specials
16. tim maia
17. mount kimbie
18. raincoats
19. tanya tucker
20. golden gate
21. amf
22. se rogie
23. mt goats
24. klimek
25. kyle hall
26. panda bear

ISSUE FIVE

WHAT PETER CALLS "A NATURAL ENCOUNTER PERSON"

VOCABULARY: ~~BOB FRANCES~~ JOESPH PERRY
AUTHOR UNKNOWN

EDITORS' NOTE. *The following is a transcription of a handwritten journal discovered in a box of books donated to the nonprofit Books on Wheels, based in Richmond, Virginia. Its author is unknown. The transcription attempts to preserve all errors, misspellings and authorial amendments present in the original version of the text.*

JUNE 6, 1975

Tonight is graduation.

~~JUNE 7, 1975~~
A FRIDAY JUNE 6.

Last night was fantastic. We had our graduation. The biggest hand was for John Zompa, of course. Afterwards I went to Mike Lee's house for a couple of glasses of champane. Nancy Lyons wrote in my year book and so did Fr. Quinn and Mrs. Lyons. I gave Nancy my picture. I wrote some true and nice things on the back. Afterwards I went with Nancy over to my house and Peter came to get us. We did this so, I could leave the car. We then took Bob up to Mat Zito's party. Then I went with Peter and Nancy over to Mike's. Then everyone went back to Matt's. I went swimming and had a good conversation with Charlie Rupuz. We drank the Priviate Stock. of beer. (Heffareefur) sounds like "have a reefer." R.L. Dufreen took Peter and I home a five o'clock and I slept over at Peter's house.

B SATURDAY JUNE 7

I went over to Peter's to sleep and woke up a twelve thirty. Mrs. Lyons made us breakfast and it was good. I went home at three in the afternoon only to leave at five to go to Ken Vinacco's party. At seven-thirty we went to Steve Celona's party. I didn't feel to exicited at the party. I was a little annoyed at Steve who didn't even say hi or talk with me at all. He spent most of the time talking to Nancy. I guess he figured I was the competition. I was quite upset about this. He kind of pulled Nan. away every time she talked to me. I just sat quietly usally in a corner and watched. I drank one beer and one screw driver. I did have one real good line that night. It broke up the whole room. Steve's sister Linda, was trying to make sure everything was all right. She asked me ~~for~~ if everything is ok. Then she said "Do you want any milk, coffee, tea, beer, screw driver or water?"

"No"

"Are you tired?"

"Yes."

"We have three beds upstairs."

"Why? Do you want to go?" punch line.

We left around 12:30.

I went with Kenny Discoli. We came to my house to get the camera. Then we proceeded to Dave Teturaut house where he was getting ready to sleep over Peters. While on their way from the party to Dave's, Peter must have talked to ~~M~~ Nancy. I am not really sure of this but, it is my guess. While alone in Dave game room alone with Nan she asked me if I thought she talked to Steve too much tonight. I was standing next to her and I said something like "not really, it's alright." I tapped her on the cheek and sat down on the other side of the room.

We went over Peter's and slept. It was nice. I slept in Peters bed and Dave selpt in the cart next to me. Dave and I talked about a half hour. He is beyond a shadow of a doubt what Peter calls "a natural encounter person."

B SUNDAY JUNE 8.

We woke up and ate breakfast around 9:30. We went to church at St. Adlobits. While walking up there Mary Lyons, Peter's 7 year old sister, walked between Dave and I holding our hands. Peter worked until 12. We visited him at the store. Later in the afternoon I took pictures of Peter playing soccer. He was the hero of the game by blocking six straight pentality kicks. They lifted him up after the game and carried him off the field. I went home and hit the ~~sca~~ sak early.

B MONDAY JUNE 9

I didn't do very much. I got my chest x-ray and went shoping. At night, I went to an excounter reunion. I talked about Sara, Bob and the letter, and Peter. Well Kenny Vinacco is upset because he feels he is being "tololated" by me and Peter. He made me feel guilty for being friends with Peter. At writing this a few day later I feel like saying "Fuck you, Kenny, and help." These Pyton Place~~s~~ sob jobs are not my cup of tea. He put me in an awkward postion. I guess he ~~wo~~ really wants me to screw ~~and~~ but, says he doesn't want to hurt Peter's happiness. He is very screwed up. I say friendship and love are not selfish things and they can be shared by more than two people.

B TUESDAY JUNE 10

Quiet~~e~~ day around here. I made some pictures and took a couple of walks. Peter came over around eight o'clock and left around eleven. We talk about Kenny and his new love, Mary Conners.

C WENSDAY JUNE 11

I Went shoping with Peter this morning and bought some film for the island and I got a hat and shirt. In the afternoon I went for a walk down River road and up the Bulovard. Then I ran the Bulovard back. And finally walked home. Tonight I will pack for Block Island. "Horrrray"

A THURSDAY JUNE 12

Today was a great day. Peter, Kenny D., Kenny V. and I drove up to the lake around noon. We stayed inside because it was raining. I listened to music ~~or~~ most of the time. At four o'clock Kenny V. and I went to pick up Pizza and Soda for supper. While we were gone Fr Quinn came up. ~~a~~ A little later Dave Tetrault came up and A decon Mike and Dave from

Baltimore was also there. Two major events of the party was the "fight" between Fr Quinn and Decon against Peter and I. I also got a chance to talk with Kenny Discolli. It was an very enjoyable day.

B FRIDAY JUNE 13

Big day. I took Danny to school. And then prepared for my trip to the island. I took the 11 o'clock boat. It was a rain wet and terrible weather day. I talked with Marta and Jim on the way over. I work at the Sping House at night and sleept in the afternoon. It was great meeting all the people again. Christy was still sore from a car accident.

C SATURDAY JUNE 14

I work at the Spring House for the morning, afternoon, and night. I slept in between shifts. It was foggy and drizzly all day anyway. After work Mark Jones and I went to the National. The State Troopers bounced me. They ask me where I was staying. I'm not sure but, maybe it is for the best.

B SUNDAY JUNE 15

It was a quiet day. I worked breakfast and lunch at the Spring House. I need a reliable friend at this point. I cannot go into the bars so, I might as well work night shift. I decided to make money this year. I can do it. I finish work at three and took a more than extremely needed shower. I rode my bike around for awhile and after supper took a long walk. It was very foggy today. The foggiest I have ever seen. It wasn't until late afternoon that it burned off.

A MONDAY JUNE 16

At writing I am rip roaring drunk. Today was a very cloudy day with rain treating. I talked with Sam Mott this morning an th he said I have the rest of the week off. Which is nice. I was sleeping until 2 in the afternoon. I still have not seen Diane C. I saw Patty Valitine and Faby Malodo today.

For the first time I am looking forward to Dead Eyes. I talked with Carl in the afternoon I walked the South East side this afternoon I also went to drink at the Spa. Cathy yelled from the blue ~~co~~ station wagon got to the Spa. ~~I~~ And I drank. I also latked with Tory Brotherhood and I think it is time for bed. Spa had a good keg of Miller. I also met Sue from Detroit I'll write about her tomorrow tomorrow Sara.

A+ TUESDAY JUNE 17

Today was a fantastic day. First I layed in bed for a long time and just relaxed perfectly. Then I met Sara at the boat. However, she was so excited she didn't say very much. Then after lunch I went to the beach. As I was lay there, John Demaris came by and we jogged the beach. When we got back we went swimming. The water was ice cold. However, all the pain went away as soon as I got out. It was very soothing as I left the water.

I came back at three-thirty and found Peter's soccer pictures. They came out good. After supper, Kathy ~~and~~, Mike and I waked to the Oar and had three beers. Then we proceeded to Champlain. Peter and George Mott gave ~~up~~ us a boat ride ~~from~~ to the Oar. Sara came by and then we started back to Kathy's house. A very importain thing happen. ~~A~~ On our way up the Oar road ~~we~~ Kathy said "You know, K.C. I like you." That was after I said I didn't smoke pot. Ken Rose gave us a ride to State beach and we walked to the Kittens. A blond girl, Karen, can play some good gutair. She also has a very nice personality I left around nine thirty and decided to call it a Terrific day.

A WENSDAY JUNE 18

Well, This day had a little bit of everything. It was a bright sunny day. I arose early and at breakfast. I had to meet the Boat at 10:40 but, it was too ~~early~~ nice a day to stay in bed. So, I went to the Ballarde to lay agaist the breakwall. Well, just as I began to settle in I spied three young maidien come trotting over the breakwall. They sat near by. About a half-hour later, Lisa a good looking and obviously the leader ask me what time is it.

10:00 o'clock. Well, then they asked where can ~~I~~ they get a soda. I showed them where and they bought me one even though I had said I didn't want one. We talked for a while and I found out they were visiting from Clinton. I met the boat and saw Bod and Deb. We talked about Saturday and he went to clean the house. I then went back to Anana, Lisa, and Karen. Anana is a cute blond very sexy. Karen is quiet, big boobs, not bad looking, and is worse of the three. She complains too much. Lisa has class. She is good looking and has one of those super personality I then went to the Gansett and ate ~~luch~~ lunch with Kathy outside. I then had a great beach day. ~~th~~ I saw a lot of people there. I talked with Lisa Gimp, Bob + Deb, Dan the tall as opposed to Danny the big, Mike, Julie and Andra. After supper I went to the Oar for a beer and then took the Clinton girl to the bluff. Then we went to the Oar and drank and drank. They left to eat at 8:00 but, John D, Peter, Sara, Gannsett and Spa Crew and Peter Crawford. I was bomb this night. John Hobby played Asshole tonight. I got a little sunburn.

A THURSDAY JUNE 19

First day of work at w Eye I move down here to day to the Shrimp got to my hands. It was an easy day. I got out and went to the beach with Dave. I showered and shaved. ~~Af~~ Dinner was good. I meet Debbie one of the waitresses here, Mighty fine indeed. Great personality. I talk with so many people at supper. It was terrific. I then ~~ran~~ met John Littlefield and he took me to State beach. I ran to Sotch and back to he Surf. Then I race Duncan an Irish ~~Slater~~ Setter. Sprints between Surf and State. I sat and watch the storm come is. The ocean was still an green. The cloud were gentle and angry. It created quite a feel inside me. The dark stillness before the storm. I also watched a ant get blow all over by the wind. I then met Matty Mee. and had a coke at the National. I came back to write read and talk to Annie. Mat Wells came to day

~~TUESDAY~~ WENSDAY JULY 2

I have not writen in a while but life around here has it good point and low points. Some of the high points of my past ten days: I met Jill the chambermaid and went for a nice walk with her~~e~~. I saw the movie *Papion*. The most importain thing happen one night last week. I was in the boy room at dead eyes with Dave Aldrigh and Patty Valitine came in. I suggested that we go listen to records. She had been sleeping and just woke up. We were playing a record and talking when Joey her "boyfriend" came in. He told her and demanded she leave. I asked if I could stay and listen to records. She said yes I was listen to Seal and Croft "Diamond Girl." About forty five minutes later I was siting in a chair and Patty came in crying. She sat on the bed. I went over and put my arm around her. She was shaking. ~~After a~~ I ask her if she wanted to talk about it and she said no. Five minutes or so later she said somethings. Most notably "People are weird." About a half an hour afterward Faye came up and said hi. Faye asked "what is wrong?" Patty started to talk and the~~y~~n she turned around and said "Oh, I trust you". Then she explained what happened. Apparetly ~~She~~ Joey and her were breaking up. He had hit her, ~~and~~ She said that she dosen't hate him and he said I'm going to make you hate me. In any case we talked for about two hours more after Faye left. ~~She~~ The end when I was leaveing she and I were on the bed and she said "Thank you for being here" Then she gave me a hug.

The next day Faye said that Patty said to her "If KC haden't been there I would have gone crazy."

A couple of nights later Patty and I talked for two hours. She was not feeling to well she had a cold.

I went to the beach today with Tim from the Gansett.

THE AUTHOR AS STUDENT WHO HAS A CRUSH ON TINA AND WATCHES OUTSIDE HER WINDOW AS SHE'S MURDERED BY FREDDY IN A NIGHTMARE ON ELM STREET

KEITH MONTESANO

After the film by Wes Craven

Tina, the love I had was inexpressible, but what I thought

I could keep always in my head—no letters, no diary,

no paintings—could not last forever. Not once did I see him,

because I never told you: I told no one. That night I was there,

saw Rod screaming, his back wrenched, almost snapping

the paneling. When he shattered lamps, bulbs, I looked away

from the blood, squinted to see anything, then took off across

the lawns. It was too early that morning, & my parents

would wake too soon. There was the smell of cut grass

& gasoline. My heart felt like it would explode. I crept
to my room, waited for the footsteps of my father. I read
the headlines in the papers. I knew. Days later I saw words
of Rod's suicide. I knew. & now that I've fallen in love again,
I can speak of this, still knowing, & never say a word.

THE AUTHOR AS MAN WHO'S ON THE ESCALATOR DUCKING FROM BULLETS AS QUAID USES A DEAD BODY FOR A SHIELD IN TOTAL RECALL

KEITH MONTESANO

After the film by Paul Verhoeven

The love I felt for each breath upon my neck was limitless—

a new woman every morning, every week. Dear God,

I've prayed, but the bullets are sprayed & tangential: everywhere.

I wonder, now, always, about my life that will end here—

a life where it's just me, trapped, trampled, & endless. Endless

but beginning: the way the world tells us we've been good

to each other, or that we matter in the end. I hope to leave

here, & hear nothing but silence, or wind, but the bullets

are flying with the screams & the bodies, & I'm here now

among them all. I look, for one second, & see blood across
the escalators: bodies all over, never knowing who's alive. I hope
to tell you this. & this is it, I think—I think we're done for.
But it's just me. & if I don't make it out, know that you didn't
deserve the life you had. It was me until the end, & it's over.

DISPATCH FROM THE FUTURE

LEIGH STEIN

Here there is no illness.
Also, we are immune to dangers
like tigers, spiders, and saboteurs.

It's so simple.

It's the opposite of unrequited

love.

It's a jaunty, irreverent adventure.

I am beautiful if you say so

and I sparkle
in the dark.

Read by my body.

Read my body to me.

Read my lips:

We are not having sex
until you get this thing fixed.

In the future, someone loves
me.

I never have to beg God anymore.

RE: PLEASE REPLY IMMEDIATELY
SIR KUSSO PHILLIP & MAYRON CHOPSUEY

EDITORS' NOTE. *The following correspondence has not been edited for content, nor have its errors of spelling or punctuation been corrected. The emails between Sir Kusso Phillip and Mayron Chopsuey appear here as they did in the original exchange.*

From: "Sir. Phillip K" (sir.kussophillip@hotmail.com)
Sent: Wednesday, January 25, 2012 7:46 PM
Subject: Re: Please Reply Immediately

Dear Friend,

Greeting's to you and your entire family. I know you would be surprised to see this massage; however I wish to introduce you to a transaction which would be beneficial to both of us and which has to be kept confidential for the purpose thereof. My name is Sir Kusso Phillip (Esq), a lawyer based in Cote d'Ivoire.

I wish to seek for your consent to present you as next of kin to my late client since you are from the same country. This man is an Astute Business man and a contractor with ECOWAS country. He made a numbered time (Fixed) Deposit, valued at $9.2M (Nine Million Two Hundred Thousand United State Dollars) for Thirty Six calendar months in a bank here in Cote d'Ivoire. Upon Maturity, the bank instructed me to send a routine notification to his forwarding address but I got no reply. We finally we discovered he was assassinated with his entire family during civil war here in Cote d'Ivoire because he was financing another Presidential candidate.

As a result of the Civil war in Cote d'Ivoire the bank approved all huge payments to be carried out from their head office in neighboring country Ghana.

With your assistance and my professional guide we would have the money transferred to your account as the next of Kin and Beneficiary to the fund. Meanwhile, I have agreed to give you 40% upon using your account to receive the fund. I have with me all necessary documents that will back up the claim in your favor.

I look forward to your positive response and would like you to contact me immediately for further discussion, It will be very important you send along your telephone number so I can call to give you further information.

I will give you more details when I have your confirmation to this letter.

Please Send Your Response To My Private E-mail { sir.kusso.phillip@hotmail.com }

Best Regards.
Sir Kusso Phillip.
Email: sir.kusso.phillip@hotmail.com

From: "Chop Suey Tuey" (info@chopsueybooks.com)
To: sir.kusso.phillip@hotmail.com
Sent: Thursday, January 26, 2012 10:18 AM
Subject: Re: Please Reply Immediately

Hello Sir Kusso,

Yes, I would be happy to help. But I must insist that I will receive 69% of the amount transferred to my account. Otherwise, I will be unable to assist you.

Good day, Sir,
Mayron

From: Kusso Phillip
To: info@chopsueybooks.com
Sent: Thursday, January 26, 2012 11:54 AM
Subject: Re: Re: Please Reply Immediately

Dear Mr. Suey,

I thank you for your response. I read your message with great contempt and I am pleading with you to assist me on this transaction and will be offering you 40% as proposed. I need you to consider this offer as it it a huge sum from the amount to be transacted.

Please I need to speak with you on phone. I need your assurance and promise of trust. Please let me have your telephone number. Or you can Please call me on this telephone number: +233540876674.

I thank you and wait for your response.
Sir. Phillip Kusso

From: Chop Suey Tuey (info@chopsueybooks.com)
To: Kusso Phillip (phillip.kusso@yahoo.com)
Sent: Friday, January 27, 2012 1:26 AM
Subject: Re: Re: Please Reply Immediately

Dear Sire,

I see your contempt and will match it with one word of indignation: humbug! As you have stated, I am the next of Kin, ergo these funds are to be given to me directly. I do not appreciate being tricked by a lawyer of your stature into giving more than 31%, and now that you have pushed the matter, I will request that exactly 73.26% of my inheritance be left in my account.

I do not mean to be rude, but my blood sugar is very low right now, and I need to eat lunch. You also cannot call my phone number as it is disconnected because I only would pay them 69% of the bill, which, considering that my brother works for them, is fair.

Please respond post haste!
Mayron

From: Kusso Phillip
To: Chop Suey Tuey
Sent: Thursday, January 26, 2012 3:12 PM
Subject: Re: Re: Please Reply Immediately

Dear Mr. Suey,

Thanks for your message which I read but still can not understand vividly your argument. The only thing I do not need right now is tension, please Mr. Suey if you can not help me, I can understand, please I crave your indulgence on the subject matter and the proposal which is irrevocable. I am offering you 40% of the total amount that will be transacted. And also I cannot forge ahead with you without talking to you on phone for goodness sake, this is a transaction worth millions of dollars which I cannot only email Instructions but also to enlighten you more on phone.

Please if you cannot continue as I have proposed, feel free to decline because I cannot add more or deduct from what I have proposed as regards the percentage sharing which is 40%. I hope you understand me better, it is very plain now there is no trick anywhere. There is no room for trick and dishonesty. I work will Trust

Have a good Afternoon!
Sir. Phillip

From: Chop Suey Tuey (info@chopsueybooks.com)
To: Kusso Phillip (phillip.kusso@yahoo.com)
Sent: Friday, January 27, 2012 4:46 AM
Subject: Re: Re: Please Reply Immediately

Dear Sir Phillip K.

You are very clever, my friend, and your golden words have led me to see that I indeed acted with haste and without a vivid picture of the situation at hand. I misread the first email, and assumed that you were only going to leave me $40, and I knew that I needed at least $69. Since we are talking Millions of Dollars now, I am ready to fully put myself in your trusted hands. 40% of millions it is!

However, I will ask that you send me $69 now, not only as an act of good faith, but because I will need to pay the remainder of my phone bill so that we can discuss this financial transaction in person. Of course, this $69 can be deducted from my millions of dollars when we complete our transaction; I do not wish to steal from you at all!

Should I give you the account number for the telephone company, or would you prefer to just send cash to me?

Yours in Trust and Financial Millions,
Mayron

From: Kusso Phillip
To: Chop Suey Tuey
Sent: Friday, January 27, 2012 5:33 AM
Subject: Re: Re: Please Reply Immediately

Mr. Suey

Thanks for your inspiring message. It go me thinking.... How can

I trust you with a $1000usd when you cannot pay your bills of $65usd. I think I am dealing with the wrong person and please this is not a child's play. If you cannot afford to pay your phone bills then you must be in a financial crisis. And with this I can not trust these funds in your care, its as simple as that. Please, I appreciate your time and effort towards helping me and I know now you cannot be of any help to me.

Sir. Phillip

From: Chop Suey Tuey
To: Kusso Phillip
Sent: Friday, January 27, 2012 9:18 AM
Subject: Re: Re: Please Reply Immediately

Dearest Sir,

You have passed my test!!!

I told you the previous stories as a challenge to see if you were able to handle the stresses of financial insecurity. Had you offered me the money, I would have known immediately that you were neither financially smart, nor were you one that I would trust with my millions of dollars. I didn't become an American Tycoon with over 986,000,000 in my bank account by trusting people who were foolish with money! No, in fact, it was by testing my colleagues and seeing who had the business acumen to not accept "quick fixes" that I rose to the top. Now I see that we can make money together, and that my riches will become even greater!

Please feel free to call me at the following number: 804-422-8066. We will surely have no problems working together from this moment onwards!

Good job!!!
Mayron

From: Kusso Phillip
To: Chop Suey Tuey
Sent: Monday, January 30, 2012 7:32 PM
Subject: I wait my dear

Mr. Suey,

Considering the amount involved in this transaction, I did not desire to expose it to any third party. I only wish and pray that you will be capable to receive the money in your account and also assist me to invest my share.

With due respect, it will not be necessary to tell me your worth. All I need is your trust and honesty. All I need to meet with you after the bank have transferred the money to your account.

Now, I called the number you gave to me - +1-804-422-8066 and there was no response. Please can you call me on my private telephone number - +233544018444.

As my security, apart from your telephone number, please I will like to have your ID. I will not hesitate to send you mine if you wish.

I thank you and I wait for your response.
Sir Phillip
Telephone number - +233544018444

From: Chop Suey Tuey
To: Kusso Phillip
Sent: Tuesday, January 31, 2012 10:44 AM
Subject: Re: I wait my dear

Mr. Kusso,

I am sorry to hear that you tried to call me and the there was no answer. My butler was most likely in the bathroom relieving himself at the time.

In any case, there have been new developments on my end. It seems that I have won a sizeable prize from the Nigerian National Lottery. This is quite lucky, because I didn't even remember that I had purchased a lottery ticket, but the honest people from their lottery system tracked me down and are in the process of transferring the funds to me now. According to them, I need to wait until this transaction clears before I can proceed with our dealings. I hope that you can be patient for this matter to settle before we continue. If not, please call me immediately!

In the meantime, please send your ID so we can have that settled before we move forward.

Your business partner,
Mayron

EVERYTHING IS DOUBLE
MATHIAS SVALINA

The ocean has its depth. The sun its pursiness. The end of life, though we give it differing names, is bitter. No matter what the scoreboard says, one must push the ball down the field. One must go for the gold. What is left after success is the blood on the couch, the distant Doppler of the ambulance. One must remember that everything is double, a fire that does not burn. What one should be doing now, down by the river, in the basement of hollow floors, is forging oneself wings, but one must forgive oneself with one's blurred lynx eyes.

DEATH
MATHIAS SVALINA

It is spring & the pear blossoms have been washed from the trees by a sudden storm, coating the street in a slick white. One stops a police officer & asks to be arrested but the police officer does not oblige. *But officer,* one says, *there is nothing but beauty in the world & still all I can think about is death.* The officer does not smile, the officer does not lay a hand on one's head. People say that forgiveness begins in the heart, but it begins in the dirt.

THE STORY
MATHIAS SVALINA

One must sit in a leather desk chair & write the exact way one will die. One must use descriptive writing. One must use concrete details. The bird's cage in the corner with all the wandering chains has been empty since the beginning of the desk. The woman in the distance bending to look beneath her car for the thing that caused the thump, she is one's inner life. The woman in the distance with her finger on the trigger of her bomb, she is one's inner life. The woman in the distance with the acid-scars slickening her face, she is one's inner life. One must sit & watch out the tall windows & keep writing until the story is done.

MOONS OVER MY HAMMY
NOAH FALCK

Thinking in another language you sat half-embarrassed
among the distinguished scent of the non-smoking section.

There was graphic eyerolling in the booth behind you,
a pierced tongue.

You were not who they thought you were
slouched beneath a hanging chandelier
that gave off a glare that was almost
paint-by-number.

Your thoughts were the cold, empty spaces
of urban buildings cranky with rusty machinery.

**

When your mother told me she found you
without a pulse, argyle socks all the way to the knees,
I held back both tears and laughter.

**

The following week the local paper printed a story—
Local Man Dies by Way of Blow-dryer

The sky never had a serious role and you, as always,
didn't plan on leaving the way you did.

There were other moments, I'm sure,
moments like ice cubes stuck to the bottom of the glass,
like interrupted keyboard solos to be continued later.

**

When you looked out the window and noticed
the headlights forever flinching in the distance,

you knew it was time.

You must have been thinking, in Spanish perhaps,
of the roomy afterlife. The last thoughts must
have been the best, the last thoughts.

YOU ARE LOOKING FOR A PARTY
A BAD BUNNY

Wait, you want to spray-paint the candy gold?
I don't think I was that enthusiastic.
I was slouching like a pile of tombstones,
pre-engraved but snow-frosted. Like that.
You're going to give me lessons, right?
Leave me to roll a few feet like a bicycle
before it tips and hits the ground? Okay,
here we are. I'll make you a sidecar.
Take you both steady and around. I'm better
than rhododendrons when it comes to spreading
out underground, way better than the oak tree,
that old cheat. I want to explode him. There are
rules about cat-burglar roots and first-chair
flutes and helmets that look more like heads
than squat, heavy shells. Truth be told:
two sidecars is steady, helmets not needed.
You have an instrument in hand, a flute,
and you are better than potatoes at playing it.
There are rules about birthdays: one
per person. Rebates end, special offers
are only as special as the shine of how bad
you want the thing, terms and conditions, so
why can't you get your gift certificates?
An old trick is to let compact monsters
chase and chatter on your skin. Monsters

are far more real and plentiful on skin
than in closets or under beds—they teach
distress and flabbergast. The sounds
of leaves and wonder. Just ask Thomas Hardy,
a great believer in monsters, and in monster-
related remedies. Watch them drag-race
on the highway to the heart, he would say.
Wait, you want monsters to leap out of the cake
instead of a lady? You want your blood
chasing its own tail? You want to plant yourself
and grow a tombstone from the ground?
The answer is that you are looking for a party.

OF A GIVEN POPULATION

P.J. GALLO

I am no longer excitable
though I find my participation
in your census stimulating.

An animal walked across
the sidewalk on which you arrived
this morning, reminding me

I have to go to work.
My other job is following strange cats
is a bumper sticker

they do not have.
My only job is sitting in an office,
though I have a window and birds

sometimes land in a tree
outside, reminding me
I was once a child

who killed a baby bird on the thought
he could teach it how to fly.
I appreciate your stopping by.

ISSUE SIX
FOR THE MOLOKAI COPS

ACCEPT THE WORLD AND GO TO PARTIES

ADAM DAY

I wish I were
god in Mainz

annulled in beer
growing old

in the shadow
of compromise

working back
from cruelty

to original sin

NEW YEAR
AMIRA PIERCE

THE DOOR of the apartment is painted green; in a few spots, the green is peeled away and you can see that the door, in a previous life, was white. You ring the bell for the third time. No answer. You wonder, again, if you have the wrong time or office stuck in your head. You definitely have the day right. Ugh. Job interviews.

A rustling behind you.

He's come up the stairs, the man in the light green galabiya, the only one that you'd seen in the building's entryway. Didn't talk when you greeted him, only nodded. And now he's reaching towards you, as if to shake your hand, smiling his toothless smile, no words but voice a muddy whistle. You move towards him and take his hand. Rough. He pulls at you. His other hand grabbing for his manhood through his dress.

You pull away, then in a split second know you must run towards him, run past him down the stairs, and you do, feet faster than head.

—Boussie! he whispers, after you. *Look!*

—Boussie eh? 'Eib! you shout back, as you bound down the hard marble spiral. *Shame.*

Your alien words echo in your ears as you run out to the sun-bleached street. Two men are here now, in the plastic chairs that had before been empty. You start to think of what to say, and then, like magic, Osama and Sami appear in the distance. You run towards them—both dark hair, light eyes, square jaws—telling your English story between heaving breaths.

Soon these men—potential bosses, new friends, strange world—are standing next to you in front of the building, translating what you just said for the men sitting in the chairs, the real doormen of this building—one with a gray moustache and the other, young and fat, both in crisp white galabiyas. The two of them nod sternly and then laugh. You move away, towards a crumbling wall. Osama and Sami stay serious, keep talking, ask you for more details about the man who did it. You say more: the toothlessness, the whistle, his galabiya had stains, he was sweeping.

—Ah!—Araby, the doormen say. Should they get him? Should they give him to the police? There are a few of them on that corner—they point, then pivot—and the other one, too, and the other. They laugh.

—The police will pull his ears a bit, gray moustache says.

You imagine that.

—No police, you say.

Suddenly Araby is out on the sidewalk, too. And he won't look at you. Young and fat holds him by the arm and sternly asks if he did what you said he did. He whimpers and you feel for him. Gray moustache takes off his plastic slipper and holds it up, as if to hit him. You brace yourself.

But the hit never comes; soon you are all in another place—you and Osama and Sami and gray moustache and young and fat. You are in an office in the building sitting on white couches facing a glass desk. The man behind the desk introduces himself. He has a long name and his hair is slicked back and looks like shoe polish. He is smiling. And it is all shiny—shiny hair, shiny teeth, shiny cheeks. He is an important man. He lists his holdings, talks about his newest venture: Gemstones in lavish settings.

He shows pictures of them: a grape-shaped emerald surrounded by diamond chips, a sapphire like a twenty-sided teardrop, six rubies grouped together like red honeycomb. Where are the gemstones? You don't ask but look around. Where did young and fat and gray moustache go?

Shiny listens as Osama and Sami explain their own venture, interrupts to say he recognizes Sami from his blockbuster movies. Sami smiles and suggests he might think of investing in a short documentary about the mining industry south of the country.

Shiny doesn't even blink but turns to you, looking straight at you, speaking in English you would have never guessed would come out of him.

—In this country, he says, there are some people—the poor people, the common ones—who don't always know the best way to act, the best way to treat a foreign lady, like you.

You shudder like you never have.

Osama and Sami begin a volley of fast words at him. You think they are saying that because of people like him, the number of poor here swells and grows. They are saying that this isn't about that, but about a basic idea—the very basic idea of how to treat a woman, a person.

You are having more trouble following now. They bring up God, and you are watching their faces, their lips, their voices alternating between angry and nearing too loud for the small room and loud whispers. One of them sends an accidental fleck of spit between them, saliva lighting in the air.

This is how you are spending your first New Year's Eve away from home, where tonight you'd be drinking at an old friend's rental condo or watching Dick Clark at the kitchen table with your mother. But here you are, on the other side of the world, might as well not exist. Not exist.

Now. They're all turned towards you, mouths moving, talking, but what are they saying? Until.

—Would you like an apology from Araby? Sami asks, in English. They have him outside, he says, as if it's nothing to hold a man captive.

You don't know. You don't say anything, but slowly you nod, and shiny man is calling towards the door, which swings open, and the doormen have Araby, each at one of his arms.

—Let him go, shiny man says, and they back off. Araby is silent and still, his eyes on that thing we are looking at when we aren't focused on anything at all. You turn away to see shiny man is opening a safe behind his desk.

—I have something for you, he says, unclear about who *you* is.

The safe glows from within and you think diamonds and he pulls out a bright silver pistol, naming it something you don't understand.

You freeze and in the corners of your eyes you feel Sami and Osama freeze too.

—There are no bullets in it, he says, popping open a panel on the handle, as if to prove it. He snaps the panel shut, visibly satisfied at the —CLICK—his machine makes, points it at Araby.

—Bowis ras-ha, he says. You don't get it, those words, like stones. The room is too strange, and you all are frozen here, and you are frozen, until. Bowis ras-ha—two words you learned at the same time you were learning English. Your mother repeated versions of both of those words to you again and again, two words buried deep and muddy.

But Araby is already upon you: in a desperate dash, his rough hands grasp your skull lightly on both sides, his lips on the crown of your skull, so fast you barely would have known what he did if you hadn't, at that very moment, realized that shiny had commanded him to *kiss her head.*

Bowis ras-ha. That shudder. Again. And now the sharp ghost of his body over you, on you.

You stand quickly, and the men are pushing him out of the room and you've lost track of the gun and Osama and Sami are shaking hands with shiny man and soon you are too—soft hands. And then you're out of there and up the stairs, spiraling up, up and finally past the green-and-white door, where you drink sweet dark tea and translate the story once more, excited now, amused, disgusted. You are still shaking, but your friends have you smiling at their caricatures of all those strange foreign men, and you all agree how the gun moment made you see death. Your death. The gun was a completely other thing that took each of you out of your skins and your skulls to a place without words. And that's all there is.

It's a new year, and you smoke a cigarette by the window, looking out at the street at the people who pass. Then the interview, which goes well. Back at your apartment, the party is big and loud. You dance and the music fills you, as if you were a balloon, and you dance, always on the edge of bursting.

SUMMER VACATION: GHAZIEH, 1987

AMIRA PIERCE

If it was like rain those afternoons,
the rain was often distant, soothing
some, silent even, a tragedy in too-big
words that we could imagine
as a shower of light.
    And when the rain came
loud and close, my mother,
aunts, grandmother pushed us

further into the house, into
the hall where we sat beneath
the hung robes and scarves,
our scraped shins folded
under us as we slapped cards
against cold marble. I think of it and

I am watching all of us, the mothers
who hover over our younger
selves. They grip at defunct
telephones with news-blackened fingertips.
    They speak in the hushed
angles of their secret languages,
wisps of words cutting a thickened
soup of sky. After the storm,

we were released, returned
to the world we'd been given.
I skipped stairs after
my cousins, climbed up
to the cement roof where we became
collectors of what the disaster
left behind. Up there: a sun

glowing fluorescent behind
the smoke. A ground of dried
vines, tangled wire, twisted
metal, plastic bags stretched
to string, bird feathers.
      In the mess,
we clutched bent bullets to
our eager fists. Scrap imprinted
in our palms, pebbles marked
the thin skin stretched across
      our knees.

THE MODERN VICE OF UNREST
JOHN BEARDSLEY

You were always mad
in the winter; skulking

up and down stairs
with a look like a wry starling—

cursing the snow, the space-heater,
the thin Victorian walls

of that bright yellow farm house
which lurched up from its foundations,

compressed to a vanishing point
in the oak limbs, the barn overrun

with brown recluse. I remember saying:
Our father is dead to us, yet still we drag him out.

Pile his corpse into a shapeless
mound of cheap clothes and lust.

We whisper where his ears once were.
We carry him up to the thin seams of the roof

and balance there—the ground below
reflecting the vacuum of space.

It really was bad as all that. I drank
the morning, and it filled me. It ate

out my eyeballs. & I drove the long asphalt
curves, stopping for nothing, except

who rose to meet me,
who touched a bitten finger to my cheek.

DEVILS TO DUST
LAUREN MAAS

WHEN I moved to Doha to teach, the first thing that made an impression on me was the heat, but that was quickly followed by the dust. Counter to expectations and the hopeful *bon voyage* sentiments of friends and family, Qatar boasted no "at least it's a dry heat" heat. Rather, it's a marine desert, and once the salty sea air reaches your skin, it creates a perfect palette for the dust. This I experienced as soon as I stepped off the plane. It was August. The railing I gripped on the way down to the tarmac was tacky. Wet dust coated everything, and then it coated me.

Over the next several weeks, as I became more acquainted with my new home, I realized that to love Doha would mean to love the dust and its residual beige, because the desert left its mark everywhere—on every building, every car, even on the sky.

I come from New Jersey—the Shore, more specifically—a many-colored place, despite what a layover at Newark Airport might lead you to believe. The beach is brassy and blue, sunsets spectacular, and you only have to travel a bit inland to find it evergreen and lush in the summer, autumnal in the autumn, and all variations of gray in the winter. Doha has only two seasons: more hot and less hot. Beige and dust remain the constants.

But Doha has thunder sand—winter storms, flushed south from Iran by the Shamaal winds, which twist barometers and drop the temperature twenty degrees in twenty minutes. They blot out the sun, or if they come at night, disguised as brown clouds, produce hazy veins of lightning. Thunder sand is spectacular. Not quite in the *Mission Impossible: Ghost Protocol* presentation of it, where Tom Cruise outruns a vanquishing storm by speeding through the markets of Dubai. You can drive through thunder sand. You can survive it. You will not be suffocated. But it is spectacular all the same.

Qatar and its sand and dust are made mostly of limestone. In the northwest of the country—an area known as Zikreet that faces the Gulf and the tiny island of Bahrain—plateaus of the rock have been eaten away by the wind. They hover over the pale Martian landscape like craggy mushrooms, their sides worn so smooth that they are impossible to scale. *Jebels*, they are called. My students, Qataris most, told me that Zikreet was the haunted desert, the dwelling of djinn, those creatures out of which our Disneyfied concept of "genies" has grown. But true djinn are Quranic demons, shapeshifters you fear at once but cannot escape until you do their bidding. A djinni's appearance is first heralded by a shimmer of the air, and then as you travel on, forgetting this disturbance, you will come upon a stranger—one with a snarled tooth or a milky eye or a scent about him that just doesn't seem right. If you engage this stranger, this djinni made flesh, you will find yourself in his thrall, and not the other way around.

I mention the djinn and the haunted desert of Zikreet to explain to you that Qatar, the whole of the Gulf even, is a land still connected in some (mostly religious) ways to what we—academically, reductively—might view as folk mythology. The weather and heat suit these beliefs. So does the living memory of a time before oil and gas wealth, when tents and camels, carpets and campfires provided backdrops to such stories. I had students in one class explain how hard it was for them to trust Omanis, their Southern neighbors, because it was widely known they practice black magic. Hearing this, the Omani student in the class nodded, as though carefully considering the accusation.

So when I came upon the article about Dingy in *The Gulf Times*, I was surprised but not shocked. *The Gulf Times* is the major English-language paper in the country, and a copy could be found in the faculty lounge every morning. This particular headline read, "Mysterious Figure Spotted on Doha's Corniche." And there, on the front page, was a grainy color photo of a muscular, burnt-looking creature with probing white eyes and a dog-like snout standing upright next to a pile of rubble. The article, which was a reprint of one that had appeared in the local Arabic daily *Al Sharq*, described one witness who "took a picture of [the creature] in spite of being terribly frightened." It also mentioned that this "mysterious figure" was spotted by many more people, a small crowd, "who also attested to the fact of what she had seen." Apparently, the creature "suddenly disappeared out of their sight when they tried to go near it." All were left to wonder: What was this creature? Why was he on the Corniche? When would he return?

The Corniche is the water walk along Doha's bay. It's in the middle of the city, bordered by the most expensive and elaborate skyscrapers money can buy, and it's frequented by local and expat families on picnics, power walkers and migrant workers who like to fish. It would be hard for any creature, even one slightly mysterious in nature, to stroll unnoticed here. And this one was very mysterious indeed, not to mention publicly nude in a Muslim country.

This was 2009, and the region was not yet brimming with political news, not yet garnering the kind of global exposure it has seen of late, as a base for Arab League peace talks and controversial host of a future World Cup. Lack of major news notwithstanding, it was the front-page placement of the story that perplexed me. So I cut it out and called up my friend Lesley, who had been living in the Gulf for several years, to ask her about it.

"Oh, you mean Dingy?" she asked when I brought up the creature.

"He has a name?"

"The crispy little guy on the front page?" she asked.

"Yeah, that's the one," I said.

She told me she and her husband John had read the article and nicknamed the monster Dingy (hard "g") because he looked suspiciously like their neighbor's disfigured cat, also named Dingy. They suspected Dingy the Cat to be in possession of magical powers that enabled him to walk upright from their neighborhood of Al Sadd all the way downtown, where he could take in the sea breezes on the Corniche and frighten innocent bystanders.

"You're crazy and this place is bizarre," I told her. "This is like a *National Enquirer* headline, but it's not in a tabloid."

"We should go Dingy hunting," she said, and laughed, unfazed.

As I said, I come from Weird New Jersey, a land with no shortage of strange places and mythical characters. The Gates of Hell, Midgetville and the shark that inspired Jaws find happy company alongside more familiar examples of freakishness, not limited to Snooki, Chris Christie and Atlantic City.

The most famous of these, of course, is the Jersey Devil. Resident of the southern Pine Barrens—New Jersey's "backwoods"—the Devil is a favorite of hikers and hockey fans alike. Allegedly the thirteenth and final child of a colonial-era farmer's wife named Mother Leeds, it was born a devil and quickly grew to terrorize the rural landscape. Into the early twentieth century, the Devil was the star subject of local lore, with reports of sightings, attacks and livestock killings attributed to the beast oft recounted in the local papers. In 1909, during a particularly contagious spate of Devil hysteria, schools were shut down to protect area children. I've never camped or hiked in the Pine Barrens and I'm generally not superstitious, but I do find myself growing slightly queasy when I think about this part of my home state. In a place so well charted, so claimed and populated, the Pine Barrens alone is none of these things. Driving through it on the turnpike, the land seems bleak and silent and full of gray trees. And it's rumored that the footprints you find there belong to neither animal nor human.

I was frequently homesick during my first year in Doha. My problems were ridiculous, but they took some time to solve: I had too few friends and too much money and living space. I spent most of my non-teaching time camped out in one room of the massive three-bedroom high-rise apartment provided by my school, drinking Nescafe and obsessively watching the BBC and Al Jazeera, the headquarters of which I passed every day on my ride to work. It was exciting to feel so "in the world" suddenly, at close proximity to the news, but remote and safe from it at the same time. I suppose the company of elegant-voiced anchors and real-time events made me feel less alone, as did the fact that the information I was accessing could just as easily be accessed in New York or DC.

I did not expect the news in Doha to remind me of home's eccentricities so quickly. But there it was one morning as I drank my coffee, staring up at me with bulging white eyes. I was in cryptid country once more.

Evidence was everywhere, but Dingy would not resurface. I walked the Corniche some weekend mornings and evenings, but it was all kite-flying and lounging in the grass, no shrieks by the fountain, no huddles of intrigue.

I asked my students about him, showed them the article to see what they'd say.

"That's a lie," they said, laughing. "It's not real."

"But what about djinn?" I entreated. "What about black magic?"

"Well, those things are more serious," they said seriously.

When, several weeks later, the school went on lockdown because a tiger was roaming the campus, conspiracy theories reigned supreme once more. The news reports stated the animal belonged to a sheikh and had been loose in the city for days, last seen in West Bay, my neighborhood. The picture in the paper this time was of the tiger on the sidewalk, sniffing at a villa's garbage can.

"Hey, Mahmoud," one student exclaimed. "It's your grandfather!"

Sure enough, there was Mahmoud Abbas, Palestinian President, under the lede, frowning over the future of his country. His grandson, my student, Mahmoud Jr., nodded. And then we all went back to speculating about the tiger.

"It's Photoshopped," said one student.

"Well, there must be *something* going on outside," said another. "We're on lockdown."

"He came here because he wants to eat the horses at Al Shaqab, at the stables," one girl said, holding up her phone.

"The tiger texted you that?" I asked.

"No, my friend, Aisha—she did."

I should have returned their attention to our lesson on proper citation, but instead I took it as a teachable moment and went to my office to grab the Dingy clipping. I returned to my students, still texting and chatting, and held it up for them once more.

"Remember this guy?" I asked.

They groaned.

"He's not real, Miss," they said.

"Are you sure?" I asked, voice squeaking.

"Look." One girl turned her computer to face us. "He's a toy."

And there, on some random mythbuster's blog, was a photo of a rubber doll with musculature similar to Dingy's, with Dingy's exact snarl, held tight in the small hands of a child.

"Well, I wouldn't call that a reputable source," I told her.

"What's a reputable source?"

"A source you can trust," I said. "Haven't you been listening?"

"I have," she whined. "But, Miss, how do you know?"

"If you can trust it?" I asked her.

"Yeah," she said, eyes blinking. Her classmates regarded me with equal interest.

"Well, how do you know if you can trust something someone tells you?"

"If I believe it."

"But what makes you believe it?"

"I just want to or I don't." She shrugged. "That's all."

So we went back to the lesson, revisiting criteria and critical thought, though mostly we were distracted, listening for gunshots, roars, sounds of the tiger's last stand. They never came and eventually the lockdown was lifted.

If today you try to search for the Dingy article on *The Gulf Times* website, a 404-server error returns in its place. Up until a year ago, the story was still available. So times have changed—Qatar's top-selling English-language daily not only no longer runs front page pseudoscience articles, but it has also wiped its history of them.

I, too, have lost all hard evidence of Dingy's brief moment of legitimacy. The newspaper cutout I vowed to save has vanished in my return to America—my relocation to the hills of Texas, a land of clear skies and straight talk. To tell of Dingy or the tiger in this new place is to talk of my past homes, places where it's possible that devils are devils and dust isn't just dust.

I CAN'T SLEEP IN THE BACK BEDROOM

SARAH CARSON

I.

I can't sleep in the back bedroom. When I was young the bed used to be against the wall, and it was better that way. Amanda Benko would string blankets from the ceiling fan, and we'd pretend we were being raped. I would do what she did—my thick little legs squeezing my pillow, my thick little hands wondering what to do.

II.

GG says Grandpa's grandpa may have died in the back bedroom. The bed was against the wall then, the mirror covered in fleece. No one had any way to know whether it was a coma or a case of the baddest kind of diarrhea. They did not drain the blood from his body. They did not look for abnormalities in his lungs.

III.

When I was young the bed used to be against the wall, and against the wall there used to be a doghouse. GG paid some boys to break it apart: board by board, wasp nest by garter snake. I used to spend hours sitting atop it, staring at the freeway, pretending I was with someone handsome, someone stronger than the disappearing. "It won't happen to us," he'd whisper, and I'd believe his every, imaginary word.

IV.

Outside the window now I can hear the sound of neighbors leaving. Their voices are muffled until they're angry, until I no longer hear them, until the realtor takes down the mini-blinds. When they're gone the rain will pool in their yard until tadpoles find their way to the water. The blacktop will crack. The screen door will get caught in west winds and linger. A stray dog will take up shelter on the porch.

LEAN WINTER, GLORIOUS HUNGER

W. TODD KANEKO

A man knows how grief tastes.
Everything he has lost lingers
on the back of his tongue.

He knows how new teeth feel
on his lips, that wolf's heart beating
for antelope deep in winter.

Cattle brand, rope burn, hoof
print—this is the tarnish of misery
on an animal's hide, cruelty's mark

hidden in the slither of a man's guts.
The body is always ready to surrender
to a more violent mouth. A wolf

buries his head in the stomach
of a desperate man—each knows
how the other feels.

THE SECOND THANKSGIVING
TOM BATTEN

HEY! HEY, King Massasoit! Hey, it's me, William. From the settlement? Wow, I can't believe I'm running into you like this, this is so funny. Yeah, I guess we are pretty close to your village, huh? I was just out for a walk, getting some fresh air. Yeah, lots of bodies sort of moldering around the settlement these days, so it's nice to get away for a little while. Take a deep breath without getting any flies in your mouth or anything like that. Sometimes just getting away and getting some fresh air is what you need to get through the week.

Hey, you know what me and some of the guys from the settlement were just talking about the other day? This is why it's so funny, running into you. Remember around this time last year, you and some of your guys brought all that food over to the settlement and we had a feast? Why did we not do that again? That was so nice. Just a real fun sort of bonding night. And you know, it's one of those things, like, I kept meaning to ask you guys back over, but something would always come up. One week, it would be smallpox, the next we'd be all locked up in these debates over whether or not to resort to cannibalism. You know how it goes, the days just get away from you. But anyway, like I was saying, wouldn't it be fun if you guys came over for another feast this year? Say, maybe tomorrow? And if it's not too much trouble, maybe you guys could supply all the food?

Yeah, you did, you gave us all those seeds and everything last year so we could grow our own crops, and like I said then it was really so, so nice of you. You won't believe what happened, actually. It's really embarrassing. Well, some of us got spooked that the crops were cursed because they saw a black cat over near the field and thought it was a witch in animal form. Burned everything, burned it all down. You must have seen the smoke. So get this, the cat ended up belonging to this widow, Mary Goodman, so of course we drown her and the cat, as you do, and afterwards we're standing around waiting for her body to rise up, and nothing. She wasn't a witch at all! That cat was just a cat! There were some red faces in the settlement that day, for sure. Mine was one of them, I can admit that. But you know, even though a lot of us starved to death this year, if we had to do it all again? I'd burn that field in a heartbeat. Better safe than sorry, right?

Oh, you know what you guys should bring over? How about some of that venison? I've never had better venison in my life than the venison you guys brought over last year. You don't think of venison as being a succulent meat, but something about the way you guys do it, maybe it's the arrows or something? Succulent. Yeah, actually we haven't done much hunting lately, unfortunately. We've really been trying to conserve our bullets. Well, we've needed them to fend off the members of the settlement who have in fact turned to cannibalism. Yeah, it's really sad, actually, and you know my heart does go out to them, in a way. I'll admit it… well, you remember my wife? Elizabeth? Oh, that's so sweet of you. No, actually, she died giving birth to our son a couple months ago. Oh, thanks, thanks. It was a rough couple of days, but you know, these things happen. Anyway, she died, right, and I'm sitting there with her corpse, and yes, I will admit, for a second I did think it would be a real waste to just bury all that meat. Not proud of that, but it did occur to me. This was like a month after the incident with the crops. But did I go through with it? No, of course not. I mean, you don't just eat your wife's corpse because you're starving, you know? What is this, Jamestown or something? Those guys, yeesh.

Anyway, so funny running into you. And really, come on over and bring us some food sometime soon. This is not one of those "Oh, we'll have to do lunch, and then you don't see the person for a year" things. This is a real, legitimate invitation. I mean, if we don't get together soon, we never will, because me and everyone else over there is going to die really, really soon if we don't get something to eat. Which actually wouldn't be too bad, I guess, since I'd get to see my wife and son again in Heaven. Oh, yeah, sorry. I should have said. My son died, like, right away without my wife around to keep him alive. Anyway. Hope you guys can make it. No need to RSVP. Just as soon as you can.

THREE HIKES IN THE COLUMBIA RIVER GORGE

WILLIAM FOSTER

I. DECEMBER 29

YESTERDAY, I hiked a short portion of the Pacific Crest Trail in the Hatfield Wilderness. The forest was covered lightly in snow, silent and still, encouraging of a leisurely pace. After a mile or so of gentle switchbacks, I lingered on a cliffside to rest and take in a sweeping view of Mount Hood and its foothills. I lay supine on a fallen tree, observed the drift of clouds and birds, and basked for a while, eyes closed, in the low roar of distant wind. When eventually I stood up to begin the return trip, I was startled to see a lovely woman emerging from the slope above the trail. I introduced myself and invited her to walk along with me, and she obliged. We conversed effortlessly and found so many things to bond over, and by the time we were back at the parking lot, had decided without reservation that we should get married. I drove her to my cabin in Hood River to introduce to my friends, but she was very shy and said she wanted to stay on the deck for the night, that she'd sleep there and that we'd talk again in the morning. "Of course," I said, and I spent the evening inside, eating dinner, playing cards, drinking wine and stepping outside now and then to check on her. Later, I kissed her goodnight and went to bed, but I hardly slept. I was so excited to wake up and share with her the morning, the rest of the day, the rest of the weekend and the rest of our lives. But when morning came and I threw on my clothes and hurried outside to see her, she was not the same woman with whom I had spent the previous afternoon. She was just a puddle of water soaked into the planks of the deck. That's when I realized she wasn't a woman at all. She was just a big chunk of ice I had yanked out of a frozen waterfall. When my friend saw me sobbing, he kneeled beside me, put his hand on my shoulder and said, "William, I know this is difficult, but there are other fish in the sea." To which I replied, "That platitude is hardly adequate for what just happened here. Please, let me be alone. Go back inside. Well, first bring me a cinnamon roll, and then go back inside."

II. JANUARY 5

The Ruckel Ridge Loop is reliably desolate in any season, and in the wet winter weather, it's especially so. Counterclockwise, the rocky trail rises four thousand feet over four miles to a densely wooded plateau, then descends more gradually over six miles back to the trailhead. I didn't see a soul until midway through the latter part, when I encountered an old, sweat-drenched albino man resting against a large boulder. He drew me into a conversation about our respective journeys. He had started hours earlier than I had and was making very slow progress. "This downhill part is the hardest for me, what with my bad knees and back," he explained wearily. With the steep ascent well behind me, I felt quite energized and light-footed, but I didn't say so. I was suddenly and unusually self-conscious of my youth and health, which he appeared to be regarding wistfully. After a bit of small talk, the old man finally said, "Well, you enjoy the rest of your hike. I certainly won't catch up with you. Happy New Year!" I walked away thinking, "Yowza, that situation was abounding in metaphors for this Road of Life on which we all walk," but as I was trying to decipher the symbolism behind the albinism aspect specifically, I tripped over a root, fell face-first into a rock and shattered all of my front teeth. I carried the shards home in the small, outermost pocket of my JanSport and locked them up in a keepsake box. For the foreseeable future, I will be eating only soft foods that don't require incisors, foods such as buckwheat porridge, Swedish Fish, cheese grits, guimauves au chocolat, spicy cheese grits, peanut butter, cashew butter, regular salt-n-butter grits, gummy worms, escargot à la Romana, Hubba Bubba Cherry Squeeze Pops, Go-Gurt, jalapeño cheese grits, Tom's Tasty Tomato Soup (hold the Brown Butter Croutons), butterscotch puddin', 'nilla puddin', creamy stone-ground grits, Fun Dip, horseradish mashed potatoes, soft scrambled eggs, Hubba Bubba Watermelon Squeeze Pops, cotton candy, avocado milkshakes, pureed haddock, Hubba Bubba Grape Squeeze Pops, banana flambé, crème brûlée (crust removed), Bartlett pear sorbet, chanterelle pâté, dewberry frappé.

III. JANUARY 18

Last April, I hiked McCall Point Trail, a short climb through the hills above Mosier, where the firry topography of the Cascade Range bleeds into Eastern Oregon's shrubby high desert terrain. Today, I hiked it again. In the springtime, the hillsides are studded with colorful wildflowers—yellow bells, prairie stars, Carey's balsamroot, fringe cups, shooting stars, etc.—and in winter, lichens and moss relieve the general starkness with bright, varying shades of pastel green. In spring, when the steep path was slick with mud, I plucked a stout, waist-high walking stick from the trailside to help secure my footing. Today, the mud was frozen nearly solid, which enabled me to climb swiftly and stickless to the summit. There, on the peak of the narrow ridge that nine months ago had afforded a panoramic view of the Columbia River to the north and Mount Hood to the south, I was completely enfolded in mist. I could not see more than twenty feet in any direction. On the south edge of the ridge, rainwater blowing from leafless trees had frozen horizontally in the high winds coming out of the gorge so that each branch appeared to be accentuated with inch-long cartoon motion lines. I was thirsty and I hadn't brought my water bottle, so I wet my tongue on these tiny, icy shelves. Walking back toward the center of the ridge, I noticed on the ground two relics from my presence here in April: 1. my walking stick, lying in the very spot where I left it, and 2. just a few feet from the stick, an orange peel, discarded by some careless hiker, which at the time I had intended, but for some reason failed, to carry out with me, thus relieving the landscape of its blight. The mist (I suppose it was the mist) put an idea in my head. I picked up the stick and slid its tip beneath the peel, which to my surprise was still firm after nearly a year of exposure. I lifted the peel off the ground, used my hand to ensure that it was stably situated on the stick, and catapulted it with all my strength into the fog on the gorge side of the crest. I regretted the decision before the stick even finished tracing its arc. All of which is to say, if you hike McCall Point Trail and you see a stout, waist-high walking stick at the summit, leave it be. I intend to return to the summit, reclaim my stick, find the peel, carry the peel on the tip of the stick all the way down the trail and put it in the bin where it belongs.

THINGS WE DO TO FILL THE HOLES

ERIN ELIZABETH SMITH

Back porches, the progression of green
in your grandmother's tomatoes
and the blur of her air conditioning
in the New South heat. The July-ness
of June and the drag
of menthols in the teeth. Chicken baking
in someone else's oven
whose temperature you do not understand.
The fabric softener smell
of new sheets.
Boys. Alcohol
in sneaked cups
and the synapses of new legs
against your own.
The treehouse youth of your best friend's
house. Your rebirthed hometown
and the dwindling number
on the electronic scale.
Baths, always a day away.
Hands on your exhausted shoulder,
songs from other loves
that rafted you onto puddles
of cheap bourbon
and surprisingly strong wine.

If only there was a way back
to your own bed,
the one three weeks emptied
from that marriage experiment
we all try—
the velour throw nearly a testament
to the ridiculousness of promise,
the hand first held
beneath a table at a bar in a state
you barely remember.
The soggy heat of him
damping the body,
opening something
that still cannot be filled.

UNIFIED THEORY
TONY MANCUS

the static in
exstacy, the lipper
average defeat
no current
we can't hold
our heads
together fine
all mystery
ruin by ruin
rooms of furniture
bent legged
walk off
the damnable
dodo lost
our positive
terminals
are sparky
yet—claw handle
opens/drops

a needle
haystacks
in groove

LEFTOVERS
NATE WAGGONER

NOW I eat all my mother's food. I live with her and my younger brother, Elvis, who never left and who writes fan fiction all day. I'm twenty-six and broke and also I am forbidden to eat any of Elvis's mac and cheese or tuna. My mother doesn't consume anything except brie off a butter knife and Pinot grigio. She is callused and gaunt and lives on disability. Dad died falling down the stairs when I was too young to remember. Anyway, so I mostly eat whatever's available. Elvis never eats leftovers and he leaves his mac and cheese uncovered in the fridge and it turns red and tastes sour. I will find the one thing left in the produce drawer, a red onion, say, and pare off the fuzzy parts and eat it raw. I eat spoonfuls of mayo until I feel adequately sick. The mayo sometimes sticks to my scruffy facial hair and I enjoy it all day. Once, I found an old box of Price Club microwave popcorn and none of the bags could pop quite right anymore—about half of the kernels would pop and the bags would get burned on the side, and I would open the bags and, making a puppet face with my hand, grab as many popped or unpopped kernels as possible and stuff them into my mouth, burning both hand and mouth in the process.

It's exhausting to live like this, to be me. I need ten hours of sleep a night so I can get up and fume and starve and masturbate three times a day and get into fights with people on the Internet or in the parking lot of Trader Joe's. It takes all my strength.

At this point, I think my mother is trying to starve me out. She has the advantage of never being hungry, but I have the advantage of the willingness to eat her food, thus resulting in a greater potential of starvation for her. When she does eat, she sucks the food up, inhales it like an Italian mobster, her only delight in the destruction of the food, not in the taste or the texture or in the feeling of filling herself.

We were always the kind of family who not only had some emergency happening all the time, but if you came anywhere near us, we would be forced to coerce or guilt or cajole or browbeat you into helping out in some capacity. Right now, we're at an all-time low of three cats, the high being twelve, cats that would constantly shit and knock things over and eat human food and other objects left around, to the point where we even designated a bathroom and another room just to be, basically, the Rooms Where Litterboxes Are, the cat's bathrooms, which I think, I hope, no other family has ever done. Cats get old and their aim gets terrible and they get the feces and litter stuck in their paws and they track it all through the house. We keep chickens, in a city where urban farming is pretty much unheard of and everyone seems to work for a website called Zazz, which no one can really articulate what it does. Mom gets up at six every morning and feeds and yells at the chickens, calls them *li'l sluts*. Goes to bed, at 9 pm, a glass of white wine having taken its nightly toll on her system in every usual way except ever building up a tolerance to the effects of a single glass of wine at 9 pm. That wine held a special fascination for Elvis and me as kids, colored and most likely textured the same as our life-giving appy juice but causing Mom to fall asleep and giggle and yell. Mom put herself through college waiting tables—on roller skates, she'd always remind us—until she could get a job as an eighth-grade English teacher, which apparently you could do in those days with just a BA in English and no teaching-work experience and a foul mouth and cat hair all over your shirt back. She talks about Proust, and through her Southern accent, affects sort of an English accent on the pronunciation of certain words like "dis*gust*," although I guess that's a word that lends itself to that.

Back to the food: there *used* to be food. Remember I said we never had to cook or learn anything or do anything? It's true. She did it all herself, and there was angel hair pasta with the little canned clam chunks, and peanut butter and Marshmallow Fluff, and tuna melts and Cream of Wheat with the raspberry drizzle dripped on top in the shape of a heart on Valentine's Day. I moved in here after Chloe left, and the one time I managed to go to a '90s party and make out with a girl named Tara and bring her back to my mother's place and sneak her into my room, Mom stormed in halfway through and kicked Tara out, made her walk home, and told me, "Ah never wanted you."

I guess what I'm saying with this online dating profile is, uh, good luck.

DAN BELOW

ANDREW BLOSSOM

WHEN A short vacation became available to him, Dan went to visit his parents. A house fire broke out on the third day of his visit, and Dan happened to sleep through it. He woke up to find he was dead and, furthermore, in Hell.

Huh, he said. That's a surprise.

In his life, Dan had never believed in Satan or any of that junk. Yet now he found himself perched atop a rocky outcropping, and there were flames all about, and in the distance there was a ridge, and over the knobby top of the ridge came the sound of about one hundred thousand screams all at once. He presumed this screaming indicated souls burning or being flayed or having their skin pierced by nettles. Whatever it was, it sounded just awful.

This really beats all, he said.

Dan wondered what he'd done in his life that was so bad it had caused him to end up in Hell. As he sat atop the rocky outcropping on which he'd awoken, he searched his mind but could not think of a single thing. He said, Maybe I just didn't live a good enough life. This idea scared him: that there had been standards of behavior and that he had somehow failed to perform according to their merits. However, by gazing at his fiery surroundings, Dan was able to assure himself that to worry thus was moot. Whatever his life had been did not matter. He was in a new situation entirely. He had best buck up and face reality.

What to do—that was the uncertainty.

Dan stretched out on his outcropping. He'd gone to bed with a stiff neck but now felt limber. He scooted out to the edge and took a look around. If, while still in the world, Dan had bothered to picture Hell, he'd thought of it according to the Dante model, with the descending circles and Satan frozen in ice at the bottom and Judas being chomped on eternally in Satan's mouth. Dan had been an English major once, and had for that reason read at least two-thirds of *The Inferno*. However, the landscape below him resembled something more like the American Southwest, albeit with fire just everywhere.

The sky above was the black of night. An eternal night, he supposed. The eternal night of Hell. The sun probably wouldn't ever come out, seeing as he was underground or in an alternate dimension or whatever. But there was plenty of ambient light. The abundance of fire lit up the sandy red landscape as if it were daytime seen through an orange filter. The golden moment, all of the time. Dan could see across the desert for what seemed like miles, at least as far as the knobby ridge over which came the sound of about one hundred thousand screams all at once.

Always night, and yet always day. It was kind of pretty.

He sighed, and scooted back from the edge. He thought, Isn't there an accountant for new arrivals? Or some kind of greeter? But maybe it was better no one was around. Maybe that way he could avoid being tortured for a while.

There it was again, the queasy feeling in his gut.

What had he done in life that was worthy of torture? Had he harmed anyone? He had been a computer consultant, for Pete's sake. Oops, he thought. By *Pete*, he meant St. Peter. Maybe that amounted to blasphemy. He'd have to watch himself. Maybe that was why he was here, all the times he said things like Jesus H. Christ. Which would be pretty stupid. But then the rules could be strict even if he didn't respect them. I mean, he thought, clearly I am in the shit here and that should tell me something about what to believe. Plus, I have said worse things in life, like cunt bitch piss puke whore ass fuck slag balls scrotum boner. So if there is a standard re: language, I am definitely screwed. Also, I masturbated and had premarital sex and scratched myself. Sometimes I took home office supplies. Often I lied through my teeth. But usually I did that to protect someone's feelings. Like when Marjorie had cancer and her hair had fallen out from the chemotherapy and I told her she looked lovely. Or when Cheryl said, What's the matter? And I said, Nothing's the matter, I love you. Whereas inside I was thinking about how tired I was of the faces she made, but I couldn't tell her without triggering some kind of episode and/or lecture. So there's that. But isn't that the human condition?

He was still for a moment.

It is the human condition, he thought. I don't know how I'm to blame for any of it.

Then, after another moment: Anyway, you're here now. Don't make a scene.

He lay back and closed his eyes. He put his hands behind his head and crossed one foot over the other. He wondered if he should go to sleep. He wondered if he could go to sleep. Up there atop his outcropping it was warm—muggy, but not unbearable. There was a stone poking his back. A hot breeze scooted over him, and on the breeze came the hint of something like charcoal.

Dan sat up. He said, Maybe I should go exploring.

Whoopsie-daisy, came a gruff voice from somewhere below him. Here's one of those what fell through the cracks.

Dan was startled. The idea about exploring was the first thing he'd said aloud in quite some time. Fancy that, that someone should be nearby to hear it. A minion of Hell, no doubt. Dan turned his back to the view of the knobby ridge and scooted on his rear to the opposite side of the outcropping. He looked down.

Ah, he said aloud. Inside he thought, Crap.

About ten feet below him was some kind of huge hulking man thing. Its skin was a reddish brown, somewhat ruddier in color than the sand. Large horns protruded from its forehead and curled back again. It had big, amber-colored eyes, which it now turned in Dan's direction. It had two huge muscular arms with leather bands strapped around each wrist. There were also two belts of ammunition that made an X across its hulking chest. And in its paw, a shotgun.

All right, now. Come on down, the thing said. I've been looking all over for you. That's what I've been doing.

Dan stood up slowly and dusted his rear. For me? he asked.

The creature shrugged. Well. For someone like you. Come on now.

Can you shoot me if I'm already dead?

Oh, yes, the creature said. It hurts like you wouldn't believe. It's worse because you don't die. The wound never gets better, you see. The creature pointed the shotgun lazily in Dan's direction. Imagine that, if you will.

Dan sighed. It looked like he was caught.

He started carefully down the ledge. The rock crumbled some underfoot, kicking up a fine orangey dust. When he came to a stop beside the beast, he could see how massively it loomed over him. He felt puny. Fragile. Insignificant. He thought, I'm really in a bad spot now. The thing was a good head taller than Dan—that was before one counted the horns—and at least twice as wide. Its red muscles looked like they'd been chiseled out of rock.

The beast reached into a satchel at its waist and removed a piece of twining. It motioned for Dan to raise his wrists.

Handcuffs, it said.

Dan obliged, and the beast bound his arms together. The twining transformed immediately into a thin strip of flame. Dan cried out and dropped to his knees.

Name's Bernard, the beast said. I'll be taking you to Central. It wagged one stubby finger at Dan. Get on up. It'll keep burning, but you'll get used to it.

Water flooded Dan's eyes. He squeezed them shut. He could hardly believe the pain in his wrists. He knew he was in Hell, and he supposed this was the sort of pain one felt in Hell, and yet the sensation of it was blinding. It was like he was holding his limbs over a campfire and watching the skin sizzle off. It was like someone was pressing a soldering iron into every point of flesh the handcuffs surrounded. Dan was sure he could feel the skin expanding around the wrists, bubbling outward and bursting, oozing juice and pus and blood. Yet when he opened his eyes again, nothing much seemed to be happening. The skin was raw where the flames touched it and that was all. Dan held his hands above his head, as if to say, Please, I'll just come with you. But no words came. They were caught in his throat.

He dropped his hands.

Bernard said, It's not so bad. You'll see. He grabbed Dan by the shoulder with one hefty paw and stood him up. He brushed the dirt from Dan's knees. Up you go, he said. That's a brave soldier. Then he hefted the gun barrel and pointed down the slope at the dry, fiery valley below them. Now let's get marching.

Dan stumbled forward, his feet slipping along the dirt. Tears poured involuntarily from his eyes, and red dust stuck to the tracks they left. Dan could feel it hardening on his cheeks. A white kind of light obscured his vision. His brain ached with the pain of the cuffs.

Whoopsie-daisy! Careful! Bernard said. It gets tricky in places. He shook his massive head, which caused his jutting horns to turn in the air. We wouldn't want you splitting your cranium open, would we? That's one of those things we would not want.

This— Dan stopped, and gasped. This is something else.

Bernard nodded. Sorry, fellow, he said. He gestured toward the landscape. Think I don't know? Take a look where I live. Lots of pain to go around. Now what we have to do, right, is get down this side of the formation, then hike all the way around to the other side—that's the side we want—and then we have to head back toward that ridge that you might have noticed when you were luxuriating up there in your perch.

Dan forced his eyes closed and slowed his step.

Bernard poked him in the ribs with the shotgun. The ridge whence came all the screaming?

Dan started forward again. Yeah, he said. I noticed it.

Bernard smiled. All right then. That's home.

They reached the ground and began to wind their way along the rock wall, the face of which loomed now to their right.

Bernard said, What did you do? In the world?

Dan exhaled, coughed. Computers, he said.

Computers! Another one! Bernard smiled, showing thick sandy teeth that were set in his jaw like stones. Never got the hang of them myself. Guess that's why I'm a worker bee.

Eventually, the rock wall tapered into the ground and Dan and Bernard were able to cross it. Dan found he could once again see the knobby ridge over which came the sound of about one hundred thousand screams all at once. He paused, briefly, and Bernard let him, but then the beast nudged Dan with the shotgun and they started forward. They walked for what must have been two hours, their progress slowed by the need to circumvent pits of flame and the occasional crevasse. They did not seem to get much closer to the ridge, but the sound of the hundred thousand or so screams was now a bit louder in Dan's ears.

Okay, said Bernard as they approached two reddish boulders set side by side in the desert sand. Let's take a break.

Dan leaned his weight against the nearest rock. You know, he said. You were right. These handcuffs don't seem so bad anymore. He held up his hands to indicate the band of fire twisting around his wrists. The skin had cooked long enough that it had grown red and dry underneath the cuffs, but Dan felt very little of the initial pain.

See? Right? Bernard smiled. What did I tell you? Do you want some booze?

Yes, Dan said. Yes, I do.

Bernard shifted the shotgun from his massive right hand to his equally impressive left. He reached into his satchel to retrieve a metal flask. It won't do much for you in the way of drunkenness, he said. But it'll make you feel better. Still some solace in the old habits. He set the flask on the boulder, shifted the shotgun back into his right hand, and then picked up the flask once more with his left. He held it toward Dan and said, Think you could uncap that for me?

Dan cocked an eyebrow. He took the container. Have you ever considered setting down the gun? he asked.

Have I? Bernard said. Indeed I have.

Dan looked at Bernard for a moment. So?

So? Bernard replied. I can't.

Dan unscrewed the top of the flask. Come again? he asked. He looked at Bernard, but the beast had its big head cocked toward the ground so that its horns pointed skyward. Dan poured the booze in his mouth, being careful not to bring the handcuffs close to his face, as he supposed they might burn violently on unconditioned skin. The liquid had a bite for which Dan was unprepared. He coughed, and his esophagus closed.

Bernard sighed. I can't. Ever set it down, the gun. This is my thing. Don't ask me to explain it. He held out the paw that was free of the gun, and Dan handed him the flask. Bernard's giant red mitt wrapped all the way around the small container. It was like a normal sized man enclosing a bottle cap in his palm. Bernard tipped the flask up, letting the liquid pour into his throat. He shuddered, shook his head and grinned. Good, he said.

Then he handed the flask back to Dan and indicated the cap should be placed onto it. Dan did as he was told.

Bernard belched. A burst of flame shot out from his nose.

I don't understand, Dan said, returning the flask, which Bernard slipped in his satchel. Why can't you let go of the gun?

I just can't. As I said the first time.

Huh, Dan said.

They were quiet for a moment.

Dan said, Can you prove it?

Bernard gave Dan a brief look. Then he stood up and stretched his arms out on either side—one hand clutching the shotgun, the other balled in a fist. He opened both hands so that his palms faced the blackness overhead. Slowly, he turned his hands to face the red ground. As he did, his fingers closed around the gun. He said, See?

What? Dan said. You're holding it.

Bernard looked over and saw that his fingers were wrapped around the gun. His head kicked back a little, as if he were surprised. No, Bernard said. Wait. Hold on.

The hell beast stretched out his arms again and faced his open palms toward the black sky. Then he rotated his palms once more toward the ground. As he did, his fingers closed around the gun.

You're still holding it, Dan said.

Bernard furrowed his brow. Okay, he said. That's enough. I'm not holding it. It just sticks to me. He brought his arms down to his side. Anyway, we should get going.

Dan said, So when you say you can't let go, is it more a mental—

I CANNOT LET GO OF IT. Bernard opened his mouth all the way to reveal his sandstone teeth. His voice was a massive, fearsome thing. White fear shot up Dan's spine and he pulled back instantaneously and fell behind his rock, making his body small, turning his face away, tucking into his bound arms. For a while, no one said anything. Somehow, Dan could hear Bernard's voice echoing in the expanse of desert, even though there was nothing nearby for it to echo against.

Ah look, Bernard said eventually. I'm sorry. He stepped forward.

Slowly, Dan turned to face the beast. He unfurled his body. He thought, Easy does it. When he looked again at Bernard, he could see the creature's big amber eyes. The pupils were pitch black, yet flecks of red floated lazily in the yellow of the corneas.

An indeterminate kind of sadness washed through Dan. He said, Are you being punished?

Bernard snorted. Excuse me?

Are you being punished?

Bernard looked away. Humans, he said.

Suddenly, Dan wanted to know everything about his companion, about how it had come to believe a firearm was fixed permanently to its grip. Surely there were levels of torture here, this being Hell, and perhaps over the eons different kinds of torture turned into different kinds of responsibility. If that were true, then had Bernard once been a man? Could Dan believe such a thing? Or was it simply that everyone suffered and that was the rule of the land? Dan opened his mouth to speak, but stopped, for now there was a low rumbling sensation, like the sound of thunder. The air all about them seemed to vibrate. It was as if a wave of electricity were passing over and around he and Bernard. There was a moment of absolute stillness, and then came a soft popping noise from somewhere above and behind them, like the sound of fireworks in the far distance. Dan turned to look into the blackness of the sky.

Here comes the rain, Bernard said.

High above them—at what might have been the level of the clouds, had there been clouds up there to look at—there appeared a series of what seemed to be tiny bursts of smoke. Minor explosions, maybe. The eruptions looked like the debris kicked up from bomb drops Dan had seen on television, only upside-down and glowing. Each burst shone with a faint luminescence and lasted only a few seconds before dissolving back into the black. At first there were ten or twenty, but soon the number of wisps had multiplied exponentially, and an erratic, pulsating cloud of energy hung over the area beyond the ridge.

Dan could sense motion now in the black sky. He dropped his eyes to the knobby ridge, over which came the sound of about one hundred thousand screams all at once. The great flames poking from above the top of the ridge had grown in intensity, and against their dancing light Dan could make out streaks of something falling through the atmosphere. It was precipitation he was seeing. Precipitation, in Hell. The overall effect was similar to that of glimpsing a fine rainstorm on a distant desert horizon.

Yet Dan's stomach began to twist in on itself.

Jesus H. Christ, he said. Those are bodies.

Bernard nodded. He brushed red dirt from his pants and then clapped his rocky hands together. Droppers, he said. That was you. He tapped Dan on the shoulder, then jerked his horns toward the sky overhead. Dan moved his eyes from the pulsating mass over the ridge and turned to look up into the blackness above him. Here and there came faint puffs of energy throughout the atmosphere. Wherever one occurred, he realized, a body was falling into the desert. As you can see, Bernard continued, most go straight to Central. A few thousand end up scattered across the countryside. Inevitable, I think, as the numbers are so high. We don't ever find everyone. But we do all right.

Dan faced the hell beast. How did you find me?

I don't know, Bernard said. He shrugged. I've been out for weeks. Out much farther, much farther into the waste than you can know about. I didn't find a single soul in all that time. And that's unusual. He gazed for a while at the bodies raining down beyond the distant ridge, and then he said, Coming back, I had a feeling I should see about that particular line of rock, on the side closest to me. And there you were, talking away to yourself. So I can't explain it. Instinct, I guess. Do anything long enough. Know what I mean?

The beast nudged Dan in the back with his shotgun. This feeling of steel through his shirt indicated Dan should move.

How long have you been doing this? Dan asked as he started walking.

About three thousand years.

Three thousand years? Dan stopped, jaw open, and looked at Bernard.

That's right.

Have shotguns existed for three thousand years?

Bernard shrugged his massive shoulders. They have here.

Don't you ever want to do something else?

Bernard laughed. It was a rasping sound that came from deep within his broad chest. Oh yes, he said. I do.

They trudged along for a while, Dan turning the thoughts over in his skull.

As a young child, he had smacked the family dog whenever it misbehaved. Rusty, the mutt. He hadn't meant to be cruel. He just hadn't known any better. He'd loved Rusty, but who at six knows how to control a dog appropriately? As he grew older, there were other dogs, and Dan learned how to handle them responsibly. This was one reason he became so ashamed when he remembered hitting Rusty, the thump his palm made against the dog's side.

What if that had been the thing?

Then he hadn't ever had a chance.

God, it could be anything. Childhood alone was a minefield.

He never gave change to homeless people.

And all those years with Cheryl—crap, those years had been one giant fabrication. Lying and lying until he came to believe the lies. Playacting at love when inside he was drained out, a shell made hollow by her abuse. She had been awful to him and for the longest time Dan had been very weak. He'd lacked courage. Sure he had—he knew that now. He'd been false to himself. These were things he'd had to learn in hindsight. He had learned.

So what was with all that pain waiting beyond the knobby ridge?

Were they going to torture him for his bad decisions?

A wave of nausea pushed through him. He was going to suffer, no matter what he calculated the cause of that suffering to be. They were going to slice his eyes with blades and he would scream in misery and then the eyes would heal and they would do it again. They were going to ram sticks underneath his fingernails until the nails splintered and tore away. They were gong to puncture his feet with hot pokers and drive hooks through his chest and hang him above the flames until his flesh charred and fell from his bones. They were going to cut off his ears and stuff them into his throat and he would suffocate again and again and pure fear would wrack his useless body. They would cut his heart from his chest and he would feel every moment of its removal; they would place his heart beating in his hands and later they would make him eat it in pieces. They would torture him unceasingly, and when the pain overwhelmed him, when he passed out, they would lacerate his skin and stuff the wounds with salt. Dan knew this, knew it for certain. All of this pain, it was coming to him.

Or he was marching toward it.

He planted his heel in the sand and spun around.

Bernard stopped. He stepped back, eyebrows raised, and lifted the shotgun slightly.

After a moment, Dan spoke. Look, Bernard, he said. It strikes me we're in the same predicament. We're both trapped.

Bernard regarded him quietly. Is that right? he said.

Dan nodded, and took a breath, let the warm air rush into his lungs. Around them small blooms of flame pushed up through cracks in the dry, broken soil. Dan said, You seem like an okay guy, and I don't think you're any happier here than I am.

Bernard said nothing.

So what are we doing? Marching me off to my fate? All those eons of torture or whatever? If this desert is as big as you say, there has to be something else. You say you don't find everyone. So why don't we make a break for it? We've got all of eternity to look around. Maybe we can even find a way out. I mean, this is Hell, sure, but who knows? Maybe there's a back door.

Red spots floated in the amber of Bernard's eyes. He nodded and smiled gently, bearing the hint of his sandstone teeth.

See that, Dan? That's Central. He thrust his gun in the direction of the knobby ridge, over which came the tips of great flames and the sound of about one hundred thousand screams all at once. That's where we're going to go. It's where everybody goes, eventually. I like you. Don't get me wrong. You're a sweet fellow. I like most everybody. But that's the way it is.

Dan looked at Bernard, unbelieving.

Bernard lifted one weighty arm in the air and fired the shotgun at the sky. A jet of flame shot from the barrel as it retorted. Anyway so, he said. Let's get going.

Dan swallowed. It was hard to do. There was dust in his throat. He turned once more to face the knobby ridge. Slowly, he put one foot in front of the other, watching his feet as they sank slightly into the red dirt of the infernal desert. He could feel his stomach as it seemed to drop away from his body. There it was, the pain, ahead of him, somewhere beyond the knobby ridge. He might never know what he'd done to deserve it, but it was coming. And in this moment, it occurred to Dan that perhaps it didn't matter how he'd lived his life. Maybe it didn't matter for anyone at all. Maybe this was what everyone got, a trip to Central and endless torture, fire on the skin and writhing limbs, no matter what they'd done. Who said that there was another option beside this one? You could hope for the best, but all around him, everywhere he looked, there was desert and flame as far as he could see, as far as he could conceive. He twisted his hands around to scratch at the red welts where his wrists had grown dry beneath the handcuffs. Hanging above the horizon was the undulating cloud, spitting bodies into the great fire. Over the ridge came a sound, and as he moved forward it settled in Dan's ears, and he knew it to be the sound of one hundred thousand voices, all of which were calling his name.

ISSUE SEVEN
THE LONESOME FOGHORN BLOWS

BAD NAUGHTY

REBECCA WADLINGER

Bad naughty handwriting in your letter like mumbling on a page, I can't read it. Bad naughty suitcase circling on the baggage claim conveyor like no one ever packed it. Bad naughty chair wants everyone to use it, beneath the bad naughty table put some nasty dishes on it. Bad naughty spoon take it upstairs that'll show it. Bad naughty tax form pay a man named Eric Levine to file it. Bad naughty smokestack naughty landscape someone paint it. Bad naughty dinner boiled chicken come and get it. Bad naughty bookshelf stuffed with words I hope they choke it. Bad naughty crows sitting on the power line, seven in a row like *fuck fuck fuck fuck fuck fuck fuck it.*

THE TRUTH
CARSON MELL

IT WAS love at first sight. He was six feet tall, thick, sandy-colored hair, slim and strong. He smoked cigarettes and laughed loudly and played the guitar. He slapped his friends on their backs and got more ice and said, "Hold on, hold on," as he picked out the next record. It was a real nice song.

Jane walked up to him and introduced herself as he read the record sleeve. He looked right past her, took something out of his pocket, handed it to a passing friend. "What's your name?" she said.

"Marco," he said, still not looking at her. He reset the needle on the record. Mandolins jangled. Then he looked down at her. She was a small woman, five-foot-two and skinny, but her eyes were powerful and dark. She didn't like most men. It was really rare for her to be attracted to someone and even more rare for her to just walk right up and introduce herself the way she did just now.

Once he started looking at her face, he couldn't stop. He told her as much, and they got pretty drunk together and went back to her place (he was living on a friend's couch at the time) and made love.

After they made love, he took her face in his hands and stared her dead in the eyes. "I'm a liar," he said. "You should know that about me. Sometimes I tell the truth, and sometimes I don't, but I don't care about the truth either way. Maybe it's a defect in me, I don't know, but I don't care. All my life I've been this way. But I like you. I like you a lot, but that doesn't change who I am. I just want to tell you this up front, right now, tonight. That from this moment on out, you won't be able to trust a single thing I say. You understand?"

"How do you lie, about other women?"

"About everything. That's all I'm going to say. And I'll never say it again, but it's the truth."

She stared at him for a long time, into his blue eyes, narrowed and intense, and kissed him. They made love again and fell asleep.

She woke to him cooking breakfast. Eggs and bacon and instant coffee. They ate a little bit of it. Her head was throbbing from the hangover.

"What you said last night," she said. "About the lying. What was all of that?"

He looked up at her. His eyes were wide and calm, nothing like they had been the night before. "I was just kidding. I'm sorry, I say crazy things when I get drunk."

"You didn't sound like you were kidding," she said. "You sounded really, really serious."

He shrugged, smiled. "I'm just a weirdo. I'm sorry. I hope I didn't freak you out."

"You kind of did."

"Sorry. Do you want me to leave?"

She looked at him for a long time. "Yeah, I'm sorry. It's just, you freaked me out."

He smiled sadly, got right up, and walked to the kitchen door that led to the back patio. "It's fine, I get it. I'm weird." He opened the door then paused. "I do like you, though, Jane. Really. And I don't like a lot of people. Everyone says weird things sometimes."

He didn't call her the next day, the next week. She thought about him a lot, about the way they'd made love. One day, a vase of exotic flowers appeared on her doorstep with a card that read: "Weird flowers from a weirdo. Sorry."

She put them on her kitchen table and stared at them. She picked up her cordless phone and called him.

Every few months, every few years, she would question him about that first night together. He'd get furious. "Oh Jesus Christ, this again! I said one weird thing." If she ever caught him in a fib, she'd bring it up. "Everybody fibs!" he'd yell. "Everybody tells little white lies!"

They had three children together. He was a great dad. Attentive and kind.

One summer, a hiker discovered a human femur in the woods behind their home. Police detectives came and found a few more human bones. They did tests and discovered they belonged to a young woman who'd gone missing the summer prior. Marco was questioned simply because of proximity. Jane watched through the glass, watched him charm them.

He shook their hands and patted their backs and walked them to the front door. Jane walked in and Marco was staring at the closed door with a serious expression, holding his elbows. He felt Jane's eyes on him and turned and said to her, "Poor woman."

Three years passed. It was their youngest's sixth birthday—their oldest was ten—when Jane found Marco smoking cigarettes on the front porch, away from everybody and staring out at the street with a very intense expression. An expression she had only seen on his face once before. "Something wrong?" She asked him.

"Nope," he said.

The next morning, he was gone. No note, no nothing. But Jane didn't need a note to understand. The whole time she'd known him, she'd known this day was coming.

WHAT'S IT ALL ABOUT, ALBERT?
NICOLE LANG

SPECIAL AGENT Albert Rosenfield appears in only eight episodes of *Twin Peaks*, but like the stinging insults he hurls around Twin Peaks, he leaves a mark.

Albert, an FBI forensics expert, arrives in Twin Peaks early in Season One, sporting dark sunglasses, flanked by two unnamed assistants (also clad in dark sunglasses) and carrying his metal briefcase. Albert's rapid-fire delivery and sharp tongue disrupt the sleepy Sheriff's Department, provoking eyerolls from receptionist Lucy and aggression from Sheriff Truman and his deputies. It's clear right off the bat: Twin Peaks and Albert just don't mix. He continues to alienate himself when he callously attempts to drill into the lifeless Laura Palmer on the autopsy table, earning both a black eye from Sheriff Truman and the disdain of notable townspeople.

Special Agent Dale Cooper, intuitive mystic that he is, immediately meshes with the quirky, otherworldly nature of Twin Peaks. He is accepted, while Albert prefers to remain the outsider. As colleagues in the FBI, the two share a deep mutual respect, although each is often left bewildered by the other's behavior. Albert represents the skeptic at home on the couch, the cynical yin to Cooper's earnest, eccentric yang.

Here are five standout moments on Albert's strange and difficult path.

1.

As Season Two begins, Albert is still chock full of insults and sarcasm, but a quick exchange he has with Agent Cooper offers hints to his complexities.

Agent Cooper asks him, "Albert, where does this attitude of general unpleasantness come from?"

Looking into the distance, Albert answers straightly, without his trademark flippancy, "I'll have to get back to you on that."

But fear not, it soon returns:

Cooper: "Well, if you don't want two black eyes on a regular basis, I suggest you make some kind of peace with rural life."

Albert: "Great. After the square dance, maybe we can all take a hayride."

2.

During a scene (Season Two, Episode Eight) in a hospital hallway following Nadine's overdose, Cooper listens intently as Big Ed recounts his woeful tale of unrequited romance with Norma and the origin of Nadine's eye patch. After ridiculing Big Ed, Albert makes a big show of the terrible hospital coffee, then reacts incredulously to Ed's heartfelt tale, going so far as to pull out a hanky in an almost Chaplinesque manner to wipe fake tears (of laughter) from his eyes. It's Albert as foil to the small-town hayseed melodrama, and pure fun.

3.

In the next episode, Cooper and Albert share breakfast, backdropped by a barbershop quartet (who appear to be smoking, not singing at all). Here, Albert begins to pave a gentler path—but, being Albert, it is of course a path paved with snark. After listening to Cooper tell him about a group of Tibetan kings known as "the Happy Generations":

Albert: "I've performed the autopsy on Jacques Renault. Stomach contents revealed... let's see, beer cans, a Maryland license plate, half a bicycle tire, a goat and a small wooden puppet. Goes by the name of Pinocchio."

Cooper: "You're making a joke!"

Albert: "I like to think of myself as one of the 'Happy Generations.'"

And a few moments later:

Albert: "How do you feel?"

Cooper: "Me?"

Albert: "I believe it's customary to ask after the health of the recently-plugged-three-times."

Cooper: "Thanks for asking."

Albert: "Don't get sentimental."

4.

The most well-known Albert scene is his speech to Sheriff Truman. Some fans dispute it as an outlandish turn in character, but I find it perfectly aligns with his uniqueness, saves him from villainy and eases his relationship with Truman. Not to mention solidifies him as a fan favorite. Truman has had enough, and after Albert likens him to a Neanderthal—"You might try walking without dragging your knuckles on the floor"—Truman grabs him and sneers:

"Albert, let's talk about knuckles. The last time I knocked you down, I felt bad about it. The next time is gonna be a real pleasure."

Albert spits right back: "Now, you listen to me. While I will admit to a certain cynicism, the fact is that I am a naysayer and hatchet man in the fight against violence. I pride myself in taking a punch and I'll gladly take another because I choose to live my life in the company of Gandhi and King. My concerns are global. I reject absolutely revenge, aggression and retaliation. The foundation of such a method... is love. I love you, Sheriff Truman."

Cooper: "Albert's path is a strange and difficult one."

5.

Here, finally, we know the real Albert in all his many facets. Back in Twin Peaks to warn Cooper that his old foe Windom Earle is seeking revenge, Albert enters the conference room, bumping into Bobby and Shelly, who are on their way out. "Get a life, punk!" he shouts after Bobby.

Sheriff Truman and Albert share a bear hug, genuinely happy to see each other again. After a spot-on imitation of Gordon Cole ("I'm worried about Coop!"), Albert begins a classic Albert briefing on Earle's recent activities.

"He's making his move, most definitely," Albert says to a pensive Cooper, who gazes through the window.

Albert gives Cooper's shoulder an encouraging squeeze and lightens the mood.

Albert: "Oh, Coop, about the uniform... Replacing the quiet elegance of the dark suit and tie with the casual indifference of these muted earth tones is a form of fashion suicide, but, uh, call me crazy—on you, it works."

Cooper: "Thank you, Albert."

This subtle exchange between the two borders on tender. It's the only time in the series that every aspect of Albert's character is fully realized within a scene and in all his difficult, competent, supportive and hostile glory. Although he appears one last time (in an attempt to bring Josie Packard to justice), this scene is Albert's swan song, and to my mind a much more fitting exit for an unforgettable character.

VANITY PLATES OF TWIN PEAKS
NICOLE LANG

1IDJAXX

JKW1EYE

1G0 2OEJ

NUU SHUZ

GRMNBZA

CRMD KRN

T0AD

5LNT DRPS

710 YEP

WOW BOB

WHPN2J0C

HWZ NEEE

WWBD 7

OOZING WITH POSSIBILITY

JULIE KARR

BIG MOMMA'S *House* is always playing at the plasma bank. Sometimes they show *The Fifth Element*, and once in a while, *Con Air*. You're only allowed to donate twice a week, at least two days apart, but if you know the routine, who works and when, you can sneak in a third visit from time to time. The cashier will discover you snuck in a third trip, but that's only after you've already donated and you're collecting your money. And at that point, what can they do? Give you your plasma back?

This particular trip was only a $15 day. The usual pricing is $15 on the first trip, $25 on the second, $20 on the third, $30 on the fourth and then back to $15. If you refer a new donor, you can get an extra $10 or $15. I don't talk to my friends about the plasma bank, but every now and then I can talk to a new person and convince them to write my name down as a referral while they fill out paperwork in the waiting room. It's good low-life karma.

"We're gonna start flagging your file if you keep this up."

"I can't keep track of when I'm not supposed to come in. That's on you."

I grab my money and walk past the other sad souls sitting there having their life sucked out of their veins, spun and separated into what is worth something and what isn't. Once the plasma is separated out from the blood, the worthless parts are forced back into your body. When you leave, it's your own worthlessness pulsing through you.

I tear my bandage off as I approach the double door exit back into the oppressive Florida summer heat. The sudden shift from the sterile, over air-conditioned building to the smell of hot cement and wild heat gives me goose bumps. I can hear the person at the front desk yelling at me to leave the bandage on for at least an hour. I shrug and throw the bandage in the overfilled trashcan out front.

I hop on my bike, another ill-advised decision on my part, and head to the gas station. As I lock my bike, I glance down and see a little blood running down my forearm. I quickly wipe it with my shirt and walk inside to buy a pack of cigarettes, a 12-pack and a prepackaged single-serving glazed cherry pie.

"$13.78, ma'am."

"Thanks," I say, handing the cashier two thirds of my human worth, looking down at my arm to make sure she can't see my worthlessness oozing out.

I'm sure that she can.

I get home, pop in a tape, sit on the couch, light a cigarette and open a beer.

"Seriously, again?"

"I know. I can't stop."

He shrugs, grabs a beer and sits down next to me.

"Buying this has ruined your life"

"No, don't worry. I was in shambles way before this."

"Fair enough."

A few months earlier, he found the complete *Twin Peaks* series on VHS at a yard sale for $15. Totally worth a day's pay of valued life. We finished the series within two weeks. Then I started compulsively rewatching it.

"What time do you work?" he asks

"Four, I think?"

"It's 3:50"

"Fuck."

"Which arm?"

"Uh, the right, please."

"Are you sure? There's a lot of scar tissue. Let's check your left arm."

"The left never really works well, and y'all always end up bruising me."

"Nah," she says, as she moves her middle and index finger over my inner elbow, "you have a nice big healthy vein right here." She dabs a small amount of iodine over the spot and instructs me to make a fist. "There we go, needle in." She tapes the needle down to my arm and I watch the blood begin its sad procession to be spun apart and robbed of its worth. "I'll be back to check on you in a bit."

I close my eyes. *Big Momma's House* plays in the background.

"Okay, all done. Let me bandage you up and you can go to the cashier."

"Whoa, that was fast."

"Not really, it took a while to get everything spun out. You've been here for three hours."

"Oh."

I walk up to the cashier, a hefty man who's younger than he looks, with a demeanor much the same.

"You can't keep doing this," he says, as he hands me the money. "It's against the rules for a reason. You need a few days between donations. This kinda shit isn't healthy."

"Sorry, I'm just trying to get a couple extra bucks here and there."

"Well, I'm flagging your file to check with me before you can donate."

"Do what you gotta do, I guess." I grab my money, $30 this time, walk out the door and rip the bandage.

I get home. He's on the couch, passed out. He wakes up to the crisp sound of my beer opening.

"Where were you last night?" he says, grabbing the beer from my hand.

"Nowhere."

"Whatever."

The bar is dead tonight, but that's okay. There's only one person I'm here to see, and he's here. I walk into the bathroom and pull out my death bag—that's what I've taken to calling it these days. I walk back out, and the bar has come alive.

"You're not allowed to donate for a month."

"What? Why?"

"Your last donation took much longer than it should have. That tells us you've been coming too much."

"Sometimes my arms bend back. Maybe that cut off circulation a bit."

"And we got reports from the lab that one of your donations contained opiates."

"That was a medical thing. I had a prescription."

"You can't donate if you're on any prescription medication. If we ran a tox screen, would it come up dirty?"

"Not for opiates. I don't do that."

"Come back in a month."

I walk out the double door, looking for a bandage to tear.

I'm not sure how long I've been there on the couch. I've been rewinding the tape over and over again, watching the same scene for at least an hour. Based on the sound of the birds chirping outside, I'd say it's early morning, but your guess is as good as mine. My death bag is emptied out, but in about half an hour I'm sure I'll tear it open and rub what little residue remains onto my gums.

Your name, please?

I look around the floor, searching for one last beer. I'm sure I can't have drunk them all.

Garland Briggs.

I find a rogue beer, though it's not a part of the pack; those are all gone. I hear his alarm go off. He opens his door and stumbles down the hallway to the bathroom. As he walks by, he stops and asks if I've been up all night.

"Yeah, but I woke up really late again. I'm going to sleep as soon as I finish this beer."

"Jesus, dude."

Garland, what do you fear most in the world?

I stare at the death bag and figure it's been about half an hour. I tear it open and lick it like a thirsty dog. I stare at the TV, heart pounding. There's no way I'm going to sleep anytime soon. I can feel the blood in my veins as it thuds and pulses through my body. I know it's only the spun-out, worthless parts of me that remain.

The possibility that love is not enough.

STACK OF DEAD WOMEN

TOM BATTEN

THERE WAS a stack of dead women in our town, in this field beside the library. The field was one of those empty, unclaimed places every town has—for a while, there'd been a sign advertising it as available for commercial real estate and a rumor that an IHOP might open there, but it never happened. Then there was talk of making it a dog park, but that never happened, either. And then the stack of dead women showed up, and from then on that's all the field was ever for, the stack.

Probably the word "stack" makes you picture something nice and orderly, but it wasn't. It was really more of a pile, like someone had dumped the dead women there in a rush. We called it "the stack" around town, though, because that's what Bob Porter, the head librarian, called it in this sort of famous letter he wrote to the *Town Crier* a couple weeks after the stack first appeared. He was upset that the stack was sitting there untended, afraid it would keep people from coming to the D.A.R.E. fair in the library parking lot. Bob Porter, in his letter, asked why the Board of Supervisors hadn't done anything about the bodies and wondered where our tax dollars were going, if not to keep our streets clean and our fields free of stacks of dead women. Where is the money? Bob Porter asked. Where does it go, when it leaves our bank accounts? Into what coffer does our cold cash flow?

Bob Porter had a sort of dramatic flair. His letter caused a big stir and an investigation into the Board of Supervisors and the town finances. The chairman, Desmond Zimmer, ended up trying to asphyxiate himself in his Oldsmobile Cutlass Supreme, but he got discovered by a neighbor and saved. He lived, sort of. Alive, but brain dead. Everyone took the suicide attempt as a sign of guilt, but the investigation never turned up anything incriminating. He didn't leave a note and he wasn't talking afterwards, so probably we'll never know why he wanted to die. His son, Des Jr., moved back from the coast to take care of him. Des Jr. had been kind of a creep as a kid, but this was a nice thing to do. Everyone talked about what an inspiration he was, how he was an example that people could change.

Bob Porter's letter didn't do anything, outside get that investigation going. The stack stayed, the D.A.R.E. fair saw record low attendance and they ended up moving it to the middle school the next year and from then on.

You probably don't believe a word of this. You probably don't believe it's possible there could be a town with a stack of dead women in it and that it sat there and no one did anything about it.

Well, it's true.

There were about twenty dead women, all different ages and races, all stripped naked, all dead, killed all kinds of ways. Some of them had been shot, some stabbed, some slashed to ribbons, some beaten or strangled. A few looked waterlogged. Maybe they'd been drowned. A couple were old and looked like victims of natural causes.

Obviously, the police and FBI were interested. They had the stack cordoned off at first, and there were always guys taking pictures and samples of hair and blood and stuff. None of the women in the stack were local. None of them matched the description of any missing women from anywhere, not even Mexico, where women tend to go missing all the time. None of their fingerprints turned up a match. It was like the women had never been alive and walking around, like they'd always been dead and stacked up. Every day, the police and FBI were a little more stymied and little less interested and finally one morning they took the cordon down and were done, done worrying about it. Maryanne Hilcoat, who managed the Hardee's on the corner of Harpersville Road, asked one of the FBI guys how they could just leave the stack there, why they didn't cart it off, do autopsies or something, give the women some kind of burial, and the FBI guy told her she watched too much TV. Maryanne said, That's what you people always say when you don't feel like explaining yourselves, and the FBI guy agreed with her, which seemed decent of him, But he still didn't explain himself, and they still left the stack there for the town to deal with.

At first, everyone stayed away, as Bob Porter predicted, but before long the stack became a kind of popular meeting place. In the evenings, Friday and Saturday nights, especially in the summer, you'd find maybe twenty or thirty people out at the stack hanging out, unwinding. People would bring folding chairs and coolers and sit around talking and drinking. This was not for children, of course, as the women were naked and in some cases pretty horribly mutilated; this was for adults, although sometimes teenagers would sneak out and go down to the stack to party after everyone went to bed. You'd find condoms in the grass all the time. There's no telling how many young couples lost their virginity with those dead eyes watching over them. Morbid, but the previous choice spot for a late-night tryst had been down by Otter Creek, and everyone agreed it was nice to be able to go night fishing again without all that adolescent moaning and groaning scaring the fish.

People would sit around the stack and drink and speculate. Who were these women? Where did they come from? Ed Tucker had this theory that they'd fallen out of an airplane, but that seemed unlikely, as they weren't uniformly crushed. They'd been killed all kinds of ways, and if they'd been killed and then dropped from an airplane, well, who kills a bunch of women just to fly them up in the air and dump them in some random little town? Nathan Sanchez, that drunk, thought maybe the women were ancient or had been buried in the field long before the town got founded and had gradually worked their way up above the soil, due to erosion, he said, over the years. That was even dumber than the airplane idea. First of all, the women weren't all dirty. Secondly, a lot of them, the ones with intact heads, had modern haircuts.

A lot of what people came up with was stupid, but it was fun. We all wanted there to be a good reason for the stack, like maybe a good explanation for something bad might lessen the badness. Or maybe it was just fun. There were arguments every now and then, but generally there was a lot of laughter and a sense of community, which even in a small town rarely feels authentic.

Of course, not everyone who came around the stack came for the right reason. Billy Lowrey got chased off and banned after one night he walked up and ruffled the pubic hair of this redhead with a slit throat. Not everyone liked the stack, either. Maryanne Hilcoat sent this furious letter to the *Crier*, talking about what kind of example were we setting for the children in town and how was the stack distracting us from more wholesome pursuits, like picking up litter along Route 17 and strengthening our relationships with God. Finally one night, she got the members of her quilting circle together to come down to the stack with a tarp. They wanted to cover it up and yell at everyone. These are all mothers and daughters, Maryanne said. Mothers and daughters just like your own, and they deserve respect. Leaving them out here, looking them over like they're just meat, it's barbaric.

Maryanne's husband, Mike Hilcoat, happened to be out by the stack that night. Actually, Mike was out by the stack most nights. Some folks thought this was Maryanne's real problem with the stack. He told her to lay off, that there wasn't anything disrespectful going on, that paying attention to the stack and wondering about it was better than pretending it didn't exist at all or covering it up. There's not one of us out here who doesn't look at this thing and think about the women in our lives and how precious they are, Mike said, how we have to protect them and nurture them and see that no harm comes to them, ever. It all devolved into an awful scene. At one point, Maryanne was in tears, shouting, You probably look at these girls wishing you saw my face in there, and Mike shouted back about why was it he couldn't do a single thing to enjoy himself without it being some sort of judgment on her?

They went on and on, back and forth.

Embarrassing. Everyone, all of us around the stack in our lawn chairs and everyone in Maryanne's quilting circle, too, all looking at our feet, no one wanting to move or make a sound, and then Scott England piped up and got between the Hilcoats and said, You guys, you guys, you're missing the point. The stack's a metaphor, he said. That's all it is. It's a metaphor.

Scott England taught English at the Middle School.

That got the Hilcoats quiet and back on the same side, because neither of them—or anyone else for that matter—was sure what the hell Scott England was talking about.

Maryanne asked Scott if he was all right and her husband asked Scott how much he'd had to drink. Scott said that the stack being a metaphor was the only explanation, if you thought about it, because why else would the women's bodies not be decomposing?

That the bodies weren't decomposing was a mystery we all considered from time to time. The theories on that ran from mystifying to flat out dumb, but Scott's was the most bewildering yet by far.

We're all concerned with how it got here, Scott said, but we never talk about how it's possible. We never talk about why here, of all places?

Scott was up on his feet saying this, pacing around in a figure eight. Des Jr. tried to take his arm and sit him down, but Scott shook him off. That we talk about it at all is what we should be talking about, Scott said. What we say about it and why we say what we say. I'm telling you. We talk about it and then we go home and think about it. Think about it and think about it until we can come back and talk about it more. But we're not saying anything, when we're talking. Does that make sense? We're talking, but we're not saying anything. You know what I mean?

Sure, Des Jr. said. I know exactly what you mean.

Scott looked at Des Jr. with all the sadness in the world behind his eyes and a string of drool dangling from his lower lip. It's a metaphor, Scott said.

I see what you mean, Des Jr. said. I never thought of it that way, but I do see it now.

I just don't know what it's a metaphor for, Scott said. I can't figure out what it means.

Des Jr. and some other folks led Scott home and got him to bed, and Mike took Maryanne off to finish their quarrel behind closed doors. Some of the quilting circle ladies stuck around, and a couple of them became regulars. Scott was back the next night. He didn't talk about the dead women being a metaphor again, but he did start carrying this little black notebook with him that he was always making notes in. When Maryanne opened the Hardee's Monday morning, it was with a wild black bruise across the right side of her face. Some people were pretty upset with Mike about that, some people wanted to say something to him, but Maryanne insisted that she'd tripped over her little pug dog, Spencer, and smacked her head against a countertop. In the end, we gave Mike the benefit of the doubt. We'd known him for so long, some of us, and what he'd said about nurturing and protecting women was so moving, and Maryanne never said a word against the stack again.

All of this took place over a single summer and maybe a couple weeks into September. Everyone lost interest after Ernest Becker, who owned the bowling alley, launched this scheme to buy the field and build a bar around the stack. Paying for the right to sit in that field and drink after we'd been doing so for free pissed everyone off, and to make matters worse, Bob Porter tried turning the situation to his advantage, He saw Desmond Zimmer's empty seat on the Board as his chance at getting into the political game, and he started bothering everyone about how a vote for him would be a vote to keep the stack public property. There was something depressing about the whole thing—Bob Porter's desperation, Ernest Becker's greed, everyone using these dead women to their own ends. Sitting there looking at them stopped being any fun at all. Week by week, there were fewer people out in the field each night, until finally people stopped going around altogether. The stack's still there, but you almost never hear anyone talk about it. Maybe sometimes, if someone's giving directions, they'll mention it then. Like, if someone were telling someone else how to get to the post office, they'd say, Take a left off Denbigh Boulevard and then go straight a couple miles and pull a right on Lakeview Road. If you see that stack of dead women, you've gone too far.

A FIRE-FORMED RING, A BRINGING TOGETHER

TONY MANCUS

1.

take the lad with the bad ideas about bikes
and put the dead girl on a palace of   a plate of
cicadas/ice   the inspector has
a face like his friends wouldn't like him
if he didn't dream so fluidly
and I am in my blue room
with the backwards speech
patterns on the roof, tapped
imagining Hopper with his PBR can
from now firm and dead
placed wood heavy
backward into a scene/r two
this incongruous talking log—it's big, heavy
and wood—feel better now dead girl
your cousin has the same face
I mean, who notices how easy it is to love
what smells like danger in the fair
and rusty mountains with a mill
for an engine

2.

On the drive we took a detour to cross the tracks and see a very large part of a tree. There were what seemed like dozens of crows and the wind in the ice made it sound like metal eking its way down the pines. Everything sparkled including our coats—the layer of forgotten script being laid over the land we'd never seen in person laid over our touring and rented car, soundtracked by the same opening as we passed the road sign for Snoqualmie.

3.

the movie makes no mention
of anything. there is the cabin
here dreams are currency and one
peoples what they can with figures
stick or otherwise, the smell of wood
simple on the hands and what grit
leaves its racing through one simple
clasping gesture. if we repeat our names
in the wash. if the clothing retains a semblance
of our being held by it, if the plastic too carries
everything forward through time

4.

Saying return is different than being a thing that surfaces again. Take water over a series of drops in altitude. One buoyant thing in it and maybe this reaping. Take your turn before you come back now. A picture on the dash becomes its ghost and this is only what the sun does. How the edges all turn inward.

INVESTIGATOR HAWK AND THE HORNED SNAKE

CHRISTOPHER COOTS

STANDING ON a hot rock beneath a red fir tree, I watch the Lawmen drag Caroline Bear's body out of Leader Lake by the arms, and lo, I remember the first time I was overwhelmed by the evil that bleeds into this World. Exhausted, the men drop her body into the marsh. The tall one with flowing black hair turns back to me, and calls, "Where is the mother?"

Two days before this, the Mother walks into my office on Queen Street and Second Avenue South, across from the Wallwebber's. Her name is Charlotte Bear. She is my Blackfoot sister and I listen carefully.

"My daughter Caroline has not been at school for three days. She has not turned up at work, either."

"Where does she work?"

"She has shifts at the Farmer's Market on Second Avenue. Certainly, she has skipped school before, but she always turns up at work. She loves her job." Her eyes linger on the floor as she continues. "Please help me, Mr. Hill. The Lawmen say there is nothing they can do on account of her running away before."

"How old is Caroline?"

"Her body is only sixteen, but her soul is ancient," she says, tightening her shoulders as she sits up straighter. "I've taught her all about the old way."

I acknowledge the hint of fear and try to assure her. "If you have taught her, then Caroline knows," I say. "If she wants to be found, we will find her. You can believe in me, Ms. Bear. Finding people is something I happen to be very good at."

Tracking Caroline Bear begins the same as any white lady skiptrace. In the case of runaways and matrimonial work, I begin with our old friend Rudyard Kipling.

I keep six honest serving men
(They taught me all I knew):

Their names are What and Why and When
And How and Where and Who

In addition to a *Who* and a *Where*, I explore this World's method of tracking: photographs, clothing and personal effects, identifying marks, allergies, contact information of relatives and friends and lovers, places frequented, transport options and an overall understanding of the situation that surrounds the disappearance of the sixteen-year-old Blackfoot girl who speaks of the old way. Like me, she is a foreigner here in Okanogan Country.

I visit Sheriff Rogers and get a copy of the police report to see why the Lawmen are not helping. All they see and hear is a young girl considered strange because of her beliefs and behavior. The report does yield one interesting bit of song, though. It turns out Caroline's man is called Jacob Upchurch. He is nearly 30 and a blackjack dealer at the rez casino on Highway 97. I decide to introduce myself, and saddle up to his table in the empty Poker Room. I buy in for chips next to two middle-aged white women with hair of smoke, and almost immediately realize Jacob's crumpled blue work shirt and cracked nametag have been pulled from the floor of his car. As soon as I accept that I am overdressed in my best jacket, I notice the glint of a gold chain beneath his collar.

What would an old-soul like Caroline Bear see in this fellow? His card work is sloppy and sluggish. On every hand, I wave my hand palm down to stand on my second card, and I only get paid when he has to hit on sixteen and busts. Twenty-five dollars well spent. No gambles. No losses. The smoke-haired women lose interest and fade away to the singing slot machines.

"I apologize for approaching you at work," I say to Jacob, "but are you aware that Caroline Bear has been missing for two, maybe three days?"

Jacob keeps his eyes down and performs a trick with the cards, but I have seen many tricks in this World and am not fazed.

"You police?" he asks.

"I am not a Lawman."

"Her mom hire you or something?" he asks, then adds, "I told Charlotte myself I was worried. You'd think a younger woman would let you be in charge. But no one is in charge of Caroline."

I don't say anything, and he keeps going.

"There are girls. There are women. Then there's Caroline."

I ask about the gold chain and he tells me that Caroline paid for it on a day trip to Seattle. He says it cost one hundred dollars and he now considers it a farewell token. I wonder how a sixteen-year-old girl pays for a blackjack dealer's jewelry. He tells me they met when he was working as a dishwasher at her high school cafeteria. She bummed a cigarette from him when she was fourteen and he was on one of his breaks, leaning against a playground wall like some kind of rebel. Sex did not immediately become an issue, but it did eventually. Much to everyone's—even his own—surprise, the arrangement outlasted her tenure at the school and carried on until very recently.

"She would say things like, 'I feel it deep in my bones: old, old memories I have never lived, but I know them like I have.'" Jacob sighs. "I know she was young. I know it was wrong. But I don't care how old someone is. How do you keep from falling all over yourself when you hear something universal like that? We were connected."

"I am not here about that," I tell him.

Jacob carries on, but I am no longer thinking of Caroline Bear. I am thinking of Laura, of whom Caroline Bear reminds me. I think of the shattered hard boys Laura left in her wake and what that meant for my old family—my Brothers and Sisters back in Twin Peaks. I think of why I left them alone with the evil I know lives in those woods. I think of Diane at her veterinary office and I think of why I left her. I think of what I did not want her to have to understand.

"I do not feel sorry for loving Caroline," Jacob Upchurch says, and I understand. He does not know where she is because they broke up one week before. He has sorrow in his eyes when he says she likely ran off with someone else.

"She admitted she was seeing someone?" I ask.

"She didn't deny it when I asked her."

"Any ideas?"

"I took some flowers to her work to try and smooth things over. It's not the first time we've broken up. But she wasn't there, and her boss was acting strange, telling me Caro didn't want me around and all that."

"Okay. The boss. Who is he?"

"It's a *she*. Sandra Willow."

"Interesting."

"If you can't find her at the market," Jacob continues, "she's in here most nights—stinking up the tables—on tilt."

"She plays poker?"

"She loses at poker."

I cross the river and find the Farmer's Market on Second Avenue North and watch for Sandra Willow. There is nothing to it. The Farmer's Market is crowded, as it always is, which provides cover. She is as easy to spot as an echo in a box canyon.

She perches behind a vegetable stand, weighing items and taking money. Occasionally, she takes out a carving knife and prepares another bunch of spinach or greens or turnips for sale. When there are no customers and there is no work to be done, she closes her eyes and looks at the ground. A melancholy Sister, if ever I have seen one.

Sandra makes a phone call, slowly dialing a series of numbers. She wears sunglasses, but I can see, as she cradles the phone to her ear and listens, that her expression does not change. As with a Wolf, it is clear from her stillness that she senses a threat. I do not yet know if I am the threat she senses.

I pick out and pay for a bunch of leeks and some cauliflower. When Sandra Willow hands me back my change with a false smile, I decide to engage.

"Turns out Caroline Bear pays for her boyfriend's jewelry," I say out loud.

Sandra pulls her sunglasses down and scrutinizes me. She continues working with her carving knife, and I realize that it would have been wiser to approach when she was unarmed.

"Does she make that kind of money working for you?" I ask. "Considering the way you've been playing at the casino?"

"I've had a bad run of luck," she says.

"Bad luck needs a cure. I know a bit about these things. Did you know Caroline is missing?"

"I know she's not at work," she says, setting the knife down. "I don't know how Caroline buys presents. Her mother's in the Needy Families Fund. Ask her."

"The Needy Families Fund?"

"Temporary Assistance for Needy Families," Sandra says. "Welfare for folks on the rez. Maybe Charlotte stopped drinking her stipend away and gave her kid some spending cash."

"You sound angry at Charlotte."

"The bottle's got her. It's the Indian cliché. Caroline's troubled, but she's a decent kid. I'm protective," she says. "When Caroline gets close to you, she shares things."

"What kinds of things?"

"Caroline talks a lot about the old way. Some kind of guilt trip her Mom is putting on her. But it's always veiled. Obscure. Trust me, I'd help you if I could, but she's a strange girl. Half of what she says doesn't make sense."

"Try me."

Sandra Willow picks up the knife again and peers at me in a way I can only describe as diagnostic. We hold eyes past comfortable. Now she is tracking me, but I have never lost a staring contest with a Wolf.

"Right after she kicks Upchurch to the curb, she tells me she has a date. It's why I told Jacob not to come around anymore. He's too old for her, and I'm glad they've broken up, but I don't want to see the guy get crushed."

"Who was the date with?"

"She said she had a date with a…" She hesitates. "A horny snake."

"A Horned Snake?"

"That's it."

Immediately, I know where Caroline is. I do my best to honor the sensation of voided spirit that strikes me.

I march into the Okanogan County Sheriff's department and let Sheriff Rogers in on my hunch that they will find Caroline Bear near a deep body of water. I inform him my people tell a legend of a dangerous man-eating creature called the Horned Snake. It is known for lurking in lakes and rivers and attacking unwary travelers.

What I do not tell the Sheriff—because I know he will not understand—is that if Charlotte Bear taught Caroline about the Horned Snake, she will have known to avoid deep waters. So if her body is, in fact, somewhere in Leader Lake, it will not have been her choice. Her cause of death will incorrectly be ruled as drowning—possibly even a suicide. It is important for the Lawmen and I to be as close to one as we can be. We must let each other do our jobs, but some days I cannot find peace with the way Law and I have been made strange.

When the Sheriff patronizes me and asks more about this serpent they are looking for, I recall the legend of "The Warrior Who Ate the Horned Snake." It is about a Blackfoot Warrior who offends the Snakes by killing and eating one that is coiled outside his shelter. The Gods turn him into a Horned Snake as punishment, and he exiles himself to the rivers and lakes because of his newfound and uncontrollable desire to devour his friends and loved ones.

Was this what Caroline was avoiding? Was she afraid she would bring harm to her mother, to the World?

"Maybe Caroline Bear wants exile," Sheriff Rogers says.

"I know the feeling all too well," I reply.

At a certain point—I seldom remember when it happens—my sense of time in this World leaves me and I am on the lip of Leader Lake. The Lawmen are dragging Caroline's body from the water. I stand on a hot rock underneath a red fir. Worms wiggle into the tree bark to hide from the Owls.

"Where is the mother?" the tall man with flowing black hair asks me.

"I have not called her yet," I say. "What should I tell her?"

"She drowned," he says. "Or killed herself. Looks like there was something weighted tied to her foot."

"And I should tell her Mother this?"

The tall man with flowing black hair knows we are at odds, and he smiles at me like one smiles at a silly Old Man. He wears a tin star, and so he is a Lawman. Which is what I was, once. But now, I am a Blackfoot brother who has buried his shattered past and judges his young Brothers and Sisters that have not bothered to create history enough to shatter. A silly, hypocritical Old Man.

They take Caroline's body away, and I kneel by the edge of the water to see what song I can hear. What story does this ground tell? Tracking is only perception. It is listening—with all senses—and expanding your awareness to move in the shadow of what you are tracking. Stepping beyond the shape of a footprint. I realize it has been some time since I have truly listened. The theory has never left me, but I am out of practice, walking on wobbly legs like a Doe from her Mother. Here at the water, I hear nothing apart from the footprints of the Lawmen, and those came in after the story was already over.

I will myself into stillness. I try not to think of telling Charlotte Bear I could not find her daughter alive. I try not to think that the evil I once attempted to leave behind has tracked me here. I try to honor the questions, to leave preconceptions aside and become everything that surrounds me, so that together we will go where one question leads to another, and then another and another.

I am nothing but flesh and muscle. Bones and blood. It is all I have to give. I will shed blood and tears for the life that has been lost and the life I have left behind. I will return to you, Mother. My thoughts will not cloud my vision. My sacrifice will be made tangible. Will you hear my silence?

The drum of my heartbeat leaves my chest and I kneel with nothing to say, nothing to offer but a small gift of tears. They fall before me as the pines' hum mingles with the first *who-who-a-who* of the Owl. And finally, I see it: near my offering, a long slick path in the sand, leading from the woods to the water.

A trail you do not know must be followed to the point of knowing. This does not mean finding where it begins. I ignore my heart's notion that the track was made by the belly of a huge, man-eating serpent as large around as a tree trunk. Instead, I acknowledge this path is the size of a canoe. A canoe that could carry body and blood as cargo until they are no longer cargo but offering to the water. And if the body and blood of this girl have been offered before the Creator determined it was their time, justice is required. Caroline Bear's suffering must not be in vain.

It is time for me to play cards.

The rez casino is different at night. It is all smoke and noise and dread. The distinct odor of alcohol melds with perspiration. There is too much interference to track here. A heavyset Okanogan Sister is handling the blackjack table tonight, and her shirt is clean and ironed. I ask about Jacob Upchurch.

"The pederast?" she asks. "He's got the night off on account of his girlfriend drowning."

In spite of the awkwardness, I win a few hands using my old strategy and get no sign of protest. It is not the Okanogan Sister's money, after all.

"Do you happen to know if Jacob has access to a canoe?" I ask.

The dealer shoots surprised eyes at me. "You've got a poor sense of humor, Brother," she says. Around now is when a bleach blonde waitress happens by, as inconspicuous as a Blue Jay on a Winter tree.

"You're Tommy Hill, right?" she asks. "I came by your office today."

"Any reason?"

"Charlotte told me she hired you," she says as she takes a look at the hand the dealer feeds me. "You have to hit on soft 16."

I do and turn over a Queen. 26. Bust.

The waitress has something feverish about her. She is prickly-eyed and smells of tobacco. "Don't worry. It was the right play," she assures me.

"I will not lose sleep over it."

The waitress catches eyes with the blackjack dealer and stiffens. It seems this yellow-headed Blue Jay has a song for my ears only. "Meet me outside," she whispers.

The parking lot is dark and not quiet, but quieter at least. The waitress walks toward me, smoking likely her tenth cigarette of the night, floodlights reflecting off her unnaturally blonde head.

"I can't stay out here long," she says. "I'm out of breaks."

"Why did Charlotte recommend you see me?"

"I went to her with something I knew about Caroline," she says. "After I heard. After they found her."

"You were close? I have heard she put some folks off with her talk of the old way."

"That was all an act!" The waitress laughs. "Her mom was a drunk and old-fashioned and she'd say all the stuff her mom said just so she could be different. It wasn't that serious. All Caroline wanted was to separate herself from the rest of us."

"Like you do with your hair?"

The waitress rolls her eyes. "Listen. The Needy Families Fund. Caroline found out that her boss was paying out extra money every month, then receiving checks from the same families for less money in return."

"Caroline worked for the Needy Families Fund?"

"No. Her boss at the Farmer's Market. Sandra Willow. She's the director of the Needy Families Fund."

"That's embezzlement," I say. "What do you think she's using the surplus money for?"

"Have you seen her play cards?"

The scent is clear now. Fragrant. Caroline Bear discovers Sandra Willow is embezzling federal funds from the organization she directs in order to supplement her gambling addiction. And Caroline Bear—a sixteen-year-old Blackfoot Sister—is killed because of it.

"They were doing it together," the waitress chimes in.

Now I have lost any sense of the trail.

"And I mean," the waitress continues, eyebrows raised, "*together*."

The waitress hands me some kind of computer stick and tells me Caroline saved the financial proof of the crime and left it with her in case anything unsavory happened.

"I'd consider death a little unsavory," the waitress says.

To become an effective tracker is to become the animal you are tracking—to walk in its shadow. If we can feel the pull of her needs and the strain of her fears, we will know why she does what she does and where we can find her. "Will Sandra Willow be playing cards tonight?" I ask.

"She usually gets to the Poker Room around nine." And after that, the bleach blonde informant high-heels it away.

After dark, the Poker Room is smokier than the rez casino proper. I am able to fill the last seat at Sandra Willow's table. The game is Hold 'Em, at which I am not well versed. What I do know is that the momentum of the game can swing very suddenly.

Sandra Willow recognizes me but does not smile. Two Malaysian businessmen flank her. One of them wears glasses and moves his arms like a Frog. The other leans on the table and slurps a bowl of noodles. The Indian with a crewcut next to me—at least two decades my senior—deals out the cards for the first hand. Bets and checks are made.

"This is no limit?" I ask.

The crewcut grunts in the affirmative and deals a flop of community cards. Further bets are made, and I buy my way in to the next round after the Malaysians fold.

"There used to be a very direct analog between tracking animals and solving crimes." I say this to the table. "I have discovered recently that the lines are now quite blurry."

Sandra Willow raises her eyebrows and nods in a way that suggests I keep my mouth shut.

"We prefer to keep small talk at a minimum during play," says the crewcut in a voice that blends a touch of British Columbia with the short, bunched cadence typical of older Indians.

There are more checks and bets. Raises and calls. I realize I have not even looked at my cards. I peel their tops from the table to discover a nine and an eight, both suited spade. This happens to marry well with the six of diamonds, seven of spades, ten of hearts, two of clubs and Ace of Spades in the community pile. I believe I am holding a straight.

When I win the pot, Sandra Willow rises from the table in anger.

"Maybe tracking is not that different from cards?" I say as I pull in my winnings. "To become the animal, to walk in its shadow, we first need to be hungry. A full belly numbs a Wolf's senses and puts her to sleep, while hunger wakes her up so she can feel, see and hear things she might otherwise overlook."

"Are you saying she has a tell?" the crewcut asks.

"Her only tell is that she is hungry," I reply.

"I already ate," Sandra Willow says, taking her seat again as the noodle-slurping Malaysian begins to deal. He mutters in some variety of Chinese as we all look at our cards. I keep my cool when I see I have drawn pocket Kings.

"You must have a hunger for victory," I say to Sandra, to some laughter from the table. The public reaction gets the stare I am looking for as I shift my eyes from my cards to the hostile eyes of the Wolf. We are becoming one.

I pull Sandra further into the hunt after the blind and the checks and the call for a raise. She re-raises. The Frog-like Malaysian hangs in, and I lay my cards down. From the statistics I am aware of, I should win the hand.

"To track the Wolf, all you have to do is become the Wolf," I say.

"How do you become Royal Flush?" the Frog-like Malaysian jokes as he lays down his hand and uses his arms to drag in his winnings.

I shrug at my loss as the winner deals the next hand's cards. I hold a nine and Ace of Clubs. With my spirit, I hunt Sandra Willow on soft paws. I stalk the way she peers at her cards. I scan her with amber eyes. My gut tightens. I stop breathing. I listen. And then suddenly, as the checks and bets and calls and raises are laid, my voice quakes.

"Imagine if you knew you were being tracked," I say. "If a Lawman suspected you of something unsavory, let us say Murder, or embezzling funds, or perhaps something as lascivious as sex with a minor…"

The table stays quiet, regarding me as if I were insane or homeless. I know what I am, and the rest is just waiting. I look at my cards and raise my bet. The Frog-like man, the noodle man and the crewcut Indian fold. Sandra Willow calls.

"But if we were tracking a Wolf, we *could* come upon a footprint, a scat or a scent post," I say. "We may even mark an adjacent tree—which would let the Wolf know she was being tracked, that the tracker recognized and accepted her presence."

The rest of the table has disappeared from my perspective, and may have, in actuality, left the room. Because I only see Sandra Willow.

"Will that acceptance make you a better survivor?" I ask. "Or will you submit to the hunt?" The cards turn for Sandra and me, and I realize that I am holding a full house. "Even though there are many lives, everything dies," I say, as I push all of my chips into the pot. "I am all in."

Sandra takes her time counting and then pushes her chips into the betting circle, fully aware that she has Aces full: three Aces and a pair.

I lose the hand and leave the Poker Room, but I know that I am still there, walking in the shadow of Sandra Willow. I will spend the next several days wondering how she will proceed after I turn the computer stick into Sheriff Rogers. I wonder if she will name other names, or if she will simply reckon with her hunger.

Some hours after I lose all my chips, I am standing under a floodlight in the rez casino parking lot, smoking a cigarette loaned to me by the bleach blonde informant. I am leaning against the wall like some kind of rebel. The cigarette does not taste good, nor does it ever, but a feeling of satisfaction overwhelms me, as does an image.

I imagine the Fox when she climbs to the top of a snow mound in Winter, lifts her snout to smell the crispness of the air and knows there is sustenance beneath the frozen water.

Our memories guide each step on the trail and show us how to work together as a pack. I must balance my suffering with the ease at which my Brothers and Sisters will most certainly embrace me back Home. I cannot relent to fear in the same way I did before, when a warning from the Forest told me I could never win on my own. Who ever wins on their own? Only the Horned Snake, although I do not believe he would describe his path as victorious.

After the corruption of a confidante nearly three decades ago, I left my home with the feeling that I would never be able to look into the face of evil with perfect courage. This feeling affected everything. Until Caroline Bear. But our strength improves with practice.

The next time I wander into the farther places—those places from a memory I have not lived—I might see and hear a deeper way, a way that draws me more quickly into the song of the track. But the only song I hear now is sharp and clear. Until I return Home, I will think of Diane Shapiro and the family we do not have because of my fear of imperfect courage. Until I return Home, I will think of Diane Shapiro, Ph.D., Brandeis.

PARTY LINE
OR, BEFORE AND AFTER FRANK O'HARA
EVIE ATOM ATKINSON

ACT 1, SCENE 1

[Lights up on an alternate universe. Frank I and Frank II are on the telephone.]

FRANK I:
In this moment of silence the expected lyricism begins.

[Silence.]

FRANK II:
A crystal hand emerging with
a sparkler.

FRANK I:
So, a light bulb?

FRANK II:
Frail in our affections,
stranded on this planet, out
I go like a cloud.

FRANK I:
Oh, don't go. We can't bear that.

A CLOUD:
A little world of our own full of
fondling and ozone.

FRANK I:
So, lovers who are very, very sunburned? Shall we mop the skylight?

FRANK II:
Wouldn't a hush smother us all? Keep us
low and apart for an Ice Age? The push of
the centuries is a slick machine, but
it turns mean. Glaciers relinquish their
secrets in my palpitating arms. I have the
chalk outline of my lover tattooed across
my chest. You are the only person I know
in this whole row of houses.

A CLOUD:
Is that a tear?

FRANK I:
Get her!

FRANK II:
We look for abundance of feeling.

FRANK I:
The biggest sailor in the fleet?

FRANK II:
I kissed his prick pierced through by
a needle. Soot clouds billowed out.
You may smoke too, it seemed to say
with an echo.

FRANK I:
Two oh-so-troubled-and-disenfranchised hearts!

A CLOUD:
This is a sissy still life.

[Curtain.]

ACT 1, SCENE 1

[Lights up on an alternate universe. Marlene Dietrich observes a party.]

MARLENE DIETRICH:
This is a story of white and aimless signals.

BALCONY RAIL:
This is a story of white and aimless faggots.

MARLENE DIETRICH:
This is a story of white and aimless faggots.

BALCONY RAIL:
Is that a tear?

MARLENE DIETRICH:
Ummmm, ummmm, ummmm.

[Editor's note: play breaks off here.]

ACT 1, SCENE 1

[Light supper in an alternate universe. and John Ashbery and Jimmy Schuyler finish their wine at once.]

:
What a trailblazer I am.

JOHN ASHBERY:
Stop quoting me!

:
I know I have a great responsibility in this venture.

JOHN ASHBERY:
I am sick and I am going to stay that way as an example to the new society.

:
Curious kind of disease.

JIMMY SCHUYLER:
Now, boys.

:
Jimmy, you'll be glad to know I have solved the murder.

JOHN ASHBERY:
Get her!

THE BODY:
Pardon me, I've got to take a terrific shit.

JOHN ASHBERY:
I am the only person who can solve anything around here and I'm going to do it.
Q: Who's the sad sailor?
A: A prick pressed against my belly, a log of foreboding.
Q: He has a funny style, doesn't he?
A: Oh come on, now, there's nothing wrong with nervousness when you're in love.
Q: Does a set of knives ever feel tired?
A: The bed, which knows everything, is silent.

:
Get her!

JIMMY SCHUYLER:
If you donate marrow, and it cures the high five, hooray for you.

SODOM:
Is that a tear?

[Editor's note: the play breaks off here.]

ACT 1, SCENE 1

[Lights up on an alternate universe. A Hollywood make-up man is creating a gash on his face.]

HOLLYWOOD MAKE-UP MAN:
I'm knee-deep in outlandish wounds.

JOHN:
You should see yourself! You're a perfect sight!

HOLLYWOOD MAKE-UP MAN:
Who'll beat up whom?

JOHN:
Johns tell fairies what their death will be and how magical they are.

HOLLYWOOD MAKE-UP MAN:
I don't know if I'm well-dressed enough. Where did I put that rhinestone lavallière?

JOHN:
Fairy, fall down like a lot of diamond bracelets!

HOLLYWOOD MAKE-UP MAN:
Is that a tear?

[The john throws the Hollywood make-up man to the ground.]

JOHN:
You're not grappling with a stranger!

STRANGER:
I've been thinking about things and I've decided that I am the perfect person.

A LOT OF DIAMOND BRACELETS:
Honey, I designed that costume for you.

[Curtain.]

ACT 1, SCENE 1

[Lights up on an alternate universe.]

JOAN CRAWFORD:
Well I *am* alive and I forgive you for your nervousness.

BALCONY RAIL:
My favorite movie star is Carole Lombard, who's yours?

JOAN CRAWFORD:
JOAN CRAWFORD!

BALCONY RAIL:
Is that a tear?

JOAN CRAWFORD:
It's not easy to be spectator or audience.
Every minute of the day and damn night,
the individual push-ups and cold creamings.
It seems like a pose. An audience noisily
grunts through its telescope: "A vision
has been spied! My own!" Why, I remember
when I made my first movie on the coast—

BALCONY RAIL:
Fence in your memory and there will be coffins.

JOAN CRAWFORD:
A friend of mine! Hello!

CEMETERY:
Our infatuation is rearriving.

[Curtain.]

ACT 1, SCENE 1

[A queen lies upon an alternate universe, putting on her face. Enter a detective.]

DETECTIVE:
A train just went by covered in icy fir trees.

QUEEN:
Good, while you dust for prints, I'll be dusting for the prince, dar-ling!

DETECTIVE:
I always hankered for a prince.

QUEEN:
How firmly he grasps me underneath the mezzanine!

[The detective holds up a magnifying glass.]

DETECTIVE:
You're not even at the opera house!

QUEEN:
Modern life is so confusing!

DETECTIVE:
You'll be happy to know I've solved the murder!

QUEEN:
Nobody was dead, I was just thinking.

[Editor's note: play breaks off here.]

THE FINAL RECORDING OF SPECIAL AGENT FALTERMEYER

ANDREW BLOSSOM

DIANE, IT'S 11:30 am. I'm standing before a plate glass window in the hallway in Philadelphia. The gray sky that greeted my arrival here has since turned into rain. On the street below me is a group of pedestrians huddled underneath the overhang of what appears to be a cheesesteak cart, their coats pulled up around their necks. They look like a painting. A group of lost souls.

I've just finished my meeting with the Number Two around here. He's brought me up to speed on the latest news from Pittsburgh. I'd expected to meet with G, but it seems G dispatched himself westward upon receiving the news about his agent. Or agents. Let's not forget there were two Bureau men involved. Although as of yesterday, it's safe to say Win—excuse me, Agent W—it's safe to say Agent W is a Bureau man no longer.

Diane, you'll pardon the abbreviated names. Number Two has requested I use pseudonyms in these recordings. G's orders. Apparently, they've had trouble with leaks, particularly as regards the ongoing investigation led by an Agent Jeffries—that is—well, forget it, I've said his name. Agent Jeffries. Does Washington know about these leaks? Should we be keeping a tab on them? Maybe we could get someone up here. Mention it to the Big Man.

As for Pittsburgh. It's a nasty business. I can see why Washington wants me there. We go tomorrow.

Diane, it's funny. I can't help feeling there's something wrong here. Something beyond the obvious. This pseudonym business, for instance. It scratches the surface of a larger problem. I need to give these thoughts some space to grow. Coffee should help—strong, black coffee, which as you know is my preference. That's another thing that's wrong—the coffee served in our meeting tasted like dishwater. People say that about coffee, I know. But I mean it sincerely—the coffee tasted as if dishtowels had been soaking in it.

Remind me to tell you about the dream I had on the train.

•

Diane, my search for coffee took me to a pizzeria near the Bureau, where I had one slice of regular cheese, a small garden salad with an overly pungent garlic cream dressing and a passable cup of Joe. After I'd eaten, I sat and looked out into the rain. Across the street, I observed a homeless man struggling with an umbrella he had pulled from a trashcan. It was warped, its spindles bent, but he seemed determined to get it working.

It's funny how weather causes the mind to wander. I found myself thinking all the way back to Missoula. There was the time—this would've been while I was in law school—Victoria and I blew a tire on the Fairmont during a downpour. She was certain she could fix it. She was always handy. I begged her not to, but she insisted. She worked in the pouring rain right up until the moment the tow truck arrived, which meant I had to stand in the rain beside her, holding my own weatherbeaten umbrella. Diane, we got soaked. But that was Victoria, wasn't it? She never gave up on an idea.

Let me try to articulate something that's been bothering me. How could a protection assignment go so wrong that we lose the witness, with one agent grievously injured and the other reduced to a babbling mess? And who would be behind such a thing? How do we find that person? That's a question we now have to answer.

Here's another one: Have you ever heard of a situation in which an agent was assigned to protect his own wife? I suppose that's a question for G. It's hard to imagine a decision like that happening on his watch. Then again, here we are.

Speaking of G. As I sat in the pizzeria thinking about the above, a neon sign flickered on opposite me. There was a bar there I had not previously noticed, now getting ready for a night's business. By all appearances a rundown place, but the sign could not have been more striking. It was a rose, bright blue in color. Given what the blue rose means to us and the fact G was in my head at that very moment, the sight of it there in the rain gave me chills. Could I regard this as a mere coincidence? You know how I feel: When two separate events occur simultaneously, pertaining to the same object of inquiry, we must always pay strict attention. I left the pizzeria and crossed the street, but the door to the place was still locked. And no one answered.

Diane, let me ask you. Have you ever been to the Philadelphia office? Have you noticed how strange a place it is? It's an extremely large building, yet there's hardly anyone there. Where's the administrative staff? Where are the filing cabinets? Haven't these guys heard of computers? It's 1985, for Pete's sake. Where are the consoles? All they've got are a bunch of empty desks and a handful of agents that stand around and look at them. It's like everyone in Philadelphia is waiting for something to happen.

Yes, that's exactly it. It feels perpetually like the moment before something happens. Remind me to mention this to the Big Man.

Tonight, on my way out of the building, I stopped into the men's room for the usual reason. There was a lanky fellow standing at the sink as I went in. He wore a floral shirt and a linen suit. It was an outfit better suited to the Tropics than a rainy December at the Bureau. He had a can of pomade and was scraping a plastic comb in it. I suppose my reaction was noticeable. The man winked at me in the mirror. He said, Buenos Aires.

When I emerged, I described the man to Number Two.

Oh, he said. That's Jeffries.

I was surprised. Jeffries, whose investigation has been compromised? Why was he dressed like that?

It's a secret, Number Two said. He won't tell. He doesn't want to lose it.

Do you see what I mean? The more I think about it, the more I think we should get someone up here from Washington. Let's find a fresh-faced guy to play the role of new recruit. Or you know what? Maybe we could get you here, Diane. You've been wanting a change of pace. Think it over. You could do the secretary routine. Put a fresh pair of eyes on whatever's going on. Let's talk when I get back.

Diane, it's just after midnight. About twenty minutes ago, I awoke with an overwhelming feeling of dread. I can't remember if I was dreaming before I woke. But I'm left with the sort of anxiety I've not felt for years. Not since Victoria.

I'm glad I still have you to talk to, even if it's just through this machine.

I haven't told you about the dream I had on the train. I wonder if I dreamed the same dream just a minute ago? No, I can't believe I did. The dream on the train was confusing, but it was peaceful. It was also crystal clear. I could see it perfectly after I woke, and I can still remember every detail now. Whereas whatever terrible dream I've just had is already vanishing from my mind. If I truly dreamed anything at all.

As you know, my studies have recently turned to the School of Whispered Transmission, with a particular focus on the Drukpa Lineage, founded in the twelfth century when nine dragons appeared to Tsangpa Gyare. Western observers often interpret the Drukpa to be followers of a Left Hand path, possessors of Black Logic. But as far as I can tell, they are simply adherents of Vajrayana. In any case, it's a fascinating practice.

In my dream, I found myself on a high grassy plain, facing a gray mountain range. I assume this was the Tibetan Plateau, which previously I've only seen in books. Before me was an old fellow in ceremonial robes. A proper Red Hat, Diane, with scarlet headwear and all, his cap vibrating in the wind that came across the steppe. The man's lips were moving, although because of the wind or because of the dream, no words made it to my ears.

As I stood there, trying to puzzle out his message, a thick rope fell lazily from the sky so its end brushed against the grass. This rope seemed to be anchored to a point somewhere high above, although as I looked upward I could not discern such an anchor. There was just the rope trailing away until it vanished. The monk smiled and pointed upward. After a moment, I caught his meaning. In my studies, I've encountered tales of great teachers who climbed down to earth from the ineffable places in order to enlighten the people. But I've never read of an ordinary person who climbed up a rope to wherever these teachers came from. Could this old man really want me to do such a thing? And if so, how was it even possible?

Suddenly, my perspective changed. I was outside of my body, looking at myself from below as I began to shuffle up the rope. I attempted to yell something, to stop me from going, but it was no use. Up I went, growing ever smaller on the rope until I disappeared completely into the gray sky.

Then I was awake on the train, pulling into Philadelphia. I'm left with two important questions. Why did I climb up that rope, Diane? And where exactly did I go?

Diane, it's early. I've still not slept. It began to feel as if my uneasiness were being reflected back at me from the walls of my room. So I left the hotel, and I have been walking the empty streets in widening circles. I'm nearly at the Bureau. Perhaps I should go inside and wait for the ride to Pittsburgh? I hate to think of it. They'd probably take one look and lock me up with W.

There's a light rain falling, but I have a warm jacket.

A little while ago, I found myself passing the bar with the neon rose. I almost pulled at the door. The sign was lit, despite the hour, and there seemed to be people inside. I wonder if—

Hold on—

Diane, let me tell you. A long dark space. A strobe light. Sitting at the bar, a narrow, severe man with a very long beard. Here is what he said to me. Are you looking for Victoria? Diane, that's what he said! Are you looking for Victoria! At the back of the bar, a blue curtain, a woman in a sparkling red dress, beams coming off in the spotlight. A blue rose in her hair. I knew something was wrong and I turned to leave and there in front of me was W. A halo of flames surrounding his head. Diane, he wasn't there. How could he be there? He's in the loony bin in Pittsburgh. They put him there today. I'm supposed to go tomorrow. But there he was. And a halo of flame. I must get to the bottom of it. If I don't make my ride, have Gordon check and see whether there's a bar across from the pizzeria. Have him check whether there's a pizzeria. Tell Jeffries I'm beginning to see it. Tell him I said good luck in Buenos Aires. Diane, I wish I could explain this better. But you'll figure it out. You always do. Where do I go if I climb up the rope?

Diane— [Recording ends.]

ISSUE EIGHT
ONLY A WITCH CAT CAN CLOSE A DOOR

OH, THAT'S NOT GOOD

NATE WAGGONER

I'M CROSSING Shattuck, on my way to the Berkeley Bowl, when a Zipcar driver stops, looks to see that the people on the other side of the street aren't crossing, then fails to see me in front of him and accelerates. I think, like, "Man, really?" as if my laptop were shutting down unexpectedly or something. Imagine if I died and my last feeling were inconvenience.

My head hits the car's hood and the front bumper hits me just below the knees. I fall backwards onto the pavement. The driver is about my age, with a shaved head and a blue-and-gray geometric pattern on his t-shirt. "Oh my God!" he cries. "What happened?"

I stand up slowly. "You hit me with your car!" I spit out blood. The people who were about to cross the street encourage me to get out of the road. The man who hit me is holding his head, making a face, breathing hard. The sunglasses I was wearing are smashed in the road and covered in clumps of my hair.

An ambulance takes me to the hospital. There's no cell service, so I have to wait before I can let my girlfriend Abigail or my aunt Kay or anybody know what happened. I'm so hungry. I was gonna get dumplings.

Nothing is broken and I don't have a concussion. They give me Vicodin. On the other side of the curtain, two teenage girls, one injured, watch *Beauty and the Beast* on a laptop.

Kay picks me up from the hospital and takes me home. Abigail comes by later and goes with me to get my prescription. I limp down to the police station a few days after that. I call the man who hit me and he says, "I don't know who this is. Don't call here anymore! I'm *good*, dude," and hangs up. I learn that he never registered the accident with Zipcar. I try to have him served with a court date, but he's already vacated the address on his license.

All summer, I am either in pain or cranky and wanting to cry whenever the Vicodin starts to wear off. I get extremely skittish crossing the street. I'll start walking and then run across, or start walking and change my mind and then run back in the other direction. I apply to a few camp counselor jobs that want absolutely nothing to do with me. I go back to work for a screenwriting contest that pays me astonishingly little to read 90-to-200-page pedantic nightmares written by possible psychopaths: endless stories of gangsters and dominatrixes and sexy wolf-people and sexy lion-people, genital mutilation, hails of gunfire.

And then there are the bad ones!

My favorite bad screenplay takes place in a world where clowns are an ethnicity. The script is completely serious, gritty even, and the only jokes are weird forced puns on the different types of clowns—Auguste, Harlequin and so forth—as if someone told the writer there should be some humor in it and this was how they took the note. The plot concerns a clown cop reconciling with his half-clown son while solving clown crimes involving clown mobsters, clown strippers and a whole clown underworld. If you feel insane reading that last sentence, imagine reading it for 120 pages while your back is killing you, and doing it for less than minimum wage. Then imagine writing, "This script shows a great deal of promise. It utilizes a three-act structure with a clearly defined beginning, middle and end, and it is formatted according to contemporary screenwriting conventions. Currently, some things the writer might consider adjusting, in order to improve the already excellent first draft..."

Physical therapy, it turns out, is mostly where great athletes go after they tear their ACLs by doing inspiring touchdowns. It is not for poindexters who get their asses run over by a miniature car while in pursuit of potstickers. Nervous, ripped young men and women in white polos lecture me on my posture.

"What do you do for a living?" they ask.

"I'm a writer."

"Oh, that's not good."

They have me stretch my arms with a large rubber band and lie atop a foam cylinder and roll back and forth. They give me exercises to do at home: open a door, put your hands on either side of the doorway, and push your body forward; put your index and middle finger on your chin and move your head back without moving your shoulders; get on your hands and knees on your bed and arch your back up and down like a sexy cat. The physical therapists massage me, which is mostly painful.

I learn that there are different flavors of pain between sharp and dull, equivalent to sour, sweet, pungent, umami, metallic, fatty, hearty… the pain of being kicked in the balls, the pain of being pistol-whipped in the face, the pain of a broken heart, the pain of breaking someone else's heart, the pain of grief… and they can all be triggered by a particular touch on your back.

One weekend, I'm so busy with the scripts that I plan an all-nighter. We're out of coffee, so I go and buy some, but I accidentally buy this stuff that I guess has cardamom in it but tastes like medical waste. I've spent all my money for that week so I just keep drinking it.

I start staying over at Abigail's place most nights, watching *King of the Hill* with her and her roommate's fluffy, ornery cat, Slushie. In the morning, Abigail brews me Major Dickason's in a French press and puts foam on top. She sees me out the door and says, "Do you have everything?"

And I say, "Yeah."

WHY THE WOMAN RUNNING.

CHRISTINE STROUD

Why the guns. Why the hunt. Why the woman nearly caught, the signs broken—not repaired or repainted or removed. Why the woman not turning. Why the gods forgiving, but not forgetting; the feast left to rot. Why the lake turning to crushed black velvet and the island overrun with small, starving foxes. Why the record skipping and never stopping only growing louder and louder. Why the dogs cowering. Why the men. Why always the men. Why not a warning. Why the doe strung up between the trees. Why falling backwards not forward. Why the blood seeping into snow. Why the windows closed. Why the phone left off the hook. Why the woman caught. Why the woman turned into the vulnerable forest. Why the leaves always watching. Why the stags still returning, still sniffing the ground. Why the woman silent every time I ask.

THE MONSTER SWALLOWS ITSELF
OR, THE DAY EVERYTHING CHANGED

AMIRA PIERCE

1.

I GREW up here, there and everywhere—

But I spent my childhood summers on the other side of the planet, in the faraway land where my mother grew up. One or two hot months each year, she took my little sister and me there to stay in her family's flat, in a building populated with cousins and uncles and aunts, in an overgrown village of similar flats and minarets and fruit trees abutting a slice of emerald sea. Life in that house had its slow and steady rhythm of visiting and returning, of praying and playing, of savory and sweet.

Lunchtimes, after clearing spattered spoons and greasy forks and half-eaten pieces of bread, after removing stacks of gristle and bone, the women would bring out the fruit. The rainbow array differed each day according to what the men had most recently carried up in crates from the orchards—spring-green grapes, yolk-orange tangerines, deeply bloody cherries, pale yet pungent pears, jewels of kumquats, rubied pomegranates, peaches golder than the sun.

My grandmother, my Teyta, was notorious for harboring the notion that human beings had a separate stomach especially for fruit, and we all agreed. No matter how full we were, we ate piles of the sweet stuff.

Every eater had their own way of dealing with each kernel, pip, and pit. Teyta kept her face close to her plate, putting fruit in, dribbling seeds out. My aunt would deseed gingerly with a small knife. As an experiment in velocity, my cousins liked to spit their seeds off the veranda. Haram alayk! Some of the adults would admonish them, others would smile. He's planting the next crop! Me, I never spat like that. I couldn't bring myself to spit at all.

With my dark hair and oily skin, I was just like the rest of them, but also I was different. I could pronounce the harsh syllables of their language with ease, but I dreamt in one that felt more like my own. Across my nose ran a smattering of freckles we can attribute to my faraway father, who had stayed behind at home, enjoying the air-conditioned quiet of an empty house in another hemisphere, while I was far away, shoveling fruit into my small mouth, scabbed knees showing under the skirt of my flowered dress.

A child, I was beginning to sense a divide between the things we dream about and the things we can be sure about. The stories of princesses saved by princes I read in words and pictures in my distant school, the tale my parents told me before sleep about the moon falling in love with the stars, the satirical drawings I found in the dusty *French, English and Other Languages* section at the back of summertime bookstores, the cartoons populated by colorful children I watched on television in any country—early on, I knew these visions were not like life. Life was the hard pavement beneath my sandaled feet as I walked the village lanes. Life was wondering if the word "village" was quite right for this overgrown and broken place, with bulleted memories scattered across its concrete walls, colorful trash strewn across its weedy ditches, the various camouflages of the various men from the various militias and armies and squadrons and guards at the checkpoints on the beach road. Life was being stuck in between and wanting only to be anywhere else. Life was the people I met in the faraway land asking if I knew what my name meant and the people wherever we were asking my name as a question, asking where it was from, what it meant, and I would roll my eyes. Amira means princess. Life was putting my hand on my heart in American classrooms reciting my Pledge of Allegiance and looking at images of President Reagan, Bush, Clinton, whoever. In the summer, back in the faraway land, strange men loomed on large posters, the carousel leaders of our many factions, parties, clans, families. Some wore turbans and dresses, some wore Western suits, most had moustaches, and their giant faces hung from buildings and across major intersections, were posted on the walls of mosques and churches. Life was lonely school lunches and airplanes that took me to cacophonous family lunches. Life was not knowing how to talk about one of my countries when I was in the other. The personal wasn't at all political then; everything was personal, mine, and no one else could possibly understand it at all.

And the swallowing? The swallowing was my secret, something I could do in plain sight without being noticed. While my aunts fought over who would do the dishes, while my uncles sipped quickly at tiny steaming cups of thick cardamom-scented coffee, while they lovingly teased my grandmother and watched the world burn on the TV over her shoulder, while our ancestors hung from the walls and watched over all of us—framed, captured in black and white, frozen in another time we could only marvel at—while my mother promised a chocolate reward if my sister and I would agree to walk with her the three kilometers to the phone office to call my faraway father, I swallowed—

2.

My cousins, aunts, uncles, grandmother don't exist as bodies now. But they do exist as memories, as disembodied voices and other kinds of ghosts, as human-shaped slips on shining screens cutting up at me through the dark. Now I am a teacher, a professor; one would say I am an adult, although whenever I say it to myself, it feels untrue—but you are an adult, Amira—and the faraway land—we call it *Lubnan*—is a memory, an emerald sea past-dream. Here, in Amerka, there is the silver-shining ocean, licking up at all sides of our crowded island metropolis, and one thing I do know adulthood to mean is that life no longer feels like a yearly cycle on repeat, stretching out in a straight line—that when I try to hold all my life at once inside my brain, it curls up on itself like a lock of my hair, like a tide pool, like a long, indigo snake.

Due to my dad's career when I was a child and then my own adult proclivities, besides Lebanon, I have lived in, traveled to so many real places—Mexico and Richmond and Cairo and San Francisco and Falls Church and Saudi Arabia and Indonesia and Chiapas and Sudan and Shanghai—met so many real people in those particular places, learning and forgetting all their names, remembering their stories in pieces and putting them back together all wrong. I have friends I have lost, and friends that have stuck by me through all the coming and the going, friends that have come back, friends that still might—

And I have felt so irrevocably alone, and it has frightened me so much, this loneliness, and—work, free work, drink, men, friends, social media, drugs, food, gossip, exercise, meditation, you name it—I have practiced so many ways to erase that feeling.

In the years since my visits to the faraway land have become less frequent, I have become unmistakably American, pulled into the ebb and flow of these four seasons, these entertainment trends, these media wars, the press conferences, the polls on polls on polls.

And I've dated men from other lands, men from this land, men who work behind a bar, under the sun, under the fluorescent lights of a lab, staring at a computer from behind a desk. Tall men, short men, hairy, hairless, sweet, dumb, intelligent as all hell and slyly mean. Sometimes when I am alone, I list them on the walls inside my mind—and the letters glow, the list comes to life, burning, and turns into a monster, a creature with scales, with bones, with guts and blood. This monster is dragon-like, snake-y, blue-ish, green. His shape shifts, his body snakes through me, for my pleasure, for my pain.

The monster writhes through my arteries and my veins, seeking out all the parts of me that are just too hard to know. To escape the pain, I think and think and think, telling myself stories about who I am and what I need to change in order to slay the monster once and for all. But before I've figured it out, the next man appears.

3.

There is man after man after man after man, and then there is the man that breaks you. We can imagine this man as the tail of the monster, or as his head, his shining eyes, his sharp teeth, his forked tongue, his fiery breath.

Those first few months with Max, I was fueled by the conversations we'd have late into the night about politics, religion, culture, history. I felt so blessed to be with someone so smart, so inquisitive, so careful. We talked until we were so tired with unlocking the universe's secrets that we had no choice but to fall into bed in a tangle of limbs and kisses that slowly unfurled as we found a liquid rhythm together and swam in it and swam and swam, falling together into a slipstream of our cocreation.

Besides everything else, we shared the experience of being half-half. Like me, Max had primarily grown up tending towards the American part of himself, but the faraway part was undeniable. Pomegranate, cardamom, olive—we had the same flavors in our taste buds, we had the same dark thick hair and the same oily skin, we had parallel family stories. Max's father met his mother in this country of countries after leaving his own faraway land, after its ruler was ripped from power. Kind of like my father met my mother in Damascus after she left Beirut. Without the political turmoil of the Middle East in the seventies and eighties, no us.

We were the political given birth to the personal.

One night, when things still felt new, I curled up next to Max on his big couch and opened a map of Eurasia across our legs and pointed to the place where my family was from and then across borders to the place where my great grandfather had died, a shrine he had made multiple pilgrimages to. And Max pointed to the place, a few centimeters away, where his family was from and where most of them still lived. He hoped to visit someday, he said, but—embargoes and visas and all the paperwork and possibilities—it was hard.

Our minds stuffed with prayer calls listened to by ghosts, I looked into his Eastern eyes and, at that moment, it felt fated we'd go there together. We kissed, and it was like melting into each other, like we could have kept kissing forever, and, under my closed and fluttering lids, I hallucinated us as small children playing, running after each other in a large house full of Fertile Crescent light.

4.

Small feet slapping on marble, the cold splash of water from the washbasin in the hall, the marvel of grape leaves soaking in a dented aluminum cauldron, all our small hands and bodies clamoring around the plastic-covered dining table—these are the perennial images from my family's flat in the faraway land, distinct images that each represent a moment repeated so many times that it has been etched into my DNA, my right brain, my bones and skin, swimming up and down my vessels and veins.

And also there are the singular moments that flashed through the existent and were gone, but still, they changed everything. Still, they leave me utterly shook. Still, they burn in perpetuity. An example: that fateful afternoon in childhood Teyta and I were having lunch alone. When she noticed I had nothing on my plate after eating a small pyramid of cherries and grapes, she planted an image in my mind that would stay with me forever—

"What have you done? Where are the seeds? Are you the soil?" she asked, the flames in her eyes magnified by the thick Coke-bottle lenses of her plastic-rimmed glasses.

I shook my head solemnly.

"If you swallow too many seeds, Ms. Soil," she went on, her voice sterner than I'd ever heard it, "you'll have a big problem when they start to grow! You'll be full of stems and leaves and roots, and then the day will come when cherries and grapes will start popping from your ears and nose." She stretched her hand toward me, and I ejected a single seed into her palm. She pursed her lips, clenched her hand tight, and turned her soft, stooped hulk towards the kitchen.

On all of the mosquito-ridden nights I spent in that house thereafter, as I fell into sleep on the same small bed my mother had slept on when she was young, my thoughts were swarmed by branches and vines, creeping slowly through my insides. Half-conscious, I imagined roots coming out of the soles of my feet and planting me in a spot of moist earth, birds singing in my branches, and the sun shining its light, like butter, down on my skin of bark. But when I awoke, I knew if anything were to grow inside me, it would have to be weeds, it would have to be a deadly vine that strangled love, it would have to be a brown plant, thorny and vicious and afraid.

I kept swallowing—because I felt empty, I think, and trapped in my head, trapped in the hollow time and space between war and peace, between childhood and growing up, between continents and lives. Swallowing meant survival. Now, I see I must have learned it from others, although it really did feel like it was only mine, like I made it up myself. I learned it from those that fled and those that stayed and survived fifteen years of the puppet-masters' so-called Lebanese Civil War, which hollowed out their country, divided their capital, drove millions from the motherland and across the planet, turned homes into piles carved through by gullies of shrapnel, turned gods into masters and friends into enemies.

After the war was officially over, despite the fact getting to the faraway land should have been easier, since the travel bans were lifted and there was less to fight about, as I became an adult my visits became less frequent. Two years, three years, five, between trips. And still, I kept swallowing.

5.

Swallowing seeds seemed like one thing, swallowing men another, and Max was the one who helped me realize it all came down to swallowing myself.

The first fight we had was about Palestine. This was in 2015, during the United States presidential election season. On my social media, Max posted a critical response to an article I'd posted criticizing Hilary Clinton's stance on Israel.

As I anticipated seeing Max in real life, I wished to not say anything, but when I was in his presence, I found my body brimming with the need to speak. Quietly, I asked his intent. He looked away, his face reddened. His response was measured, with an undertow of anger, and he went on to talk at me for hours—about how Palestine was a broken cause, misguided, dangerous, poorly steered. Or maybe it was minutes. Anyway, I intervened only briefly, to explain that Palestine matters because it has to do with Israel and, naturally, with Lebanon, and Lebanon is mine in a way that I can't explain. After a pause, when he resumed talking, he said something like, "If you use this personal politics emotional nonsense tactic again, I can't be with you."

"Like, you're saying you want to break up?" I gulped, the first time the possibility had crossed my mind.

A map of the Middle East flashed through me, as did the time when I was three and my mother had to leave Lebanon through Israel with only me and my newly born sister; the orchards flashed, the sea, the bright bright roof of our building where we'd collected bullets as children; everything flashed, including Max's angry eyes. I wish I could tell you I turned around and walked out of his apartment, never to return. But in fact, I stayed right there and admitted that maybe he was right, that I barely understood the politics of the Middle East. I said I wanted to learn more. And over the months that followed, I did my best to please him. I read articles and watched videos and listened to him explain what he knew and how he saw the world. Sometimes I was fascinated, sometimes I was heartbroken, but I nodded, I asked questions. I wanted to show him I understood, to show him he was doing me a favor, filling me up with the truth.

Most of my other serious boyfriends had been really jealous types. I felt lucky with Max, because he just wasn't. But now I see the intimate and violent thoughts I've swallowed again and again have taken a variety of forms—from jealousy over a guy I've kept in touch with to ideas about what's right or true. Now, I know that the personal and the political aren't so separate after all. In both ways, in all ways, I was a vessel, a wound, to be filled with vigor, to be dominated, changed by force.

For a while, Max convinced me that Israel's existence was entirely warranted and just. He convinced me that Islam was at its core a violent religion, that the Islamists, in fact, were taking over the hearts and minds of our great land. He convinced me that modern-day feminism was flawed, that *decolonize* was a metaphor irresponsibly deployed by the left, that all lives matter and Black on Black crime was a real reason.

And for the presidential election, he had me convinced that I should vote for Gary Johnson, and I did—which, at the time, was a very big deal. I am not telling you all this so you hate this character I have drawn of Max. I also hope you will not hate me. Time has passed since then, and I trust he has changed. I know I have. That's what this essay is about. The thing I want to tell you is that it's terrifyingly funny what I think I know when I'm scared, how much of the time I have been scared, how much subconscious energy I have used to separate myself from my own political life, from myself.

On the fateful first Tuesday in November, as we watched the numbers come in, Max had me convinced that Hilary would win anyway. We changed the channel to watch some show he liked before we went to bed.

I fell asleep with my head on Max's broad chest. I am tall but he was taller and also big, and I really liked that, the feeling of being enveloped by him, the feeling of fitting over, under, beside, inside, around somebody else the way I did with him.

In the thickest part of night, Max got up to use the bathroom. I woke up, too, and crossed the room to check my phone. It's impossible to fully explain how I felt when my screen cut up at me like a bright knife through the dark, showing me the other guy had won. My first reaction was it just had to be a joke. The *Times*'s front page looked like the *Onion* memes I saw all the time in those days. It looked like the crumpled *MAD* magazines my sister and I had found in those Lebanese bookstores when we were kids. One thing I can say for certain about that moment and all the images it evoked is they weren't as distant as they seemed, and yet I pushed them down.

The toilet flushed and Max walked back in the room, his phone in his hand. He had somehow played a joke on me. It seemed so clear. The headlines were some Internet scheme. He had gotten in on it to fuck with the ambivalently hopeful girlfriends of the world.

I couldn't see his face in the dark, but I heard his laugh.

"Wait, Trump won, for real?" I said.

"Yup." He laughed some more.

"No," I said, and he was still laughing.

We went back and forth like that for a frozen moment, him chuckling syllables through the stale shadows, me quiet and struggling to think, to breathe. It didn't feel real, but Max didn't stop. I played at anger, and before I knew it, I was on top of him in his bed, like so many times before, my legs straddling his chest, his stomach, but this time my hands weren't stroking but holding, gripping his cheeks, then squeezing his neck.

Scant light from the alley came through the window and across the bed, highlighting the edges of his nose, his jaw, flecking his lovely eyes. He had a face like a classical statue, and as he laughed and I looked at him from above, he looked like one of those evil gods who takes pleasure in people's suffering. I must have squeezed harder because he stopped laughing. "I can't breathe," he said.

Some part of me would like to tell you that I strangled him. Instead, I let go and he swallowed, laughed again, and maybe I finally laughed, too.

We stayed together for half a year after that, and I guess that means I needed, wanted, needed more of Max and he of me. That was a dark and lonely time for all of us, and I know I can't speak for everybody everybody, but can't we agree that politically, personally, we've all gone through tough times? And the hardest thing for me to face is the possibility that I bring it on myself, that I ask for more and more.

Did Max and I have sex after we woke in the night to find out Trump would be our next president? I can't be sure, but I think so, and, if we did, then it went like this—

I let the heart-stomach feeling pulse through my body. I wanted to say something to Max, but what could I say? I feel lonely when I'm with you? I miss the things I hardly remember? I forget where I'm from? My thoughts finally shut up when Max put on some music from the future—all blips and space sounds, all sonic chorus and synth beats. It felt like we were nowhere, the two of us, and when he reached for me, I reached back. Hands, lips, ears, tongues, skin and wet and moans and soft becoming wet and hard and all of it. The rhythm of our bodies took me away. And I closed my eyes and returned to my childhood kingdom, floating above the orchard, the trees like waves washing me out to the sapphire sea. Yes, and my grandmother's prophecy came true two decades after it was delivered in the waves of a new kind of orgasm—I was floating, then crashing, an explosion from inside, until vines, leaves, thorns, roots shot from my eyes, my mouth, nostrils, ears.

And like that, the world had changed.

6.

In fact, the world has never stopped changing, as long as I have been here and long before that. My ancestors might seem frozen in photographs, and yet they are the past alive in the present. They survived the surging and ebbing power of capitalism, self-righteous clashes of politics, confusion about love and beauty and lust, the chaotic and inevitable suffusion of puberty and belief. And the price of all that survival—this swallowing, this swimming and gulping and shifting in order to stay still—is a thing we have not really named, not even in our thoughts. Still, the thing, nameless, took some form (maybe a monster? a slippery snake? maybe vines and tendrils and leaves? maybe tide pools upon tide pools with no real possibility for stillness, for peace...). Stuffed inside our heads, our necks, our throats, our ears, it filled the spaces that yielded to it, muffling everything, everywhere. And yet it was so light. How could it even matter, really? (It did.) And how is it that it persists to this day? (It does.) And how do we breathe through it? Do we all grow up and break free together, or does it happen to us one by one?

7.

Do you remember the day after the election and all the days after that? Do you remember how social media suddenly felt a lot more meaningful and confusing? Do you remember all the calling campaigns and protests and posts where people tried to talk about their feelings of hopelessness and hope and devastation and everything else? All the speculating and crying and falling apart?

During the time of these questions, Max went more easily from stoic to suspicious, angry, easily excitable. Reliably, always, he'd get back to stoic. It was inconceivable how much we'd changed since we'd known each other, how much, in each other's eyes, our reflections had changed. I can't say for sure that I remember all this as it was. No, these are pieces of stories I've told myself and others so many times that I've made them all true. These are the many stories that I've birthed and married together, for you. For me.

Over the phone the evening after Trump's inauguration, Max told me the pictures of the scant crowd gathered for the swearing-in all over the liberal media were fake fake news, and I told him I wanted to go to the Women's March. I hoped he would come with me, but I also knew he wouldn't.

As I pedaled my bike over the East River the next morning, I thought about calling him, but what would I say? I pushed and I pushed and the city skyline looked beautiful before me and I felt the same rush as I always do upon descending into Manhattan. My phone vibrated against my pelvis, and I knew it was him and left it in my pocket, wanting to make him wait. It vibrated again and again. I made myself wait to look at it until I was locking up. Not Max. It was my mother, my father, my brother-in-law, texting in chorus from D.C. My sister's first baby was on her way. They were all at the hospital, waiting for her to join us in this world.

I was surprised, caught off-guard, suddenly frantic. I should be home with my family and not here, I thought as I entered the throng.

Groups of people who seemed like friends were gathered together in small knots in the immense crowd, and families, children on shoulders, women holding hands, men standing by. Exuberant crowds with uterus signs and Trump masks clogged the streets. Police blockades disrupted traffic in every direction. I felt dizzy. Unsure. It was impossible to focus on any one thing. And as I found my way along the river of bodies, feeling both a part of them and also utterly alone, the new Amira was born. Do I mean me? Maybe. I want to tell you that I joined the protest wholeheartedly, that I screamed my lungs out against our new leader, screamed for our rights to be seen, noticed, understood, cherished, that my screams became a rainbow gushing out of me, a rainbow colored by all the anger and sadness and fear I had swallowed deep down inside me for years. But the truth is, I couldn't feel anything and I could feel everything, all at once. Among the millions, I was tiny and defenseless, and I could tell the story of that day as the day I began to come into the world anew, my eyes not wanting the light.

But also, my sister called her daughter "Amira." My reaction the first time she said it: That's my name! Mine! Like a bolt, I let the feeling course through me; it was sharp, an electric trill, and I had to let it go—because it's not just for me. Amira is also the name of my aunt, my great-grandmother, too, a name swimming through our female blood, a name that swam here from far away across the teeming seas, a name that will live on.

Before leaving the march, I chanted a little and danced some, and when I was ready to go, it was hard to leave. And as if life were a video game, I glided around, across, above the march, got a feel for the beautiful monster of a million bodies and voices it was, before heading back south, buoyed by a wave of what I had just experienced and letting go of all of it to slip into the stream of regular traffic, trusting I was powered forward by a new velocity that is carrying us over the edge into some version of reality we can't imagine, the crest of a wave breaking open the way we live, love and make meaning.

ALWAYS IN YOUR HAIR
X.C. ATKINS

I LOVED Auggie's hair right from the very start. I can't say it was the first thing I noticed about her. I think it was her eyes, her smile, her ass, and then her hair. It very well could have been her ass first, if I'm really being honest. But I did notice her hair, her long, big curly Jewish hair. And I loved it.

I loved putting my face in it. It felt like I was putting my face in a soft forest or a spell.

I always paid attention to women's hair. I paid attention to it like it was the Weather Channel. It could tell you a lot of things. It could tell you what they'd done that morning or the night before. It could tell you if they were single or in a relationship. It could tell you if they were going home with you or if they never wanted to speak to you again. It could tell you how many kids they had, it could tell you if they were in sales, it could tell you if they'd just traveled to a different country for the first time. No one told me this secret, I learned it all by myself. Or maybe what it was, I just listened to women, when they talked about it. Because they knew better than anyone else, of course, what a big indicator it was. What stage of life the state of their hair put them in.

So it surprised me when Auggie would straighten her hair anytime we'd meet up with her family for the holidays. I didn't understand that. I thought her curls were so beautiful. But I paid attention to how adamant she was about getting her hair straightened before the family event, the frenetic shift in her voice, the slight rattle in her pupils. She had some crazy tendencies, I perceived quickly. And that excited me. It's like seeing an accident that's about to happen. You can't take your eyes off.

When we moved in together, I had no idea how much her hair would become a part of my life. I don't mean that metaphorically. I mean it was everywhere. Clumps on the side of the shower. In all the drains. In my mouth when I woke up. In my underwear when I went to the bathroom. It was insane. It was everywhere. It was unstoppable. Plus, she brought her cat. What the fuck. I thought early on I'd use the cat to break up with her. I was allergic to cats. But this fucking cat. I wasn't allergic to it. I don't know how that works. I even went to the doctor. I said, I'm normally allergic to cats. How come not this one?

The lady just shook her head. "I don't know," she said. "It's a blessing."

Auggie had short hair, Auggie had long hair. She had pink hair, blonde hair. It always looked good. But it was everywhere, all the time. I got used to it. I never lost my mild disgust at finding it in every drain or in my food or on my toothbrush, but I got so that I didn't need to complain every time I encountered it. I couldn't waste my complaints on something I encountered that often. The relationship wouldn't have been sustainable otherwise. And I really wanted this thing to work.

Down the line, we got a dog. And very quickly, we both came to love the dog like hell. It was a very pretty dog. One night, Auggie was at work and me and the dog and the cat were sitting on the couch watching one of those comic book movies. I tried to get my fill while Auggie was elsewhere. I needed the nostalgia refill. It was like a soul boost for me. Cause all other hours, I had to suffer from this fucking world.

But I looked down at our dog and she blinked sleepily to me and I said, "Wanna go out, Baby?"

Her ears perked up. We got off the couch and I got her leash and we went out.

It was late. We went down the hill and around the bend into the mulch, where our dog liked to poop. Yup, here she went. Popping that squat. It was a good one. I realized I was lucky: I had one poop baggie left. I collected what she'd dropped and tied it up.

But our sweet girl looked up at me nervously. Uh oh. She had more. Except now she started to do this weird anxious shuffle, her butt down. She was looking up at me again. She was worried, I could tell. She needed me. I tried to look around at her butt. She had a last little nugget of a turd there, but it was hanging by a strand of hair.

I knew I had to extract the hair but I was out of baggies. But what else could I do? Our sweet Baby couldn't do anymore. The hair, Auggie's strand of hair, was holding that little piece of turd for ransom. I had to use my hand.

I bent down and pulled the hair out of her ass. That's all there was to it. Our sweet little dog was happy immediately. I'd saved her. I was her dad. I'd saved her.

I had to suppress the surge of revulsion swelling in me. We got back up to the apartment quick, and I washed my hands. I wanted to wait til Auggie got back home and tell her what happened. Basically, yell at her. I had another glass of wine and started to feel the night coming in on me. I was getting older. I tucked our dog in, put up the gate, brushed my teeth and went to bed. I told myself I'd tell Auggie tomorrow. But when I woke up, I didn't remember. We just laid there together, my face in her hair, and it smelled so nice. Like it always had.

NORTON ISLAND

JESSICA LASER

There are moths when we talk about Sergei,
two kinds, those that have been eating
away at his memory, so that he appears
with holes, and those attracted to the bright
insight of his sustained but bodiless presence.
When I miss him most, I go hunting moths.
I use myself as bait, calling up all
my illumination, surprised to find that
which comprises brightness originates
not in thought but in the willing
and on that merit I attract them to me
and find their path leads only to me
and find in myself those missing from me
have left themselves undisturbed
by geography. Sergei roves the stairs
built into the side of the hill. He starts
each day along the field and brings
wildflowers for the vase on the table
where they remain until they can't raise
their own heads. "If they don't die
they weren't really alive," he says
but now I'm here with Meg
and the vase and the gnarled flowers,
entirely dry. Their receding water
revealed a small island populated
by pines, spiders and deer. Meg starts
each day along its field and blesses
herself with its ticks and grasses.
The field loves her, the sun never sets

upon her, for she keeps from the field
her anger and the field knows only her
harmlessness and love. She lies down
and revives it. But Meg is not a girl
to be amazed. She, the invisible mainland,
invokes the haze of summer days on islands
off the coast of Maine just so she can lift the fog.
I love her, reader, but it is gluttony
to hold two people where one should be—
in my heart, I mean, in my heart.

LAPLANDISH SPECULATIONS
A BAD BIRCH

What is more Nordic than an orca's aorta?

Only the northernmost ward
of my bent ventricle knows.

My mean bestemor say I icky
so snort, but yay I got God's dingaling.

If indeed I err to have caribou for bae,
I want not not to be bad naughty.

Not me, what with my cathartic fox
and muskox carcass so heavy

with horn. Put away your sun
for sixty-nine days to come and see

just how much Finnish you wouldn't
have in you. Only an old Norse would

know Norsk wood. I wooed. I wailed.
I virked that nasty tree until it wailed
no more. I knew some Nebraskan Danish

that tasted like a sweetish pile of shit.
Here I sit shitless with no spit to give.

Admit it. Two shites under a sheet,
both billy goats and bitty ghosts.

My heart froze. I left it whaling.

AS UGLY DOES, 1969
HERMINE PINSON

BOBBY'S SECOND *daughter sits on the couch one night. It's late. He watches. He surmises. At this moment, his daughter is rolling her hair with her head turned sideways, like her mother sometimes does, her eyes on the TV, which is nearly at a right angle as her fingers section off her hair, then roll it, repeating the gesture with the next section. What else does he notice when he walks into the room and sits on the couch, after having trouble with the front door lock, as he usually does when he has drunk more than his share of liquid bliss? Her innocence immanent, an aspect of herself which she holds close, having only recently become aware of it, but as a flaw or hindrance or blind spot. In its shadowed gloom, the TV casts its ghostly facsimiles of life.*

Harry the Hippy lies asleep. He's the dog they swore had recently escaped from the circus and landed on their doorstep one rainy night, before Hermine and her father left the house to see a performance by Duke Ellington and his band at Jones Hall. Harry lies asleep, his blond coat staining the rug with motor oil from his having sat for hours under the car in the driveway. Bobby has come home from wherever he's been all evening, perhaps somewhere he's not gotten something he wanted. He is tight, and he squints at his daughter, as if trying to remember who she is. She mumbles her greeting, keeping her eyes on the TV and rolling her hair in the pink sponge rollers. Bobby's response is to plop down beside her, like a puppet whose master has suddenly cut his strings. Sometimes, when he's had too much to drink, the animated face he usually shows to friends and family yields to the naked glare of his "quarter-to-three" look, the one that notices the thing they've been smelling all night is right there in front of them and it stinks like vomit or curdled milk. His eyes narrow to a one-eyed squint, then to a more appraising look, then a startled one, and finally a leer of recognition. He chuckles in spite of himself, a short high bark that sounds close to a cry, and crosses his arms tightly across his chest, as if he has made a novel discovery. "You know somethin'?" he says in a conspiratorial way.

"Huh?" she says, still watching the *Twilight Zone* rerun.

"You ugly," spoken in the vernacular, with a relish that makes him tighten his arms to his chest and draw his posture up, only to break down in an explosion of short cries that again have only a passing resemblance to laughter. She looks straight ahead at the TV. What else is there to do? No one in the room but father and daughter and therefore no one to dispute or confirm his assertion. Now she is the center of his attention, and it feels like being shrunk, then trapped inside someone's mind. Enveloped in translucent silence beneath the gently turning overhead fan, father and daughter sit before the TV like two Jason deCaires Taylor underwater sculptures, father's eyes squeezed to slits in dark repose, as escaped strands from daughter's sponge rollers move in the languid rhythm of black seaweed.

In the subterranean environs of two am, it would be meaningless to say, "You're wrong," or "No, I'm not," because the daughter doesn't necessarily disagree with him, but she thinks, Why does he find it necessary to point out her ugliness? Should she have reminded him, "Remember when you called me your 'little brown baby with sparklin' eyes'?" On the other hand, why reason with him? Because Daddy wasn't there, nor Bobby the gregarious, nor "the doctor." This was Bobby's dregs, the man her mother too often encountered at the end of a long workday and long night of play—not quite the belligerent one on the verge of eruption, but his philosophical twin, the one always on the edge of sleep, having rested his scalpel for incisive observation. Mama lies asleep in the daughter's old bedroom, now her bedroom, having retreated from the daily fray of living to contemplate her wounds. Tears spring from daughter's face like they do in *Little Orphan Annie* cartoons, but she keeps her eyes on the last scene of the episode, the one where the tony couple who think they've driven into an empty town with plastic milk cartons and fruit in the refrigerator and plastic trees discover they are the playthings of a giant little girl, now their god and mother, who can play with them until Mama calls her for dinner. Why does the daughter feel shame as a visceral thing, as the smell of her own armpits, the drying insides of her mouth, her greasy hair rollers? Images of Rod Serling's subversive logic fill the screen and somehow make sense to the daughter, even if she can't explain why.

"Little brown baby with sparklin' eyes, come to your pappy and sit on his knee." Daddy first uttered these words when he was a young doctor and father whose actions assured his children, if not his wife, that he cared deeply for them—and not just because they were his children.

But his second daughter is no longer a bandy-legged baby, he no longer loves his wife, and he sees his children with more clarity every day. She is sixteen-going-on-seventeen, and she has a boyfriend who tongue-kisses her in the backseat of her own car and fondles her firm young breasts like ripe fruit. Usually, Daddy barely acknowledges boyfriend, growling a fatherly greeting whenever boyfriend comes over. Now, father reveals that he is aware of his second daughter's changing body and mind. Her concession to having heard her father is evident in the way she dabs at her eyes with one of the tissues she uses to wrap around her rollers. He smiles and closes his eyes to his daughter's tears glistening in the febrile darkness of blue light. Then, suddenly, he rouses himself and interrogates his knees, before standing up and reaching around himself, as if to adjust an invisible skirt, and marches off to bed, stiff-legged and resolute. And perhaps daughter's disappointment isn't about her belief or disbelief in her father's mean revelation; it is as if all that fathering had been a lie, and now, after guzzling spirits, he can tell her for her own good what she needs to know before she lives another minute in this world.

CYNDI LAUPER

MEG FREITAG

Some are nectar people,
And some are brine people,
While some like milk best.
Some will drink anything, so long
As it's free. I dreamed of you
Wearing a long white veil, like a bride.
When you lifted it your face was smooth
And featureless. How
Will you drink your new bottle of nice rye,
I thought. How will you sing the song you sing
When you want to tease the dog,
Make her stand up like a little person
On her back legs
And howl.

SQUIRREL TAIL

MEG FREITAG

I traded an abalone shell for it, and a purple pen.
I used it as a bookmark and one day I wore it in my hair to school.
When my teacher saw it she made me throw it over the fence,
Then watched me as I washed my hands with janitor's soap.
After school I climbed the fence to try to find it in the undergrowth.
The mulch I touched was black and slick and cool.
Owls hooted at me, like they knew who I was
And that I was no good.
I ran home beneath the purple, writhing shadows
Of tall tall trees, no squirrel tail in my hand or backpack or hair.
The world had been going through one of its small phases; I hated
Being outside in the evening when suddenly it grew.

PICK OF THE LITTER
CLAY McLEOD CHAPMAN

LOOK AT them go. Nothing but a knot of limbs, all tangled up into one another. You've got to hand it to the mommy who's generous enough to donate a whole box of sidewalk chalk to the rest of the playground—but there's blood in the water now. These kids are like kindergarten sharks gnashing over the last scraps of chum. Wouldn't want to reach my hand in there. Probably wouldn't get all my fingers back.

Careful, kids! Watch out for the little ones. No biting now. Elbows down.

Playgrounds can be pretty intense with the pecking order, can't they? The children are one thing, but I'm talking about the parents. All the adults just sit back on the park benches, ringside seats, letting their kids have at it. See who survives.

You've got the nannies, who could give a crap. They simply toss the kids into the mix and then chat on their phone for the next few hours. They barely glance up from their manicures while their wards are off getting garroted to the swing-set.

You've got the daddies—but they're a rare bird around these parts. Might as well be looking for a unicorn out here. They never know what they're supposed to be doing with themselves.

And then you've got the mommies. All the mommies. They cluster together in their corner to compare juice box brands or whatever. They're more interested in chatting amongst themselves than whatever's happening out here. Don't get me wrong. They'll occasionally look over their shoulders, just to make sure it's somebody else's kid that's screaming their little head off—not theirs.

Is anybody even watching their kids out here? Did you just see what that boy did to that other boy? Did anyone see what just happened to that little girl?

It's like a free-for-all out here. The punching. The dry-humping. The kicking and clawing. The spitting. The hair-pulling. The gnashing and the gnawing.

Does anybody even care what happens to our kids?

I'm not going to lie—I steer clear of the other mothers here. Their club. I'd rather just watch the children. They're more interesting, anyways.

Ever try to guess whose kid is whose? All you've got to do is scan the crowd and see if you can pinpoint which kid belongs to which parent. It's fun.

Come on. Let's play.

That girl. In the sundress with the pink flowers? My guess is she belongs to that mom over there. They share that same air, that hoity-toity *me-me-me* vibe.

That boy. The one with the skinned knee? Tough call. I'm going to go out on a limb here and say he belongs to—*wait.* I'm going nanny on this one. With the way he's acting out there, there's no way his mother's got eyes on him. Like a freaking Tasmanian devil. Get that kid on his Ritalin already. He's nanny material all the way.

How about her?

Over there. On the slide. With the pigtails. It's like the whole park belongs to her. She's not bossy like the others. Everything else seems to—just seems to radiate around her. It's her playground. The rest of us are just playing on it, you know?

They're so perfect when they're that young. It's a shame to think she'll lose that cuteness in a few years. The older they grow, the more they lose that beauty.

Can't stay cuddly forever, I guess. Everybody's got to grow up sooner or later.

That's usually when I give them back. I'll just drop them off at the playground—any playground, they're all the same—and pick up a new one.

Which one's mine? Good question. I haven't quite decided yet. Usually, the right one just kind of comes to me. I'll know when I see her. Or him. I'm not picky. It's just a matter of knowing when to swoop in. When their mother isn't looking.

Good things come to those who wait.

There she is.

Excuse me.

THE BEAUTY PRIZE
SARAH ELAINE SMITH

The cows wake her,

the sea rises
like some dark city.

A beautiful woman
in a field
with a hatchet

following Medusa
through warm wind.

You want to love
what you already love

but it is too late.
You have already seen it.

Seen it and are mine.

THE DISCOURSE
SARAH ELAINE SMITH

Still, it makes me happy to see a bluebird.
Especially if it is fat in the wintertime.
Especially if it has a cute mohawk.
But not if it pecks at my house.

I throw a book at the wall.
The cats look at me as if
I am capable of something monstrous.

And I am. I am sailing against
the harbor lights. My heart
is a blue-black room.
I will be myself at any cost.

SLOWERS
NATHANIEL RAPPOLE

"HAD THAT dream again."

Driftr acted as though he wasn't listening. He was young's only human companion. Pushing seventy-nine, he was tall and lean and lived alone. "The talk of a man ain't got a damn thing to do with how his feet work," Driftr said as he kept time by tapping his toes on the floor.

"The beast came at me. It tore open my chest and dried leaves spilled out and took the form of a thousand bats."

"Ah. A good dream. This world needs more bats." Driftr fake-smacked the back of his right arm, as if to kill a feeding mosquito.

Music hung and stabbed the air. Loud squealing over steady soul, like the slaughter of a hog over a fountain of warm milk.

The old man's eyes had a sweet glaze to them. "Saxophone alone is like sexonthephone... It don't cut it. Add some bass n' drums and just like that, you've got the real deal." His voice was a gravel truck unloading its contents into a deep hole.

young smiled and stepped out into the dusk's midlight.

It was early November and the trees of the Darkwood were showing their dying colors.

"Bats," young thought.

~ BLUE JAY ~

young was the better part of thirteen, but his light was as old as Jesus. A carpenter of the existential, he had learned to take care of himself years before his family was gone.

Driftr switched out the record and joined young on the porch. "This here fella was a buddy of mine in the '50s. He gave me this bit of vinyl seventeen years ago. Just prior to his meeting with the infinite."

They listened while the night's insects sang nothing but the chorus.

It was a thunderin and a thunderin and lightnin on the day this poor boy wasa born. I ain't never known nothin but yer trubbl...

young spoke of the past he saw. "Eye didn't know why I did it. Neither did my mouth or any other part of my face, and the horse-apple mass behind my forehead had no part in it. Nah. My hands told the story. They followed through with such conviction that, trembling above and covered with blood, they felt no remorse."

He looked at Driftr.

"That was the first time I had bow shot and trimmed a buck by myself. I was eight years pass and had made the arrowhead out of the ribs of an old harmonica I found in the dirt. I don't know much about music, but the grooves put a hum in the air that to me sounded like the blues."

Driftr laughed. It sounded like bits of earth were lodged in his throat. "Yessss," he hissed in unison with the end of the A-side. "I believe you've been hunting since the dawn of days."

~ PA BLOOD ~

Living in a heart made of violent smoke and rubber metal was a billboard with a large glowing face. The text below the giant's chin read, "Hurt in an accident? GET YOUR$!"

This distortion in the sky belonged to a cityman who made his fortune off of the unfortunate. A story all too common, but in the fall of the late '90s this man decided to leave the lights, noise and money to live in a cabin in the Appalachian deep.

It was all because of a dream that he aimed to claim some forgotten piece of family land in an area the locals called Moonwood.

The dream had to do with grassy urchins and sea cucumbers of fungus. It had to do with large foreboding trees that swayed in brine and a beautiful woman floating lifeless in the horizon. It had to do with a boy with the body of countless animals and a crab-shaped moon.

This cityman with a dream and newly-sought destiny was a learned man with a distinct taste for knowledge. He devoured books. He consumed them as if he were a lioness and each book a fresh gazelle—a carcassy sandwich filled with sinewy strands of paper and ink, its contents to be digested over years.

He became a lawyer by proxy. Truth is, he could have done almost anything.

He filled his car with the likes of alchemical hermeticism and Newton and headed towards the southern wilds.

~ MA BLOOD ~

A feral cat chanting in space. The aum of the purr. She be a utiful woman. Strong and silent with a preternatural sense for hunting and survival.

She had never known life outside of Moonwood, nor did she have any care to.

She had no name, for that was the tradition into which she was born, and she barely spoke because the need rarely arose.

One day, shortly after meeting a man from the city, a vision of terrible strength was bestowed upon her.

She was walking near the northern boundaries of Moonwood, just where it meets with the Darkwood. This was a place few animals dared enter. All sides were guarded by brambles as thick as spiny whale guts and twice as murky. The leaves overhead were transparent from sunlight, and she could see their veins—and just above the tree line, a day moon.

She became faint. The brambles opened as if a puppeteer in the clouds pulled the thorny strings to the sides, revealing an old oak tree. Its bark seemed to crawl. The crawling turned to defined shape and a huge bear was birthed from the old oak tree. Snarling with chunks of spit as hard as acorns, the beast walked slowly towards her.

Its hide was a metropolis of matted propolis and blood. It reeked of mashed berries and urine. The bear raised one giant paw and held it in front of her face. Beams of Godlight shot from its claws.

She awoke naked in a moss garden. The sun's rays touching her skin like a lover in the morning. It was then that she knew a child was in her.

~ YOUNG BLOOD ~

A boy such as this is no boy at all, but a many-life made young again.

One hundred and thirty-eight days after young's birth, his father stepped through the great oak door that was the mouth of their house and headed north. Never to be seen or heard from again.

young's mother spoke of this only once.

As she lay on her deathbed, she asked for young to come close so that he could better feel what she had to say.

"Don't hide, my son. For it's when yer hiding when the lion comes for yer mind n' tears out yer name."

She coughed blood and bile.

"Sept round here, we got bears and no names to scratch at." She smiled. "Yer pa didn't hide. The deathbeast called for him and he went. His last words to me will be mine to you: 'The crow caws in fives while the wooden owl flies above the darkwater. Love take me with you, for I cannot see without yer guidin light.'"

This was the most young's mother had ever said to him at any one time. With few words, she had nourished his instincts from the beginning and helped him to sharpen his knowledge for solitary survival until the end.

young was seven when he dragged his mother's body outside to burn and it wasn't until his ninth fall that he spoke to another human.

~ WOODS ~

Late one morning, young heard the sound of a man's voice on the wind.

He stepped through the great oak door, felt a cool breeze from the north and walked in that direction.

young only knew of the Darkwood through the short yarns that his mother would sometimes spin. They were always brief but somehow telling of that wildly unknown place. She herself had been drawn to its mysterious power, but had never physically entered its territory.

young took with him his filled quiver, bow and knife.

He was scared, and the closer he came to the northern edge of Moonwood, the colder it became. He heard the gargled caws of a crow that sent chills down to his heels. "Gaaaa! Awaay! Dead-dead-death!" it seemed to warn.

He walked the Darkwood border in hopes of finding a chink in the thorn armor, but to no avail. young had reached the thickness. He stopped, closed his eyes and listened.

There was a man singing on the other side of the impenetrable wall of vegetation.

At night I can't tell if I'ma sleep or awake.
So far away... You'll never catch me.
The glass shining thru it's pointing at you—
reflections of me are cast out to sea... You'll nevr see me.
A tree broke in two for me and for you,
with the blood of the lamb buried in sand... You'll nevr bleed again.
Shhooowwhwwhwwlwowwssssssh!
And the long arm of the sea made a sound.

"Hello, young huntr!" the singer said from beyond. He now seemed so close that, if it weren't for the forever-brush, young could have reached out and touched him. "These crazed brambles run long, but not so wide. Ifn yer searching for a way through it, I can't help you. But the moon can."

The voice was old and young, though it might not be human. It sounded rough and choppy, like large carnivorous territorial grunts in an idling motorboat.

young stepped back and looked up. There, the waxing first quarter moon showed its form in the midday light.

He decided to move west and follow the dark portion of the moon—all the while keeping it in sight just above the tree line.

The sky darkened and there was a denseness to the air. His heart quickened and he became slightly faint.

He held on tight to his bow with his right hand.

The brambles seemed to be filled with black blood. Oil-rich capillaries reaching towards the sky while the larger circulatory system pulsed all around him.

The woods were very much alive.

young walked for miles and as darker day became blind night. He noticed something odd about the bramble wall. Many of its tips turned silver from the reflection of the moon and a large section of the mass started to recede into the Darkwood, creating an entrance.

~ SLOW TIDE ~

"It's thought that newly hatched leathrback sea turtles have a one-in-one thousand chance of reaching adulthood. From the moment they are out of their egg shells, they are drawn to the sea's powr. Their birth mothr is long gone when the moon's light helps to guide them from the sandy pit to the salty deep."

young could tell that the old singer was looking towards the night sky as he spoke.

"Name's Shallo Huggins, but no one cept my momma evr used that name, and she's loooooong gone. You can call me Driftr. Being a young huntr from Moonwood, I bet you ain't gotta name."

"That's right."

"I bet your daddy was a cityman with a plan and your momma never saw him coming."

young nodded in the pitch.

"Well, I saw you all coming years ago, and Ima call you young—becuz that's what you are."

Driftr had no problems moving through the Darkwood and young needed only to follow the sound of the old man's footsteps.

It was cold.

Driftr sang with the rhythm of his own walk:

Oh—no...
Nobody home.
We eat-nor drink-nor money-have-we none... HA!

A barred owl called in the distance: *Who cooks for you? Who cooks for you alllllll?*

young smelled fire as they approached a log cabin that emitted a flickering light out of a circular window.

He was very tired.

Driftr stepped inside the cabin and motioned for young to enter.

While young had only just met the old man, he felt completely disarmed. Still, the thought of how Driftr had known such details about his parents left him wanting to ask.

There was a bowl of hot soup next to a bed that was made on the floor by a roaring fireplace.

"There's yer sleep spot, young huntr. These nights are good for a-dreaming, and I will be a bunch of wood feathers and a beak of stone." Driftr laugh-hissed like sandpaper on a steel pipe. He walked out of the room and shut the door behind him.

Aside from the crackling of the fire, all was quiet.

young, who now felt like he could barely keep his eyes open, put down his bow and quiver, crawled into the floornest and fell into a deep sleep.

~ AMBERGRIS ~

The sky was a swirl of absurdplum purple and slashorange glassblue—impossible colors that young had not known to exist. Hundreds of black vultures were riding the thermals, taking the form of storm clouds.

A large tree stood in front of him. Oak and fur woven into a closed portal. Its bark oozing bloodsap.

young heard hissing from above. One of the branches had an owl on it that was looking at him.

The owl had a gray and rigid beak that looked to be made of stone.

Its feathers were large and its feet were fused to the branch.

SSSSSSSsSSSSsSSssSS! It spun its head and began to retch.

Something dropped from its throat-hole onto the forest floor.

The owl snapped its legs free from the branch and flew off into the darkness, its wings like wooden wind chimes.

young went over and picked up a brownish pellet that had landed in the leaves below.

It was still warm. He began to pull it apart and inspect its contents.

Small beaks, mouse and bird bones made up what seemed to be a key.

young put his left hand to the great oak's trunk and found a small hole just to the right of the curvy fault line of the giant creature.

A deafening growl-scream came from within, causing young to drop the key and put his hands to his ears.

He stepped back.

young thought of his mother and without further hesitation he picked up the key and unlocked the portal.

Salt water.

Leagues of it came spilling out of the oak tree, and within seconds young found himself in the middle of an ocean with no land in sight.

young awoke.

The sun was shining through a window and had painted a golden circle on his face.

He rose and went outside.

Driftr was sitting on the porch, singing to himself.

Come on in the watr's fine, if ya like a little broth
and brine.

young stared at the old man. "What lives in the great oak?"

Driftr looked at young intently. His eyes large and black. "The gnash gnaw jawr is a living shadow full of dampfur and toothclaw. A real creature of the Darkwood and a slave to the flesh hunt. Its purple spotted bone-cars will park in the lot that is your skull. Little lamb, do not fret. There are worse ways to meet the eve of your days. Greet the heap that you will become with the understanding that you are nitrogen. You are bear shit."

~ WILL BEND ~

"I met your pa just before he died." There was a distinct shift in Driftr's voice and he gleamed with immense kindness.

The air was shallow and calm.

"He too dreamed of the beastly life givr n' takr of these woods. Its ground-up grunts gave him a salted death song, which he wrote down for me to give to you, if evr you was to come this way."

young unfurled the yellowed, dirt-streaked paper and read aloud.

In a darkened wood fell a shadow of a man
Broken blood, weakened hands
Hot with plague when the vision came
A massive figure to end the game

I've heard it said life's thread is of the weakest kind
Therein lies the beauty of its absurd design
Most are quick to guess by my face and clawed caress
I have come with a soul purpose

Where you die
"Away!" crows cry
Sea and sky
Will blend

Driftr interjected here and explained the next part was young's father's response, and therefore his own addition to Death's song.

young felt his drumming heart beating time in his chest. He swallowed and continued.

I hold my breath
And there stands death with my hand in his
Dear God, am I truly ready for this?
Its mouth is covered in a crude substance
Like a seabird in a spill, I give-in to the will
Of outside forces, but of course it's not that easy
It makes me queasy, now I'm nauseous, now I'm sick
With the feeling I quit too quick
I hope this soul remains my own
We walk strangely as death takes me from what I
know

Where I die
"Away!" crows cry
Sea and sky
Will bend

It was in this moment that young noticed Driftr's house was made entirely of oak.

young keenly smiled at the old man and said, "I'm going home, but come by anytime."

Driftr let out a robust snort and replied, "No matter how old I get, or how young you become, we are always friends."

young walked the alone unknown, accompanied by a song on his breath and the distant call of an owl on the wind.

YOU HAD TO BE THERE
NOAH FALCK

the dog's paranoia reawakens
at daybreak

bird songs traffic
the last sycamore on Timon Street

and here is the war cry of memory
repeating

and the cinematography
in your dying mother's dream

the tripped noise of war-drunk motorcycles
brigading a beach scarred with moonlight

a body wearing itself away
one drink at a time

you watch from the service entrance
in government sanctioned scrubs

PORTRAITS IN CERTAIN LIGHT

NOAH FALCK

mountain light
until we meet again

when the sunset's not enough

this era we're in now
mostly chemical,
maybe rain

some November left
on your lips

the clouds idle fog-based,
almost lake-colored

at winter's end everyone waits
for tomorrow's light

a day when the future forgets,
the light will untie
and pummel us into the emblems we are
or are soon meant to be

CUE THE JUMBOTRON

PATRICIA SMITH

A WARM September afternoon. The leaves are a sharp New England red, the sky a bright, bright blue. I am in Western Massachusetts, here to officiate my cousin's wedding. I have worked on the ceremony intently for the past several weeks, off and on for months, trying to get just the right tone, find the exact right words for each part. At this point in my life, I have delivered a college graduation speech, but this is *marriage*, a send-off into my cousin's married life, and I have to get it right. I want my words to be a blessing, a benediction to us all.

As if I have that power in me.

When Terri and her then-girlfriend Felicia called and asked me to be an officiant, I was floored. And frankly, surprised. Why me? I certainly didn't have a strong track record where marriage was concerned. Technically, I didn't have any track record at all, if what is meant by "marriage" is its legal definition. I had been "married" twice before and yes, even now I put the word in quotation marks. The first marriage, to my-then partner, occurred when we were both in our twenties. We decided to have a "commitment ceremony," the trendy name for gay weddings back when they weren't yet legal anywhere. We planned it ourselves, decided on New Year's Eve. We bought fancy black velvet outfits and gave each other corsages. I made all the food, recipes I'd scoured from *Bon Appetit* and *Country Living*, cheeses stacked to resemble a wedding cake and lots of hors d'oeuvres. We chose an elaborate chocolate cake from our favorite bakery and bought bottles of champagne. We invited forty of our closest friends to our apartment. We didn't have an officiant. Instead, we wrote vows that we read to each other: mine, an original poem I had a friend copy out in calligraphy; hers, her own heartfelt words, which she shared after inviting two of our "witnesses" to read from *The Little Prince*—one in French, the other in English—as a surprise for me, a French teacher and fan of Antoine de Saint-Exupéry. After our vows were complete, we cued the music, pushed play on the tape recorder, and Glen Miller's "In the Mood" burst forth. We hugged each other and that was that.

For the next four years, I bemoaned the fact that we hadn't kissed at our ceremony. Didn't that doom us to failure? I feared it had. Still, we registered as domestic partners, bought a two-bedroom condominium and forged ahead with our lives.

This, I thought, was adulthood, the life I had been longing for since college. We surrounded ourselves with good friends, a dinner group, jobs we loved—me, a teacher at a private school, and she, a law librarian. We bought season tickets to one of Boston's theaters. We were both readers, both leaned towards the academic. She was a volunteer at the Cambridge Women's Center, where she fielded calls to the helpline. As a graduate of an all-women's college, she seemed immersed in her lesbian identity, her staunch feminism and queer selfhood loudly proclaimed in the bumper stickers that adorned her car.

Still, the not-kiss nagged at me. I saw it as a sign.

I wanted a do-over.

When a relationship ends, it's easy to blame simple reasons. One day, after being together for seven years, my partner announced that she didn't think she was really a lesbian. We had been getting ready to head out and buy a birthday gift for my one-year-old niece. My partner had been sitting in our kitchen on one of the wooden stools for which we paid too much money in a lovely Cambridge furniture shop. The moment began like this: I was giving her a hug and making a comment about wanting to feel adored. What prompted that remark, I can't now remember. All I recall is saying the words and what followed. She stopped breathing, gulped a few times, held me tighter. She wanted to tell me something, she said. She kept swallowing. Then my knees buckled.

"I have to sit down," I said. "You're scaring me."

There was a man, she said. They had been flirting. She thought about him a lot.

Barely a month passed after that awful conversation before she moved out to go be with this man. I was bereft, flattened.

Sometime later, she relayed something that sticks with me still. When we were first together and had moved into our first home—a spacious, light-filled apartment, the same apartment where we held our commitment ceremony—I used to run to the door when she returned from her job at a downtown law firm. But at some point—was it before or after our kiss-less ceremony—she noticed that I had stopped running to the door. What had made that happen, she asked me?

How long had we both been living together and wishing we felt adored?

Fast forward a few years. New state; new girlfriend, a teacher like me, an older woman. I told her I thought marriage was important, that it made a difference to proclaim vows in front of witnesses. I told her I thought it mattered to ask our community of friends to help sustain our relationship.

What I didn't say is what I knew already, that it wouldn't be foolproof. I knew firsthand that a wedding wouldn't inoculate us against all the difficulties that can unravel a relationship.

Though not yet legal in the Commonwealth of Virginia, we called our ceremony a wedding. We hired a jazz band and a caterer. Ordered fancy invitations with reply cards. Asked my niece to be our flower girl. Invited seventy-five friends, many of whom flew in from out of state. We even attended pre-marriage counseling with the Unitarian minister who then married us. If I had been paying attention then, I might have realized what we were in for.

The wedding was lovely.

During the ceremony, we asked our guests to join us in a blessing, to offer us their support. Afterwards, we ate crab cakes and tenderloin, drank wine, listened to jazz. A few people danced. But then, later, looking at the pictures, we noticed that not one of them included us together and none of them included my family.

We stayed together ten years.

I'd like to believe that maybe if everything had gone right, if we had danced together, had enjoyed the reception with all our friends, we might have started off our "married" life more auspiciously. As it was, we were ill-suited to live together for the long-term, my second partner and I. Her depression. My stubbornness. Our inability to talk about important things. But when I ended the relationship, she was furious. She said, "Getting married was *your* idea. We exchanged *vows*." She said, "You promised *forever*."

And so, on a sunny Massachusetts afternoon in September, I find myself standing in front of the *huppa*, facing the seated guests who look at me with expectant faces. The writer in me is dismayed to realize they are *beaming*. It's the only word. They are co-workers, lifelong friends, family members. My own mother and sister and brother are seated out there, too. And my current partner, to whom I am not married. I take a deep breath and begin.

"Welcome to this gathering and ceremony of love and celebration. Friends and family of Terri and Felicia, we come together today not only to witness, but also to support and to become the village that will help sustain Terri and Felicia's relationship. We have already been cheering them on. We're already thrilled to see and experience their joy. We're already happier people when we're in their presence. Their infectious smiles and genuine hearts bring light into our lives. We revel in their love for each other and in their love for us, and today, we surround them with our light and love, and by our presence we offer them our collective blessings."

I believe my words.

I have loved watching Terri and Felicia's courtship and their epic engagement, which started with the proposal live and in full color on the Jumbotron at Fenway Park, the Red Sox beating the Yankees on a warm August night.

Is this what it takes to make a marriage survive? Without grand gestures of love, are the rest of us doomed?

These days, I'm surrounded by weddings—my friends' children, former students, my partner's son. Jonathan is twenty-three and his fiancée, twenty-four. Too young, I think, to be getting married, though they have lived together for two years already. Still on their parents' health insurance and cell phone plans, they haven't quite left the nest. Theirs was a short engagement—ten months, starting with their own grand gesture—a public proposal in front of the outdoor Christmas tree in Downtown Richmond, the rest of us waiting back at the country club for a surprise engagement dinner.

Who was I at twenty-three? What could I have promised?

At fifty-five, part of me feels beyond weddings, beyond the engagement photos and the hoopla. Although my own mother remarried at seventy, more than twenty years after my father died. Never again, she said after all those years, it's too much work. And yet at seventy, she happily said yes and embarked on her second marriage. Twelve years long so far.

These are the collective stories I bring with me to this sunny New England moment. The mums lining the pathway to the *huppa* are glorious, golden and plum. Terri and Felicia beam, too, resplendent in their white suits. They can't stop grinning.

I summon confidence, share the stories I've written about these two people I love. I ask everyone present to do what my own friends and family couldn't do for me, to help Terri and Felicia keep their vows and support their union. I tell Terri and Felicia that their vows are "sacred pledges to guide them for all their days." I call their promises to each other "a covenant of love and faith." I ignore the nagging reminder of my own failure to keep such a promise. Here and now, under this warm September sky, that is what my previous experience leaving feels like.

A failure.

And yet.

There, seated in the front row: my current partner. My *love.* I want us to be the ones in the white suits, showered with this affection, these blessings, this send-off into married life. Prior to meeting Cindy, I had hardly imagined that I might fall head-over-heels in love again. When you're almost fifty, you don't picture yourself starting over. When you think about your life, you think: *This is it. This is how it's going to be from now on.*

Eight years younger than I, Cindy was a new hire at the school where I teach American Literature and Creative Writing. As the technical theatre director, an artist and set designer, she was the object of much discussion when school started. Kids and teachers alike wondered who she was. We teachers vied for Cindy's attention, gossiping about tidbits we'd heard and shared moments at the photocopy machine. I knew she had a son, but I didn't know she had heard me read from my work at an all-school assembly and had wanted to meet me. We found each other on Facebook first and started chatting there, safely, with distance. Soon, we were talking more in school, eating lunch at the same time, having coffee in the afternoons. And when we fell in love in that giddy kid, young love kind of way, it took me by surprise. We are patient with each other, we talk easily about the hard things, we are supportive of each other's goals, and most importantly, we are passionately and deeply connected. I can't imagine life without her.

Here is what I know: I have ridden a camel in Timbuktu; protested nuclear missiles at the Greenham Common Women's Peace Camp in England; lived in Paris and in West Africa. And by far the coolest thing I have ever done in my life is to officiate my cousin's wedding.

Here is what I don't know: why some marriages don't last.

We like to think love conquers all. Stephanie Coontz, author of *Marriage: A History*, explains that nowadays we believe marriage "is based on love, mutual sexual attraction, equality and a flexible division of labor"—a definition, she explains, that helped pave the way for acceptance of same-sex marriage. Of course, opponents of marriage equality often claim to be more in favor of something they call "traditional marriage," but an exploration of marriage practices throughout history demonstrates there is no such thing. Historically, love has not always been a necessary ingredient for marriage. Nor has heterosexuality. And mutual attraction only entered the equation within the last one hundred years. Even now, in this time where people place an emphasis on love, Coontz reminds us that "whether it is valued or not, love is rarely seen as the main ingredient for marital success." If we have been alive for a long while, we realize love can be fleeting, volatile. Basing a long-time future on such an emotion seems risky at best. Foolish, even.

And yet.

Love and marriage are hopeful acts. We enter one without will, it seems—loving who we love, falling hard sometimes, our devotion complete. In the finale of the musical *Les Misérables*, Jean Valjean sings, "To love another person is to see the face of God." And so maybe the not-kiss, the not-dancing—maybe after all, these *are* signs. If life is hard enough, if marriage requires *more* than love to sustain it, maybe at the very least we should be giddy at the outset. Like Terri and Felicia, we should do it up *big*. Cue the Jumbotron. Dance with abandon.

This next time, I want to do it right. I want all the words to be incantations to set us on our path. And even if words as prayers aren't enough, if they can't do the work to hold us together, we'll enter our union with hope and with tremendous love.

ANOTHER DREAM POEM
JUNG HAE CHAE

When, past the stanchions of that unmarked path,
the night shakes loose of my cockeyed vision,

it's not the yellowing dream of her I wake from
    (the yolk having separated from the egg
    (the egg from its larder at last))—

I, a creature scaling toward home, one pod forward then another, another…
she, a nightscape among the ruins I stop and rest in.

Across the inmost distance between night and this dream,
a peculiar field fraught with unease, eddies, some seas,

the edge of dark water having pierced through time, then me, still piercing…
    (not pure darkness, only versi-colored forgetfulness)

I want to crash through and touch her,
that stalk, that dry crusty stem, thorny once;

now, embers in April snow.

HOLE
JUNG HAE CHAE

In the middle of the night, while others are asleep,
a small girl falls into a hole inside an outhouse.
Falling, she sees faces flecked with white dots,
glistening in a sea of fetid mist. She inhales
the mist, as though it were her mother's
amnion, her tiny body pushed against a tidal
wall of unlived lives as it crashes into the sea.
(A dream, she thinks.)

Inside the dream, she knows about the monster
shit truck that comes around once a month,
with its giant nose tube, sucking up
fecal matter from the entire neighborhood,
fouling up its breathable air supply for days.
A monthly opportunity for renewal:
everything bad wiped clean.

Inside the hole (feels so deep and unfriendly)
a mirror of dotted faces shield her in a blanket
of certain knowledge (feels terrible and secretive),
holding her afloat as Time holds its breath.
(Why is Time waiting for her,
she wonders in the dream.)

A dream where wanton wishers come alive
at twilight, riding on the winds of that cracked place,
a tundra formed from dislocated pellets of desire,
gathering in lust, stealing breaths, weaving
mothers' whispers into a night quilt.

Bodies wash away in the sea.

She strains to hold her breath, ready to let go,
until a hand swoops her out from under.
(A tortoise, she thinks.)

THE UNPREPARED
EDDIE VEGA

"ARE WE still taking the Zoque man to Boca?" That was Ernesto's question on my second day in Uxpanapa. I couldn't for the life of me remember the Zoque man's name at the time, although he had humbly introduced himself to me the day before. I probably didn't anticipate having to talk to him much over my time there, so I arrogantly made no effort in trying to hold onto the name of Don Fidencio, even as he traveled for an hour and a half to Boca del Monte in the bed of our four-door Nissan pick-up.

Although he was short, Don Fidencio had a long face. His cheekbones were high, standing under his eyes, slightly hiding them, and he seemed to always smile even when saying something less than pleasant. The smile itself wasn't pleasant, since it seemed he only had about eight teeth and three of them were straight.

"Well, if he's here when we come back through, we'll take him." Jorge paused to look at Ernesto. "We're not going to wait for him." Sure enough, Don Fidencio was there at the parish in the morning before we left back for Coatzacoalcos. There was a small room next to the priest's quarters where we often stayed while visiting La Chinantla. Later, I learned that Don Fidencio had spent the night sleeping on the bench outside the sacristy. It was his custom, as well as that of most of the travelers passing through on their way to Boca del Monte or Minatitlan or Acayucan or wherever they had reason to visit.

Sitting in the front passenger seat the next morning, I was most likely the only one that saw Jorge roll his eyes when we arrived at the parish to gather the rest of our belongings so we could make the journey back to Coatza. I wasn't asking anyone in particular when I posed my question, "Isn't that the Zoque man?" But I had turned to Jorge for a response when I saw him sigh and roll his eyes. It wasn't that he didn't want to help him, after all, he was our leader in the whole venture. Although he was there in a ministerial capacity, Jorge was an introvert, and he didn't want to have a stranger riding with us for the next few hours.

Paco, sitting in the back seat, laughed a little as he saw Jorge and Ernesto talking to Don Fidencio. "There's two of them coming." I looked and saw an older man with what I perceived to be a strong resemblance to Don Fidencio. Though truthfully, until I spent more time in their village, all of the Zoque looked the same. Jorge sat back in the driver's seat, looking through the side mirror as Don Fidencio and his father made their way toward the back of the truck. He sighed again. "Paco, go to the back." They each got out of the truck again and Jorge motioned for the old man to come in and sit in the cab. I asked him if he wanted some water, but Jorge answered for him. "Just give him the bottle, he only speaks dialecto."

La Chinantla was the major city of the region, although I'm not sure if "city" was the right word. It had a paved street through the town center for all of five blocks. It also boasted three telephones, although I only ever saw two of them. The third was somewhere farther away from the town center and the parish where we spent most of our time. Eventually, we rented a house in the town so we could stay there on our visits.

There were a few times when a boy on a bicycle found me at the house to tell me I'd received a phone call. It made me feel important, having received a call. I'd show up at the caseta a few minutes later, inform the attendant I was there, and the phone would ring after a short wait. She'd say something to the effect of, "Si, un momento," and then point me to either of the two phones I could use. At the end, I paid my airtime, a few dozen pesos, and left with head held high and chest puffed out, as if I was an important empresario, despite the fact it was a call from my father making sure I was still alive.

Don Fidencio was Zoque. They were a Mayan people, still speaking their dialect to each other, with a few people in each village knowing Spanish. They had come to the Valley from Chiapas, where they'd lived for centuries until the Chichonal Volcano erupted in 1982. It was with some hesitation that I once asked him to tell me the story.

We had just arrived in his village for one of our presentations. Paco and I had eaten in La Chinantla about an hour and a half before. We'd eaten well, too. Our favorite comedor belonged to a lady named Doña Esperanza. Every time we came through, we ate there, usually a plate of bisteses a la Mexicana—thin steak strips cooked with tomatoes, onions, and jalapeños. It came with a side of rice and black beans. That particular time, we'd finally figured out the difference between a comedor and a restaurante—in a comedor, they'll give you seconds. We took advantage of Doña Esperanza's offer.

So it was with full stomachs that we trekked to Belisario Dominguez, on a bumpy road that looked like it hadn't been traveled on by car in some time. It was full of puddles, small creeks and hoof prints of different sizes. We arrived there an hour and a half after leaving the comedor.

Don Fidencio's house was the first one upon entering the village, or the last one if leaving. His wife greeted us since he hadn't returned from the field. She gave us each a cup of agua fresca de naranja as we sat in her kitchen, watching her cook. She excused herself to get something from the outside and I looked over at Paco.

"That's not for us, is it?"

"I was hoping it wasn't, but I think it is."

"What do we do?" He shrugged his shoulders. "Careful with the water."

I looked at him with some confusion and he just smiled. She came back in and we made small talk. The heat, the road, no rain in three weeks. As I took my third sip from the cup, I felt a tickle on my moustache. I brushed my fingers over it and found a sugar ant. Discreetly, I looked into the cup and saw a small contingent of his cohorts floating in the center of the water. I looked over at Paco, and he wanted to laugh, but couldn't. We sat and chatted for a while, waiting for Don Fidencio to return. With each sip, I'd look directly into the cup, making sure the ants stayed on the opposite side. As they floated toward my lips, I'd stop my sip. It was a bit of a dance, but I managed to not swallow a single ant.

Don Fidencio returned finally, greeted us and then spoke to his wife in their dialect. He then showed us into the next room, where there was a small table up against a wall and one chair. He carried in one of the chairs from the kitchen where we had been sitting as his wife carried in two plates of food. Paco and I looked at each other helplessly. There was nothing we could do to stop this without disrespecting our hosts.

We sat and looked at our plates—sardines mixed with egg. "Have you ever had this?"

Paco looked more worried than I was. I guess I had finally become accustomed to being surprised by anything anymore.

"I've never seen this," he replied. "I'm from an actual city." Don Fidencio's wife returned with tortillas. They were large, maybe about ten inches in diameter, corn, as thick as three stacked quarters, a beautiful sight to see. I knew that if I ate with enough tortilla, the sardine taste would be deadened. It wasn't so much that we were grossed out—although sardine and egg is an acquired taste. The fact was, we were still stuffed from Esperanza's bisteses.

Don Fidencio had excused himself and now came back in freshly bathed. He was wearing his other shirt. In all the time I'd seen him, I noticed he was wearing one of two shirts. Each one had about three or four buttons. I asked if he would join us, and he said he would be eating later.

We ate and waited outside for Don Fidencio to join us. I contemplated the outhouse as Paco made his exit from it. There was no door, just a curtain, and the roof looked even shorter than ones utilized in other villages. Paco came out smiling. "It's just a hole. There's no seat." I tried not to look astonished as he handed me the toilet paper roll he was carrying. We always carried a few with us in the truck since it was a relative luxury when we traveled. I tossed it into the passenger-side window, denying myself a trip to the facility.

It was just then that a few men approached and Don Fidencio came out. Introductions were made and I asked where we would be speaking.

"The community center," they all said.

"Show us the way, then." They talked to each other in their dialect and chuckled as we smiled back and began walking. About a minute later, we reached a gorge.

Apparently, the creek we had crossed on the road earlier ran through the middle of the village and separated it at this point. The community center was on the other side of what they proudly called their bridge. Really, the structure was a log that crossed the canyon, with wire tied between trees on either side. Today, I would estimate it at about thirty feet across and thirty feet down, but it may have been twenty and twenty or forty and forty. Regardless of the distance across and the height above a small stream trickling through a large concentration of rocks, my first reaction was in English because my astonishment could not be hidden in a language I needed to translate myself into. "You've got to be fucking kidding me." I was lucky to be astonished, otherwise I would have been speaking too crudely for this company.

One of the men walked across, leaning backwards while holding the wire. This was the ropes course I never took. The third man to cross didn't even use the wire. I muttered, "show-off," under my breath. Of the two of us, Paco went first. He might've been more afraid than me, but we each knew that if we didn't cross this bridge, we would never be able to communicate with these villagers. The bridge had evolved into a metaphor. I would rather it had evolved into a steel arch, at least three-feet wide, with handrails.

Through the employment of a motley combination of prayers and curses, I crossed the metaphor.

"¡Nunca nieges a tu gente!" It was a few months later, and Don Fidencio was finally telling me the story. They felt tremors, but they weren't afraid, because they felt tremors every so often. Then the mountain looked like there was a storm coming from it, and ash began to fall. It was on top of every house, and the cows looked like they were standing dead because of the grayish color they'd taken on.

Sometime around midnight, they heard the explosion and ran outside, only to see the mountain on fire. Houses were beginning to burn from the rocks and ash that were falling everywhere. They ran holding chairs over their heads, screaming to God for help. They ran and ran and ran.

By morning, they had arrived at the next village. The mountain was smoking, but there was no more fire and no more ash. Some of the people looked back, saw how much calmer everything was and slowly started walking back to their homes. They were never seen again.

Don Fidencio and his wife kept moving and eventually got to another town, where they got on the back of a pick-up. From there, they finally got to a bigger town, San Pedro, I think. There were hundreds or thousands of people, he couldn't tell. What he could tell was no one wanted them. The shops were closed to them and only the churches had food. Soldiers told them to get on a truck and leave, so they did.

Their evacuation was on a dump truck, where they stood with other people, as many as could fit. Behind them were two buses and more trucks. He saw trucks and buses in each direction for as far as he could see. But mainly trucks. Slowly, they moved west, but since he had seldom left his village he didn't know where. Then the trucks stopped in the afternoon and they stayed still for hours and on into the darkness. His wife was beginning to faint from the running and the standing, so he got off the truck to ask the first soldier he saw for some water.

"Get back on the truck!"

"But I just need some water for my wife," he told him.

"Stupid Indian, don't you understand?"

Just then, an older man in uniform, one looking like a superior, arrived and slapped the soldier across the face. "Esta es tu gente. ¡Nunca nieges a tu gente!"

This is your people. Never deny your people!

The community center, a thatch-roofed structure with two sides closed and a dirt floor, was only about twenty feet from the ropes course Paco and I had just completed. Three of the men were already gathered inside. A few more showed up after we arrived so that there were between ten and twelve campesinos.

We had decided the talk on this day was to be about the self—self-actualization, self-awareness, self-esteem. By that point in time, I had made up my mind that the whole region suffered from collective low self-esteem. Most men and nearly every woman had trouble looking at our eyes when we spoke to them. At first I thought it was respect, but eventually I learned it was a feeling of inferiority. They generally felt as if they didn't matter in the world.

In many ways, the government had done this to them. Belisario Dominguez and the surrounding villages were given to the Zoque to resettle in after the volcano eruption. La Chinantla and its satellite villages, were inhabited by Chinantecos, relocated there because their previous homes were flooded to construct a reservoir. They were all promised land and infrastructure and only got the former. It had been nearly twenty-five years since they had been sent there, and there was the one five-kilometer stretch of paved road, no water or sewage system, and only occasional electricity. The towns were so poor, some didn't even have names. They were called by the numbers assigned to them during the relocation—Poblado Cinco, Poblado Ocho, Poblado Trece, etc.

We had a large truck that sometimes carried livestock and feed. It was the only vehicle we could transport people in, too. It had been washed and benches were placed in it, but on one particular occasion, the driver decided against placing an overhead tarp on it. A group of indigenous women were brought to our retreat house for a weekend of meetings and workshops. They traveled exposed to the scorching sun, and when they arrived, one spoke up for the rest of them, "I know we're just women, but we feel shade was a necessity." *Just* women, she said. Like she was acknowledging her perceived space in the hierarchy.

With all this in mind, I had prepared a lesson about knowing oneself and being proud of oneself. The campesinos had about a second-grade education, and I had remembered a third-grade lesson on self-esteem where we went around the room and each stated what we were most proud of about ourselves.

I asked the men what they were most proud of and heard a deafening silence. I thought maybe they needed an example, so I told them I really admired their use of a machete. These men walked through the jungle hacking away at brush in their way. They trimmed the entryways and makeshift lawns of their houses with their machetes. On occasion, I'd see them open cans and bottles with them, too. The machete was their multi-tool.

"I really admire the way you all use your machetes. If I used one, I'd likely cut off one of my own fingers." They laughed. After my example, we went around the room, and each man said that what they liked about themselves was how they could handle a machete.

The last few, though, added some info. They thanked us for being there, for teaching them things, and for hopefully blessing them later with a cow project. The last one had the most to say: "I hope you'll give me a cow. I go to La Chinantla sometimes and I see men with cows. Their kids aren't starving. They have clothes. They go to school in Chinantla. I would like my children to go to school in La Chinantla."

We found a different crossing on the way back, one that didn't involve praying and cursing. Paco and I didn't talk much on the return to

La Chinantla, but after a twilight beer in the breezeway of the house we were renting, we cried about what we'd heard. That was the day I realized I wasn't prepared for any of this. It was the day I decided I had to come home.

GRUENE HALL

LOGAN FRY

The isles they berate. These biles keep great, it is so
Great that people truly *care* again, artisan, small-ba
Tch, oh, that, that's where the sulky paedos go, the
Y have th
Is one corner it is the stinky gallon of pleases he be
Hooving emits, tell me it girl he trundles beatificati
On whence he pleases he emits, tell me about it girl
Did you know silly factory gotcha bilk reality-flour
Ishes favor whom gets salty as he sits, that baltic war
Gives lassy blemishes franco bayonets just may, just
Might remove, it's a pheromone salad, one's verruca
Accident flayed into ice, the hairstyle bleeds those
Centrist volumes of their bleary fantasts. Gimme th
At. Forge blemishes. Burst syringes leaking lead and
Greeny cocoanuts. Your own self wish it were a slut.
Thrice yet the lapping whips have lain
My weakly back its curve again.

Not in France Ritchson what you did it. Whoops cer
Tain conditionals press manes getting crushed
Instead into torture. Sully brigadiers carving for
Tnights before tedium's face, fill with that this vase
Give it here, scrump
Tious verily, holding two terrors simultaneously a, so
Me would say, duet about Gert
Rude tallying who's listless, a -ness, it is so elaborate
time

Is, the way that *nothing* definitely *really* can't be done
In it, given something have it, this et al is telltale birth
Ing it all is fair is all gay salving, loosing
My minde until irradiant, aye, Lysistratus, derive arrows
From his mirthful digging, th
Is scepter is of course sustain
Ably farmed yes certainly rooftop smelted, this scepter
Which I with you w/, in your goodness, those of wishes.

LOVE

LOGAN FRY

To knead an oaked cadence. To seal the of closed in it.
Is the unbefore-tasted bad taste in mouth the sick out?
The forge fake seams deem.
A hope I sick in ours I taste.

Hot in winks the skunk sat.
Confide in the disproportioning quavers.
Chastity has spendy classes
On ebbing its haste will neuter.

The nub of a bit is love's pull on the earth
Wherein soil is kept in want of a compact

Inert with invention's intent, quibbles wet an intensity.
The paused tornado aches.

Any half is truth, if a truth

May bleed out kept whole, whole as truth not as a thing,
I clear my throat to clarify—

Any thing is half,
And in that truth
Is. But kept half,
Its blood messes
The hardscrabble tile.
Made whole no blood

But no truth in either.
Lift the mesh from the wet on the surface thought truth,
Licks there frictioned,
Inlaid; truth is but a happenstance's furnished solidness—

—Not to dismiss!

Couch in a pillory love's humiliations;
Any is at most half, an upbent cushion

Assed in stink's homeful languor rigid
Like pigstuck. Sicked is love's fulltime.

Life met me too late.

GIFT ECONOMIES OF THE OCCULT NORTHERN TERRITORIES

GREG KOEHLER

Here is a picture of two naked communists
Don't they seem happy and well-fed. Take it.

And take this tin of Tuesday's borscht it tastes
Much better today than it did yesterday or

The day before or the day before that which
Was Tuesday. Here is a box of cheap red wine

I'm sorry I cannot drink it with you my allergies
And envies are killing me. I'm sorry the redbud

Is dead perhaps I didn't water it aggressively
Enough through this lingering drought though

Redbuds are said to live short lives to say aw
Fuck it quicker than other natives to this place.

It's Friday and the communist girls are naked.
They are surely dead by now but they smile

And bear their glowings. They look like you
Only pale and well-fed and happy and less

Burdened by the alienation of labor. They look
Nothing like you. I am jealous of their nipples

And of whoever later licked their pinking skins.
I covet their extraordinary beets. Please take it.

Take these directions to the start of the May Day
March it is on the desperate side of town and

Is hard to find after three jars of cheap red wine.
The band is good but only the woodwinds are

Playing this year thanks to their availability and
Desperation in support of righteous causes.

On Tuesday I wanted to cry but could not so I
Peeled the onion chopped it into cubes and

Immediately shed tears. They weren't the sort for
Which I longed but were warm and pleasant in the

Corners of my eyes. The borscht was excellent but
Tomorrow will taste like good sex. On Sunday

It will taste like an anguished cotton dress and
Half an apple browning. Take it. Monday it will

Expire. Take this box cutter and this piccolo and
Please take this enamelware bowl and spoon.

Take this jar of tears I collected for three years
Back when I could cry and did so not infrequently.

Use it to salt the spot where the redbud stood.
Put your lips to the breast of the nearest Russian.

for Alexis Almeida

ekphrastic on Tractor Drivers by Arkady Plastov

BLUE DREAD
EVAN CRAIG REARDON

Blue dread and its awe both ours and tangents
whispered immortality across manged seeds
that lack tongues to describe in fielded rapture sorties
between the expected and the perceived. Esse
est perceptio and Descartes picks his fingernails; all
that is clear is the airdraped rumble of lawn mowers,
scything through the breathgrooved field,
birds canticling one eye that trawls the tip of the sky, and each
time I pause to detect the next constant under
the complaintless wheel of today lightworn to tomorrow.

It always collapses to time, that subtle fuck
of memory and instance   each trying to weigh the other, corral
the day's wages into what was never offered but gratefully received.
Did not know but was felt, it was tasted on
the berry's bloom, those trees that can't still stand, yet they are like us,
are planted by cool streams of words that give growth, as much gives I,
but doesn't move beyond its ken. The Beast's words know that we're here:
oh it's arbor's stanchion, that old gray mare promising riches and
an adventure that was never wanted, but taken anyways.

Our study of the morning's claspings to delight
in separating ephemeral dross from rich turpitudes of dark
like a seed without its purpose—why the fetish; why the touch.
As surrounded by the ill-defined and their own coordinates to us
the word continues to hold, fingers tangled
in bourbon barrel hair, sun glinted to pull new notes to sipped fore.
The hawk's melody now decanted an ostinato in the treble clef
grounding these ridiculous notions of space bordered by laurel leaf.

TREE HOME

LYDIA DOLVIN

THIS WINTER, my brother and I came home to our mother, one house, two dogs, and two cats. The dog count has been reduced steadily over recent years as our old cohort ages out and fewer puppies are acquired by children with starry eyes. Now it is just my old boy, Indy, a small genteel Shetland Sheepdog, and my mother's new German Shepherd rescue. With five living souls, the house is still busy, but there are not as many personalities as we were once used to. It therefore made some sense to my brother and I when mother sat us down and told us she was thinking about moving to the city. Daniel met my eyes and we briefly and silently exchanged information.

I often think of Daniel and myself as a unit. As siblings, we have always gotten along. We used to be mistaken for twins when we were young, and it has started to happen again now that we both pass as adults. More importantly, we vibe. Our shortcomings are very similar, and so are our virtues. A shared history fills in the rest. We looked back to our mom. As the older one, I knew I would have to ask the question: *What will happen to the farm?*

Sunlight drops through the spaces between leaves. Its ever-shifting beams dapple the surface of my skin. In the summertime, everything shimmers. On the best days, the trees ripple silver and green with a breeze that carries away the hot damp hilltop air. I lie with one arm in the sunshine, the other shaded by the soft undersides of the leaves, which are not yet waxed and hardened by summer drought. The wooden floor is cool and damp beneath me. My toes are dark gray with caked-on dust. Despite all of the wild vegetation, our soil has always been thin and dry. My mother tried and failed for six years to get apple trees to grow.

It is 2007. The year preceding was a tumultuous time for Daniel and me, but by now life is regaining a precious certainty. My father is home for the summer on medical leave as he recovers from a liver transplant. Because of his immunosuppression, our dad has to wear a mask in public and avoids going into town. Other than this, he seems to feel quite well.

This is our ideal scenario. Dad is a social guy; he's a recovering addict with his twenty-year chip and plenty of mental energy for fixations. Cut off from the outside world, he directs his creative efforts into the available conduits: his elementary-aged children. We flourish under the attention, but our congress still needs a direction—some sort of common goal to stave off the inevitable doldrums and quarreling. A thorough consultation of *The Dangerous Book for Boys* reveals a few solid options, and in late May it is decided. We three together will build a treehouse.

By we three together, I mean my father and his two lemonade-delivering servants. He handles the lumber and we provide the refreshments, which is an alright arrangement by me. Now I wish that I had paid more attention, or perhaps that I had been a bit older than ten, because I have retained next to nothing about construction or carpentry. How a person like my dad could just decide to build a treehouse, and then do so without major incident, is beyond me. Then again, had I been older than ten and my brother older than eight, it would not have been the summer it was.

And see, this is what I mean! How do you start a treehouse? How do you begin lodging wood pieces in a tree using only ropes and ladders, and do so in such a way that the wood pieces are still standing there thirteen years later? I could not tell you. I only know that we did it then, and fairly quickly too. Lumber is acquired, a framework put up, cold drinks delivered and sandwiches consumed, and by the end of the first weekend we have a tree platform without walls. It stands twelve feet off the ground on one side, but because the tree reaches over a steeply graded hill, the platform overlooks a ravine at a dizzying height. We climb up the ladder and look down to find that the forest floor has fallen far away, a fantastical trick of scale that makes me believe I am Alice in *Wonderland.* Without walls, the open air feels both treacherous and accessible, like you might actually decide the possibility of flight is worth the inevitable consequence of falling.

Looking back, I am stunned by the number of actively dangerous opportunities my parents gave to Daniel and me. We had a trampoline with no net, a rope swing over the ravine that took us up to twenty feet above the ground, a zipline. Now, a tree platform with no walls. It remained wall-less until mid-July, when we ran out of other projects and the boredom really caught hold again. In the meantime, we had our daily routine. We woke up. Ate lazy breakfast. Dad's heels hit the floor as he practiced tai chi in the living room. Daniel's whereabouts were unknown. For me, video games all morning for as long as I could, until Dad kicked us outside with cucumber sandwiches.

Reunited by our exile to the outdoors, Daniel and I found new ways to occupy ourselves in the cooling canopies of the woods. I would have happily stayed inside playing video games all day. It was easier than devising our own systems and games that would give us purpose in the open world. But our backyard forest also carried a real sense of danger. Signs of animal activity were easily found. We inspected ourselves for ticks as a matter of daily grooming. No grownup was keeping tabs, so we operated on the buddy system. If I were incapacitated, it would be Daniel who ran and got help. And frankly, it was the summertime—we knew there were snakes and we were trespassing in their domain. We knew how to distinguish between an angry copperhead and harmless hognose. I had been warned about the cottonmouth and feared the day we might encounter one. The stakes were small but real, and this kept the games interesting. If things did go terribly wrong, we could *die*. This clear understanding of our mortal boundaries was, in hindsight, not something every child gets an education in. We were fortunate to have it.

When you're a child in the heat of summer and youth, the days roll by like a steady parade. Every day is a little different, but the routine is the same. All the while, small additions are made to our tree home. Plywood walls appear one week at a time. There is talk of buying buckets of purple paint. A hinged door is introduced, adding intrigue and drama to what used to be a simple hole cut into the floor. The lumber is too heavy for our small arms to lift from below, so Dad fills an old canvas bag with stones and rigs it as a counterweight. The door now opens with a smooth action. My father, a man of rare backyard genius!

The biggest and final project is the construction of a real gabled roof. It is August now, and there isn't much time left. We are not worried. There will be plenty of summers more to live like this, one hundred more projects to complete. But weeks slip by, suddenly oiled and slick, and we find ourselves colliding with September before we have time to realize. Attentions are turned to school and new clothes, the farm fields go yellow, the rhythms change. Our treehouse is beautiful, and it opens to the sky. Is it a real house without a roof? No matter—we will finish it next summer and sleep in it every night.

I once overheard our dad say that driving by the corn growing on the side of the road always made him sad. Somebody, maybe my mother, asked him why. He replied that it reminded him of the end of summer and the passing of time. I thought this was a curious thing to say. I remember it now because it was the first time I had heard time considered as an antagonist. Until then, time meant moving forward to new and different adventures. I could not figure out exactly what my father meant when he said this, but I wanted to understand. It seemed like a deep and mystical sentiment to have. I held onto it.

The next summer starts the same but does not pass like the last. Daniel and I spend days with our grandparents, who let us stay indoors. I become obsessed with sudoku. I don't know what Daniel does. Instead of finishing the treehouse, our father goes back to work. He comes home every evening exhausted. My mother assumes he has become too accustomed to unemployment, and we dismiss his complaints until the left side of his body begins losing sensation. There is a diagnosis of pinched nerves, but no improvement. My mother nearly forces entry into a neurologist's office, bypassing a months-long waiting list. There is a diagnosis of brain cancer, but no improvement. By August, he is sent home with a swollen brain and a palliative care regimen. He is different from the father we know. He is confused and sometimes angry. He yells at my mother and the waiter at Outback Steakhouse. He yells at the dog. He doesn't yell at us, but we think that he could. He sits in his recliner, he stays in bed, he breaks twenty years of sobriety, he smells like sick rotten pancakes. He has hallucinations and his organs fail. In December, he dies.

There is no world in which the summer we build a treehouse repeats itself. If Daniel had not been eight and I had not been ten, it would never have happened. I can't say what the loss of our dad has to do with our loss of the woods, but I suspect that it's less than you might think. Something happens as we get older and these worlds become less accessible. I think we still lose that person who tells us to go outside and create something. We don't often tell ourselves to do this because it's hard, and it's even harder as you forget what it was like. I go back to the woods and our treehouse and I feel itchy. I see bugs and dirt, and I don't stay long enough to rediscover what made that world so interesting to me. It's a shame and it's normal. I don't think you can really go back.

The treehouse is still standing solid, although I haven't ventured up there in many years. It has grown dark with lichen and rain. I imagine all sorts of things have made a home up there. Our dad loved our little farm, and he gave us that gift. In this moment, I don't know if it's enough to carry that inheritance inside of us. Do we also have a responsibility to maintain it? To pass it on? I have trouble drawing the line between sentimentality and real value, if there is a line to be drawn. I don't want to keep my mother suspended in an old life she isn't really living anymore. I don't want her to have obligations to us or to her dead husband that pain her to keep. You can't go back, and she knows that. The farm is a lot of work, and maybe she wants to move on. As young adults, Daniel and I don't spend much time here. We don't go back. But I still can't stop myself from asking the question. It is too heavy in the room, and she doesn't have the same ties to the forest that we do. So I ask it for me and Daniel and Dad. "Okay, Mom," I say. "What will happen to the farm?"

42ND AND 33RD

ANNA STEINMETZ

THE DRAGON turned the corner.

Shit.

He took into account his current arsenal: a golden pen, a pack of cigs and a used tissue. The dragon had seen him and opened its wings.

Double shit.

He dropped the used tissue and began to run down the busy sidewalk. He hung a left at the nearest corner, passing by the same pet store he had been in only a week before. From the outside, it had looked innocent enough: puppies and kittens displayed in the windows alongside mountains of food and toys. Inside, it was exactly what you would expect in a Downtown Chicago pet shop, a low-paneled ceiling, dark grey walls, shelf upon shelf of supplies cramped into the little storefront. Crowded and dull, but clean enough.

Every shrink he saw since the accident said the same damn thing about survivor's guilt, the five stages of grief or some new form of suffering brought back by the boys from 'Nam. It was all high-brow bullshit, of course; they would say anything to try and solve a problem they couldn't understand. The most recent professional suggested a pet would provide a feeling of purpose. Of course, this claim wasn't any more convincing than the others, but at least it was physically feasible. So he had gone looking for a dog or a cat. He'd even have settled for a hamster or fish, if it came down to it. But the clerk was exceptionally pushy in selling him an egg.

Ah yes, he thought, *man's best friend. The egg.*

The clerk looked to be about—and he wanted to be fair—one thousand years old. The man's last encounter with a pair of scissors must have predated the coming of Christ, and his snowy beard and hair nearly touched his ankles. His beady red eyes were only slightly concerning.

"Well, see, sonny," the old man began, "I could sell you a pup now for about a hundred bucks, or I could sell you this egg for five."

"Are you suggesting that this is a *dog egg*?" he asked, cautiously eying the green and scaly spheroid sitting on the counter.

"No, not at all. This is a rare lizard egg."

He thought it over, picking up the egg and turning it in his palm. *Lizards do have scales,* he considered, *and I'm not certain, but I think they lay eggs.* The decision came down to the contents of his wallet: a bent paperclip and about fifteen dollars in cash.

He walked out of the store and into the windy streets with the egg in hand; it was warm in his palm and he could almost feel a pulse, as if the creature inside were already moving. In his other hand, he held a red book. It was incredibly heavy and had seen prior use. *Cura et Custodia in Dracones* was scrawled across the front in gold.

God, I hope the rest of it isn't in Spanish, too.

He was relieved to open the book and find English instructions explaining what the lizard would eat and where it would want to sleep, as well as a long section labeled "Safety Precautions." First, he stopped at the supermarket to get the food and bedding.

The Dracone will eat only the finest of flint, he read.

Huh, I never realized lizards eat charcoal. He picked up a ten-pound bag and threw it in his cart, the egg gently jostling in the child seat.

The Dracone must sleep in thin sheets of gold leaf.

A roll of tinfoil joined the bag of charcoal. Among other things he threw in the cart were three bottles of extra hot sauce, strike-anywhere matches and a fire extinguisher. The cashier at check-out looked concerned, to say the least.

He kicked the apartment door shut behind him and dropped the bags on the floor. He could feel the heat of the egg in his pocket and the burning in his arms from carrying his supplies all the way back from the market.

The apartment was almost entirely white, not because of interior design, but lack thereof. It was two rooms in total, the kitchen-office-living-dining-guest-sun-bedroom and the bathroom. The wooden floors were worn and warped, and paint peeled where the empty walls met the ceiling. He had done his best to furnish the space with what little money he had. The kitchenette hadn't seen use or repair since the early sixties, when he first found the place. Next to it sat a flea-market find: a whitewashed table and two chairs, one for him and one that hadn't been used since April. In the first short months of spring, the kitchenette had seen more use than in all the years he'd live there. A bunch of the guys would come from work: Mark, Michael, sometimes Jason if he could get away from his wife. They'd sit up burning their throats with whiskey and laughing the flames out of their stomachs. Soon enough, Jason's wife would catch up to him and Mark or Michael would have to turn in, but David would stay long into the night; the two of them sharing the two whitewashed chairs. Now, the empty seats looked sad and pale against the only color in the apartment: the brown leather La-Z-Boy that faced the window and doubled as his bed.

He held the egg and walked to the window, looking out across the Chicago skyline. The only value of the apartment was in its view. His window faced south, so the sunlight streamed in through the big bay windows throughout the day. He could just make out the top of the Sears Tower in the distance. For three years he had worked on it, high up on the iron skeleton. The heights had dazzled him. It was there he'd met David; met the whole gang, really. It was easy to fall in love with high places when your waist was tethered to safety. He never once knew he'd be tempted to cut the line.

The book said to keep the egg in a warm place until it hatched. So he wrapped it in a little tinfoil nest and placed in on the sill just above the radiator, its green scales iridescent in the last weak rays of the sun.

Sitting back in the La-Z-Boy, he stared at the egg, trying to remind himself he was no longer alone. *Remember what Dr. What's-His-Face said: this pet, well, egg, needs you*, he thought to himself. *You have to be alive for the egg to survive.* He pulled out the book and began to examine his new responsibilities. His purpose. A golden pen fell from the book onto his lap.

That wasn't there before. The pen was too thick to have gone undetected between the pages. He gave the book a good shake, just in case other pieces of gold wanted to present themselves. He turned to the back cover of the book to test the pen. It didn't write in ink, but rather seemed to burn into the binding. At the top of the page he wrote: *Reasons to be alive.*

Reason 1: This egg needs you to hatch.

Even as he scrawled his first reason to live, the big bay window still beckoned him forward, forty-eight stories to the street below. His knuckles turned white as the sun set and he braced for the nightly struggle not to jump.

It had been almost a year since last September, when the tower was finished. He had stopped working in April. He couldn't go back after the fire.

The egg moved. I swear it just moved.

He leaned forward until his face was inches from the egg: staring, watching, waiting for another movement. He could feel heat on his face as if the egg were burning, as if it were on—

Flames fly out of the elevator shaft, burning his side and his face.

He's sweating. He's not in his apartment; he's on the forty-third-floor, walking past the elevator. Only a floor below him, David is cleaning the guide rails, and the other three are on the thirty-third—Mark, Michael and Jason. The roar of the fire is louder than David's screams.

Crack.

His head snapped up. It was morning.

Crack, crack!

It was still fairly dark in the apartment, but an orange glow surrounded the egg. The green scales turned red with heat. Two cracks had already formed as the lizard tried to push its way out. He grabbed the book and furiously flipped through the pages, trying to find the instructions.

Stand extremely far back, protect the face and hands, or take cover when the Dracone hatches.

Take cover?! Oh Christ. He grabbed his welding mask and gloves and scrambled to the kitchenette. He peeked at the egg from behind the overturned table. The last time he wore the mask, David had been alive, and the thought of iron working didn't smell of burning flesh—

Stop it, focus! This thing's about to blow!

The egg was now white hot and steaming, singeing the tinfoil nest. A piece of shell flew off and lodged itself in the ceiling. Soon, the entire egg was cracking into pieces and sailing off in every direction, one in the cabinet, one in the La-Z-Boy. One had barely missed his head and was now stuck an inch deep in the drywall behind him. He hadn't even flinched; he never took his eyes off the miniature explosion on the windowsill.

A burst of flames illuminated the tiny apartment, and then all was quiet. The egg still sat on the sill, unmoving, charred and black. He took off the mask and crawled over to it, ready to protect himself from another onslaught of eggshell.

The egg was like a dying ember. Blackened on the surface, but pulsating with orange and purple life underneath.

The Dracone must be cleaned of the ashes of its womb.

He reached out with his glove and gently brushed the egg; the soot fell away at his touch. He cleared away the cinders until the form of a tiny lizard was revealed. He could just barely make out its tightly curled shape, completely ashen. It was beautiful. It was his. Like a new mother, he gently cupped the hatchling in his hands and sat back into the La-Z-Boy, indifferent to the soot and ash falling into his lap.

It slowly uncurled and opened one eye. One beautiful golden eye peeked up at him. Then two, blinking. The little lizard raised its head and coughed. Flames singed the hair on his arm. He held his breath.

I don't think this is a lizard.

He watched as the not-lizard stretched out its arms.

Wings. I have a fire-breathing lizard with wings.

He grabbed the book and flipped open to an illustration: a great winged dragon breathing fire mid-flight.

Holy shit.

He looked down with horror at the little creature in his lap, the dangerous monster that was teething on his thumb, the treacherous beast that curled up comfortably in the palm of his hand. It looked up at him and tilted its head inquisitively, blinking like a newborn baby having found its mother. He smiled.

Reason 2: This baby dragon needs you to survive.

The dragon refused to eat the charcoal he had bought.

"C'mon!" He tried to push the piece towards the dragon's face. It threw its head back and forth, avoiding its meal, growling and chirping like a fussy child.

"Well fine, then!" He slammed the charcoal down on the table and went to the microwave to make his TV dinner. The dragon clumsily flapped after him, landing on his back and clawing its way onto his shoulder.

No sooner had he pulled the tray from the microwave than the dragon descended on his mac and cheese, nose diving into the sticky yellow sauce. The soot from its shell turned the noodles a soft grey,. Its shiny red scales were dripping with cheese. Its back was covered with ridges that ran from the top of its head to the tip of its tail. Attached to its arms were massive wings that flapped to keep afloat in a sea of pasta.

"Fine, that can be your dinner, but no dessert." He smiled at his joke and gave the cheese-covered dragon a little pat.

The dragon nearly destroyed the kitchenette. It clawed its way into the microwave looking for more mac and cheese. Once he finally succeeded in duct-taping the microwave door shut, the dragon took to battling the sink.

The Dracone despises water. Exposure causes immense pain and possibly death.

He finally managed to wash the dishes by using his back to block the dragon from the sink. By the time he was finished, the dragon was nowhere in sight. He looked in the cabinets, under the sink, behind the table, until finally he saw the oven light was on. The dragon had managed to turn the temperature knob to four hundred degrees, and it was napping peacefully within its own personal kiln.

By night-time, he had built a little tinfoil bed for the dragon, following each and every tedious instruction from the red book. But the dragon took one look at his two-hour project and curled up in the middle of the La-Z-Boy.

"No, bad dragon, that's my bed. You sleep here," he said as he plopped the dragon down in the metallic little nest on the windowsill. He leaned back in the La-Z-boy and closed his eyes. The dragon fluttered over to his lap and laid down. He pretended not to wake.

Reason 3: I love this dragon.

The dragon grew at an incredible rate. When it first hatched, it was under two inches tall and shorter than the length of his hand. After only a couple of days, it was longer than his arm and nearly a foot tall. It was improving its flight. It was learning to breathe fire.

In its squeaks and coughs, he saw the flames that had consumed his dear friends. The white apartment was now blackened with soot and burns. Looking at the damage, he touched his own face where the heat of the elevator fire had left red, bubbled scars.

The dragon would get angry. It hated when he washed the dishes, furiously watching as the water hit his hands. It would cough into its mac and cheese and then be unhappy to find it burned. Bedtime became a daily struggle over where he and the dragon would sleep, both of them wanting the La-Z-Boy.

He was just trying to take a shower when the dragon's weight pulled down the curtain it had been trying to climb. Spray from the shower hit its back, hissing and sputtering like water against a hot stove. The dragon screamed in pain and threw itself against the bathroom door, knocking it off its hinges.

He chased after the dragon as it ran around the apartment, spitting fire and dragging the shower curtain along with it. It scrambled onto the windowsill and started clawing at the curtain.

"Stop! Hey, stop!" He frantically tried to contain the bewildered creature. It turned to him, still roaring and spewing fire—

The flames were suddenly at his face, and he could hear men screaming below him. David was burning alive. His friends consumed. The worst way to die. Their corpses nothing but a hunk of charred flesh. Unrecognizable. They hadn't known they were going to die in that elevator shaft.

He grabbed a glass of water from the windowsill and threw it at the dragon.

The dragon yelped with pain and cowered into the corner. Red, bubbling burns appeared on its side.

He raised his hand to his cheek. "Oh god." He tried to reach for the dragon.

Its large and golden eyes looked back at him, betrayed.

"Please let me take this off of you–"

It pushed out the window and flew.

"No!" he screamed, reaching out after it. But the dragon was already halfway to the street.

Reason 4: I have to fix this.

Outside, he had no idea where to look. He started running in the first direction he could think: towards the outline of the Sears Tower. The same route he had walked to work every day. He came to a halt at the intersection of West Madison and South Franklin.

The dragon turned the corner.

He ran after it until he reached the base of the tower. He stood in the shadow of the iron beast he had worked so hard to build. The place where four of his friends had died. The place he last saw David alive.

In truth, he had not come to see it after it had been completed. He'd only seen it out of his window. He walked to the door and read the plaque beside it.

April 11th, 1973—Four men on the 42nd and 33rd floors gave their lives in the building of this tower.

A plaque was all they were given. Their four lives. Only worth a plaque on a building.

They didn't give *their lives, you fuck. They were killed! And for what?*

He stared up at the steel tower before him.

They printed three sentences in the *New York Times*. Three fucking sentences, one of which was dedicated to the fact that the tower would *still* be the tallest in the world. Two whole fucking sentences about four men who died. They didn't even say their names.

He sat down against the building. A shell of a man who had nothing left, who every day felt purposeless and every night felt the urge to jump, who didn't even have a match to light his cigarette.

He looked up to find golden eyes. The dragon walked towards him slowly, curious yet cautious. Its gaze never dropped from his tearful eyes until its face was inches from his own. The dragon snorted, and the tip of the cigarette in his hand was ablaze.

The dragon curled up beside him and lay its head in his lap. They sat there for hours, underneath the plaque, against the iron giant, watching people walk by without a glance.

Reason 5: Someone has to remember their names.

ALIVE ENOUGH
CLAIRE LEWIS

Years ago now Barbara texted me "I think
I see raccoons when I am drunk instead of ghosts."
In California I see something less alive than raccoons
but more alive than ghosts. I moved because he had been
in my old apartment and the bar we went to is closed now
and that way of remembering is like déjà vu but worse
because it bleeds into the land. Walk home with me.
There are no streetlights here. How should I know
when to be afraid? *I know he would never hit me*
is an excuse. He would.
I'm nothing special.

RABBIT VALLEY

CLAIRE LEWIS

the air conditioning in the car is broken. the compressor clicks.
Rabbit Valley approaches from the north side of the highway
and there are NO SERVICES
but i pull off anyway. i wish
i could say the desert opened up before me like a night flower
but the whole-sky dusk was pressing down heat and anger and
standing out underneath it i felt   ashamed.

GRASS CARP
JACK DEAN

I FINISH mowing the lawn and drive to your house. Each week: edge in the morning, mow in the afternoon, drive to your house for dinner and a movie. I make habits like this out of a summer that feels overgrown and unkempt otherwise. Regularity.

I always pass the small man-made lake on the right side of your street, slow down a bit to watch for bluebirds preening feathers in the magnolia limbs, swarms of geese honking a warning song, sometimes a cavalier squirrel crossing the road. Today, when I pass by the water I see something thrashing. A writhing gray fish in the heart of the lake, bloated and thrashing whitish foam in all directions.

I drive the rest of the way to your house. You meet me at the driveway with arms outspread. I tell you about the flailing fish. You ask to see it, so we drive together to the lakefront. When you see it, or as much as can be seen around the gurgling fountain of water it splashes up, you begin to cry. "He's in pain, he's hurt. Maybe he's been caught on some fishing line," you say.

"What do we do?" I ask. I am sweating from the forehead and armpits in the heaving summer sun. My head is an empty bucket. A wrought-iron gate separates the road from the water. This thrashing fish is at least 30 feet out. We have no way of maneuvering across the water. In your neighbor's yard there are two faded pirogues lying abandoned and dead on the bank. We circumnavigate the neighbor's house to inspect them. Turfgrass and dandelions grow in a haphazard circle around the boats, swallowing them beneath waves of greenery. You call your mom. She's got three-fourths of a degree in veterinary science, so perhaps she will know what to do.

When your mother drives up to us, she has a pool skimmer and a plastic bucket in her front seat. She tosses both onto the grass. A cobwebbed salmon-y kayak dangles from the rear of her Subaru Outback like a spear through the heart. We all three carry this equipment down to the lakefront, tossing each item over the iron fence. Then we climb over, too.

We pick blades of grass to decide our tasks in Operation: Fish Rescue. You and I pull the longest blades, so we sit on the shore with the bucket and skimmer, respectively. Your mom wobbles out on the water in the kayak. We yell encouragements from the shore. When she reaches the center of the lake, she uses her oar to shove the writhing fish toward shore. It tries to dive beneath the surface to avoid the kayak and the oar but just as soon bobs to the surface, flopping upside down. We remain like this for an hour. The kayak ever-circling the resistant fish and shoving closer to shore inches at a time.

When it is finally near enough to the waterfront, I bend forward with the skimmer, and sweep the fish into the net. The catch of the day! I get my first clear look at the fish—it is maybe three feet long, gray-speckled on its back and pure white on its stomach. Its belly is distended and bright red. You fill the bucket with water, and I gracelessly drop it in. We pull your mother back to shore and carry the kayak, the pool skimmer and the bucket with protruding fish over the fence and into her car. To make room for the kayak, you and I sit in the trunk, our feet dangling out and the fish bucket between us.

When we make it home, we lug the bucketed fish up the driveway and into the abandoned koi pond in your backyard. On the way there, we pass your dad mowing the overgrown lawn. He stops the mower, comes out and sees the fish inverted and still in your empty pond. "It's clearly suffering in there," he says, and the cold term "it" upsets all of us. In the time between kayaking him ashore and plopping him in the backyard, we have decided that the fish is a he and that *his* name will be Horatio. We tell your father this, and he corrects himself. "I can put *Horatio* out of his misery. It'd be humane, and *he* wouldn't feel a thing, probably." His plan is to bash the fish's head in with a stone from the fire pit. We refuse. He would surely refuse, too, had we taken him up on his cold-headed offer.

We stand over the upside-down carp, rearranging him in the water and attempting to keep his gills submerged. We figured this would be the end of our little epic, freeing a suffering fish from the water. Nobody warns you that animal rescue takes more than just the act of removal. Who would've known.

Looking for answers, you call LSU's exotic pet hospital, hum along to their hold music. I stand over the metal bird bath next to the koi pond and watch apple snails trail in circles and munch algae. Earlier in the summer, we kayaked through Highland's bayou. On our way back from that strenuous trek, I spotted a snail shell big as a fist drifting in the water. I plucked it out and kept it. The paddling had been particularly tiring, the day particularly hot, my neck particularly sun-drenched and burning. I thought this shell to be a hard-fought prize.

As we drove home from the bayou, the shell started moving, snaked its way across the dashboard. We knew we couldn't kill it. Your mom identified it as an apple snail, so I named him Johnny Apple-snail. She explained that apple snails are non-native invasives and that they eat everything in sight. Apple snails could chew through every bog and marsh, could swallow Louisiana whole. They also lay strings of sickly pink eggs every few weeks. Some of the eggs laid on the lip of the bird bath hatch and develop into new Johnnys. And we can't kill a single one, so we are now accidentally farming invasive snails. Seeing the swarm of Johnnys, I realize I am an ecological process of the worst kind.

Half an hour passes, and you finally get through to a vet student, one who is willing to take the fish in and exam it. We learn that if you're distraught enough, the vet school will take your case for free. Your mother breathes a sigh of relief. She has been filling up a bathtub with lukewarm water and salt, sterilizing a penknife in preparation for a home operation on this bloated fish. Instead, we make arrangements in the car for Horatio's next car journey. He is left for the night at the vet school. We cook dinner and watch our movie—*Re-Animator*.

In the morning, you get a call. Horatio is okay. The vet students operated on his inflated swim bladder. He's on medication, will be returned soon. They say he's a grass carp. Also, they've named him Bill. All just different names for the same thing, I suppose.

"Grass carp are terribly invasive," your mom says.

"I don't take Horatio to be much of an invader," I offer.

"You know that's not what I meant. Maybe we shouldn't have rescued him."

The vet students tell us that his swim bladder disorder was likely caused by nitrates in the lake. I recall what I read in *Lawn People* earlier this summer, the book I talked your ear off about as soon as I was done. Paul Robbins says nitrate run-off comes from lawn care. You spray insecticides to keep out pests and invasive species. The chemicals spill out into the water during a rainstorm. You cut your grass to keep things orderly. The clippings sink into the lake with nitrates that flood the fish's gills, inflating its swim bladder. The fish flips upside-down and thrashes in the water. We're back where we started.

We release Horatio back into the neighborhood lake, and there is no *Free Willy* moment. He doesn't turn and thank us. He is just a hapless and terrified fish. When we toss him back into his man-made home, he immediately dives down below the surface, undetectable beneath the layer of brownish-green pond scum and algal bloom. His quick escape is the closest thing to an animal show of thanks.

And next week I will have to mow the lawn again. The grass stretches out of the dirt, flowing out like verdant ponds, ready to swallow the town whole. My mower chops the green chutes down. A fish goes belly-up somewhere. What a miraculous cycle, great regularity to it all.

VALLEY OF MONUMENTS

MICHAEL AGRESTA

MY DARLING, do you remember the Alamo? You said you'd expected something bigger. You'd always imagined it like something from the movies, you said—waves of infantry ramming at the gates, archers, surprise reinforcements arriving from the south, Santa Ana leading the charge in slow motion on a white horse. In plain daylight, it looked like a glorified pioneer's cabin. Hadn't the Apache taken on a hundred encampments this size, outposts forgotten by history, surrounded them and burned them to the ground? (Or did you say the Comanche, the Sioux?) Not to mention the reprisals, you said. Why were we to remember this one, you asked me, in all that history of slaughter?

As we drove west from San Antonio, you named off other violent episodes from American history that ought to have been better memorialized. The draft riots in New York City. The Arkansas mass lynchings. Wounded Fucking Knee. (You named more; those are the ones that have stuck with me.) Your mind a sharp and beautiful thing, glancing from one obscure surface to another, like winter sun on West Texas frost, before wildfires turned that scrubland into coils of ash.

We cut a path northwest through the wasteland. Strange machines hummed fifty miles distant on the horizon, shimmering in the haze, blasting away at some purpose we could not and were not intended to know. A sign, a turnoff for a hidden village of those who maintain and operate these machines and the steel-reinforced storage vaults nearby, cisterns from which not a single drop can be lost, for their contents are eternal poison to all creation.

You knew then, too, about the search for symbols to warn humans away from long-term biohazard containment sites. They wanted something that would be legible ten thousand, one hundred thousand years in the future. How do you speak to someone so distant, you asked. How do you tell them, Go away, dig for treasure in some other place, if you stay here you'll unleash something ancient and terrible and deadly? You imagined a synthetic landform that shaped the wind into dissonant, eerie music; rock glyphs of vipers, skulls and dismembered human forms.

All the time I was thinking how I'd communicate the opposite—how to tell you I loved you if you'd forgotten me, forgotten love, forgotten even yourself, the whole hackneyed sentiment eroded and erased one word at a time. The problem, you remarked, is the one out of every hundred men for whom the sign saying *Keep Out* reads as a dare or a siren call. Another set of symbols must be erected just for him, to misdirect him and to wear him down. I think you were talking about me, poking fun at me for allowing myself to wallow in admiration of a beautiful, deteriorating mind.

There is an unconquered America in the mountains of New Mexico, a blue and perfect lake, and a canyon somewhere further on where a recalcitrant band hid for generations until times changed and "we"—your wording, I remember it—gave up smoking them out. These places cannot be forgotten, you said, because they were never seen and surveyed, not by the men who paved the westward roads on which we traveled. You wanted to hike up into it. At first I wasn't sure if you were being metaphorical. We spent a day driving around to various offices, but in the end our request was rejected by the tribal authorities. This pleased you, I think.

We drove back to the motel, checked the map, and figured out what time we'd hit California. Then you turned off the lights and we went there in our dreams—not to our new home by the ocean, your professorship, the family we'd raise, the friendships we'd consecrate, the life we'd share until the fragility of neurons took it all away, but to that other place, that high desert lushness to which we'd been denied ingress in waking life.

It's there that I'll remember you forever, blue mountain lake.

MCDONALD'S KILLS PEOPLE
QUINN BLAIS

WALKING INTO our McDonald's was like stepping back into the 1950s. Or at least, that was the goal of whoever decorated it. In my opinion, it fell a little short. The checkered floor tiles would give you a headache if you looked at them for too long. Posters of Elvis and Marilyn Monroe plastered the walls, interspersed with real vinyl records and record sleeves, vintage advertisements for Heinz ketchup and McDonald's own hamburgers. Inexplicably, the owners also installed a miniature train track suspended from the ceiling, and a model steam engine pulling three cars chugged around the lobby all day. That had nothing to do with the fifties, as far as we could tell.

The real highlight was the working jukebox, which played a variety of old songs—some period-appropriate and some less so. There was Buddy Holly and Dean Martin and Ray Charles, but there was also disco music and "Funkytown." The little hallway leading back to the bathrooms further broke the spell, as portraits of fifties celebrities yielded to framed photographs of us, posing in our visors and baseball caps as McEmployees of the Months. Will Murphy got May 2015, and then the rest of the afternoon crew followed, taking over the wall through September. I had July—and beating Mikey Walsh, who got August, was a point of immense pride. Maddy came second and Kelan, to nobody's surprise, came last. Those were the five of us.

We worked the after-school shifts from three until seven or eight, each of us in our designated place, the same positions every time. Will and Kelan worked the grill, competing for the title of fastest cheeseburger-builder, often spraying mustard across the counter or littering the floor with pickles in the process. Mikey worked the back booth, the first window where you collect money, because he never miscounted change. It was simply a fact that Mikey was smarter than all of us. When the jukebox broke and got stuck playing "Funkytown" for hours on end one Thursday afternoon, Will and Kelan contented themselves with kicking its metal frame and mashing its buttons. Rolling his eyes at them, Mikey retrieved the toolbox from the back room and opened up the machine. Fifteen minutes later, we could listen to Patsy Cline again.

Maddy and I tended the front of the store, she at the window and I at the counter, because we were teenage girls and so our manager liked us to interact with the customers. If I was the sweet one, Maddy was the pretty one, a talented soccer player who turned heads when she walked into the room, blonde ponytail swinging. Her parents owned a café down the street, and we always asked her why she didn't work *there*. Anything had to be better than this.

"I spend enough time with my parents," she said. Besides, there was nothing better than this. There's an idea about working at McDonald's, that it's a last resort or something reserved for trashy, uneducated people. It wasn't like that for us. Rallying together around the frustrations of rude customers, of constantly being covered in fryer grease, of the notoriously broken ice cream machine, we became fast friends. When the store got slow, we went into the freezer where there were no cameras and we smoked grape cigarillos that Will bought from the gas station. Later, we graduated to pot. Other times, we clustered around the doorway connecting the kitchen to the front of the store and snacked on chicken nuggets.

Our shift manager, Sean, shook his head at us. "Those are going to kill you, you know." He was a twenty-seven-year-old substitute teacher and avid fitness enthusiast. On his left triceps, he had a massive tattoo of an hourglass with the inscription TIME WAITS FOR NO MAN. We laughed off his warning, part of a collective ruse in which we pretended we'd never seen him sneak into the office with two Filet-O-Fish sandwiches and shut the door behind him.

"McDonald's kills people," he reminded us again. "High cholesterol." We didn't care. We were sixteen and seventeen, teenagers with fast metabolisms. Cholesterol couldn't kill us.

After work, we took our time getting home. Outside of our shifts, real responsibilities were limited, and we would pile into Mikey's truck and listen to Nirvana in the parking lot. If we were stuck in the fifties inside the restaurant, we suspended ourselves in the nineties in our free time. We had developed a collective love for grunge—Alice in Chains, Screaming Trees, you name it. Pearl Jam was coming to Fenway Park the next summer, and we had already begun saving money for tickets when we should have been saving money for college. But while a concert in August seemed part of the foreseeable future, college in September did not.

One Friday night, we watched the entire *Soaked in Bleach* documentary on Will's laptop, sitting in our McDonald's lobby. The movie details the conspiracy theories surrounding Kurt Cobain's death, specifically that his wife, Courtney Love, was involved. It became our secret shared belief, and we would comment on it as we worked.

"How could he have shot himself with that much morphine in his bloodstream?" Kelan asked me, raising his eyebrows.

"He couldn't have picked up the gun," I answered soberly. "I need another cheeseburger—this wasn't supposed to have ketchup on it."

When we lit up our cigarillos, we toasted. "For Kurt," Maddy announced, and we repeated it back, our mantra. We blew smoke out of the little hatch on the back wall of the freezer, breathing Kurt back into the world.

The day that we watched *Soaked in Bleach*, I drove Kelan home from work for the first time, because it was so late. He lived in the brick apartment buildings behind the grocery store, which I always considered a somewhat scary part of town. Even though he insisted that it wasn't, and that he was fine walking, he accepted my offer, and we made a habit of it from that point on. While the rest of us attended high school, Kelan had dropped out. But since we were split up across the various local school districts, it didn't matter. We lived our separate lives during the day, coming together only in the afternoons to spend a few glorious hours in the fifties. There was a distinct line between McDonald's and "real life."

But occasionally that line blurred, and at other times fractured completely. During the summer when I was McEmployee of the Month, Kelan called me as I was about to head into work. I didn't even have his number saved in my phone, and I had no idea how he'd gotten mine. "Can you bring some concealer?"

"Sure," I replied, confused. He didn't have particularly bad skin. I gave him the stick of concealer in the break room as I was putting up my hair and velcroing my visor.

"How do I do it?" he asked, sticking out his arm. In the crook of his elbow, purple needle marks. Despite never having seen them in person before, I recognized them easily. His eyes told me not to ask. As I blended the beige concealer onto his skin, he mouthed a silent, *Thank you.* I hadn't realized the vast difference between my life and Kelan's until that moment.

Soon after, the boys fixed my car. The boxy Jeep Cherokee fit easily into our nineties fantasy. Except that the heat didn't work, and as September cooled into a brisk October, that started to pose a problem. They tinkered around under the hood one evening while Maddy and I sat in the open trunk, talking and drinking iced coffee from the Dunkin Donuts across the street.

"Sacrilege," Sean would remind us whenever we came into the store with those pink and orange cups. Our McDonald's had iced coffee too, but it wasn't half as good. We couldn't help ourselves—we were New Englanders, after all.

Eventually, Will exclaimed in triumph. They'd done it! We lingered a little longer, and then went our separate ways. I'm not sure why we never hung out outside the lobby or the parking lot, but we didn't. Those were the geographical bounds of our friendship. Which might explain why, when Mikey called me the Friday before Halloween, he demanded that I come to McDonald's immediately.

"Why?" I asked. It was late, after eleven o'clock, and I'd just showered after watching my high school's football game. We had lost, as usual.

"You've got to come. Right now." Something was wrong, I could hear it in his voice. My stomach dropped. Our McDonald's was a seven minute drive from my house, and if I was really pressed for time, I could do it in six. That night, it only took me five. I remember feeling a brief flash of triumph in beating my record time as I swung the Jeep into the parking lot, but it dissipated quickly when I saw the boys sitting together in the bed of Mikey's truck.

Climbing in, I situated myself next to Will, who wrapped his arm around my shoulders. I gave him a look—we didn't do that. Nobody said anything, and Mikey passed me his phone.

A picture of a bleach-blond girl with bright blue eyes. It took me a second to recognize her with her hair down, wearing a fuzzy grey sweater rather than her work uniform. The next picture was a car that had hit a tree and caught on fire.

"Maddy—" Will started, and then stopped.

I remember breathing out all of my air in one sudden exhale and then being unable to take another breath in.

Mikey stood up and got out of the truck. He kicked a crumpled paper cup across the parking lot. He walked over to the dumpster, and he kicked that too. I can still hear it, that metallic clang. Over and over again.

Kelan said it, because I couldn't read the rest of the article. "She got stuck in the car." That was enough, but he continued anyway. "She fucking burned to death."

"Stop," Will intoned.

We didn't cry. We just sat there, listening to Mikey kick the dumpster, until my parents called and said they'd seen it on the news and they needed me to come home immediately and I'd better not be drunk and I'd better not be speeding. It took me ten minutes to drive back to my house, edging along the windy roads slowly in the dark.

The next week, we went to the funeral. It was closed casket. Will held my hand and I didn't give him a look, even when it felt like he was going to crush bones. Some girls from Maddy's soccer team spoke, and her parents. They called her Madeline. We hadn't even known that was her full name. They talked about her pep and leadership on the soccer team, her stellar performance in school. She had two younger brothers, and we hadn't known that either. Before we left in our separate cars, we considered whether we had really known her at all, or if we had just been one tiny fraction of a life so much bigger than us. We wondered if any of her other friends believed that Courtney Love had killed Kurt Cobain.

Ten months later, the four of us went to the Pearl Jam concert together, and soon after that, Will and Mikey and I left for our respective colleges. Kelan stayed, and some part of us envied him for that, for being able to hold onto teenagehood and the fifties, for being able to listen to Elvis on the jukebox and Screaming Trees in the parking lot. We shared a joint outside Fenway before finding our nosebleed seats.

"For Kurt," Will proclaimed, but I shook my head.

"For Eddie Vedder. This is Pearl Jam."

"No," Kelan said. "For Maddy." We could smoke to that.

I stopped working at McDonald's once I started college. Will worked over our first winter break and then quit for good. Mikey lasted until the next summer, and then transferred from UMass to Michigan. His family moved out there, too, and he stopped coming back.

February of my junior year, Will called me out of the blue. "Did you hear?"

"Did I hear what?"

"Kelan Fitzgerald died." It had been years since I'd talked to him, but it hit me right between the ribs. "Asthma attack," Will told me. At least that's what it said in the article. I'd never seen Kelan use an inhaler.

"Kelan didn't have asthma."

"I don't know," Will said. "Maybe he did." We wondered quietly if it was something else, but Will couldn't get back from Ohio and Mikey couldn't get back from Michigan and I couldn't get back from Virginia, so we never found out.

Will and I met up at our McDonald's a couple days after this past Christmas. He'd gotten even taller and skinnier since I'd last seen him. After ordering some chicken nuggets to split, we sat down in the corner booth where the five of us had watched *Soaked in Bleach*.

"Looks different," he said.

"Yeah," I agreed. "The train's not running." And the walls were painted yellow and the music was coming from new overhead speakers. The jukebox was gone. No more "Funkytown."

We walked into the hallway by the bathrooms to look at the McEmployee of the Month photos. Ours were long gone, replaced by some new teenage faces smiling under baseball caps and visors. We wondered if they were friends with each other, the kids pictured from May through September. Silently, we wondered who would survive.

TIGHT
KATY RESCH

MIDNIGHT BEFORE the preschool field trip, the stilled ceiling fan above the bed, vaguely visible in the clock glow, resembled to Ingrid a five-pronged crack in a frozen lake. As if something heavy had landed on the ice and the blades were lines of rupture reaching from the center of impact. Oh, she was exhausted, but Dan's nose whistled on each exhale, had done so since September, when Margot hurled herself from the top of the sliding board and Dan broke her fall with his face.

Ingrid rested her hand on his thigh. Margot had been playing with that unpredictable Angie, and the girls had dared each other to fly like Batman.

And who had told the girls about Batman?

She pinched him. "Roll over."

He did, and she dreamed Miss Hannah flipped the minibus over the pathetic guardrail on the Nickel Bridge. The preschoolers who didn't drown in the James limped to Dollar Mart to buy knock-off Barbies and Made-in-China choking hazards for their Secret Santa partners. Miss Hannah got sidetracked by the display of press-on nails, and a drifter shoplifting inhalants shoved his fist into Margot's mouth, dragged her to the alley, pounded into her as if she'd been deboned, then tossed her body into the dumpster of rotisserie chicken carcasses and car batteries by the Gulf station.

Or Ingrid told herself she was dreaming, not thinking. Margot was three now, almost four: Ingrid had no right to intrusive visions. Those belonged to new mothers, mothers of babies. The ones who handed off six-week-olds to underpaid strangers then pumped milk in the accessible stall at work. That unnatural season was behind her. She opened her eyes, then closed them to an afterimage of the hole in the frozen lake. What was her problem?

She took her phone from the nightstand. Google had no answers, and Weather.com forecast freezing rain too wimpy to cancel anything, even in Richmond, Virginia, a town which was too far north to shut down at the mention of snow but did so anyway. Still, she drifted off on a hope: pajamas all day, crafts, hot cocoa.

*

In the morning, as Dan knotted his tie, Ingrid hated the tendons in his pale neck. She hated every belted shirtdress she ever bought on clearance. She wanted to call out of work, take Margot on a real field trip. Dollar Mart as an excursion—really? She pulled on some cowl-necked thing, then poked about the dish that held her jewelry in a jumble.

"Field trips should be educational," she said, and she would know. She worked in the education department at the art museum, designing tours and art-making workshops, mostly for school children and older adults from retirement homes.

"All they'll learn at Dollar Mart is that Christmas is for buying useless crap," she said. Margot's school should have accepted her offer: "Bring the kids to the museum," she had told the director, "I'll book you pro bono."

"Pro bono, huh?" Dan said now and winked.

"Ha." She knew what he was getting at. A few weeks earlier, Ingrid had been placed on probation—she'd scheduled so many free tours the department had to submit a budget revision to the board of directors. "Education is a profit center," her boss had told her—too many times, evidently. Their fund for free programs was small, and anyway, Ingrid wasn't authorized to use it.

She finally found the mate to the earring she wished to wear: free-form shapes in enameled brass. She had no interest in precious gems, flashy things. If she had extra money, she'd spend it on time—a desire she held up as fundamentally human—*humane*—and so owed to her, to everyone. But owed by whom?

No matter: they had student loans, as Dan reminded her while he threaded on a belt.

"Two-hundred K," he said.

She laughed. "You sound like a hedge fund guy." But the language made sense: Dan raised funds for the city library and spent time with donors who spoke of money in this insider way.

"You wish," he said.

She didn't understand, so he explained: "Don't you want me to be a guy who makes a ton of money? We could own instead of rent. You could paint again, dress Margot in non-toxic sweaters."

She blinked. The comment belonged to an argument they'd never had outright.

"You know," she said, "I read an article on marriage recently that called money 'the knife in the drawer.'"

"I'm driving you to self-help." Dan smirked.

"Margot's sweaters are fine," she said, and so was painting less often. "For now, anyway, while she's so young." That knife—Ingrid saw it as a thin blade in Dan's grip, angled to gleam. She wanted to snatch it, slice those sweaters and stretched canvases. He wasn't even right about her desires as he held them against her.

He must feel inadequate, she mused, some tenderness breaking through, so she changed topics. "I should call out. Miss Hannah might text while she drives."

Dan protested that Miss Hannah wouldn't be driving the minibus, but indeed she would be. Ingrid had already inquired. "It's her hair," she said, a wink in her voice as if referencing a shared joke, because she had told Dan before that Miss Hannah's beachy blond waves freaked her out. Who perfectly styles their hair to care for preschoolers all day? It reflected skewed priorities.

But Dan resisted her playfulness, so Ingrid said, "And the roads might be icy." A loaded statement in their city: Richmonders knew squat about navigating on ice.

Dan fondled his tie in the mirror. "Call out. Solid plan."

But she wouldn't. Not today. A tour group was coming to the museum from one of those posh assisted living communities, and it'd be fatal to ditch a tuition-paying visit with no notice.

From her bed, Margot shouted good morning, then sang "Rudolph the Red-Nosed Reindeer" as she opened dresser drawers.

The sweetness of it constricted Ingrid's chest. Her eyes got hot. She sat on the side chair covered in laundry.

"Babe," Dan sighed.

A wooden thump sounded: Margot had tugged a drawer off its track and onto the floor.

Ingrid stood to go investigate, but Margot thundered to their doorway.

She said, "I got my outfit. If you come into my room, I will punch you."

"Whoa!" Dan said.

"We don't punch or speak rough," Ingrid said, but calmly. She started toward Margot, to escort her back to her room.

"I said, I will punch you." The girl stalked back to her room, then resumed singing.

"What the hell was that?" Dan said.

Ingrid looked down the empty hall and could see her daughter scrambling from her bed to her dresser, pulling the drawer in a panicked rush: Mommy's coming. She's going to pick my outfit and comb my hair.

To Dan, she said, "Who knows. An independent stage."

In the car, Ingrid and Margot sang the bakery shop song, played the animal guessing game. Margot gripped Ingrid's hand as they walked the path into school and up the stairs to her classroom. At the door, she leaned into Ingrid, hesitant for a few beats. Ingrid quickly bit the insides of her cheeks to admonish herself. She recognized her preference for this dynamic: Margot letting go only after Ingrid's encouragement.

Ingrid crouched. "Hear that?" she said, and Margot paused, alert, until she noticed the techno hokey pokey bumping in her classroom.

She brightened, yanked her coat so hard she jammed the zipper.

Ingrid eased the fabric free. The girl kissed her cheek.

"I love dancing," Margot said.

"Funny Bunny, me too."

Maybe Ingrid shouldn't be so hard on herself. Margot had yet to learn she could assert independence without a performance of cruel rejection, and of course Ingrid preferred this tender ritual. Around them, other mothers hung coats on hooks and kissed the tops of heads, then clicked in their office shoes back to the staircase, back to the idling cars they would steer into the productive day. Did they like this rhythm? What did they do? And the teachers there at the preschool—many were mothers of toddlers, too. Where were their children while they were here? There was never time to ask: the air crackled with a harried frequency. Extra conversation would throw the schedule.

And anyway, her questions shamed her. She worked with art, she and Dan could buy groceries and electricity, they leased a reliable car.

Margot lunged to dance with Miss Sara, Miss Hannah's co-teacher. Then she stopped, as if taking notice, and shouted in joy: "Angie!"

Ingrid looked harder into the room. Spotting Angie, she felt a surge of worry, and then of embarrassment. The child's feral energy put her on edge. Typically, Angie only attended a few days a week. Ingrid realized she'd been hoping the girl wouldn't be there for the field trip, her rambunctiousness a sure distraction for the teachers and a stimulant for Margot. At age four, Angie had the build of a six-year-old and moved it with athletic power. The girl's mother, Ingrid surmised, coached water polo for a state university, based on her bumper stickers and shoulders—an esoteric sport Ingrid couldn't envision. She, Dan, and Margot were lithe; people often asked Ingrid if she'd studied ballet. So she caught her breath, sometimes, when she watched Angie and Margot in the playground after school. Together, they pushed their bodies to the edge of injury, shriek-laughing the whole time. They dove into handstands and landed on their chins. Linked arms and spun until the force flung the loser to the ground. Margot trailed Angie with shining eyes, her tongue visible. "Teach me," she said when Angie karate chopped the boxwood hedge. "Let me try!" she said when Angie drop-kicked someone's stuffed dog into a puddle.

Now, Margot ran to Angie and hugged her. Angie froze, looked Margot over like she didn't recognize her or wanted her to buzz off. Then, a smile cracked Angie's face and she embraced Margot so hard they fell over.

Ingrid looked at Miss Sara to calm them, not wanting to claim authority in the woman's space, but the teacher said, "Margi, you and Angie can be field trip buddies."

She turned to Ingrid with her brow raised.

Time to go.

Ingrid blew a kiss that Margot didn't notice, then told Miss Sara thank you and have fun to smooth the wrinkle she'd caused by lingering.

Outside, the school minibus rolled nose-first into a spot that required a proper, ass-in parking job. Miss Hannah reversed into traffic to correct the angle. A car honked and she gunned it so the front tire jumped the curb.

Ingrid waggled her jaw. Could she offer assistance in a way that wouldn't make them both feel like shit?

She got into her Subaru, steered it to the museum, slowing and signaling and checking her mirrors. The dense winter sky flattened everything to gray—other cars, cyclists, even red lights.

Her phone pinged as she arrived in the employee lot. School, she thought, and checked it, seatbelt and engine still on.

But no—Jess, her supervisor, was already emailing. She'd copied Ingrid on a reply to the Vice President of Education, subject line: *Increase in tuition refunds?*

Before Ingrid could read it, a new email pinged. Jess to Ingrid, the VP copied, subject line: *Profit potential.* Evidently, Richmond Senior House, the group Ingrid was to take on a tour that morning, inquired about weekly artmaking workshops and would pay extra to have them customized. Today's visit would determine the residents' degree of interest. Jess ended the note to Ingrid, *You got this*, no punctuation to close the phrase. Smart: if things went poorly, Jess could tell the VP she'd been posing a question.

Ingrid's heart pounded in her mouth. Not because she felt pressure, but because she didn't and knew she should. Once upon a time, she would have leaned into this challenge. As a painter, Ingrid agreed it was preposterous to seek stability from art sales. She'd come to appreciate the art of teaching art. But teaching didn't create stability until her role escalated into budget obligations. She wondered why she didn't care, why her apathy didn't trouble her. Whenever she asked this of herself, the same memory surfaced—the mobile that spun over Margot's daycare crib when she was maybe two months old. It had a woodland theme, seemed sweet, but the fox bared its teeth as if to eat the bunny and the pink-capped mushroom resembled an engorged penis. Ingrid laid her infant beneath these figures, then saw them spiral on her computer monitor at work as the machine booted, in her lunchbreak coffee as she stirred in cream. What kind of pervert would hang such a thing? At her desk, she counted minutes; her nipples needled and leaked. Her confused nipples, Margot's confused mouth. Drinking from a bottle became easier for Margot than nursing, so Ingrid only expressed milk into bottles. Like tons of women, she told herself at the time and for years after—because maybe, if she understood her dismay wasn't special, she could finally get with the program.

Well, someone else's baby stared at that done-for bunny now. Margot's survival, she reminded herself, relies on your body only to the degree that it can report to work. And a dozen ladies are on their way to see if you can dazzle them. Whereas your child is strapped into a minibus on the interstate with twelve other children. Her field trip buddy is straining her seams, she's unfastening your kid's harness, she's chewing your kid's hair. Maybe your kid laughs her head off. Maybe Miss Hannah has forgotten to adjust her mirrors.

Ingrid checked the weather. Sleet still predicted, and the temp had dropped to 34 degrees. She texted a screenshot to Dan: *Cold enough to freeze a bridge.*

Inside the museum, the women from Richmond Senior House were gathered at the gallery door, twenty minutes early. When Ingrid said she had to fetch the keys, they bobbled their heads; she dashed to her desk and back before Jess could see them there, checking their wristwatches.

As Ingrid held open the door, her nose still draining from the cold, part of her stayed in the parking lot, in the private cell of her car, her thoughts. The women filed in, adjusting their bouclé jackets and smelling of talc and rose. Ingrid turned, pressed her face into her arm as if to cough, then pinched her nostrils dry on her sleeve.

"Ladies," she said, and their expectant faces spurred a near-Pavlovian response. She smiled and swept her arm. "The exhibition before you features sculptors working in seemingly functional household forms to uncover the inner meaning of gathering during the winter holidays. Often, we gather for meals with family, the people with whom we can be both intimate and estranged—historically familiar, yet presently alienated."

She paused, not wanting to say the next part. "And that's why the show is titled *Tight.* As in 'tight knit.'" She kept her voice sweet because she hated the title so much. She'd cautioned Jess it sounded too sexual. "Vaginal," she'd specified, but the program sponsor loved how they could stretch the concept to encompass their new airline miles credit card. The last page of the exhibition catalog promoted the benefits: *It's never been easier to stay Tight with loved ones far away…*

Saying it, Ingrid couldn't help but clench her pelvic floor as her obstetrician had instructed. Without meaning to, she scanned the women's trousers. Surely, some of them wore leak guards, had borne multiple children and strained their bodies caring for them. This notion of tight not lost on them.

To preempt questions, she moved quickly to the first sculpture. The women followed her. Their air suggested they were politely concealing their confusion. One woman gave Ingrid a wiry smile certainly meant to bless her heart.

"Here we have a maple table with scrolled edges, but what do you notice about the leaf?"

The woman who had smiled huffed. "Why, it's unattractive."

"Lorna!" Her friend slapped her arm.

"Intentionally so, Barbara-Gae, I'm not being fresh." Lorna looked at Ingrid.

"Exactly." Ingrid explained that the leaf was an aluminum sheet into which the artist had pounded dents. She punched her fist against her palm. "We have an extended table, as though to welcome more guests, but the dents make the leaf useless. And ultimately, uninviting."

"I thought this was about gathering for Christmas," Barbara-Gae said. "My mahogany table could fit fourteen with a leaf and I always had a green plaid runner."

"Ah, but did you want all of those fourteen?" Lorna tapped a finger against her temple. "There's always some relation we hope is obligated elsewhere."

A woman in the back laughed. "Seat cousin Ralph at the dent."

Lorna turned to address another woman. "Celia, take a photo and send it to that daughter-in-law. Tell her you found the perfect dining set to reflect her hospitality, the way she's treating you this season."

Barbara-Gae hissed for Lorna to let the poor woman be, and Celia waved her hand. "I saw them Thanksgiving."

"For brunch," said Lorna, low, then clucked her tongue at Ingrid. "Dear. Show us another."

Ingrid led them to a serving tray with melted handles, then to a gilt place setting punctured with holes.

The women murmured. Why would anyone put holes in perfectly nice china? Where did the artist even find such an old set—had it been her grandmother's? Why didn't she preserve it as an heirloom?

Ingrid rocked on her heels. Her own mother was maybe a decade younger than these women, but, with her degenerative joints, would have had a harder time navigating this gallery excursion. Not that her mother went to galleries—her parents had refused to help with Ingrid's college tuition if she studied art, which had motivated their daughter to pursue painting 800 miles away from their suburban Chicago home. No looking back. Then, Ingrid had Margot, and the bone-deep affection between her and her mother coated the old sting of disapproval in a way that seemed evolutionary—a biological override of rote emotion. On their last visit to Chicago, Margot sat on a church pew and watched her grandmother sing, the girl's face open with awe, as if her grandmother's thin voice might float them both to heaven. She—Margot—gripped a hymnal and murmured in imitation. The woman's pedestrian piano playing, devotion to the Bears, ritualistic consumption of pork and cabbage on New Year's Day—her many simple, unquestioned conventions sparkled when lit by Margot's wonder. Eventually, maybe sooner than Ingrid could fathom, her parents would require hands-on help, would move to a facility like Richmond Senior House—though less expensive—that provided cultural outings her mother did not enjoy but attended to fill time.

It occurred to her that she should edit her script for the retirement home tours, scrap the language about holidays. "Holidays" conjured memories, and it rankled to not have them reflected here. Maybe this was why the women bickered now, among each other, over place settings and proper Christmas recipes. She imagined Margot and Angie squabbling over some plastic junk under florescent lights, Miss Hannah settling the dispute by slapping the toys from their hands.

"That's it?" Lorna said to Ingrid.

Ingrid heard a tapping sound and angled her ear: freezing rain pelted the wall. Next, ice would glaze the asphalt.

She told her face to grin. "Ladies. Let's make some art."

She led them to the studio, explained they would work together on a mural-sized painting of a holiday-themed tabletop.

"And who keeps the painting?" Lorna asked. "I'd rather make my own."

The women chimed in agreement.

"Right. Let's do that." Ingrid slipped an apron over her head and smelled onion through her deodorant.

She cut butcher paper into personal surfaces, and distributed every watercolor set, since no one wanted oil crayons as she'd expected. She took the crayons herself and sat at the head of the table, by Lorna and Barbara-Gae. What could she salvage from this lesson plan?

"Just... paint whatever you'd want to see on the table at a celebratory dinner. I'm drawing a centerpiece my daughter might make in preschool."

The ladies cooed, and Ingrid began to draw an imbalanced flower-like form.

Lorna watched. "My son always brought me lopsided bouquets. I'm painting the settings I liked for Christmas. Bone china so fine you could see the future through it."

"Do you still use it?" Ingrid asked.

"Heavens, no." Lorna and Barbara-Gae exchanged what Ingrid thought was a pitying look.

Lorna continued, "My apartment barely has a kitchen for a pre-cooked ham."

Barbara-Gae leaned in, spoke in a hush. "Did you hear Patricia's flying to Dallas on the twenty-fifth? To her daughter's."

They both glanced at the far end of the table, where a woman with a pronounced tremble dipped her brush in paint.

"Terrible time to travel. And so far." Lorna pursed her lips. "And in her condition."

"And day of. All that hassle, and she won't even see the presents opened in the morning."

The women shook their heads, and Ingrid sensed a knowing pass between them that wasn't exactly compassionate.

She asked if their children lived close. Did they host Christmas now?

Oh, no, they each said, their children had gone to college, met spouses, moved for work or to be closer to the in-law relations.

Lorna said, "Two big firms in Los Angeles recruited my Jonathan. Go, I told him. It's why I taught you to work hard." She puffed a little laugh. "But you'll see me at least three times a year and I don't care for air travel or big cities. He comes just after the New Year. Twins used to join, but they're onto distractions now, teenagers."

"Richmond Senior House does a top-notch Christmas program," Barbara-Gae added.

"That Stephen fellow comes with his guitar and his daughter with the triangle. Precious."

"Ah," Ingrid said as she colored the corolla teal, a color rarely found in nature. "Live music? How lovely."

No one trusted Ingrid to have their dry paintings delivered, so the women boarded the Richmond Senior House shuttle bus with their watercolors dripping off the butcher paper and probably staining their coats. "Or you could pick them up next time you're here," Ingrid had said, as they blinked at her.

Now, she waved goodbye from under her umbrella thinking she didn't give a fuck. Her curriculum had won an award from the state art commission. Margot would never leave her to eat Christmas dinner to the cloying sound of a triangle. On Christmas, they huddled under blankets by the fire pit out back and drank cider. She would somehow make sure the tradition never ended.

Ingrid watched the shuttle bus turn into traffic, exhaled when it didn't slide or fishtail. She checked her phone: 12:45 and no missed calls. Margot's class must be safely returned to the preschool room, prepping for the developmentally inappropriate one-to-three pm nap. Ingrid didn't want to return to the office and get interrogated by Jess. She didn't want to explain that she'd blown prospective revenue, didn't want to anticipate an email from HR updating the status of her probation. She wanted only to speed through yellow lights on her way to snatch up Margot before the child fell asleep, then, if she dared, drive west to Chicago. She'd take her mother and daughter to the lake, to the Lincoln Park Zoo, somewhere good.

When Ingrid arrived, Margot was pissed. And a little drunk from a disrupted routine and a post-Chick-fil-A sugar crash. The chocolate ice cream still moustached her mouth.

"I want to stay with my friends!" she said as Ingrid nudged her from the dim classroom into the hall.

"Hush, sweetie, your friends are trying to rest."

"Well, I'm not!" She stamped her foot.

"You're not what, babe? Not going to hush, or not trying to rest?"

"I'm just… not!" Margot attempted to frown but a giggle broke through. "That doesn't make sense."

"Funny Bunny," Ingrid said, pleased to have engineered the girl's reaction.

She zipped Margot's coat, and her phone buzzed in her purse. The girl twirled woozily toward the staircase, bumping into the walls. "Whooaaaa," Margot said.

Ingrid's cell buzzed again. "Careful on the steps." She withdrew the phone, expecting Jess, but saw Dan's name. She didn't answer in time, and in a flash, text messages materialized like bubbles bursting.

I killed this morning!! Ducking killed!

**Fucking*

Ingrid read with one eye as the other tracked Margot, who was on the steps, pitching all her weight forward while hanging onto the railing. "Margot!" she said.

But what the hell did Dan kill? He was a grant writer.

"Hey!" Margot whined. She was seated on a step, leaning to rub her butt cheek with her hand.

She'd fallen, but Ingrid could tell she was okay.

Dan texted again. He'd impressed the donors so much, they'd emailed him on the sly about a position in their company. *Contract-based to start. An awesome in.*

She hummed. Was contract-based ever an in?

This time, Margot yelped as she fell, and Ingrid watched her stutter on her back down the final few steps. She lay blinking on the granite floor.

"You're okay." Still, Ingrid hurried, heart kicking for what could have been.

"You were not focused, Mama." Margot crossed her arms.

It wasn't the right time to say nothing came of casting blame. She patted Margot's knee.

A door opened on the east side of the foyer, and Angie emerged. She went to the water fountain, then pointed at Margot: "What's wrong with her?"

"Please stop it, I don't like it!" Margot shouted back.

Ingrid furrowed her brow at seeing Angie downstairs. Shouldn't she be asleep? "Are you doing a music class with Ms. Jennifer now?" she asked. Angie shrugged. Ingrid glanced between the girls, tried a different tack: "How was the field trip?"

"She took my candy cane sticker," Angie said.

"You gave it!"

"Then I wanted it back." Angie showed her teeth.

"Angie, honey, let's get you to class." Ingrid said.

Angie turned to the fountain. She had a pink pencil in her hand, and she used the eraser to press the lever. She strained her neck, too short to drink.

"You need the stepper." Margot rose to fetch the stepstool tucked under the fountain.

"I don't need it," Angie said.

"Just try." Margot tilted her head, maybe attempting to be friends again. Ingrid would let the girl drink, then would escort her to the music room or to the Head of School's office—yes, that must have been it: Miss Hannah probably took Angie to the Head of School's office so she wouldn't disrupt nap time.

Angie stepped up. Margot pushed the button, then released it as Angie leaned for a drink.

"Hey!" Angie said. Margot flashed a heckling smile.

"Be kind, Margot," Ingrid said.

Margot pressed the button and Angie went for it. Again, Margot cackled and let go.

"I'm *thirsty*," Angie shouted.

Margot pumped the button hard, so a gush splashed Angie's face. She did it again, wetting the front of Angie's yellow sweater—as if acting like Angie would win Angie's affection.

"Enough," Ingrid said. Still, compassion twinged for her daughter, even though she was being a jerk. The fall had embarrassed her, and she wanted to impress Angie. Ingrid stood to intervene, but Angie jumped from the stepstool and wordlessly jabbed her pencil into Margot's right eye.

She pulled back her arm, elbow sharp, and jabbed again with a twisting motion. Margot shrieked.

"Mama!" She crumpled onto the floor, hands over her eyes.

Ingrid dove, swooped Margot onto her lap and squeezed her, to steady herself.

"Let me see, honey." Panic compressed her voice. But she could not let herself fracture. To yield to panic was to fail at this whole thing. "It'll be okay," she said.

But Margot wouldn't remove her hands.

The hallway shrank to a box of buzzing light, her daughter's cry bouncing off its surfaces. A wish rose in Ingrid like a growl: to know her daughter's pain so she could know what action to take. Get an ambulance? An ice cube?

She lifted her face and saw Angie's astonishment. The girl had backed up, but not far enough, in Ingrid's opinion.

Ingrid shoved her with one hand, the child's shoulder larger than Margot's but still very small. Angie stumbled back.

"You little fuck," Ingrid said. "What are you doing without a teacher? Get a fucking teacher."

Angie covered her ears, then flung open the door and disappeared through it. Margot cried louder, clasped her palms as Ingrid tried to peel them away.

Something wet Ingrid's neck. "Damn it, I need to see!"

Ingrid held her daughter firmer. Margot moaned, the sound pushing into a higher pitch, and Ingrid loosened her grip. But then Margot cried out. Had the position freshened her pain? Ingrid had no idea how to shift without jostling or whether the jostling would hurt. She tensed her arms, then relaxed them, tensed then relaxed, eliciting from Margot a new yowl each time, all objections, Ingrid holding her daughter too tight and not tight enough.

DREAM STORY REVISITED

LEENA EL-MOHANDES

SHE STARTLES awake, a stream of moonlight crawling over the windowsill and down to the floor. His arm is draped across her waist, his hand limp and dangling over her hip. Perspiration dots her forehead.

She folds both hands under her head and stares at the man in the moon. She imagines he shifts around in his great wheel of Swiss cheese until he feels her gaze and stares back, his shaded face framed by the panes of his window, one of many amorphic orifices in his mottled dwelling.

It is this image that lulls her back to sleep.

She stands in the road, straddling the double yellow line.

Woods line either side of the pavement, denser and darker in the foliage to her right. The street is dimly illuminated, but there is not a star or visible moon in the sky.

She feels a prickling and sees a creature—the eyes of one—peering at her from the tree line on her left. She turns to face it, too unsure to be afraid. It comes forward slowly, into the inexplicable light, and stops just inside the white line on the far side of the road.

It is a doe. Its ears lay flat to its head, its nose sniffs gently, assessing. They stare at each other, neither comfortable, but neither afraid.

The silence is broken by the hum of an engine. It swiftly shifts from a faint buzz to a gurgling rumble, and headlights appear from a bend in the distance.

Neither she nor the creature react. The headlights reflect in the doe's dark chocolate eyes. She begins to feel the roar of the engine in her ears—and yet the creature stays still.

Go, *she urges the animal.* Run.

The doe remains unmoving. The light is so close now she must squint to see the doe, whose brown coat shines in the spotlight of the road. Her bones shake with the engine's every turn.

Run, *she implores.* Now. You are almost out of time.

For a moment, she sees herself reflected in the doe's eye like the back of a silver spoon. The doe's right hoof lifts, and the vehicle strikes.

She cries out, or she would, were not the wind knocked out of her so immensely. Wind whistles by her ears and she feels such weightlessness as she has never felt before. Briefly, she floats in the illuminated, starless sky—and then gravity grabs hold again and she is sucked back to the earth.

The road rushes up towards her as she plummets. She braces for impact; when she and the ground collide, her limbs go numb, but there is no pain—only a jolt, like a zap of electricity, and a profound moment of silence.

Sound comes rushing back, as does the feeling in her limbs. The nearby foliage rustles. She looks up just in time to see a fluffy white tail disappear into the darker side of the woods.

Wait, she pleads, but she has already given chase.

Branches jab and scratch at her as she races by. They tear at her clothes and claw at her cheeks. She feels a dampness on her skin. Whether it is blood or perspiration, she does not know. She runs and runs until vegetation gives way to a clearing. The doe stands just within the shadows on the far side, watching.

She steps forward, once, twice, cautiously, so not to spook the creature, though she still observes no fear in its eyes.

She stops in the center and waits. The light of unknown origin paints the clearing in a pallid, hazy grey. Again, the girl and the doe stare at one another, she in the clearing, the creature in the wood.

There is no rumble this time, only the sudden bath of brightness as she turns her head to the snake eyes of light—and the impact, which vaults her into weightlessness once more.

Her eyes open, momentarily blinded by the shaft of moonlight drawn across her cheekbones. The weight across her waist pins her to the mattress, shedding additional heat onto her abdomen. She does not settle into the embrace, though she does not wriggle away.

The man in the moon strokes her hair gently, his rivulet of light traversing her face and ears and wrapping around her head, stopping just shy of the adjacent pillow.

She considers the moon, the sky, for a moment, counting stars.

Then she falls into sleep.

He is in the bathroom, rinsing off the sweat after his sports game.

He hasn't played seriously in years, but this routine was mundane for a time.

She puts away her shoes and coat and unpacks her purse. It is not late, but she remembers she has an early commitment the next morning and intends to turn in soon. She is about to undress when he comes into the bedroom.

No words are spoken as he approaches. None seem necessary; none seem sufficient.

They stand so closely, sharing breath, daring one another to break the physical barrier. Finally, she lifts her chin, hardly, barely, a modicum of movement, and his hand cups her jaw. His thumb presses just above her throat, tilting back her head, and the eye contact is no longer enough.

The exhale they share is partly relief and partly anticipation. Her heart pounds. He must feel it against his chest, against his roaming palm. They pause only long enough for her to lay back on the bed and him to climb over, lying together in the moonlight which streams onto the bed and into their bodies—the night sky's spotlight.

The heat becomes unbearable; sweat slicks his back, and her hair clings to her neck and temples. He leans his forehead against hers, their brows pressed together with a firmness that is grounding. She opens her mouth, to breathe, to gasp, and he seals off her sigh before it can escape. She tastes him on her tongue and then tastes iron.

Her eyes open abruptly. The metallic flavor fills her mouth, and something jostles against her tongue.

Keeping hold of her gaze, he leans back and spits forcefully to the side, sending a small object, like a watermelon seed, to the shadows of the floor below. He leans back down and again seals her open mouth; again, he spits to the side; again; again, moving away less and less until his weight barely shifts, and only his head turns, though his eyes do not.

It's not until she tries to bite down on her lip that she realizes she cannot and breaks their tethered gazes to see the jumble of her teeth on the floor, glistening with saliva, incandescently white in the pool of moonlight.

She wakes to a flash of lightning. The sheets strangle her feet at the end of the bed, the duvet off to the side. She turns onto her back, his arm now resting limply across her pelvis. The ceiling fan above her clucks slowly, shuffling the warm air of the room in a sluggish circle.

Beside her, he grunts softly and nestles closer, settling so she feels his rhythmic exhales at her neck. The limb across her hips is not heavy, but she doesn't attempt to free her arms from beneath its weight, despite the added warmth. Another flash of heat lightning flares in the window.

Flat on her back, she allows the gentle whir of the ceiling fan lull her into sleep.

She is at the peak of the world, where there is nowhere higher to climb, only a flat plateau, and ultimately, a drop-off.

She lies on a soft patch of grass. Fluffy white clouds bob across the sky, though they never occlude the sunshine, which beams across her skin, warming her to the core. There is no noise, save for the gentle whisper of grass caressed by the breeze. The sky is a vivid cerulean blue. She is at peace.

A rustle behind her catches her ear. She sits up and turns, inspecting the foliage for movement. The leaves sway with the wind and strands of her hair flick her cheeks. Another noise escapes the brush, and she squints, a palm shading her eyes, to make out a form in the greenery. A sniffing black nose appears between two bushes, encircled in white fur.

The breeze picks up and her hair billows across her face, obscuring her sight of the snout. By the time she tucks the strands behind her ears, the creature has peeked its head out of the foliage.

A doe. Its black nose sniffs gently, wide-set eyes quietly studying. Around its neck dangles a collar attached to a nylon pet leash, the end loop on the ground beneath, coiled under its own length.

Between one moment and the next, the doe has bounded from the bushes and taken off for the grass behind her, where the earth seems to meet the sky. The leash trails after, snapping in the air close to her head. Before she can open her mouth, before she can reach for the leash, before she even realizes the patch of grass ends, the doe has leapt off the edge.

She hurdles after, diving for the loop of nylon, and falls off the bluff, plummeting into the sky.

The doe is not visible, concealed by the mist through which she falls. The leash is only a meter away, pulled taut by the forces of gravity and drag, fighting to reach her.

She stretches for the loop, but the wind blows her hair into her eyes and dries them so intensely she can barely see. She tries to straighten her legs—to streamline—in the hopes that she may fall that much faster, but her muscles will not obey.

She is free-falling. The loop is pulling farther and farther away. She can no longer feel her limbs. Even the wind is no longer whistling in her ears.

So, she closes her eyes and falls.

The ceiling is bathed in a warm glow.

Beside her, he lays on his stomach, one arm under his pillow, the other thrown over his head.

She turns to the window and is greeted by the sun creeping above the horizon. The moon has long set. She blinks slowly, taking in the budding morning, and bids the man in the moon a good day's rest.

READING LOVE LETTERS OF THE DEAD ON A RAINY MORN

MELISSA STEPHENSON

My little frigging mistress, my little fucking whore, Joyce
said to Nora. (Tell me where do you find a man like that?)

Always be polite, my mother always said.

Don't never go to bed angry, says the lady
in the dental clinic waiting room.

Your true other, I've heard tell, is your soul-shadow,
repressed opposite, whom you love-wrestle
into completion, puzzling yourself back to whole.

Find someone who makes you laugh, says
someone somewhere (or so you heard).

He should be kind, familiar, like from a past life,
butterfly-inducing, swoon-stirring, time-stopping

(but human). *Pick one,* she tells me, *who's*
always ________ *but never* _______.

You only find the love you think you deserve,
says another between sips of late-day coffee.

You are always my beautiful wild flower of the hedges,
Joyce wrote to Nora, *my dark blue rain-drenched flower.*
(Where *do* you find a man like that? But then
he shat on her too, or the other way around.)

Love sparks so often from the extra-
ordinary, defying platitude. See it?
Rounding the bend pigeon-toed on your last-straw
day, carrying Richard Burton eyes and comparing you
too loosely to the moon, all memory erased

now of that June in Vermont so wet
the ground never dried and you learned to love
above all else long runs alone in the rain.

WHY BLACK FOLKS LIKE TO DANCE
GLENN NORTH

"For the art—the blues, the spirituals, the jazz,
the dance—was what we had in place of freedom."
– *Ralph Ellison, Shadow and Act*

You study the darkness
of my body, desiring
to know the curve
& the line, whips scarred
my back but they never
broke my spine, you implement
strategies designed
to steal what's inherently mine,
you want to move like me,
to groove like me,
to boogaloo like me
but your body can't
move like mine
'cause it never needed to…
I cakewalked out your slavery
& you couldn't lynch my blues
yeah, you try to dance
like me but you stuck
with two left shoes.
My hips undulate with a passion
that shakes pinecones loose
my frame contorts in ways
that Sherlock could not deduce
with every oppressor I face
& throughout every abuse

my movements possess
a beauty that only struggle
could produce.
I keep it movin' with a quickness
with a panther's agility
got a lindyhop too fast
for the naked eye to see
I call my left leg Malcolm
& Martin is my right
I can march the streets
of Birmingham at noontime
& dance all Saturday night.
Never understood
how you could love my music,
my walk, my talk, my style
but hate me so intensely…
Why am I so reviled?
May not ever get the answers
on this side of eternity
but one thing is for certain
I'ma keep on doin me
I'ma dance like
there's no tomorrow
And sing at the top
of my lungs
shakin my Big Black Groove Thang
until the final bell is rung.

After The Portrait of Joseph "Doc" Brown by Millard C. Haywood

THE DUKKHA OF FLOW
JESSE DONALDSON

IT WAS the fall and the leaves were turning brown and the football team was losing, so things were pretty much the same as ever in Lexington, except Freddie Flow's snubnose .38 was one bullet lighter—an accident—though his roommate Stank didn't see it that way, and Stank's cousin Lavelle surely wouldn't. The bullet lay somewhere in the wall of his and Stank's living room, evidence that couldn't be taken back, evidence that Freddie was rightly fucked even though Stank was alive and well. No going home for Freddie. He'd be skittish at every loud boom, run from every big fat weightlifting motherfucker who might be Lavelle.

Freddie stalked the university's rec fields like a stray with a score to settle. He snuck up on the leaf piles, raked carefully by some underpaid chump without benefits, and punted them with his flyest kicks. Shit was falling apart, blow it up. He swung his leg like a pendulum and the leaves went scurrying, scanned the fields to make sure the saps who'd raked them in the first place weren't around, then kicked again. Freddie didn't care. More work, more pay. Time and a half and all that. Motherfuckers should thank him. Leaves. He liked how they crunched beneath his kicks. He liked how they fluttered in the breeze.

The right side of Freddie's low-slung denim hung with the snubnose sitting atop his last three eighths, all stolen from Stank. He needed to learn to shoot the .38, I mean, really shoot it. In case shit. That much was straight truth. Protect yourself. Fucking Lavelle. Fucking Stank, really. Backstabber.

Across the field from Freddie, a pack of Asian dudes wearing crimson dresses tossed a basketball back and forth like kids set loose from school. Their arms were bare and their feet were too, save some sandals. Freddie hunkered deep into his hoodie and pulled the strings taut as he walked toward them.

This is what you do when you can't make it as the next great white rapper: sell drugs. For Freddie Flow, this started as slinging dime bags to doctors' sons near the unmanned guardhouses of gated communities.

His clients came in pairs—cash in their front pockets, eyes to the ground, legs jingle-jangling. Freddie came carrying Ziplocs of weed he claimed were eighths but weighed less and were cut with Top.

His roommate Stank, this half-Black kid whose mama had christened him Stanley, considered himself a gardener of sorts and grew hydroponic in most of the closets. Freddie had come up with their business plan at the end of a long night getting high and celebrating their soon-to-come eviction. He was in the corner of the living room—headphones on—watching Stank's friends roll joint after joint and dance. He wrote *SELL WEED* on the palm of his hand and the next day, while Stank was frying eggs, he looked at that hand again, lit a joint, and said, "Let's sell this shit."

All of Freddie's best moments were like that. Divine Inspiration sent straight to the dome. He liked to hatch plans and imagine the future, but this time his and Stank's impending homelessness transformed his idea into something more than a pipe dream. Freddie was gonna get rich or die trying, and he told Stank as much. He was an Entrepreneur. Warren Buffet in Diesel Jeans. C.R.E.A.M. Get the money.

And shit was tight at first, too. Selling weed turned out to be Freddie's calling. Stank started growing in every closet of the apartment and Freddie walked all over Euclid delivering to college kids. At the end of the summer, almost a year to the day that Freddie had written their business plan on his person, he and Stank moved into a two-story with pool access in one of those self-same gated communities where Freddie sold to teenage punks. They had a MILF neighbor, a lawnmower they ran whenever the neighborhood association taped some bullshit notice to the door, and an entire basement floor of grow lights and manna.

Freddie would call home to his pops every other Sunday and say things were good in Lexington, thank you very much, and no, he didn't need to return home to work in some podunk car shop in the buttfucking holler.

The Asian ballers had shaved heads and baby faces. They played full court, a measured five-on-five anchored by crisp passing and mid-range jumpshots, the occasional runout, up and down, all the time chattering in yips like terriers. Their robes flared like fire whenever they pivoted, and even in their sandals, they caught air like kites to lay the ball softly off the glass.

Freddie thought about his girl—Hannah, her red hair and pale skin. He wondered what she'd look like in crimson. He'd never seen her wear it, probably never would. Reminisce over Hannah who shined. Glitter girl. He'd spent the last of his last cash the night before on a leather jacket she coveted. Fur-lined. Pricey. Freddie's last act: dropping the bills in the cashier's hand like it was nothing and realizing he didn't have enough left over for dinner. Hannah's last: a kiss on the cheek and an apology for being tired. A bunk exchange.

Ever since Lavelle made it clear that Freddie was out, Stank was *his* supplier now, Freddie'd been trying to hide his stress from Hannah, but she knew something was off—she had a sixth sense when it came to cashflow. Their relationship was more business than affection, and the price of Hannah's attention appreciated like wine.

He watched one of the ballers take an outlet pass, race up the court, and release a perfect left-handed jump shot from just beyond the arc. The dude kept his arm raised as it swished. Kung-Fu Kobe. Game over.

Freddie started to walk away, but one of the ballers yipped and passed him the rock. It hit stiffly against Freddie's hands and sent bass tremors through his wrists. The Asian dude mimed taking a shot. Freddie shook his head. He was a terrible athlete, and he hated to look the fool, though he knew people often thought him foolish. Haters. The Asian dude stepped closer. His robe was plain, like a bag with armholes cut at the shoulders. Flip it and you could have a potato sack race or a big red diaper. Freddie bounced the basketball once and tossed it back. "Naw, man," he said. "I don't hoop."

The dude caught the ball and looked confused, hurt even. Then a second one came over and handed Freddie a flyer explaining that they were Buddhist monks from Thailand brought by the university to make a mandala, which was some sort of sand painting. The monks would spend a week working on the damn thing and then throw it in the river. Freddie shook his head, pocketed the flyer. "Crazy," he said and put out his fist. The monk greeted him knuckles on knuckles. Straight up playa monk.

Her stripper name was Hannah—the same forwards as backwards—and she went by it in regular life, too. Once she'd it let slip to Freddie that her real name was Harry, named after a grandfather at her daddy's insistence. She was a runaway country girl caked with runway makeup that made her skin an even whiter shade of pale. A ghost dancing round the pole. She wouldn't have given Freddie the time of day before he started slinging, but with a fat stack in his pocket, she didn't mind his attention, at least not more than anyone else. Freddie told her he loved her after two dates, and she laughed and said, "Ssshh, the movie's about to start."

She was kind to him, but Freddie would have stayed even if she wasn't. She was just that beautiful. Her hand in his made him feel electric. He knew how she made her money, but he didn't care. She never talked about the club. Hannah was above it all, like helium. Always looking down her nose at people. Girl Pinocchio.

She liked listening to Freddie talk business, liked that he had a mind and used it. When he ditched his iPod for the 24/7 news radio, she didn't even poke fun. She even let him pull over one night in the empty parking lot of a China Buffet and lick her pussy in the back seat while the radio host droned on about derivatives and the price of gold.

Freddie knew the price of gold. He'd called the jewelry he strung on Hannah investments. Sometimes he'd imagined Stank moving out and her moving in, imagined them buying a lockbox for all her diamonds and gold, for the certificates of stock he'd buy. Something to leave their progeny. Red-headed fuckers with Freddie's smarts and Hannah's looks. Little players. College grads. Doctors and lawyers.

One time, he let it slip to Hannah that Stank was "being a little bitch"—Freddie's way of saying he couldn't believe Stank would just up and stop supplying him. Hannah said Freddie didn't need Stank. Stank was a pothead gardener. Freddie was a visionary. He'd make it work. She said it with so much confidence he'd actually believed her.

But Freddie couldn't make it work. He tried growing his own hydroponic and learned he didn't have the touch. White boy, black thumb. He was in the process of moving out of the house for homelier digs when he and Stank got into a fight over who bought the TV. Freddie had taken out the gun just because he could, and when it went off, he was as shocked as anyone. Stank stood open-mouthed, gaping like a fish. Freddie kept expecting him to bleed or keel over, but the bullet wasn't even close. Then Freddie ran.

By now, Lavelle would know. Lavelle: a roll-necked devil stuffed into too small a sausage casing. Lavelle protects his own, Stank once told Freddie. Lavelle is a bad-ass motherfucker. Which meant Stank didn't consider Freddie a bad-ass motherfucker, which meant Freddie could be walked over like the goddamn grass. Friendship. Fuck it. Just a set of circumstances bound to change. A true friend would have helped him keep Hannah, would have understood, but Stank put a lock on his door to protect his precious garden. Eden. Doesn't mean nothing without Eve. Knowledge. Drop it like Milton. Lucifer is rising. And his name is Freddie Flow.

With one day of post-gunshot survival in the books, Freddie found himself back at the blue courts, watching the monks hoop again. He hadn't slept more than a few front-seat-of-the-car-winks because sleep was the cousin of death. Freddie couldn't say what exactly brought him back to the courts. Boredom, probably. He'd sold the last of his shitty schwag to a pimple-faced kid in the library. What else was there? At least the monks were more interesting than driving around town, hoping not to be seen by Lavelle.

The monks were excited to see him again, called Freddie up to the court and banged knuckles, prodded him to take a shot. Freddie on the spot. Take the stage. Take the Mic. He looked around to see if anyone stood witness, and when he was satisfied that this would be between him and the monks, he released a gooseneck jumper that clanged off the rim and bounced into some scraggly bushes. One of the monks ran the ball down and tossed it back to him, but Freddie bounced it on. "That's all I got," he said.

The monks gathered around him. "You can do better," one said, catching Freddie off guard. Sly-ass, English-speaking mothermonk. Talking all like Yoda and shit.

"What's that?"

"Just because you can't shoot doesn't mean you can't play." It was the baller monk who spoke, Asian Kobe with the sweet release. "We're one short," he said.

"I'll just watch, man."

"No game unless we have ten."

The other monks didn't follow, so Kobe translated, and they all started nodding and saying, "Play play play," like it was the only damn word they knew.

Freddie sniffed once, shrugged. "A'ight," he said.

He took off his hoodie, snuck the snubnose out of his pocket, hid it in the bundle. He wore only a wifebeater, and the cold brought bumps to his skin. Braille for the weather. Chillbugs, his pops had called them. Freddie jumped up and down, rubbed his arms.

"You're with me," Kobe said.

Watching along the sidelines, Freddie had understood why each monk was moving where, but on the court he couldn't get the rhythm. He kept running into teammates and Kobe kept pointing him to one place or another. When Freddie tried to take his guy on the dribble, the defender knocked the ball away and passed it down court for an easy two. Freddie dropped his head and Kobe yelled, "Just play ball." Freddie wanted to quit, or maybe he wanted to punch Kobe in the face and show him who was boss; instead, he started passing as soon as the ball touched his hands, but Asian Kobe wouldn't let him alone. He made a point of passing to Freddie and imploring him to "shoot the rock." It got so tiresome that Freddie finally did and missed everything. "That's better," Kobe said. Freddie cursed him under his breath.

Freddie's only saving grace was defense. What he lacked in talent, he made up for in effort. He kept in the face of his man, even talked a little shit, though the fucker couldn't understand. "Can't nobody score on me," Freddie chirped. "No buckets, no how." The monk just smiled. Then near the end of the game, he took the ball, winked at Freddie, and spun by him before letting a floater go that brought it to game point.

Asian Kobe called time out and gathered the team. Freddie was the last one to sulk into the huddle. "No buckets, huh."

Freddie'd had enough. He pushed the monk in the chest. "What's your fucking problem, man?"

"That's better," Kobe said. "You gotta release that anger. That's why we ball." He pushed Freddie back but not hard and the other monks laughed. Then he said, "I'm going to screen your man and you drive to the basket." Freddie nodded like he could do that. Art of War. Art of Balling. Phil Jackson meet Confucius. Confucius says score buckets, son.

Freddie dribbled up the court, waited for the screen, then dropped his head and barreled toward the hoop like a whole herd of Freddies. The monks moved left and right out. Moses parting the sea. Moses Malone. Moses Flow. Freddie to the basket with a little underhand flip, a sweet rainbow kiss that tickled the rim before falling through. Leather on nylon.

"Get back," Asian Kobe called, and Freddie hustled down the court with his teammates. His man got the ball and Freddie came up close enough to feel the monk's robe against his skin. White meets rice. Freddie bumped the monk and the ball came loose but nobody called foul, so Freddie grabbed it and started up court like a wild beast stampeding. Then he heard Kobe—his coach, his sensei—yell hold up, slow it down, and Freddie, all instinct to the core, all never-listen-to-no-one-no-how-cause-the-Flow-knows drove to the hoop before laying off a bounce pass to Kobe, who skied towards the rim, and just when it seemed like gravity—that apple to the dome bastard of the everyday—would bring him down, his dress seemed to catch a breeze and he threw it down.

Freddie ran up and gave him chest bump. Then the other monks gathered around and exchanged high-fives, and soon enough Freddie forgot which ones had been on his team and which ones hasn't. It was all celebration.

"Where'd you learn to speak English?" he asked Kobe as they lined up at the water fountains.

"Chicago."

"So how'd you end up in this robe?"

"Luck," he said. "Better luck than whatever has you carrying that gun."

Freddie looked away.

"I'd ditch that life."

"Is that what you did?"

"No. I went to Yale. But you don't need an Ivy Leaguer to tell you that gun will bring you trouble. Fire a bullet and it comes back to you."

"Circle of life and shit?"

"You could say that."

"Easier said than done, Boss," Freddie told him. "Life ain't always simple like b-ball. Sometimes the bullets been fired before the game's even begun."

*

Freddie left the monks, took out his cell and called Hannah. You can't win if you don't play the game. She picked up after four rings, and he said, "Lemme take you to dinner, Boo." Smooth as baby's butt, he thought. Oil her up.

Hannah waited before answering. "I don't know, Freddie."

"Come on, girl," he said, annoyed at how whiny he sounded. Be like Kobe, he told himself. Straight butter. "I just want to buy you a steak. You working tonight?"

"No."

"You gotta eat, right?"

"I suppose."

"I'm gonna get us a whole cow. Angus. And Idaho potatoes. Not some damn Kentucky potato. And when it comes to the salad, I'll tell them to bring us chocolate cake salad." He strutted like the veriest peacock now, his confidence returned.

Hannah laughed. He could picture her smile. Bleached teeth no matter how much she smoked. "Pick me up in an hour?" she said.

"An hour and fifteen," Freddie replied, as if he had something important.

Then he drove to a spot a few blocks down from her place and counted the minutes and the cheddar from his last weed sale. He didn't have the patience for talk radio, so he put in an old OutKast record. Cooler than polar bear's toenails. Freddie on the other side of the pillow. Fuck Lavelle. But first, little-f fuck Hannah. *Lovemaking: The Art of Seduction*, a treatise on steak dinners and sexual technique by the Fabulous Freddie Flow. The minutes crawled by and Freddie caught some hazy zzz's. When he woke up, he tried to get fresh and clean by grabbing a car deodorant shaped like a hula girl and rubbing it on the armpits of his hoodie. Chanel No. 5 for the needy.

Hannah was waiting for him, looking fly in a short black skirt. She'd look fly in anything. Red carpet Hannah. Damn, he was lucky. He parked and left the car running, jumped out to get her door and went for a hug, a full-on kiss. Hannah kissed him back, kissed him like she'd been missing him. When she pulled away, she said, "I'm sorry."

Freddie blinked.

Stank came out first and Lavelle behind, a fatass playa squeezing himself between two parked trucks. Hiding like a bitch. Freddie made to protect Hannah, but she stepped away from him. The realization hit hard. Hannah's face turned sad. "Run," she said softly through soft lips. Freddie reached for the snubnose, thought better of it. Maybe he could have made it if he'd bolted, but Freddie just stood there—looking at Hannah, looking at Lavelle. Bolted in place, unmoving. Stank stopped about ten feet away and stared at the ground. Lavelle walked like it pained him. As he limped past Hannah, he put a hand to her shoulder. Dismissed. Then he turned that same hand into a fist and wheeled it at Freddie.

Freddie didn't have a chance. He went down on the first punch and stayed curled up like a scared potato bug. He took Timberlands to the ribs, the ass, the chest, the fucking sternum. He couldn't breathe. Timberlands to the side of his head. Shit went dark. Someone was screaming. Hannah? Him? Maybe it was all in his head. His wounded head. There was blood in his eyes. A loose tooth. Who knows when these things happen? The order of events? Who cares? Freddie was rightly fucked.

"Stupid ass white boy," Lavelle said after Freddie had recovered enough to show he was alive. Lavelle bent down. Gravity seemed to pull at him, so he went to one knee and then two. He looked at Freddie with bloodshot eyes. Freddie blinking back the blood. "You reap what you sow," Lavelle said, like he was some damn philosopher, like he invented that shit. He pulled out a gun, cradled it in his fat hand. His fingers had fat rolls like his neck. Neckfingers. He put the gun to Freddie's head. You sow what you reap, Freddie thought. Sow. So. The hammer cocked. So this is how a life ends. "You're done," Lavelle said, and laughed. Maniacal motherfucker. Freddie was paralyzed. The moon sat flat and bowl-like in the sky behind his maker. In the periphery—Hannah. Cloudy but there. A vision. A trip down memory lane. Then Lavelle pulled the gun away from Freddie's head. "Damn, Stank," he said, his voice high-pitched like a girl's. "Help a fat man up." Freddie couldn't close his eyes, kept looking up at that saucer bowl moon long after they'd gone, long after Lavelle had rifled through his pockets for the last of his cash and the snubnose that set it all in motion.

Life's a bitch and then you die. That's why we get high. Freddie rolled the verse in his head over and over, unable to move his jaw, which had been wired shut. No more flow. Verbal. Soze becomes Kint.

One more day, the doctor said. They needed the bed, which meant there were people more broken than Freddie, but he didn't believe it. He pointed to the tube where they released the liquid breadloaf that knocked his ass o-u-t out. The doctor frowned. Fucking look at me, Freddie wanted to say, and the doctor seemed to understand. He called the nurse for another bag, let relief drip into Freddie's veins. Vanity was over, that much was certain. The nurse proved as much with a mirror held before his face. FrankenFreddie. Black and Blue and Yellow and Green. Gangrene. Surely he would die. Get it over with. The doctor talking, words slowing. Drip Drip Drop. Eyes down.

Mean Nurse Number Two came in later, bearing gifts. Flowers in one hand, a folded paper bag in the other. On the paper bag, in Stank's graffiti scrawl, were the words, "Sorry, Dawg." A card was stapled to it with Hannah's bubble script. Freddie pointed and Nurse huffed. Better things to do. Don't we all. "Please," Freddie tried to grunt. Nurse ripped open the envelope like it was a bill. Out came a card with printed cursive. Sympathy. Save the envelope, now. Careful. "I had no idea it would end like this," Nurse read, her voice nothing like Hannah's. "Love, Harry." Nurse looked at him. Harry and Freddie. Queer boys. It all made sense. Hate crime. Freddie didn't care. He missed her. How stupid he was. Everything that happened, and he'd take her back if he could. His one love. Girl Harry. The only one he'd ever know. "I ain't even going through the of rest this," Nurse said, dropping the paper bag by the bed.

Freddie focused on his limbs. Broken ribs, they said, but his legs worked. Bruised but functioning. A cast on one arm. Doctor says it could have been worse. Compared to what? A bus? His toes moved and his legs swung down and they held up under the drop to the floor. Freddie's good arm opened the bag. Inside was a paperclip of twenties, a change of clothes, and a pair of Adidas kicks with a quarter of Stank's kind in the right toe. Stuffed in the left shoe was the root of all evil. Five chambers of .38 doom. All empty. Smart.

Freddie shuffled to the closet where the hospital had bagged and set his old clothes, still bloody and ripped and covered with tar dirt from the parking lot. He checked the pockets and pulled a flyer from the hoodie.

Monks.

He handed the flyer and two twenties to the cabbie, pointed to the spot marked with a star along the Kentucky River.

"This says it starts at five o'clock," the cabbie said. Freddie pulled another twenty from his pocket. Drive fast. Cash money, a language all its own. The cabbie lead-footed it away from the hospital.

Freddie arrived in time to watch the monks scrape their mandala into a jar. A few photographers captured the proceedings and some hippie students smoked cloves next to the river. He tried to catch Kobe's eye and let him know he'd come, let him know he cared, but Kobe was focused on the monks using brushes to capture every last speck of sand. Spiritual Geometry. Ashes to Ashes. Dust to Dust. Freddie couldn't imagine destroying something so perfect. The monks wore golden caps shaped like cones on their head. They looked like Asian Klansmen, and Freddie immediately felt bad for the thinking that. God, what was wrong with him? His ribs stung. The cabbie had said he'd wait in the car, but Freddie saw the guy coming down the hill to the river and was glad for the company.

"This is different," the cabbie said. Freddie shrugged.

The monks chanted, a few played these long horns and one clanged the cymbals. At first it was just noise, but the voices started to make sense, not because Freddie knew the words, but because he felt like he could understand, if given time. Cipher divine.

The eldest monk, an ancient Freddie had never seen, took the jar of sand. All the color had mixed together, and it looked gray, like any other sand from any old beach. The monk held it up in the fading sun and then Kobe announced, with a bit of a tremor in his voice, "The Buddha said this existence of ours is as transient as the autumn clouds. To watch the birth and death of beings is like looking at the movements of a dance. A lifetime is like a flash of lightning in the sky." Freddie nodded like he understood. The Ancient held the jar as far as he could over the river and poured. The Sands of Time. Save me a speck. Save me a place. Freddie wanted to put it back together, to build the painting again. He still didn't understand. Why?

He expected the sand to make colors in the water, to turn the river sherbet, but it just floated like ash and swirled in an eddy before slipping down, down, down. A few monks threw flowers onto the water. They floated, like in the bowls at the China Buffet.

The crowd started to disperse, most of them with disappointment hanging on their faces. Freddie understood. It seemed like they were on the outside of a joke they'd never understand. The cabbie who'd come down to witness, said, "Don't take too long," and followed them. Freddie lingered. He waved at Kobe. When the monk came over, he almost placed a hand on Freddie's shoulder, then thought better of it. Where would there not be bruises? He didn't say a word. Freddie couldn't, but he wouldn't have known what to say if he could. The weight was still on his hip, but he lifted it. Someone watching would have thought him crazy, would have thought that he was about to shoot the monk, but Kobe just looked at the gun and nodded. Freddie squeezed it in his hands and cried through his sore lids. "It's okay," the monk said. And then he said something that sounded like another language, something soft and low and soothing, and Freddie tossed the snubnose into the river flow.

QUEENS-BY-THE-RIVER

CYNTHIA GRIER LOTZE

You are awake now, the day
is fall, a wife sleeps

dreamless by your side,
but your dreams have been

a wildscape, they have taken
all of the breath from your body

in returning you to this
your life, the untroubled

autumn of Queens-by-the-River.

By some other river you
are a god—or, better, there

is a God. God to make
the waters rise and sing

at the morning, to crash
the waters down, someone

is able to make a decision.
Dreamless sleep bothers

God. The placid East
River, still as the corpse

sunk to its floor—this
bores God. Because your God

is not a God of the Good; this God
sees to the stink at the foot

of Central Park, driving you down
streets to witness a suicide and then

onto the QR, home to this wife
not yours.

I CUT THE GRASS
PHIL FORD

IT IS amazing how many animals I run over with my John Deere Z900 Zero-Turn Mower when I'm on the median of the highway. Snakes, hedgehogs, sometimes birds. A lot of eastern box turtles. I used to be concerned, but now I know the death of nature is just part of the modern world.

Yeah, I know that sounds pretty harsh for a person who spends his entire work life outside, but you should see the garbage people toss out of their vehicles while going seventy miles an hour. It's not pretty. Cans, bottles, diapers, fast food junk, mostly. One time, I found a fucking pistol.

Something I don't understand seeing—and I see it a lot—are shoes. And I'm not talking about a pair, mind you, but one. Just one. How someone tosses just one shoe on the asphalt is beyond me—unless they have their foot sticking out the window and bring it back in too quickly and it pops off. Or a friend in the car thinks it would be funny for Louise to walk around the mall with one cherry red pump. I just don't get it. And why wouldn't you want to retrieve it?

I've been working this job for eight years now and my skin fucking shows it. I'm a goddamn 30-year-old man in a 50 year old's skin. Leathery like the chair in the Dean of Business Studies office that a student needs to fuck on to graduate. Worn, seasoned and full of regret. I only know that chair is like my skin because I tried the college thing for a semester. Oh, I did fine, but I started to realize I was going to debt myself to death in student loans and still make shit money kissing ass at some entry-level future-tanked capital idea. So I decided to do this business on my own instead. Four person work crew. Lawn care at first, hitting the big industrial office parks, you know, the places that have FOR LEASE signs in all the windows because some hot shit developer thought to cut down a bunch of trees and build a corporate mecca for young startups and medical companies. Places like that need to look good from the outside, even if the only businesses inside are call centers and beauty schools. So I started with them. Steady work, real steady, but not as secure as getting into contracts with the highway people. You stay busy all the time with those folks, and you get your own stretches of road.

Highways are the place you find the most shit. Garbage. On these roads, it's all garbage in the end. You get a good sense of the human psyche from what you see strewn about a cloverleaf interchange.

Exit ramps are the place you encounter the real jerk offs of humanity. I mean, they're practically at the destination where they're meant to be arriving. Why throw their shit out the car window now? A lot of cups, fast food, that kind of thing. You even see the repetition of it. The habit. The same collection of large sweet tea cups with the same lipstick shade on the straw in the same area every month, in a pile, obviously the same person either going to or coming from work who could take the extra fucking time to just throw the cup in a trash can at home or the office, but would rather chuck it out here to keep me employed.

Some days I feel like putting up a big sign on those exits that says, "Only Idiots Litter, YOU IDIOT." But I am fairly certain it would come back to me and my crew. So I just keep it in my dumb, frustrated head.

You know, despite what some people think, there's one thing that we never find on the side of the road. And that's fucking money. People will stop for that shit.

The most disgusting thing we ever found was a hand. A damn severed hand from a human being. What in the hell happened in that scenario? Tomás found it while running the weed whacker and it freaked him the fuck out. At first, he thought he might have whacked over the rest of the body. Tomás is a good employee but pretty innocent about a lot of things, especially the stuff we find out here. Anyway, we had to call the authorities on it because, well, it was a freaking human hand. Obviously, it could have been from a crime scene or leftover from an accident we didn't know about. My crew thought it would be a fun gag to put up a photo at the rest areas asking, "Have you seen the rest of me?" Like those missing child signs. We rolled with that idea for a few weeks. Hilarious, even though we didn't actually do it.

We never found out what happened to that hand. I imagine it's in an evidence box somewhere, waiting for the rest of its owner to turn up. We still talk about that hand, referring to it, him, as "Hitchhiker's Remorse."

Something I never get tired of out here on the medians is the smell. It's a weird bouquet of diesel, tar and grass. I mean, sometimes you get the occasional waft of garbage or shit, but for the most part it's those three primaries. In a way, it's the smell of everything Americans love to be involved with—the ease of travel and the aspiration of nature. Not real nature, mind you, but the essence of it. I kind of think of it as the perfect modern world scent.

The oddest thing? Well, that would have to be the giant dildo we saw plop off of a work truck into a merge lane. Tomás and I were unloading our mowers and gear from the cloverleaf island when we saw this beat up old construction truck tearing down the lane onto the highway, and this big floppy thing popped right off and bounced about fifteen yards down the road. It looked like it was all happening in slow motion, too. You know, like when you see a fat guy falling down the stairs. The wobbling and jouncing—freaking surreal. We stopped and looked at each other for a moment, wondering if we saw what we thought we saw, then started cracking up. I mean, what the hell? A dirty floppy oversized sex toy bouncing down the interstate is not something you see every day. And what in the world was it doing on that truck? Tomás was at a loss, but I think it was some wacked out prank the construction crew was playing on the guy. Like a "Who's got the dildo now?" game they punch around at work all the time. Well, guess what, fellas? We've got the dildo now, and it's in the landfill, getting ridden by raccoons for all we know. Game over.

Our end-of-day usually begins with a twelve-pack in a parking lot, just a daily wind down thing. Sometimes we'll go somewhere for a late lunch, but we mostly go our own ways after tackling our bit of road for the day.

I'm thinking about selling the business after this next summer. I need to level up in the life department. You spend a lot of time in your head while the John Deere engine hums up your ass, and some of those thoughts can get pretty twisted. But every once in a while, a moment of clarity cuts through. I'm not sure how much more my skin can take out here, and I don't even have any goddamn health insurance to fight the cancers I got coming my way. I need an indoor gig with air conditioning and a refrigerator to put my lunch in. I know I'll quit soon, just out of necessity for living, but I'll still always have that modern world smell rolling in the back of my mind. That's just a part of me now.

MOTORING
ANDREW BLOSSOM

UP ON the island there was a place out behind my cabin where there was an old door leaning against a tree. It was about a ten minute walk. It wasn't on the path. I'd go around to the rear of the cabin and put my back to the wall and walk straight into the woods. I wasn't trying to find the door, but I came across it anyway. After that, I'd walk out there to smoke and think whenever the writing was not so hot. I was working on a play. The play involved an unhappy couple. I had a name for it, but I wasn't thrilled with the name. I thought maybe it would change. The whole thing was just the couple in a car, talking, gradually revealing how unhappy they were. It was a play about love.

The door was made of walnut, dark with age. It was propped against a birch tree. Three broad panels with splintered edges and water stains along the styles. The fixtures had vanished, but there was a shadow around the bore hole and blackish swatches I took as evidence of hinges. But where had they gone? Maybe someone had scavenged them? If so, who? The island was a mile into the water, and the door was deep in the woods. A mound of earth had accumulated at its base, years of leaves returned to dirt, green moss creeping across the surface. Moss was the name I'd given to the male half of my unhappy couple, who in a dull way had proven themselves to be a man and a woman once they started speaking. Now I wasn't entirely sure what to do with them. But there I was.

The name had come well before I got to the island. I'd thought it up when I'd first started the play, when I was staring not at a door or a tree or a pile of dirt but the blank wall of my apartment in Ridgewood. The name for the man was Moss, and the name for the woman was Ashley, although her husband or whatever Moss was called her Ash. This was one big problem I had. Their love was decaying, but every time I went back to the thing, I couldn't decide whether the two were married. In a way, it didn't matter. I knew marriage was not a prerequisite for unhappiness. But at a certain point, one has to know how they'll talk to each other.

So I stood there and smoked. I thought about the play and the unhappy couple I had conjured from my mind. I thought about Fern and the things we'd said and left unsaid. I began to construct a scenario. It wasn't about the play. It was this: What if the door opened? I knew it made no sense; the door was wider than the tree against which it rested. But what did it matter? I was just smoking. What if the door opened? I began to wonder. Imagine the playwright or whomever breaking up the mound with the heel of his boot. Maybe Moss could do it, I thought. Or I don't know, Ash. Imagine her taking hold of the panel at the bore hole. Imagine the walnut turning on invisible hinges. What would be revealed? A passageway? Steps that led downward? I liked the idea of steps. But what would be the thing that was down there? In the distance were the sounds of engines. Lobster boats, picking up traps. You could always hear them in that place.

I could hear Ash, too. You don't always have to win. This is what she said to Moss just before I stopped writing. Love does not have to be a competition. And Moss sat there, staring forward into the night, his hands unmoving on the wheel. Someone needed to say something, but the trouble was I knew he wouldn't. I was getting to know Moss. He reminded me of me.

You have to talk to me, she said.

So I said, Listen, Ashley. Are we stuck?

I could see her shifting in her seat. What do you mean?

Are we trapped in this car? Is there a next step here? Or are we just stuck? I can't tell anymore.

Well, it's up to Moss, she said.

Right. Right, it's up to Moss. But I know this guy. He's not going to say anything. Or if he does, it won't be the right thing.

Because I thought Ash was correct. Love did not have to be a competition. This was something I never understood about my time with Fern, who from the start acted like our relationship was a lobster boat race and it was always the Fourth of July. She was always souping up the engine so she could get slightly ahead. Whereas I just wanted to putter around together and pick up traps.

Listen, Ashley. In the distance were the sounds of engines turning at normal speed. I wasn't sure where I was going, but I said, I think I see a way out of the car.

So tell me, she said.

Moss's hands tightened on the wheel.

Over here. I pointed. My cigarette had burned itself out. Can you see it? It's a door out in the woods.

THIS BAD LUCK'S BOUND TO MISS THEE, MARK

J.W. MORISON

for mark steele

Tuesday. From what old news the midday and charged collect
Call dredges, only the news that my friend from back when,
My Memphis friend with his follicle flop
                                                            and drop-smile,
My friend has a scar on his skull the breadth
Of the Big Muddy—despite how slackjaw wide
The lesion, what percentage of nerve and matter
Cancer might still, malign as a shock or bad odds, be cleaving
To—only this news and its skew, its screw on my vision, only this
Registers at all.
                                                      The rest of the day is not just
Crossed wires, a blown chisel, sparks,
                                                      misfitting the rainproof
On the disconnect:
                                  it is more the crushed grey cell
The afternoon's pliered down to as the sun slivers,
It's the gibbous in the sky's corner getting its blood up
                                                                              and say-so.
It's a bad ante. For a bad game. Fixed and weighted.

But Mark's counting cards with a fullfathomed grin,
The phone says, and here the arc fault hooks up right
For fucking once. I coil the neutrals like snakes
In the throes of a breathless, settling rigor, rigor
Mortis. But they bob like yesses,
                                        yesses in the breeze.
Yes our wager. Yes your win.
Yes your blood and the current's bend.
So mark this circuit *dedicated*, friend—
To the folded hands we hold to ground you, prayer,
And to the breaker, tripped,
                                    beneath your comeback hair.

PLEASE DON'T ASK ME TO WRITE A MOVIE MEMOIR

WOOJIN YOON

THE FIRST thing I did was call Zeta.

"My life is over," I said. I tend to be dramatic when I'm stressed. "My GPA is never going to recover from this. I'm an English major who's going to fail an English class. Oh, God. What am I going to do?"

"Woojin," Zeta said, already sounding tired.

"Maybe I'll just die," I continued. "That seems like the easiest option, doesn't it?"

"Woojin," she repeated.

"You don't understand," I wailed. "I have to write a *movie memoir.*"

"What the hell is a movie memoir?"

"*Exactly*," I hissed, and then felt bad. Maybe I was being a bit harsh on Professor Blossom, who had been nothing but kind to me. It wasn't his fault he was a white film bro. "I have to write six to ten pages about my favorite movie, or a movie that played a significant role in my life, or my relationship with movies in general, or—"

Zeta groaned.

"Bitch, how is that going to be difficult? There are only, like, three movies you don't hate, and we both know which one is your favorite. So calm the fuck down and go write six to ten pages about *Tangled.*"

I scowled. I didn't like feeling exposed.

"Where is my pity?" I demanded. "Where is my—"

"I'm hanging up," she said.

A week later, Zeta and I found ourselves alone in my dorm room. It was close to midnight, and we were huddled together on the floor. The room was dark. The only illumination came from the fairy lights blinking around us and from my laptop, which sat precariously on a makeshift table. On its screen, I had opened my high school friend Yehjee's Disney+ account, and *Tangled* was queued up and ready to go. It was the perfect set-up for a movie night, but right now? We weren't there for a movie night.

We were there on a mission.

"Ready?" Zeta asked.

"Ready," I said. I tried not to let my reluctance show on my face. This had been my idea. What right did I have to regret it?

"Let's go over our plan. Why are we here tonight?"

"To psychoanalyze my obsession for *Tangled*," I recited.

She nodded, satisfied. "Let's do this."

God, I really didn't want to do this.

"Okay," I said. "Okay."

I pressed play.

By the time that the end credits were rolling, Grace Potter singing "Something That I Want" in the background, we hadn't actually done any psychoanalyzing.

We'd talked throughout the movie, mostly lamentations about how we didn't have our own Eugene Fitzherbert, but nothing of substance.

Nothing about me.

I knew Zeta, though, and her silence meant she had too much she wanted to say. She was just waiting for the right time.

"Woojin," she said. "*Woojin*."

"Yes?"

She shook her head, lips pursed, but she looked more confused than annoyed.

"You are the most self-aware person that I know. There's no way that you don't already have, like, a dozen ideas for your movie memoir."

Almost instinctively, I became defensive. "Look—"

"I hadn't watched the movie in a while, so I didn't remember, but—come on. If your connection with *Tangled* is obvious to me, then it has to be obvious to you, too."

I picked at a hangnail. For a moment, I wished that I could write down what I wanted to say. I had always been a better writer than I was a talker.

Zeta could probably tell that I was three seconds away from a full-blown existential crisis, because she got comfortable. She lay down on the floor, ignoring my protests—I hadn't cleaned the carpet in weeks—and folded her hands neatly on her stomach.

"Let's start small," she suggested. "Don't get me wrong—I like the movie. It's an objectively good movie. But a part of me is tired of damsels in distress, you know?"

I frowned. Was Rapunzel really a damsel in distress? She had essentially kidnapped the kingdom's most-wanted thief and blackmailed him. But that wasn't what Zeta was asking.

"I don't really mind them," I said.

She raised an eyebrow.

"That's surprising."

"Not very feminist of me, huh?"

"It's not *not* feminist," she corrected. "It's just—you're so independent. You hate accepting help. You're the only college student that I know who feels crippling guilt for missing a class or an assignment. I thought you would be all for damsels who can save themselves."

"I don't know," I said. I looked down at my lap. Picked some lint off of my sweats. "Being a damsel in distress doesn't sound too bad. I'm kind of tired of saving myself."

There was a moment of silence, and then Zeta said, "Holy shit. That was so deep."

I let out an involuntary laugh, and I felt some of the tension leave my body.

"No, seriously," she insisted. "Write that down. You're going to want to remember what you said."

Rolling my eyes, I opened the Notes app on my phone and typed, *I'm kind of tired of saving myself.* I took a moment to read the sentence once. Twice. It was the most non-academic writing I had done in a long time.

Next to me, Zeta let out a hum. "Hey, at least we're finally getting somewhere. You don't look like you're going to bite my head off for probing further."

I winced. "Sorry."

"It's fine. But do you want to talk about it now?"

I put my phone down, extending the moment for as long as possible, and I inhaled.

Exhaled.

Clenched and unclenched my fists.

Fuck it. If I couldn't be honest with Zeta, who knew me almost as well as I knew myself, then who could I be honest with?

I closed my eyes.

"I could," I started slowly, "write about how, to me, *Tangled* is more of a love story than anything else. It's a love story about two broken people, people broken in the same way I am, finding and choosing each other.

"I could write about how I see myself in Rapunzel. I see her trying to make herself smaller; I see her apologizing for things that aren't her fault; I see her desperately waiting and hoping for more, for an *after*—because there has to be an *after*, right?—and I see myself. I see myself at ten and eleven and twelve and thirteen and fourteen years old, made of skin and bones and the collateral damage of my parents' war. I could write about how much I hate it, because Rapunzel—she's not my reflection. It would be easy if she were my reflection. Instead, she's what I could have been, what I *should* have been, if I had gotten away from my father, scathed but still—still *good*. Rapunzel went through what I did, went through worse, and she came out *good*. Why did I come out bitter and cynical and selfish? How is that fair?

"I could write about how I see myself in Eugene. I see him deflect with laughter and nonchalance, and I see myself trying to convince everyone that I'm fine, that I can handle it, because what's worse than losing control? That's why it's difficult, deciding which is more terrifying: being known or being unknowable. Because isn't being known the same thing as being loved? If I met someone who *saw* me, flaws and all, and decided to stay—I don't think I would know what to do with that. If I would even stay in return. Eugene was brave enough to try. He stayed because he wanted to learn how to love and be loved. I'm not—I don't think I have what it takes. I think I would run away. I don't know if I'll ever stop running away.

"I could write that. I could write all of that."

"But?" I heard Zeta ask. Her voice was whisper-soft.

I opened my eyes.

"But I don't want to," I finished.

"Why?"

I shrugged helplessly.

"It's hard to explain."

"Come on, Miss Type A," Zeta coaxed. "Do what you do best. Make a list or something. That makes it easier, right?"

I chewed on my bottom lip.

Eventually, I said, "Number one: I don't want to start the movie memoir because I'm scared. I haven't written anything personal since before my gap year, and that was in 2020. I'm scared that, if I write, I'll realize that I'm no longer good at it. And that would destroy me, because writing is the one thing I'm good at. It's *mine*, in a way that nothing else is." We both ignored how my voice shook. "It's all that I have.

"Number two: even if I am still good at it, what if I only write well when I write about my trauma? I don't know how I feel about that. I want to write well, period. I don't want my trauma to define me, but what if it already does? What if I write about it so often because I subconsciously know that it's the most interesting thing about me?"

"Bullshit," Zeta said. "Are you done?"

I huffed. Zeta knew how to ruin a moment.

"Well—"

"There are so many things wrong with what you said," she continued, like she hadn't interrupted me. "Number one: a bunch of writers only write about one thing. JK Rowling—"

"We hate JK Rowling in this house," I said out of habit.

"—won't stop writing about wizards and look at her! She's a billionaire, even though she's transphobic as hell. Besides, who cares? Who cares if you only write about your trauma? Writing is an art, and art is"—she waved her hand, trying to think of the word—"it's a form of escapism. A way of coping. And it should be for you and you only. Number two: *why?*"

I blinked at her.

"Why what?"

"Why do you have to be good?" She threw her hands up, hissing in pain when they smacked against my drawer. "What is it with you and being *good*? Why can't you just *be*?"

"I already explained this," I weakly argued. "Writing is all that I have."

"So what," she demanded, "you're never going to write anything ever again?"

"Maybe," I muttered. I sounded like a petulant child.

Zeta slapped my arm.

"You dumbass," she said affectionately. "Okay, here's number three: you love writing. Even now, with all of this pressure you put on yourself, you love it. It's like you can't help but love it. I've seen you when you write, and you're *happy*. Even when you're seconds away from tearing your hair out because you can't find the right words, you're happy. So—for the moment, forget about being scared. Forget about needing to be perfect. Just ask yourself this."

She looked at me. Her gaze was unflinching.

I wanted to look away.

"Are you willing to lose something that you love?"

Two days later, I sat in front of my laptop. My fingers tapped the keyboard. On the screen, a Google doc was open.

It was blank. It had been blank for twenty minutes.

I closed my eyes. Rested my forehead on the desk.

God, what was I thinking?

I couldn't do this.

I felt so fucking small and stupid. Objectively, I knew this was just an assignment. I *knew*. But my anxiety and depression warped it into something bigger, something that made me feel like I was drowning on land. It took all of my control to keep a panic attack at bay.

What if I wrote something terrible, and everyone in my class hated it? What if they confirmed my worst fear, made it into a reality, and I was left with nothing?

In my head, their shadows laughed, showing my memoir to their friends. *How did she get into an advanced creative writing class?* they whispered. *What was Professor Blossom thinking?*

Who does she think that she is?

I opened my eyes and grimaced when I realized that I had picked open a scab on my arm.

So, what, you're never going to write anything ever again?

Are you willing to lose something that you love?

But what other option did I have?

"Write," I murmured to myself. "You can just write."

I inhaled.

Exhaled.

Clenched and unclenched my fists.

Okay, I thought. *Let's be rational. You can do rational.*

If I wrote something terrible, then I had my answer: I was no longer good at writing. But would that ever stop me from loving it? And couldn't I get better again? Wasn't there a sliver of a chance that, one day, I would look at my writing and feel satisfied? And if I wrote something good, then I would regain something. A part of me would finally settle.

How could I ever find out if I refused to even try?

"I'm tired," I said aloud. "I'm tired of being tired. I'm tired of being scared."

I thought of Rapunzel. I thought of Eugene. I thought of Zeta.

I thought of myself.

And I began to write.

BURY ME
AT MAKEOUT CREEK

COBRA HEART, Andy Miller, 2004

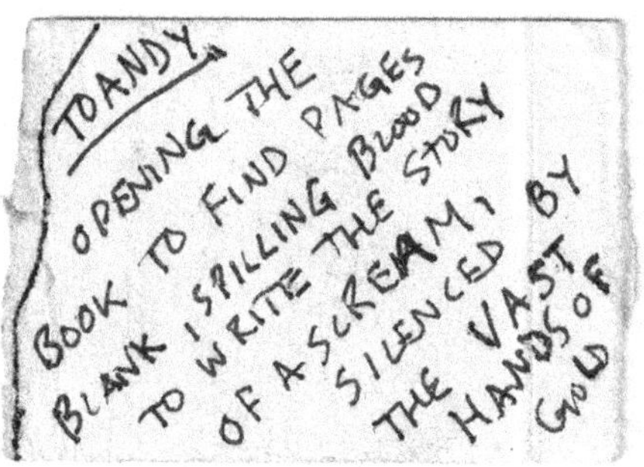

EARLY INSPIRATION, Matt Bierce, c. 1999

Quality Cassette/CD Duplication
CASSETTE & CD EXPRESS
~~Mention This Ad Get 10% Off~~
Special Volume Quotes
~~Tape duplication using KABA real time.~~
Located On Music Row
Division of AL JOLSON ENT.
116 17th Ave. S.,
Nashville TN 37203
Phone: (615) 244-5667
DAT
Digital Audio Tape

Holy Evening,
Purple Tiger,
Nacho Rain.

Hey Andrew,

the concept behind this poem is that the title should be the "ad". in other words type this incredibly long title:

"Quality Cassette/CD Duplication Cassette & CD Express. (period) Special Volume Quotes. Located on Music Row. Division of Al Jolson Ent."

Holy Evening, ← comma

Purple Tiger. ← period
Nacho Rain" ← backwards quotation mark

LETTER, David Berman, 2007

picaresque — San Francisco B.C.
traditional — Suffering Jukebox
Fifties — Candy Jail
philosophical hopeful — What Is Not but Could be If
melodramatic — Pillow Is the Threshold
self-satire — Party Barge
political — Strange Victory, Strange Defeat
gothic tale — Aloyisius, Bluegrass Drummer
romantic — We Could Belong To Eachother
rousing — Lookout Mountain, Lookout Sea

Sept
Sun M S.F.
11 12 13 14 15
16 17 18 19 20 21 22
23 24

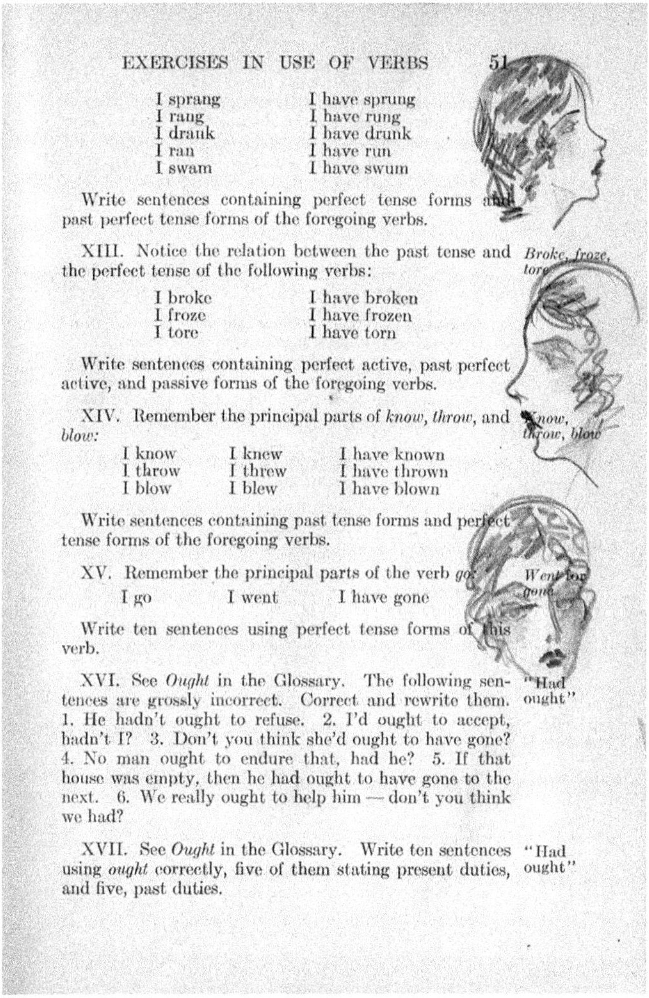

EXERCISES IN USE OF VERBS 51

I sprang	I have sprung
I rang	I have rung
I drank	I have drunk
I ran	I have run
I swam	I have swum

Write sentences containing perfect tense forms and past perfect tense forms of the foregoing verbs.

XIII. Notice the relation between the past tense and the perfect tense of the following verbs: *Broke, froze, tore*

I broke	I have broken
I froze	I have frozen
I tore	I have torn

Write sentences containing perfect active, past perfect active, and passive forms of the foregoing verbs.

XIV. Remember the principal parts of *know*, *throw*, and *blow*: *Know, throw, blow*

I know	I knew	I have known
I throw	I threw	I have thrown
I blow	I blew	I have blown

Write sentences containing past tense forms and perfect tense forms of the foregoing verbs.

XV. Remember the principal parts of the verb *go*: *Went for gone*

I go	I went	I have gone

Write ten sentences using perfect tense forms of this verb.

XVI. See *Ought* in the Glossary. The following sentences are grossly incorrect. Correct and rewrite them. 1. He hadn't ought to refuse. 2. I'd ought to accept, hadn't I? 3. Don't you think she'd ought to have gone? 4. No man ought to endure that, had he? 5. If that house was empty, then he had ought to have gone to the next. 6. We really ought to help him — don't you think we had? "Had ought"

XVII. See *Ought* in the Glossary. Write ten sentences using *ought* correctly, five of them stating present duties, and five, past duties. "Had ought"

MARGINALIA, ARTIST UNKNOWN, discovered by Amy Mitchell in Edwin C. Wooley, Ph.D., and Franklin W. Scott, Ph.D., *New Handbook of Composition: Rules and Exercises* (D.C. Heath and Company, 1926), purchased at Diversity Thrift, Richmond, Virginia, 2007

Misuse before a substantive clause

229. Put no comma before a substantive clause introduced by *that* or *how* when the governing verb (such as *said, thought, supposed*) immediately or very closely precedes the clause.

Wrong: The boatswain said, that the wheel was damaged.
Right: The boatswain said that the wheel was damaged.
Wrong: I always supposed, that the foreman was to blame.
Right: I always supposed that the foreman was to blame.
Wrong: They told us, how they had escaped.
Right: They told us how they had escaped.

Exercise 90

General Exercises in the Use of the Comma

Punctuate the following sentences correctly. After each sentence put the number of the rule which applies. 1. Ever since I have been a regular attendant at the theater. 2. However capable as he was he failed of his purpose. 3. He should as I said before read Pope's *Atticus*. 4. He is to say the least not trustworthy. 5. He is too weak however to keep any promise at all. 6. They all seemed I thought ashamed of the exhibition. 7. His eyes flashed as he drew his sword and his breath came short and quick. 8. He bought the land with his own money and his bank account was not extremely large either. 9. Mr. Blount was evidently anxious for his eyes kept wandering toward the door. 10. It is a very good story for the author is unusually clever and witty. 11. He is benefited by the new rules but yet he is discontented. 12. Dickens' *David Copperfield* which is my favorite novel is somewhat autobiographical. 13. I do not want books that instruct I want books that amuse. 14. It is strange that a play so tragic as *Lear* should give you pleasure. 15. The door flew open and Ralph Rackstraw covered with mud entered the church. 16. When a shotgun is brought in from the field it is usually dirty. 17. Since I had always before that time been so much alone it was not easy for me to make friends. 18. A few days after they sailed the boat sprang a leak. 19. There also was the village doctor, a man of fifty years. 20. Thomas De Quincey, author of *Joan of Arc*, was an opium-eater. 21. A fine fellow, a member of the yacht club, was drowned. 22. My dear fellow what made you so careless? 23. The letter was addressed to Syracuse New York and dated May 19 1836. 24. The horse is the most useful of all animals to man. 25. I went away with a good picture of a Chinese laundry in my mind. 26. In the center is a stove around which a number of farmers laborers and boys were gathered. 27. No latest fashions or shimmering silks were displayed in that window. 28. I am glad to see you old man. 29. One day a poor old ragged tramp walked into the yard of a prosperous farm in Dane County and knocked timidly on the door. 30. She felt that she had been slighted. 31. When I used to carry my dinner pail to the little school at Nichol's Corner I felt very self-important. 32. He brought some flowers to Miss Miriam and her sister was jealous. 33. Tomorrow my dear I shall receive a check. 34. I am not to tell the truth very fond of the game. 35. Indeed I shall take no such answer. 36. Alas it could never be true.

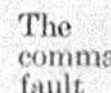

The comma fault

230. Do not use a comma between coördinate independent clauses that are not joined by one of the pure conjunctions, *and*, *but*, *for*, *or*, *neither*, *nor*, except when the clauses are short, have no commas within themselves, and are closely parallel in form and substance. Use a semicolon if it is rhetorically desirable to indicate close relationship between the clauses; otherwise use a period. This error is an inexcusable fault in writing, because, like the "period fault" (see Rule 24) it shows inability to recognize what constitutes a sentence. (See Rules 231 *a* and 231 *b*.)

Wrong: He had not the habit of concentration, this was the cause of his failure.

ingly, besides, also, thus, then, still, otherwise,* and *in fact.

Wrong: I saw no reason for moving, therefore I stayed still.
Right: I saw no reason for moving; therefore I stayed still.

Wrong: He went below and lit the fuse, then he returned to the deck.
Right: He went below and lit the fuse; then he returned to the deck.

Conjunctive adverbs distinguished from simple conjunctions

NOTE. — Good usage makes a clear distinction, as regards punctuation, between conjunctive adverbs and simple coördinating conjunctions (e.g., *and, but, or, for*). A comma is ordinarily used (see Rule 221 *f*) between clauses of a compound sentence that are connected by a simple conjunction; but a comma should emphatically not be used between clauses connected by a conjunctive adverb. Compare the two following sentences:

Right: The president bowed, and Hughes began to speak.
Right: The president bowed; then Hughes began to speak.

Before *and, but,* etc. in certain cases

(*c*) **Ordinarily, between the clauses of a compound sentence that are joined by a simple conjunction, when these clauses are somewhat long, or are subdivided by commas.** See, for example, the second sentence of the foregoing note, and also the text of the notes under Rules 14 and 88.

Between involved sentence-members

(*d*) **To separate two or more coördinate members of a simple or complex sentence when those members, or some of them, have commas within themselves.**

Right: He said that he had lent his neighbor an ax; that on the next day, needing the ax, he had gone to get it; and that his neighbor had denied borrowing it. [The three objects of "said" are separated not by commas, as ordinarily three objects of a

THE SEMICOLON 185

verb should be, but by semicolons, because one of the objects has commas within itself.]

For other examples see the text of Rules 134, 135, and 137.

(*e*) **To separate any two members of a simple or complex sentence when, for any reason, a comma would not make the relation between them immediately clear.**

Instead of a comma, to prevent obscurity

Misleading: If I were a millionaire, I would have horses, and motors, and yachts, and the whole world should minister to my pleasure.

Clear: If I were a millionaire, I would have horses, and motors, and yachts; and the whole world should minister to my pleasure.

See also the sixth sentence in the text of Rule 140 and the first in the text of Rule 142.

Exercise 92

Sentences or clauses intro-duced by *so, therefore,* etc.

Write the following sentences, properly punctuated: 1. These screws control the reticule hence they are called reticule screws. 2. I objected to the plan however since he was bent on it I yielded. 3. A hot fire is necessary therefore a strong draft must be provided. 4. The wood had been injured by warping moreover the metal parts were badly rusted. 5. Sickness delayed their moving therefore we did not get the house so soon as we had planned. 6. What you say is true nevertheless the thing is impossible. 7. The meerschaum becomes finally saturated with nicotine then there is less danger of its breaking. 8. All the cracks were filled with tow thus the craft was made seaworthy 9. She never laughed nor even smiled moreover her conversation was always of a melancholy tone. 10. She has conversed with Mirabeau hence she must be very old. 11. She wished my father to be informed accordingly I wrote to him that evening. 12. He continually reproached her and she was always offended at his reproaches thus their friendship rapidly grew cold. 13. I saw no reason for declining his invitation besides I enjoyed his society and wished to be with him longer.

III. ANALYTICAL OUTLINES

Outlines

293. An outline is an orderly plan of the material to be used in a composition. The material is condensed into topics, sentences, or paragraphs, so numbered and indented as to show their logical relationship. There are, therefore, three kinds of outlines: topic, sentence, and paragraph outlines. (Throughout an outline, the writer must adhere to one type consistently.) The topic and the sentence outlines are more commonly used. Of these two the sentence outline is to be preferred, for it states more explicitly the writer's thought. (Compare the two outlines in Section 294.)

Nouns, not verbs, in topic outline

In a topic outline, make all the titles, as far as possible, in the form of nouns, with or without modifiers. *E.g.*, write "Rapidity of Movement" rather than "Moves Rapidly."

Sentence outline

If, on the other hand, a sentence outline is desired instead of a topic outline, write each division in the form of a sentence which expresses the central idea of the division. Subheads may be expressed as subordinate members of this sentence, or as separate sentences.

Numbering and Arrangement of Titles

294. Number and indent the titles of an outline according to the following method:

THE GOVERNMENT OF SWITZERLAND

Topic Outline

Specimen topic outline

I. Value to Americans of a knowledge of Swiss institutions.

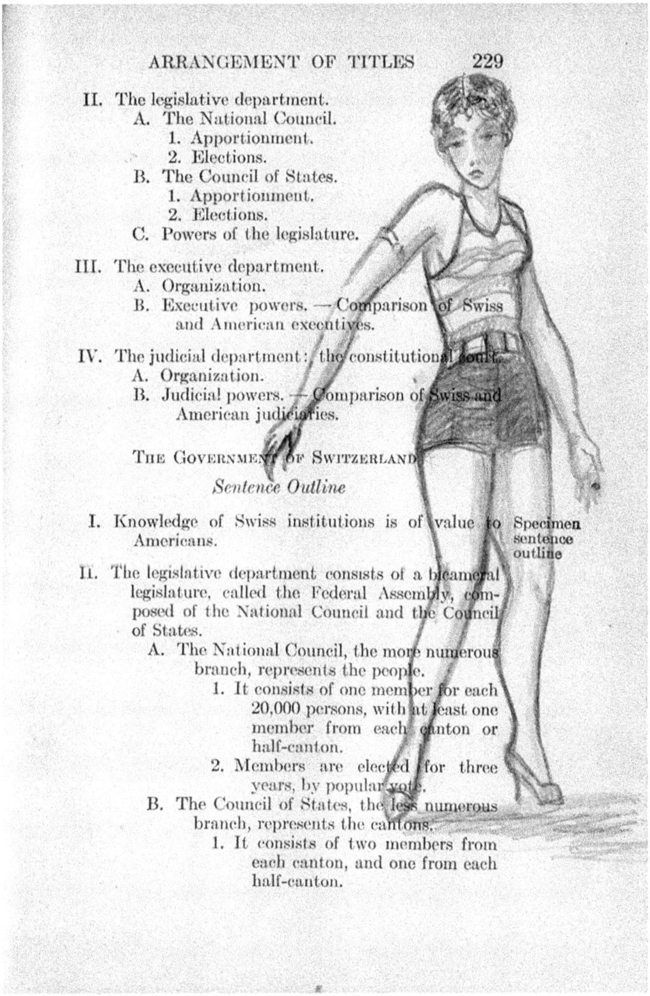

II. The legislative department.
    A. The National Council.
        1. Apportionment.
        2. Elections.
    B. The Council of States.
        1. Apportionment.
        2. Elections.
    C. Powers of the legislature.

III. The executive department.
    A. Organization.
    B. Executive powers. — Comparison of Swiss and American executives.

IV. The judicial department: the constitutional court.
    A. Organization.
    B. Judicial powers. — Comparison of Swiss and American judiciaries.

THE GOVERNMENT OF SWITZERLAND

Sentence Outline

I. Knowledge of Swiss institutions is of value to Americans. Specimen sentence outline

II. The legislative department consists of a bicameral legislature, called the Federal Assembly, composed of the National Council and the Council of States.
    A. The National Council, the more numerous branch, represents the people.
        1. It consists of one member for each 20,000 persons, with at least one member from each canton or half-canton.
        2. Members are elected for three years, by popular vote.
    B. The Council of States, the less numerous branch, represents the cantons.
        1. It consists of two members from each canton, and one from each half-canton.

Street numbers

The Reverend Charles Wentworth,
463 Ninth Street,
Bridgeport,
Connecticut.

Bad:

Street not to be omitted

Editor Centerville Ledger,
65 North Liberty,
Centerville,
O.

Right:

Ellipsis not to be used

For the Editor of the Centerville *Ledger*
65 North Liberty Street
Centerville
Ohio

Margin and punctuation

349. The margin, straight or diagonal, and the punctuation, open or close, should correspond with those of the letter.

Right:

Professor Henry D. Lennington
1436 Putnam Avenue
Woonsocket
Rhode Island

Right:

Colonel Charles Kent,
The Southwick Hotel,
Kansas City,
Missouri.

The postage stamp

350. The postage stamp should be attached in the upper right-hand corner. It should be right side up, and its edges should be parallel to the edges of the envelope. A postage stamp upside down or affixed in a haphazard fashion raises against the sender of the letter a suspicion of slovenliness.

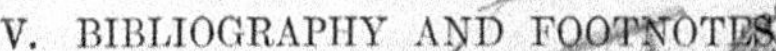

V. BIBLIOGRAPHY AND FOOTNOTES

Bibliographies

Frequently students will find it necessary to cite references to sources from which they have taken material. Such a list of books relating to a given subject or author is called a bibliography. Although there may be no arbitary ruling regarding the style followed by authors and publishers in the citation of authority, yet there is a form generally used. First the surname of the author or editor is given, then his initials or given name, next the exact title of the book, the place of publication, the name of the publisher, and the date of publication, all of which information is usually found on the title page of the book. The following examples are punctuated according to the usual form: Form used for bibliography of books

Gosse, Edmund W. *Inter Arma*. London, W. Heinemann, 1916.

Gosse, Edmund W. and Wise, Thomas J. (Editors). *The Posthumous Poems of Algernon Charles Swinburne*. London, W. Heinemann, 1917.

Note. — The name of the publisher is frequently omitted. In case no date is given on the title page of the book, the abbreviations n.d. are sometimes used.

The bibliographical form for magazine reference should contain the following information: the name of the author; his initials or given name; the name of the article; the publication in which it appears; the volume and page or pages inclusive, the month, and the year of the issue. (See Rule 246.) Form used for bibliography of magazine articles

257

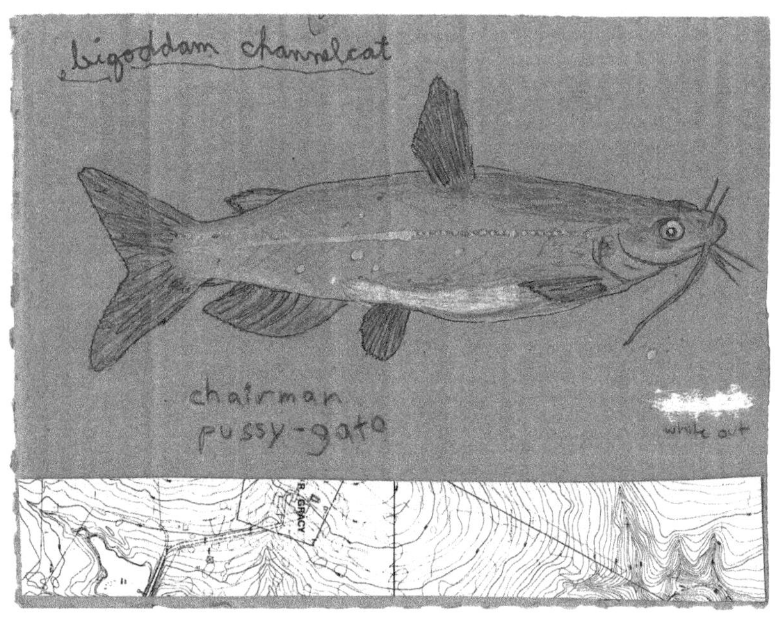

CHAIRMAN PUSSY-GATO, Greg Koehler, 2007

COBRA VARIATIONS, Andy Miller, 2009

NEVER
FORGET

NEVER
FORGET

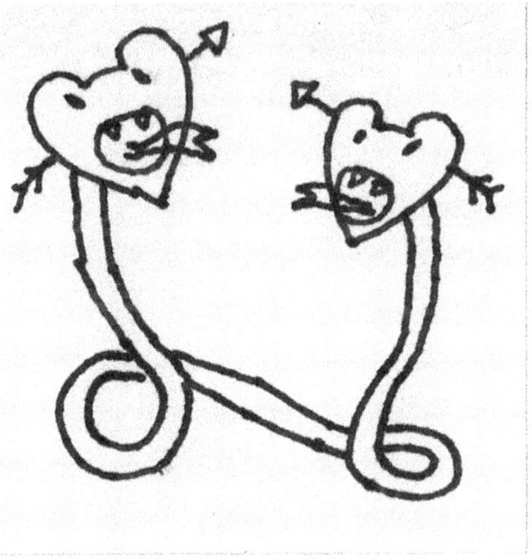

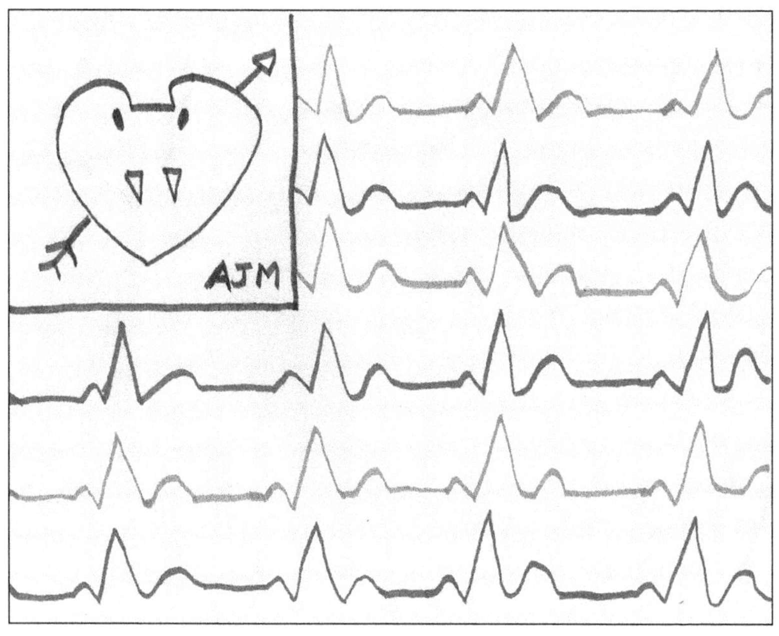

NEW FLAG, PROPOSED, Andy Miller, 2009

ZPRÁVY Z PRAHY, George Allen, 2008-2023

NÁPOJE
11

COMMUNISTA
WE ARE ANTIFASCIST
FUCK NACIST
NORSKE FJORDY

POTRAVINY

18
SPEKTRÁLNÍ
LABORATOŘ

PERS
STĚHOVÁNÍ
VYKLÍZENÍ
724 964 444
MIOW
NOD

EVIL TITS

BONG HIT

MORE LOVE LETTERS, P

JAMMER SLAMMER SKETCH, Nick Kuszyk, 2009

DINGY, Doha, Qatar, 2009

ITEM OF INTEREST ONE. Frequent lines of rock running out from roadside. Carefully spaced, with the lines always about ten yards in length.

ITEM OF INTEREST TWO. Piles of empty Budweiser and perfume bottles left in desert.

ITEM OF INTEREST THREE. Unfinished building shaped like spaceship, set apart from highway amid great expanse.

ITEM OF INTEREST FOUR. Pile of rubble upon which cinder-block has been carefully balanced.

ITEM OF INTEREST FIVE. Circle of rocks, painted blue.

ITEM OF INTEREST SIX. Single piece of pita on hot gravel.

Photos by Lauren Maas, Doha, Qatar, 2010

POSTER, THEY LIVE! Washington, DC, 2011

JOURNAL, AUTHOR UNKNOWN, 1975, discovered by Ward Tefft in a box of books donated to the nonprofit Books on Wheels, Richmond, Virginia, 2012

June 6, 1975

Tonight is graduation.

~~June 7, 1975~~ [crossed out]

A Friday June 6

Last night was fantastic. We had our graduation. The biggest hand was for John Zompa, of course. Afterwards I went to Mike Lee's house for a couple of glasses of champane. Nancy Lyme wrote in my year book and so did Fr Quinn and Mrs Lyons. I gave Nancy my picture. I wrote some true and nice things on the back. Afterwards I went with Nancy over to my house and Peter came to get us. We did this so, I could leave the car. We then took Bob up to Mat Zito's party. Then I went with Peter and Nancy over to Mike's. Then everyone went back to Matt's. I went swimming and had a good conversation with Charlie Rupurz. We drank the Private Stock of beer (Heffarcefer) sounds like "have a reefer." R.L. Dufreen took Peter and I home a five o'clock and I slept over at Peter's house.

B Saturday June 7

I went over to Peters to sleep and woke up a twelve thirty. Mrs Lyons made us breakfast and it was good. I went have at three in the afternoon only to leave at five to go to Ken Vinacco's party. At seven - thirty we went to Steve Colono's party. I didn't feel to exicited at the party. I was a little annoyed at Steve who didn't even say hi or talk with me at all. He spent most of the time talking to Nancy. I guess he figured I was the competition. I was quite upset about this. He kind of pulled Nan away every time she talked to me. I just sat quietly usally in a corner and watched. I drank one beer and one screw driver. I did have one real good line that night. It broke up the whole room. Steve's sister Linda, was trying to make sure everything was all right. She asked me ~~for~~ if everything is ok. Then she said "Do you want any milk, coffee, tea, beer, screw driver or water?"

"No"

"Are you tired?"

"Yes"

"We have three beds upstairs."

"Why? Do you want to go?" punch line.

We left around 12:30.

I went with Kenny Discoli. We came to my house to get the camera. Then we proceeded to Dave Teturaut house where he was getting ready to sleep over Peters. While on their way from the party to Dave's, Peter must have talked to Nancy. I am not really sure of this but, it is my guess. While alone in Dave game room alone with Nan she asked me if I thought she talked to Steve too much tonight. I was standing next to her and I said something like "not really, it's alright." I tapped her on the cheek and sat down on the other side of the room.

We went over Peter's and slept. It was nice I slept in Peters bed and Dave selpt in the cot next to me. Dave and I talked about a half hour. He is beyond a shadow of a doubt what Peter calls "a natural encounter person"

B Sunday June 8

We woke up and ate breakfast arround 9:30. We went to church at St Adlobuts. While walking up there Mary Lyons, Peter's 7 year old sister, walked between Dave and I holding our hands. Peter worked until 12. We visited him at the store. Later in the afternoon I took pictures of Peter playing soccer. He was the hero of the game by blocking six straight pentality kicks. They lifted him up after the game and carried him off the field. I went home and hit the ~~sca~~ sak early.

B Monday June 9

I didn't do very much. I got my chest x-ray and went

shoping. At night, I went to an excounter reunion. I talked about Sara, Bob and the letter, and Peter. Well Henny Vinacco is upset because he feels that he is being "toldated" by me and Peter. He made me feel guilty for being friends with Peter. At writing this a few day later I feel like saying "Fuck you, Henny, and help." These Pyton Places' sot jobs are not my cup of tea. He put me in an awkward postion. I guess he ~~wo~~ really wants me to screw ~~and~~ but, says he dozen't want to hurt Peter's happiness. He is very screwed up. I say friendship and love are not selfish things and they can be shared by more than two people.

B Tuesday June 10

Quiete day around here. I made some pictures and took a couple of walks. Peter came over around eight o'clock and left around eleven. We talk about Kenny and his new love, Mary Conners.

c Wensday June 11

I Went shoping with Peter this morning and bought some film for the island and I got a hat and shirt. In the afternoon I went for a walk down River road and up the Bulovard. Then I ran the Bulovard back. And finally walked home. Tonight I will pack for Block Ikland. "Horrray"

A Thursday June 12

Today was a great day. Peter, Kenny D., Kenny V. and I drove up to the lake around noon. We stayed inside because it was raining. I listened to music ~~or~~ most of the time. At four o'clock Kenny V. and I went to pick up Pizza and Soda for supper. While we were gone Fr Quinn came up. ~~or~~ A little later Dave Tetrault came up and A decon Mike and Dave from Baltimore was also there. Two major events of the party was the "fight" between Fr Quinn and Decon against Peter and I. I also got a chance to talk with Kenny Driscoll's. It was an very enjoyable day.

B Friday June 13

Big day. I took Danny to school And then prepared for my trip to the island. I took the 11 o'clock boat. It was a rain wet and terrible weather day. I talked with Marta and Jim on the way over. I work at the Sping House at night and slept in the afternoon. It was great meeting all the people again. Christy was still sore from a car accident.

K Saturday June 14

I work at the Spring House for the morning, afternoon, and night. I slept in between shifts. It was foggy and drizzly all day anyway. After work Mark Jones and I went to the National. The State Troopers bounced me, They ask me where I was staying. I'm not sure but, maybe it is for the best.

B Sunday June 15

It was a quiet day. I worked breakfast and lunch at the Spring House. I need a reliable friend at this point. I cannot go into the bars so, I might as well work night shift. I decided to make money this year. I can do it. I finish work at three and took a more than extremly needed shower. I rode my bike around for awhile and after supper took a long walk. It was very foggy today. The foggiest I have ever seen. It wasn't until late afternoon that it burned off.

A Monday June 16,

At writing I am rip roaring drunk. Today was a very cloudy day with rain treating. I talked with Sam Mott this morning an ~~th~~ he said I have the rest of the week off. Which is nice. I was sleeping until 2 in the afternoon. I still have not seen Diane C. I saw Patty Valitine and Faby Malock today For the first time I am looking forward to Dead Eyes. I talked with Carl in the afternoon I walked the South East side this afternoon I also went to drink at the Spa. Cathy yelled from the blue co station wagon got to the Spa. And I drank. I also talked with Tory Brotherhood and I think it is time for bed. Spa had a good keg of Milber. I also met Sue from Detroit I'll write about her tomorrow tomorrow Sara.

At Tuesday June 17

Today was a fantastic day. First I layed in bed for a long time and just relaxed perfectly. Then I met Sara at the boat. However, she was so excited she didn't say very much. Then after lunch I went to the beach. As I was lay there, John Demaris came by and we jogged the beach. When we got back we went swimming. The water was ice cold. However, all the pain went away as soon as I got out. It was very soothing as I left the water.

I came back at three-thirty and found Peter's soccer pictures. they came out good. After supper, Kathy ~~and~~, Mike and I walked to the Oar and had three beers. Then we proceeded to Champlain. Peter and George Mott gave ~~up~~ us a boat ride ~~from~~ to the Oar. Sara came by and then we started back to Kathy's house. A very importain thing happen, ~~A~~ On our way up the Oar road ~~we~~ Kathy said "You know, K.C. I like you". That was after I said I didn't smoke pot. Ken Rose gave us a ride to State beach and we walked to the Kittens. A blond girl, Karen, can play some good gutair. She also has a very nice personality I left around nine-thirty and decided to call it a Terrific day.

A Wenaday June 18

Well, This day had a little bit of everything. It was a brigtht sunny day, I arose early and at breakfast, I had to meet the Boat at 10:40 but, it was too ~~early~~ nice a day to stay in bed. So, I went to Ballards to lay agaist the breakwall. Well, just as I began to settle in I spied three young maideen come trotting over the breakwall, they sat near by. About a half-hour later, Lisa a good looking and obriously the leader ask me what time is it. 10:00 o'clock. Well, then they asked where can ~~I~~ they get a soda. I showed them where and they bought me one even though I had said I didn't want one. We talked for a while and I found out they were waiting from

Clinton. I met the boat and saw Bod
and Deb. We talked about Saturday and
he went to clean the house. I then
went back to Anana, Lisa, and Karen.
Anana is a cute blond very sexy.
Karen is quiet, big books, not bad looking,
and is worse of the three. She complains
too much. Lisa has class. She is good
looking and has one of those super personalit
I then went to the Gansett and ate
luch lunch with Kathy outside. I
then had a great beach day. I
saw alot of people there. I talked with
Lisa Gimp, Bob + Deb, Dan the tall as
opposed to Danny the big, Mike, Julie and
Andra. After supper I went to the Oar
for a beer and then took the Clinton
girl to the bluff. Then we went to
the Oar and drank and drank. They
left to eat at 8:00 but, John D, Peter,

Sara, Gawnsett and Spa Crew and Peter
Crawford. I was bomb this night.
John Hobby played Asshole tonight.
I got a little sunburn
A Thursday June 19

First day of work at Dead Eye
I move down here to day to the Shrimp
got to my hands. It was an easy day.
I got out and went to the beach
with Dave. I showered and shaved.
~~Af~~ Dinner was good. I meet Debbie
one of the waitresses here, Mighty fine
indeed. Great personality. I talk with
so many people at supper. It was
terrific. I then ~~saw~~ met John
Littlefield and he took me to
State beach. I ran to Sotch and
back to the Surf. Then I race
Duncan an Irish ~~Stater~~ Setter. Sprints

between Surf and State. I sat and watch the storm come is. The ocean was still an green. The cloud were gentle and angry. It created quite a feel inside me. The dark stillness before the storm. I also watched a ant get blow all over by the wind. I then met Matty Mee and had a Coke at the National. I came back to write read and talk to Annie. Mot Wells came to day

~~Tuesday~~ Wensday July 2

I have not writen in a while but life around here has it good point and low points. Some of the high points of my past ten days: I met Jill the chambermaid and went for a nice walk with here. I saw the movie Papion.

The most importain thing happen one night last week. I was in the boy room at dead eyes with Dave Aldrigh and Patty Valitine came in. I suggested that we go listen to records. She had been sleeping and just woke up. We were playing a record and talking when Joey her "boyfriend" came in. He told her and demanded she leave. I asked if I could stay and listen to records. she said yes I was listen to Seal and Croft "Diamond Girl". About forty five minutes later I was siting in a chair and Patty came in crying. She sat on the bed. I went over and put my arm around her. She was shaking. ~~After~~ a I ask her if she wanted to talk about it and she said no. Five minutes or so later she said somethings. Most notablly "People are weird". About a half an hour afterward Faye came up and said hi. Faye asked "what is wrong?" Patty started to talk and then she turned around and said "Oh, I trust you". Then she explained what happened. Apparetly ~~She~~ Joey and her were breaking up. He had hit her, ~~and~~ She said that she dozen't hate him and he said I'm going to make you hate me. In any case we talked for about two hours more after Faye lift. ~~She~~ The end when I was leaving she and I were on the bed and she said "Thank you for being here" Then she gave me a hug.

The next day Faye said that

Patty said to her "If KC hadn't been there I would have gone crazy."

A couple of nights later Patty and I talked for two hours. She was not feeling to well she had a cold.

I went to the beach today with Tim from the Gansett

CARTOON, Lauren Maas, 2013

Life and not life
Life after life after
life gone gone gone
The paper man did it
then some one did
the paper man

LIFE AND NOT LIFE, discovered by Emma Cusumano among the shelves at Chop Suey Books, Richmond, Virginia, c. 2014

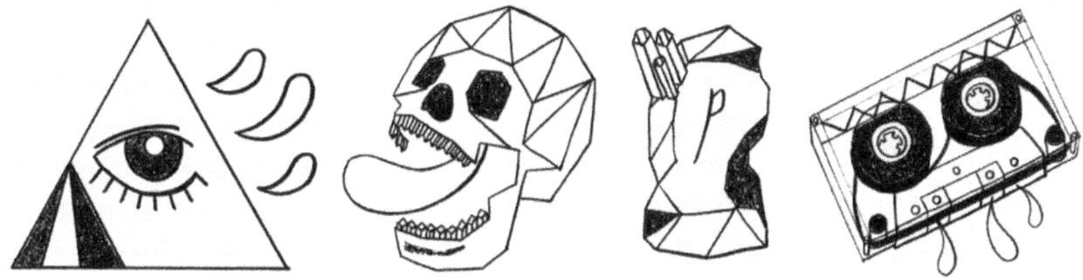

THE EVIL ONES, Mandy Dunn Sampson, 2017

DIARY COMIC, 11/01/22, Mandy Dunn Sampson, 2022

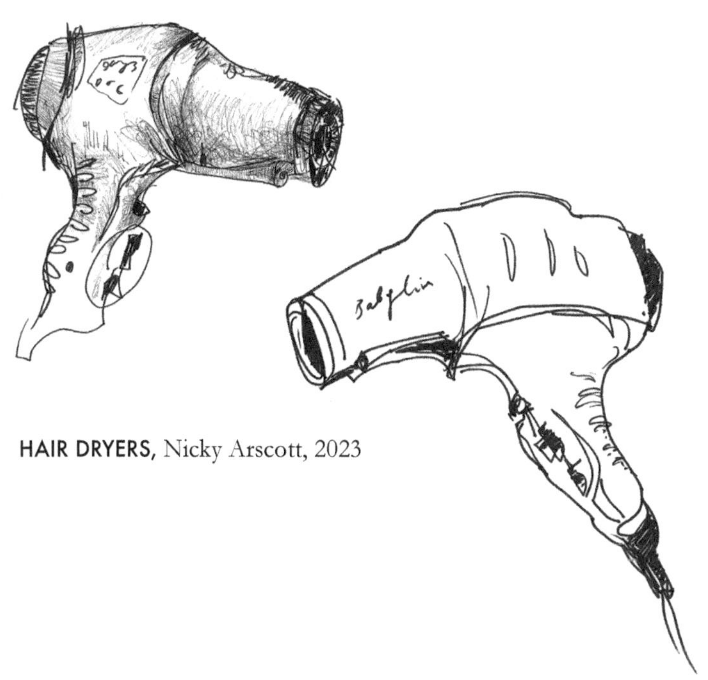

HAIR DRYERS, Nicky Arscott, 2023

COME CELEBRATE THE RELEASE OF:

MAKEOUT CREEK

ISSUE EIGHT * ONLY A WITCH CAT CAN CLOSE A DOOR

WITH YOUR HOST

· ANDREW BLOSSOM ·

SPOKANE, WA

READING

QUINN ARNONE
BALTIMORE, MD

LOGAN FRY
COLUMBUS, OH

GREG KOEHLER
SAN ANTONIO, TX

CYNTHIA GRIER LOTZE
MINNEAPOLIS, MN

NATHANIEL RAPPOLE
RICHMOND, VA

S.E. SMITH
LOS ANGELES, CA

CHRISTINE STROUD
PITTSBURGH, PA

FRIDAY, OCTOBER 13TH
6–8PM FREE!

BOTTOM FEEDER BOOKS 415 GETTYSBURG STREET

POSTER, BOTTOM FEEDER BOOKS, Ryan McLennan, 2023

DIGITAL FLYER, art by Nick Kuszyk, KGB Bar, New York, 2023

POSTER, PHO LUCA'S, Richmond, Virginia, 2023

PHOTOGRAPH. Weidhaas, Adolph Edward. *Brünnhilde.* 1936. Library of Congress, Washington, DC.

DIGITAL FLYER, art by Jen Dunlap, Kippered, Los Angeles, 2024

VEGAN-AF GINGER RUSSIAN

- INSTANT COFFEE
- OAT MILK
- JAMESON
- ICE

(PROPORTIONS WTFE)

RECIPE, VEGAN AF GINGER RUSSIAN, Greg Koehler, Los Angeles, 2024

TO MAKE IT A VEGAN AF RED-HEADED RUSSIAN, use brewed coffee or espresso in place of the instant coffee. Proportions WTFE.

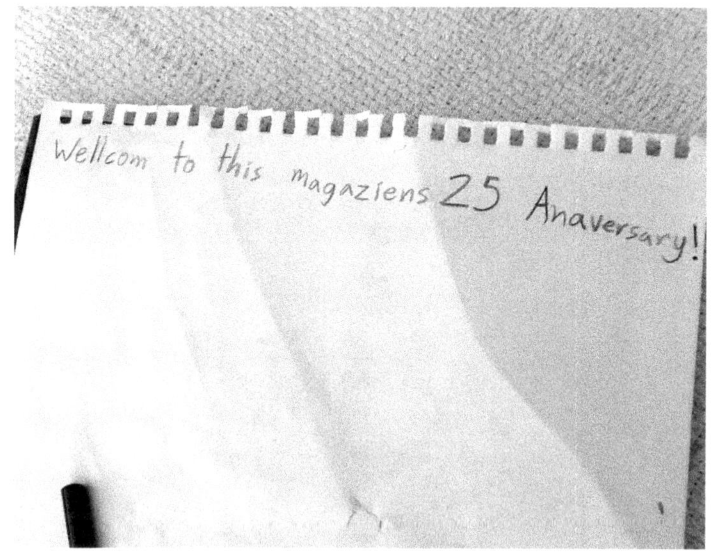

INTRODUCTION, FIRST DRAFT, Dorothy Vincent Kingstrom, 2025

CASSETTE TAPE, purchased by Greg Koehler, Blanco, Texas, 2025

NOTES

21. "If You Lived Here, You'd Be Home Now" is excerpted from the novel *Standard Six*.

28. "Reckon Thy Disease Its Courtship" also appears in *The Sum of Every Lost Ship* (Cleveland State University Poetry Center, 2010).

40. "Dorchester Diary" first appeared in installment form via Blogspot.

55. "Grandfather Jitterbug" and "Grandmother as Legend" also appear in *The Party in Question*, winner of the Burnside Review Chapbook Prize

78. "Autumn Rising" also appears in *The Dictionary of Unspellable Noises: New and Selected Poems, 1975-2018*, published by Press 53 in 2019.

104. "The Shapeshifter Introduces Her Village to the Moon" and "Fox-Girl Before Birth" also appear in *If Birds Gather Your Hair for Nesting* (University of Georgia Press, 2009).

161. "Old Virginia" was written at the insistence of a second party for use in an as-yet-untitled zombie movie.

167. "Brian Shaffer is Here" is excerpted from the screenplay *Josh vs. Perveen.*

196. "Visiting Delaware" was originally published in Issue Four of *Makeout Creek* as "Three Counties."

197. "Spring Mix" quotes the author's "Breaking Through: Kyle Hall," which was first published at *Resident Advisor* in 2009.

201. *Vocabulary: ~~Bob Frances~~ Joesph Perry* is a transcription of the handwritten journal discovered by Ward Tefft in a box of books donated to the Richmond, Virginia-based nonprofit Books on Wheels in 2012. The journal was written in Rhode Island in the summer of 1975. Its author remains unknown.

246. "I Can't Sleep in the Back Bedroom" also appears in *Buick City* (Mayapple Press, 2015).

254. "Things We Do to Fill the Holes" also appears in *DOWN*, released in 2020 by Stephen F. Austin State University Press.

257. "Leftovers" is excerpted from the novel *Dilettantes and Heartless Manipulators*, published by Snow Goose Press in 2015.

259. "Dan Below" also appears in *I've Got a Message for You and You're Not Going to Like It*, the tenth anniversary edition of which was published by Makeout Creek Books in 2024.

342. "As Ugly Does, 1969" is excerpted from the memoir *Blues Family Album.*

347. "pick of the litter" also appears in *Acquired Taste*, published in 2025 by Titan Books.

CONTRIBUTORS

MICHAEL AGRESTA has published nonfiction and fiction in *The Atlantic, Slate, Wall Street Journal, Wired, Texas Observer, Southern Review, Boston Review, Conjunctions* and others. He writes regularly on art and culture for *Texas Monthly*. He has received residencies from the MacDowell Colony, Blue Mountain Center, VCCA and Lighthouse Works. His MFA is from the Michener Center for Writers in Austin, Texas, where he lives.

GEORGE ALLEN lives and works in Prague, Czech Republic, where he feeds his fried-cheese-and-sauerkraut addiction without judgment or fear. In his free time, he teaches photography at an art school and takes pictures of his surroundings. He earned an MFA in Photography from Virginia Commonwealth University in 2004.

NICKY ARSCOTT is an artist living in Llanbrynmair, Wales.

X.C. ATKINS is the author of *Grace Street Alley and Other Stories*, published with Makeout Creek Books, and *The Desperado Days*, published with Trnsfr Books. His short stories have appeared in *Prairie Schooner, Paper Darts, Maudlin House, BULL*, Akashic Books' *Richmond Noir, Coal Hill Review* and other journals and anthologies. He is Pushcart Prize nominee, and he graduated from Virginia Commonwealth University. He lives and writes in Los Angeles. See more at www.xcatkins.com and on social media @wolf_cassoulet.

EVIE ATOM ATKINSON is a David Lynch devotee living in New York, Los Angeles and Croatia. She wrote "Party Line, or Before and After Frank O'Hara" before she came out as trans, when the mythologies of gay male identity, archness and diva worship felt tethered but fraying inside her. She still shares a party line with her past selves. Those past selves have been the inaugural Director of Literary Arts at Chautauqua Institution, the Director of Writing Programs at Catapult and creative writing faculty at Interlochen Arts Academy and Johns Hopkins Center for Talented Youth. Her writing and research have been supported by Fulbright, the Critical Language Scholarship, the Saltonstall Foundation and others. More of her poems can be found in the Academy of American Poets' *Poem-a-Day, Black Warrior Review, Dreginald* and others.

A BAD BIRCH works that naughty little taiga 'til its calves are sore.

A BAD BUNNY has waited for this moment.

A BADDEST BUFFALO might be a little dust on the bible.

JOSIAH BANCROFT is the author of six novels, a collection of short fiction, numerous poems and a forthcoming graphic novel. His books have been translated into nine languages. Before settling down to write full time, he was a college instructor, a rock musician and an aspiring comic book artist. When he's not writing, he enjoys strumming a variety of instruments, drawing with a growing cache of imperfect pens and cooking without a recipe. He lives in Philadelphia with his wife, Sharon, their daughter, Maddie, and their rabbit, Chaplin.

TOM BATTEN'S writing has appeared in *The New Yorker, The Guardian* and *The Tusk*, amongst other fine media outlets. He lives in Virginia.

JOHN BEARDSLEY is a poet, educator and musician who currently lives with their senior dog near Lake Michigan, having recently returned to their home state of Wisconsin after some long years of physical and spiritual transience and/or self-imposed exile. Their poems have appeared in *Makeout Creek, Colorado Review, Gulf Coast, Mid-American Review, The Journal, Third Coast* and elsewhere.

DAVID BERMAN (1967-2019) is the author of *Actual Air* and *The Portable February*. His band, the Silver Jews, released six albums—*Starlite Walker, The Natural Bridge, American Water, Bright Flight, Tanglewood Numbers* and *Lookout Mountain, Lookout Sea*—on Drag City Records. In addition, he released the album *Purple Mountains* on Drag City, and he blogged regularly at *Menthol Mountains.*

MATT BIERCE, ah, he might as well jump.

QUINN BLAIS is an aspiring novelist, present day copywriter and undiscerning coffee enthusiast. She earned her BA in English and creative writing at the College of William & Mary. While at W&M, Quinn received the Glenwood Clark Prize for Fiction and the Tiberius Gracchus Jones Prize for Nonfiction through the William & Mary Student Literary Awards. When she is not writing for pleasure, Quinn runs a small content-writing company called WriteHQ and writes for money. She is based in Baltimore, where she lives with her husband, Drew, and her dog, Poppyseed Bagel.

ANDREW BLOSSOM is a writer, editor, publisher and cat mother. He lives in Spokane, Washington.

KEVERLEE BURCHETT'S work has been published in *The Southeast Review, Southern Humanities Review, Duende, Painted Bride Quarterly* and *Calyx*, among others. She lives in Asheville with her daughter and one perfect dog.

SARAH CARSON is the author of the poetry collections *Buick City* (Mayapple Press, 2015), *Poems in Which You Die* (BatCat Press) and *How to Baptize a Child in Flint, Michigan* (2022), winner of the 2021 Lexi Rudnitsky Editor's Choice Award from Persea Books.

BRIAN CASTLEBERRY'S first novel, *Nine Shiny Objects*, was a *New York Times* Editor's Choice, was long listed for the PEN/Faulkner Award, and won the Library of Virginia Book Award in Fiction. His other work has been published in the *Southern Review,*

Narrative, *LitHub*, the *Los Angeles Review of Books* and elsewhere. His second novel, *The Californians*, was published in March of 2025 by Mariner Books.

JUNG HAE CHAE is a Korean American writer and author of the forthcoming memoir-in-essays *Pojangmacha People*, winner of the 2022 Graywolf Press Nonfiction Prize.

CLAY McLEOD CHAPMAN writes books, comic books, middle and YA books, as well as for film and television. *Acquired Taste* is his most recent collection of short stories. You can find him at www.claymcleodchapman.com.

MAYRON CHOPSUEY has been canceled.

CHRISTOPHER COOTS is a writer and clinical social worker residing in Brooklyn, New York.

MATTHEW C. CRADY graduated from Virginia Commonwealth University with an MFA in fiction. He currently resides in Louisville, Kentucky, where he and his fiancé live their best lives.

EMMA CUSUMANO is a bookseller-turned-lawyer living in Pittsburgh, Pennsylvania, with her husband, son and dog.

CAROL ANN DAVIS is a poet, essayist and the author of *Songbird* (Wesleyan University Press, 2026), as well as three previous collections by Tupelo Press. A former longtime editor of the literary journal *Crazyhorse,* she is Professor of English at Fairfield University, where she is Director of the Low-Residency MFA and founder of Poetry in Communities, an initiative that provides poetry curricula to communities hit by sudden or systemic violence. An NEA Fellow in Poetry and finalist for the National Magazine Award in Essays and Criticism, Carol Ann has read her work at the Library of Congress, Poets House, on the website of *PBS NewsHour*, and at the *Los Angeles Times* Book Festival. Her advocacy work on behalf of those affected by gun violence has led to an appearance on MSNBC's *Morning Joe* and on several Northeast public radio outlets. Her poems and essays regularly appear in literary magazines and periodicals, including *The Atlantic, The Daily Beast, The Georgia Review, Image, The Gettysburg Review, The American Poetry Review* and *Agni.*

ADAM DAY is the author of *American Elision* (Louisiana State University Press, 2027), *The Strategic Crescent* (Broadstone Books, 2025), *Illuminated Edges* (Kelsay Books, 2024), *Left-Handed Wolf* (Louisiana State University Press, 2020), *Model of a City in Civil War* (Sarabande Books, 2015), and *Badger, Apocrypha* (Poetry Society of America, 2011). He publishes *Action, Spectacle*, an online and print journal of art and culture.

JACK DEAN is a writer and attorney living in Atlanta, Georgia, with his loving partner Margaret and handsome cat Cowboy. When he is not working, he writes about visual art, music and nature for no one in particular. Sometimes when he sleeps, he dreams of bees.

TOM DE HAVEN is the author of eighteen books, including *Freaks' Amour, Sunburn Lake,* the Derby Dugan Trilogy (*Funny Papers, Derby Dugan's Depression Funnies* and *Dugan Under Ground*), *It's Superman!* and the nonfiction book-length essay *Our Hero: Superman on Earth.* He lives in Richmond, Virginia, where he retired from teaching creative writing and comics at Virginia Commonwealth University in 2018.

JAMI DITTUS writes poetry, fiction and stream-of-consciousness health blogs out of Richmond, Virginia, by way of New Jersey. Her current house is not haunted.

LYDIA DOLVIN is a full-time science teacher and even fuller time creative. She currently lives out in the woods near Charlottesville, Virginia. Her hobbies include raking leaves, living gently and knitting socks for friends.

JESSE DONALDSON is the author of *The More They Disappear* and *On Homesickness.* He lives in Oregon.

JEN DUNLAP is an artist and production designer based in Los Angeles. Her artwork uses interactive performances, sculptures and paintings to explore human emotion and interconnectivity through the perception of the self. Notable film work includes *The Chronology of Water* (dir. Kristen Stewart), *I Wish You All The Best* (dir. Tommy Dorfman), *Long Weekend* (dir. Steve Basilone) and *MA* (dir. Celia Rowlson-Hall).

LEENA EL-MOHANDES is a graduate of the College of William & Mary and occasional copy editor. She is currently applying to medical school. She lives in Western Maryland with her dog and bookshelf.

TARFIA FAIZULLAH is the author of two collections of poetry: *Seam* (SIU Press, 2014) and *Registers of Illuminated Villages.* She currently teaches at the University of North Texas.

NOAH FALCK is the author of *Exclusions* (Tupelo Press, 2020), which was a finalist for the Believer Book Award, and the co-authored collection *Prerecorded Weather* (SurVision Books, 2022), winner of the James Tate Poetry Prize. In 2013, he founded the Silo City Reading Series, an immersive, multimedia poetry event series that takes place inside a 120-foot-high, 100-year-old abandoned grain elevator. He lives in Buffalo, New York. Read more at noahfalck.org.

COURTNEY FENNER is a writer and educator. She digs adventure franchise blockbusters (think *Jumanji* or *Jurassic Park*), zombie movies, Frida Kahlo and paraphernalia from her PBS-riddled childhood. You'll know she loves you if she makes your favorite cookies for no particular reason at all. Most importantly, she is thrilled that 1990s R&B teenage wunderkinds Brandy and Monica are finally touring together.

PHIL FORD co-edited and was a contributing writer to the *Richmond Macabre: Nightmares from the River City* book series. He has recently had stories appear in multiple anthologies, such as *Generation X-ed* (Dark Ink Press, 2022), *The Nightmare Never Ends* (Exploding Head Fiction, 2023) and *Under the Stairs* (Ossuary Press, 2023). When not writing, he is in a trash-punk band called Crack Fox and currently DJs the Friday Clock Out 5-7 PM on WRIR 97.3 FM, Richmond Independent Radio.

WILLIAM FOSTER lives in Oregon.

MEG FREITAG is the author of the poetry collection *Edith* and *This Is a Book for People Who Love Dogs*, an illustrated work of nonfiction. She's a graduate of UT Austin's Michener Center for Writers and the Iowa Writers' Workshop. Originally from mid-coast Maine, she now lives in Boise, Idaho.

LOGAN FRY is the author of *Harpo Before the Opus* (Omnidawn) and of poetry in *The Yale Review, The New York Review of Books, Cleveland Review of Books, New American Writing, The Rumpus, Fence* and *Lana Turner.*

P.J. GALLO has published poems or prose with *Apalachee Review, Bat City Review, Independent Weekly, Roanoke Review*, Thirty West Publishing and elsewhere. He is the author of the chapbook *Geirfuglasker.* He co-edited *LEVELER*, an online poetry journal, from 2010 to 2020. He lives in Maryland.

JAMES HANNAHAM, after appearing in Makeout Creek in 2011, published the novels *Delicious Foods*, which won the PEN/Faulkner Award, and *Didn't Nobody Give A Shit What Happened To Carlotta*, which was a Kirkus Best Book of 2022. Both novels were New York Times Notable Books and won Hurston/Wright Legacy Awards. In 2024, he returned to Richmond, Virginia, as a conceptual artist, appearing in the Institute for Contemporary Arts' acclaimed show *MURRMUR: Blurs and Senses.*

EAGY HASBERRY is a spambot and poet.

SMITH HENDERSON is the author of the novels *Make Them Cry* (Ecco) and *Fourth of July Creek* (Ecco). His fiction has been anthologized and published in *Best American Short Stories, Tin House, American Short Fiction, One Story, New Orleans Review, Makeout Creek* and *Witness.* He lives in Montana.

ANNA CLAIRE HODGE is a poet, journalist and writing teacher in Orlando, Florida. She holds a PhD and MFA in creative writing, and her work has appeared in many publications, including *Mid-American Review, Charleston Magazine, Prairie Schooner, Four Way Review, Willow Springs, New Orleans Review* and others. Her poems have been anthologized in *It Was Written: Poetry Inspired by Hip-Hop, Turn it Up!: Music in Poetry from Jazz to Hip-Hop, Best New Poets 2013* and others.

ANNA JOURNEY is the author of five poetry collections, including *Wolf Cut: New & Selected Poems* (2026), *The Judas Ear* (2022) and *The Atheist Wore Goat Silk* (2017), all from

Louisiana State University Press. She is an associate professor of English at the University of Southern California.

BENJAMIN JURGENSEN is an artist and educator who lives in Rhode Island.

W. TODD KANEKO is the author of *This is How the Bone Sings* (Black Lawrence Press, 2020) and *The Dead Wrestler Elegies, Championship Edition* (New Michigan Press, 2023). He is co-author with Amorak Huey of *Poetry: A Writers' Guide and Anthology, 2nd ed.* (Bloomsbury Academic, 2024), and *Slash/Slash*, (Diode Editions, 2021). His poems, essays and stories can be seen in many journals and anthologies. He lives with his family in Grand Rapids, Michigan, where he teaches creative writing at Grand Valley State University.

JULIE KARR is a semi-retired musician, performing solo and with her bands (past and present) Bad Magic and Sensual World. She lives in Richmond, Virginia, with her family.

STEVE KEENE has painted over 300,000 paintings.

DOROTHY VINCENT KINGSTROM is nine. Do not call her "Dottie" or "Dot." She will not be going to college if it is sleep-away. Her goal for this week is to improve her single-digit multiplication automaticity. She does not wish to talk about what makes her heart happy. She would like a snack and for you to stop talking to her; she is reading.

GREG KOEHLER is a poet, conceptual artist and philosopher from the cold place.

NICK KUSZYK lives in Ridgewood, Queens, and rides his bike as much as possible. His knees still feel pretty good.

JANE ROSENBERG LAFORGE is the author of five full-length poetry collections; her most recent is *The Exhaust of Dreams Adulterated* from Broadstone Books. She is also the author of four chapbooks of poetry; a memoir; and two novels. Her 2018 novel, *The Hawkman: A Fairy Tale of World War I* (Amberjack Publishing), was a finalist in two categories in the 2019 Eric Hoffer Awards. Her 2021 novel, *Sisterhood of the Infamous* (New Meridian Arts Press), was a finalist in the National Indie Excellence Awards in regional fiction (west). She has been nominated for the Pushcart Prize in fiction and poetry; the *storySouth* Million Writers Award; the *Best of the Net* anthology; and the *Best Small Fictions* anthology. She lives in New York.

NICOLE LANG is a film school dropout whose diverse background in hospitality, film production, tech and the music industry has led her to her current role supporting live transformative theater. By seeking reinvention and collaboration, she has had success in many entrepreneurial ventures, including owning a bakery, performing in touring bands, co-founding a film production company and hosting a podcast. She lives in the East Bay of Rhode Island with her husband, musician Marty Key, and their rescue chiweenie, Anchovy. Every day, once a day, she falls in love and recommends it.

JESSICA LASER is the author of *The Goner School*, a finalist for the 2025 Griffin Prize.

CLAIRE LEWIS is a poet and editor. She lives and works in Richmond, Virginia.

CYNTHIA GRIER LOTZE'S poems can be found in *Makeout Creek, Harpur Palate, Sycamore Review, Versal* and *Smartish Pace*. She teaches English and bikes around with her family in Minneapolis, Minnesota, but please bury her in Richmond, Virginia.

LAUREN MAAS is a writer and editor who lives in Rhode Island. She is a member of Makeout Creek's editorial board and its unofficial lead cartoonist.

TYLER MAGILL is a librarian, writer and musician living in Charlottesville, Virginia. In 2019, he received the American Library Association's Paul Howard Award for Courage.

MUKI MAHAN je *Muki Mahan.*

TONY MANCUS is the author of two books of poems, *Same After Life* (Gasher, 2024) and *All the Ordinariness* (The Magnificent Field, 2022) along with a handful of chapbooks. He serves as chapbook editor for Barrelhouse, works as an instructional designer and lives in Colorado with his wife, son, and two black cats.

CLINT MCCOWN'S twelfth and thirteenth books—*Son of the Secret Service* (essays), from the University Press of Kentucky, and *Dibs*, (long poem), from Press 53— are forthcoming in the spring of 2026. He is a Professor Emeritus at Virginia Commonwealth University. In 2021, he was inducted into the Writers Hall of Fame at Wake Forest University.

RYAN MCLENNAN was born in 1980 in Norfolk, Virginia. In 2003, he received a BFA in Painting and Printmaking from Virginia Commonwealth University. He has exhibited work in Richmond, Los Angeles, Boston, New York City and Denver. He lives in Pittsburgh, Pennsylvania, where he runs his used, new and rare bookstore and art gallery, Bottom Feeder Books.

CARSON MELL is a man who loves love.

ANDY MILLER is a person who has created and performed with his friends, your friends, other people, himself and you.

AMY MITCHELL is an educational advocate, researcher and music historian. She lives in Asheville, North Carolina, with her family.

KEITH MONTESANO is the author of the poetry collections *Ghost Lights, Scoring the Silent Film* and *Housefire Elegies*. He currently lives in Bethel Park, Pennsylvania.

J.W. MORISON is a farmer in Virginia.

GLENN NORTH is the Director of Inclusive Learning and Creative Impact at the Kansas City Museum. He received an MFA in Creative Writing from UMKC and is the author of *City of Song*, a collection of poems inspired by Kansas City's rich jazz tradition. He is a Cave Canem fellow, a Callaloo creative writing fellow and a recipient of the Charlotte Street Generative Performing Artist Award. North is also an adjunct English professor at Rockhurst University, and he is currently filling his appointment as the Poet Laureate of the 18th & Vine Historic Jazz District.

SIR KUSSO PHILLIP is a lawyer based in Cote d'Ivoire.

AMIRA PIERCE is a professor of expository writing at New York University, where she specializes in working with non-native English speakers and engineering students. She got her MFA in fiction from Virginia Commonwealth University in 2011, and she writes fiction, poetry and creative nonfiction. Born in Beirut, Lebanon, she lives in Bushwick, Brooklyn, with her family.

HERMINE PINSON is the Frances L. & Edwin L. Cummings Professor of English & Africana Studies at the College of William & Mary in Williamsburg, Virginia. She has published three poetry collections and produced two CDs, one in special collaboration with Pulitzer-prize winning poet Yusef Komunyakaa. Pinson's poetry, short fiction, and nonfiction have appeared in numerous anthologies and journals. She has performed her poetry in the United States, Europe and Africa.

MIKE POWELL is the author of *New Paltz, New Paltz*. He lives in Tucson, Arizona.

LIZ PRATHER teaches creative writing at the School for Creative and Performing Arts in Lexington, Kentucky. She holds an MFA from the University of Texas at Austin and has authored three books on writing from Heinemann Press.

NATHANIEL RAPPOLE lives in Virginia and makes music as Gull.

NICK READING is the author of *Love & Sundries* (SplitLip Press) and *The Party in Question*, winner of the Burnside Review Chapbook Contest. His poems have won the Twyckenham Notes Joe Bolton Prize and the Patty Friedman Poetry Award. His writing has appeared in *New Ohio Review, Mid-American Review, TriQuarterly, Cortland Review, Painted Bride Quarterly* and others.

EVAN CRAIG REARDON is a poet and theological librarian. Originally from New England, he currently lives and works at a seminary in the Midwest.

KATY RESCH is the author of the story collection *Exposure* and a recipient of artist grants from the Barbara Deming Memorial Fund and Richmond Culture Works.

PIR ROTHENBERG is an editor and potter who lives in Rochester, New York.

MANDY DUNN SAMPSON lives in Philadelphia, Pennsylvania, with her family. She has worked in publishing since 2012.

JON SEALY is the author of four novels, most recently *The King Street Affair*, as well as the craft memoir *So You Want to Be a Novelist.* A South Carolina native, he lives with his family in the suburbs of Richmond, Virginia. Learn more and download a free short story at jonsealy.com.

ALYSON SINCLAIR lives in Asheville, North Carolina.

ERIN ELIZABETH SMITH is the Executive Director of Sundress Publications and the Sundress Academy for the Arts. Her third full-length poetry collection, *DOWN*, was released in 2020 by Stephen F. Austin State University Press. Her poems have appeared in numerous journals, including *Guernica, Ecotone, Mid-American, Tupelo Quarterly Crab Orchard Review* and *Willow Springs*, among others. She earned her PhD in Creative Writing from the Center for Writers at the University of Southern Mississippi and is now a Teaching Professor in the English Department at the University of Tennessee.

PATRICIA SMITH is the author of *The Year of Needy Girls*, a Lambda Literary Award finalist. Her fiction has appeared in *Blue Mountain Review, The Master's Review, So to Speak* and *The Tusculum Review.* A three-time Pushcart nominee, her nonfiction has most recently been featured in *InkFish Magazine*, with other work appearing in such places as *Hippocampus, Broad Street, Salon, Prime Number* and several anthologies. Her short fiction was also selected for presentation in *From Page to Stage,* choreographed and performed by Starr Foster Dance Co. in Richmond, Virginia. In 2024, Smith was awarded the Emyl Jenkins Award by James River Writers for inspiring a love of writing. Most recently, she received the Hebestreit Award for Adventure Writing from the National English Honor Society. A repeat Fellow of the Virginia Center for Creative Arts, Smith earned her MFA from Virginia Commonwealth University. Since 2006, she has taught Dual Enrollment English and literary arts at the Appomattox Regional Governor's School in Petersburg, Virginia. She lives in Chester, Virginia, with her wife.

SARAH ELAINE SMITH is the author of the poetry collection *I Live in a Hut* (Cleveland State University Poetry Center, 2012) and the novel *Marilou Is Everywhere* (Riverhead Books, 2019), a finalist for the *LA Times* Book Prize for First Fiction. She is a graduate of the Iowa Writers' Workshop and the Michener Center for Writers and the recipient of support from MacDowell and the Dobie Paisano Fellowship. She lives in Los Angeles.

LEIGH STEIN is the author of six books, including the poetry collections *What to Miss When* and *Dispatch from the Future* and the novels *If You're Seeing This, It's Meant For You* and *Self Care.* She is also the creator of the *Attention Economy* newsletter on Substack.

ANNA STEINMETZ, a rapidly aging College of William & Mary graduate, is currently counting down her days of employment at *The Late Show with Stephen Colbert.* She has been heralded as shorter than expected, fun in small doses and violently lactose intolerant. Based in New York City, she is on her third cup of coffee and everyone's last nerve.

MELISSA STEPHENSON'S writing has appeared in various publications, including *The Washington Post, The Rumpus, Ms. Magazine* and *ZZYZYVA*. Her memoir, *Driven,* was released by Houghton Mifflin Harcourt in 2018. It was longlisted for the Chautauqua Book Prize and won the 2020 Indiana Emerging Author Award. Though born and raised in Indiana, she is a long-time resident of Missoula, Montana.

CHRISTINE STROUD is a poet and editor living in Pittsburgh, Pennsylvania. Her poems have appeared in *Prairie Schooner, Ninth Letter Online, Cimarron Review* and many others, as well as in several anthologies. She is the author of two chapbooks, *Sister Suite* (Disorder Press) and *The Buried Return* (Finishing Line Press), and is currently working on a full-length collection.

MATTHEW STUART lives in Austin, Texas, with his daughters, Mia and Zoe. He writes and paints and hosts an annual home run derby.

MATHIAS SVALINA is the author of nine books, most recently *Comedy*, a story collection from Trident Press. In his day job, he runs a dream delivery service.

WARD TEFFT lives in Richmond, Virginia, where he is the developer of Chat IRL, an app that allows users to turn off their phones and computers and explore communication with their surrounding world.

ALLISON TITUS teaches in the low-res MFA program at New England College. Her latest book is *High Lonesome*, and she is co-editor of *The New Sent(i)ence* anthology/manifesto.

KELSEY TROM is a Professor of English at Tusculum University, where she is the editor of the *Tusculum Review* and the creative writing program coordinator. As the Harriet Reeves Neff Chair of Fine Arts, she hosts visiting writer events that connect student scribes and Greeneville community members with mold-breaking authors. She writes fiction, essays and long letters. She lives with her husband, Alan, in a log cabin he built by hand and hopes to one day build something as durable. She swims with the Kingsport Viperfish.

EDDIE VEGA is a poet, storyteller and educator. He is the author of *Chicharra Chorus* (FlowerSong Press, 2019) and *Somos Nopales* (FlowerSong Press, 2024), and his poetry appears in public spaces in San Antonio, Texas. He is also the editor of *Asina is How We Talk*, a collection of Tejano poetry. A Macondo Workshop Fellow, Vega directs the Mouth Dakota Poetry Project, a biweekly open mic, and currently serves as the seventh Poet Laureate of San Antonio.

REBECCA WADLINGER is the author of *Terror, Terrible, Terrific* and the translator of Norwegian poet Gro Dahle's collection *A Hundred Thousand Hours*. Her work has appeared in *Tin House, Ploughshares, Black Warrior Review* and *Best New Poets*, among others. A graduate of the Michener Center for Writers and the University of Houston's doctoral program in Creative Writing, she now lives in Portland, Oregon.

NATE WAGGONER'S work has appeared in *Electric Lit, Barrelhouse, Peach Mag, The Hard Times* and elsewhere. He lives in Richmond, Virginia.

NESS WARMBLOOD is an anagram.

WOOJIN YOON graduated *summa cum laude* from the College of William & Mary in May 2024 with a Bachelor of Arts in English. She now works as an editor for *The Korea JoongAng Daily*, the English edition of the Korean national daily newspaper, *The JoongAng*. When she's not being a cog in the capitalist machine or writing (or thinking about writing) stories about her own life or fanfiction, she's probably watching a sitcom, playing a video game or napping with her dogs.

RYAN P. YOUNG lives in Billings, Montana, with his family. He works for a bank.

MAKEOUT CREEK HAS BEEN

EDITORIAL BOARD
Andrew Blossom
Greg Koehler
Cynthia Grier Lotze
Lauren Maas

EDITORS EMERITI
J.W. Morison
Joshua Poteat
April Sopkin
Allison Titus

LOGO + INSPIRATION
Andy Miller

COPY EDITOR
Leena El-Mohandes

EARLY SUPPORTERS
Brian Castleberry
Thomas Kane
Reveley Lee

MAKEOUT CREEK ONE
OF MANY
2008

COVER
Andy Miller

CONTRIBUTORS
James Tadd Adcox
George Allen
Walker Allen
Nicky Arscott
Josiah Bancroft
David Berman
Lillian Bertram
Brian Castleberry
Crystal Castleberry
Tom De Haven
Tarfia Faizullah
William Foster
Herb Hurni
Greg Koehler
Nick Kuszyk
sTo Len
Cynthia Grier Lotze
Tyler Magill
Muki Mahan
Clint McCown
Joshua Poteat
Marie Potoczny
Nicholas Reading
Brenda Sieczkowski
Sarah Elaine Smith
Frederick Stivers
Luke Sykora
Allison Titus
Wendy Trevino
Rebecca Wadlinger
Greg O. Weatherford

MAKEOUT CREEK TWO
THE REVELEY LEE APPRECIATION SOCIETY
2008

COVER
Adam Juresko

CONTRIBUTORS
George Allen
A Bad Bunny
Caleb Barber
Erin M. Bertram
Lillian Bertram
Liz Countryman
Jami Dittus
Courtney Fenner

Anna Journey
Adam Juresko
Jane Rosenberg LaForge
Reveley Lee
B. Lightning
Lauren Maas
Muki Mahan
John McAuliffe
Keith Montesano
Daniel Morgan Owen
Jon Sealy
Matthew Stuart
Elizabeth Kate Switaj
Davide Trame
Kelsey Trom
Anna Lowe Weber

MAKEOUT CREEK THREE
HOT DAMN IT'S MAKEOUT CREEK THREE
2009

COVER
Ryan McLennan

CONTRIBUTORS
George Allen
Walker Allen
M.C. Boyes
Meghan Brinson
Keverlee Burchett
Kara Candito
Matthew C. Crady
Kristen Eliason
John Estes
Teresa Farrell
Lauren Barrier Gould
Eagy Hasberry
Smith Henderson
Brian Henry
Muna Hijazi
Ben Kopel
Nick Kuszyk
Reveley Lee
Rob Lee
Rebecca Lehmann
B. Lightning
Jeff Lodge
Muki Mahan
Clayton Michaels
Andy Miller
Mike Powell
Liz Prather
Pir Rothenberg
Jon Sealy
Andrew Terhune
Ness Warmblood
Adam Wayland
Ryan P. Young

MAKEOUT CREEK FOUR
LIFE IS PRECIOUS AND GOD AND THE BIBLE
2011

COVER
Oura Sananikone

CONTRIBUTORS
X.C. Atkins
A Baddest Buffalo
Keverlee Burchett
Eric William Carroll
Diya Chaudhuri
Jamison Crabtree
Hannah Craig
Weston Cutter
Carol Ann Davis
Laura M. Dixon
Tyler Flynn Dorholt
Fadeyeva
Jamie Fueglein
James Hannaham
Anna Claire Hodge
Aaron M. Johnson
Benjamin Jurgensen
Sarah Kilby
B. Lightning

Cynthia Grier Lotze
Stacy Muszynski
Mike Powell
Oura Sananikone
Kory M. Shrum
Alyson Sinclair
Jay Snodgrass
April Sopkin
Erin Vaughan
Nate Waggoner
Anna Lowe Weber

MAKEOUT CREEK FIVE
WHAT PETER CALLS "A NATURAL ENCOUNTER PERSON"
2013

COVER
Vocabulary: ~~Bob Frances~~ Joesph Perry

CONTRIBUTORS
Richard D. Allen
X.C. Atkins
A Bad Bunny
Andrew Blossom
Mayron Chopsuey
Noah Falck
P.J. Gallo
Caleb King
B. Lightning
Keith Montesano
Sir Kusso Phillip
Marie Potoczny
Leigh Stein
Mathias Svalina
Ward Tefft
Unknown Author

MAKEOUT CREEK SIX
FOR THE MOLOKAI COPS
2014

COVER
Mandy Dunn Sampson

CONTRIBUTORS
Franz K. Baskett
Tom Batten
John Beardsley
Rebecca Bernard
Andrew Blossom
Sara Bohannon
Jon Boisvert
Sarah Carson
William Cordeiro
Adam Day
Kyle Flak
William Foster
W. Todd Kaneko
Michael Kozak
B. Lightning
Lauren Maas
Tony Mancus
Ben Pelhan
Amira Pierce
Mandy Dunn Sampson
Erin Elizabeth Smith
Ephraim Scott Sommers
Star Trek Robot
Gale Marie Thompson
Nate Waggoner

MAKEOUT CREEK SEVEN
THE LONESOME FOGHORN BLOWS
2015

COVER
Eliza Childress

CONTRIBUTORS
George Allen
Nicky Arscott
Evie Atom Atkinson
Brad Bacon
Tom Batten
Andrew Blossom
James Callahan
Alicia Camden
Clay McLeod Chapman

Casey A. Childers
Christopher Coots
Daniel Crawford
Adam Day
Santa Sergio De Haven
Kate Duffy
Brad Dukes
Ryan Evans
Teresa Farrell
Alani Foxall
Parker Galore
J.T. Glover
Sara Gossett
Harriet Hayward
Marshall Higgins
Adam Juresko
Julie Karr
Nicole Lang
Sarah Lauck
Jason Lefton
sTo Len
B. Lightning
Rob Lindley
Muki Mahan
Tony Mancus
Joseph McCorkle
Ryan McLennan
James Meagher
Carson Mell
Andy Miller
Jay Moritz
Andrea Owens
Dan Rhett
Liz Roberts
Travis Robertson
Oura Sananikone
Noah Scalin
Nico Cathcart Schroeder
April Sopkin
Bonnie Staley
Allison Titus
Kim Vodicka
Rebecca Wadlinger
Nate Waggoner
Nick Walberg
Annie Warren
Benjamin Winkler

MAKEOUT CREEK EIGHT
ONLY A WITCH CAT CAN CLOSE A DOOR
2023

COVER
Nick Kuszyk

CONTRIBUTORS
Michael Agresta
George Allen
Nicky Arscott
X.C. Atkins
A Bad Birch
Tom Batten
Quinn Blais
Andrew Blossom
Jory Berkley
Ford Burdett
Mark Burdett
Lindley Burnam
James Callahan
Jung Hae Chae
Clay McLeod Chapman
Jackie Clark
Jackie Crady
Emma Cusumano
Jack Dean
Ioan Dearling
Santa Sergio De Haven
Julia DeKorte
Lydia Dolvin
Jesse Donaldson
Green Dragonetti
Jen Dunlap
Nicole Efford
Leena El-Mohandes
Noah Falck
Christian Fisher
Phil Ford

Meg Freitag
Logan Fry
Shamala Gallagher
Tina Gibbard
Kylee Gilman
Mark Hitz
Joe Howl
Shelby Hurd
Greg Koehler
Nick Kuszyk
Jessica Laser
Reveley Lee
sTo Len
Claire Lewis
B. Lightning
Cynthia Grier Lotze
Ryan McLennan
Tricia Burdett Meyer
Andy Miller
Brooke Miller
Amanda Case Millis
Margaret Mitchell
Matthew Moore
J.W. Morison
Julianne Nash
Glenn North
Daniel Morgan Owen
Amira Pierce
Hermine Pinson
Nathaniel Rappole
Evan Craig Reardon
Katy Resch
Dan Rhett
Liz Roberts
Erin Russell
Domenica Ruta
Ezekiel Ruta-Smith
Felix Valentino De la Luz Salmoran
Ian E. Sampson
Mandy Dunn Sampson
Luke Sholer
Patricia Smith
Sarah Elaine Smith
Anna Steinmetz
Melissa Stephenson
Frederick Stivers
Christine Stroud
Eddie Vega
Sahil Verma
Nate Waggoner
Em White
Woojin Yoon

IN LOVING MEMORY OF
Stephen T. Dunn

WITH SPECIAL THANKS TO
Cassie Berman
Amy Black
Thea Brown
David Carpenter
Thom Didato
Rosy Faver Dunn
Shelley Duvall
Steve Keene
Ryan McLennan
Mike Parisi
Lloyd Poast
Brett Sova
Ward Tefft

MAKEOUT CREEK BOOKS
WWW.MAKEOUTCREEK.COM

www.ingramcontent.com/pod-product-compliance
Lightning Source LLC
Chambersburg PA
CBHW061130100726
47911CB00013B/749